The Best of Pulphouse:
The Hardback Magazine

THE BEST OF
PULPHOUSE

The Hardback Magazine

Kristine Kathryn Rusch
Editor

St. Martin's Press
New York

THE BEST OF PULPHOUSE: THE HARDBACK MAGAZINE.

Design by Richard Oriolo

Library of Congress Cataloging-in-Publication Data

The Best of Pulphouse : the hardback magazine / edited by Kristine
    Kathryn Rusch.
        p.   cm.
    ISBN 0-312-06564-7
    1. Fantastic fiction, American.   2. Science fiction, American.
3. Horror tales, American.   I. Rusch, Kristine Kathryn.
II. Pulphouse.
PS648.F3B48   1991
813'.0876208—dc20   91-4350
                                                                CIP

First edition: September 1991

10 9 8 7 6 5 4 3 2 1

For Dean Wesley Smith and Debra Gray Cook
—this book is ours, guys.

And especially for Bill Trojan
—we couldn't have done this without you.

Contents

Acknowledgments

This book would not exist without help from:

Bill Trojan, Philip Barnhart, Nina Kiriki Hoffman, Jon Gustafson, Mark Budz, Lynn Adams, Alan Bard Newcomer, Kevin Kenan, Stephanie Haddock, Jerry Oltion, Adrian Nikolas Phoenix, Jonathon Bond, Greg Freeman, Becky Connor, Todd Vandemark, Kevin J. Anderson, Charles N. Brown, Richard Curtis, Gordon Van Gelder, Kij Johnson, Harlan Ellison, Charles de Lint, Edward Bryant, Jack Williamson, Steve Rasnic Tem, William F. Wu, and all the book dealers, subscribers, writers, and readers who have believed in us from the beginning.

Foreword

When Dean and Kris first began talking about Pulphouse Publishing I was fascinated by their vision, their idealism, and their naivete. I felt a great deal of trepidation about what they were proposing because I had read a number of articles and books on how to start a new business. The opening step alone seemed intimidating: researching the laws and regulations of any particular field. And then, after the legalities are taken care of, there is the conventional wisdom that wields a very long and heavy stick to maintain order, and conventional wisdom is flouted at the risk of great peril.

Everyone knows there is a real need for conventional wisdom, that it was invented in order to keep us all from making hideous, costly, embarrassing, stupid mistakes. There is the big overall kind of conventional wisdom that tells you not to pull the chair out from under the only rich uncle you have. Then there are the lesser edicts that go under the umbrellas of finance, mining, agriculture, and so on; each area has its own bible of conventional wisdom that serves its observers very well. Publishing is no exception.

Conventional wisdom says that publishing is a capital-intensive business. You need the money up front to pay the writer, wretch that he/she is in demanding payment for what should be freely shared. You need to pay the editors, the printers, the binders, for advertising (if any, and usually there isn't except for those books that don't need it anyway, but that's a different article), shipping, office help, stamps, telephone service, waste baskets, and so on. All this must take place long before a book is sold and money flows back into the publishing office. Capital-intensive.

Pulphouse didn't have a sou.

Convenional wisdom tells us that to start a business, at least one of the principals should have been in that business for years, serving an apprenticeship. If not actually inside that business, then that person should have been close enough to know exactly what happens, when, and how. Many editors leave editing to become agents, for example; they know what's happening, and to whom.

Pulphouse didn't have anyone who fits that description.

Conventional wisdom today says that although the editors don't really love all those look-alike books, *in the tradition of*, *following*, *sixteenth in the series*, *so much like X that her mother couldn't tell the difference*, or the kind with Big Author writ large (and actual writer somewhere or other—if you hunt you may find it), the beleaguered editors are forced to publish all the above again and again because the market demands this. After all, they have to show a return for the investors, and only the old, tired, familiar, comfortable, nonthreatening guarantees that return. Schlock sells. Everything else is a gamble.

Pulphouse publishes unknown writers shoulder to shoulder with known writers and demands only that what they write and submit be fresh and new. It actively seeks the boldly original, and publishes it with fervor and success.

Conventional wisdom knows the short story is dead, and has been for a century or two at the very least. Editors groan at the mention of a new collection being submitted by the writer. Collections don't sell, they lose money, no one buys them. Televison has replaced the original short story.

Pulphouse is solidly built on a foundation of short fiction.

Conventional wisdom says that there are too few hours in the day and too little office help for publishers to respond to writers directly or quickly. Many publishers no longer even accept unagented material. Three months, six months, a year, two years to reject your manuscript, or even take it, all are acceptable because they are doing the best they can with limited eyes and hands and money. Poor dears. (Of course, if they joined the latter half of the twentieth century and began to use computers, they might have time enough for individual responses—but that, too, is a different article.)

Pulphouse people read what arrives in the mail, they answer letters, they send back material—information packets, notes on stories, and advice for rewrites. They do it all swiftly, within weeks.

Conventional wisdom says that to succeed, publishers must adopt the attitude of big business: obsession with the bottom line and with tax matters, endless sales meetings, and all the other paraphernalia. As publishing has become more and more multinational in character, the categories of fiction have become narrower, more readily identified. A pound of romance, a yard of mystery, a gross of horror, an acre of fantasy: you should never be surprised by what you have bought. After all, a pound of eight-penny nails is exactly the same wherever you get it.

Pulphouse is obsessed with writers and their written work. It is obsessed with quality fiction, short stories and novels that are not forced into convenient procrustean beds. Pulphouse will surprise you, delight you, perhaps astound you from time to time; possibly it will even anger you. Today it is not what it was yesterday, and tomorrow it will be different from today. A pound of Pulphouse fiction is quite definitely not like another pound of Pulphouse fiction.

And that's as it should be.

—Kate Wilhelm

Introduction

I can never pinpoint the exact moment when the craziness started. Perhaps it began the first time Dean Wesley Smith and I gazed at each other (across a crowded kitchen in New Mexico—add violins or an ominous orchestral rumble, depending on your point of view). Perhaps it started during those late night conversations in his apartment in Eugene, conversations that began with "Why doesn't somebody . . . ?" and ended with "Yeah! What a great idea!" Sometimes I think that we both were individually crazy (I did, after all, work for seven years at a very political, listener-sponsored radio station for relaxation—

and Dean, well, Dean gave away *free* 52 issues of a magazine he wrote, edited, designed and published) and when we got together, the insanity reached critical mass.

No matter. The spark of Pulphouse Publishing might be lost in the sands of time, but the memories remain. We started *Pulphouse: The Hardback Magazine* for a variety of reasons. Dean's first novel, *Laying the Music to Rest*, had just been rejected by a major publisher because it couldn't decide how to market the book.[1] A number of my stories had been returned by my regular editors because the stories were "too weird." We complained that there weren't enough markets —especially markets open to unusual work—and we decided to do something about it.

Of course, we had no idea what we were getting into.

We did have some experience. I knew, from my radio days, that in order to be experimental, we could not be tied to a subscription or advertising base. Too many subscribers revoke their subscriptions because of dirty words or sex scenes. (Just that year, an editor had warned me that even though he was publishing one of my stories, he was worried that he would lose a lot of subscribers because of a scene in which a woman rapes a man.) Too many advertisers tried to control content they viewed as potentially harmful to their product or their image. I had also spent my years at the station editing a nightly newscast. I understood that content had to flow together and that deadlines were firm.

Dean, on the other hand, published a writer's magazine for a number of years. He knew that there was more to a magazine than its editorial content. Design, marketing, and a unified vision were important. His years as an architect gave him both design skills and an understanding of the importance of details. His law and business experience helped with the publishing side.

We studied the market and decided that, with our skills, we could put together a hardback book filled with short stories by name and unknown writers and sell it to the collector's market. The collecting field was going through a boom during that period, and would go for anything unusual and different; a hardback magazine with the freedom

---

[1] The editor who did publish the book, Brian Thomsen, didn't have that problem. He published the book as science fiction. It wound up as a finalist for the Bram Stoker Award for best first horror novel of the year. Evidently, there were people who liked it regardless of whatever label it wore.

to publish stories in any (and every) genre seemed to us to be unusual—and worthwhile. We didn't expect to sell a lot of copies, but we set our price structure so that we didn't have to. We called the book a magazine instead of an anthology because it was quarterly, available by *subscription*. Originally it was going to have interior advertising and more columns. (Look inside Issue One. Our one and only ad appears there, and shows why we decided against advertising.)

Dean spent hours and hours, sometimes going days without sleep, designing the look of the magazine. He also read slush. I read manuscripts too, and contacted writers. Jack Williamson agreed to let us reprint his essays on writing. Steve Rasnic Tem and William F. Wu sent us wonderful stories. Kij Johnson was the first new name to rise above the slush pile. We grew excited with our growing project.

Then we tried to contact other writers, and discovered that we couldn't explain what a "hardback magazine" was. Dean had already decided to do a mock-up of the magazine. Detail-oriented perfectionist that he is, he wanted everything to be exactly right on the first issue. That meant we needed to have a practice step in between.

A Pulphouse tradition, Issue Zero, was born. Issue Zero (which we have done on all of our projects since) is a mock-up, done to show exactly what the project will look like, and to work out the bugs in the system. Issue Zero of the Hardback Magazine shows that we expected the magazine to be smaller in size and scope than it turned out to be. It also proved to be the smartest thing we did.

Dean used Issue Zero to attract bookstores. I sent copies of it to my favorite writers. Many responded with stories. We gathered an impressive line-up: Kate Wilhelm, Charles de Lint, Edward Bryant. Then I got my phone call from Harlan Ellison.

Actually, it wasn't a phone call. He left a message on my answering machine. "I received your Pulphouse loss leader," he said. "I want to talk to you about it." He left his phone number and hung up.

I called him back before I had time to worry about what he wanted. (After all, the back of my brain reasoned, we did call *Pulphouse* a "Dangerous Magazine." Was he objecting? Were we too close to *Dangerous Visions*?) When Harlan came on the line, my worries evaporated. He was effusive. He thought we were brilliant, absolutely brilliant, to do a mock-up of our product, and for that reason alone, decided to contribute a story to our effort.

He later explained to me what we had done right. Not only had we some impressive names already in our roster (including people who rarely wrote for anthologies), but we proved that we could produce a product. So many magazines appear as announcements in writers' publications and as invitations to writers, but somehow disappear around payment and production time, that writers and agents naturally mistrust any new publication. Most would-be magazine publishers never realize the costs involved. We, at least, were thinking about production as well as editorial content.

As the list of contributors for the first issue began to grow, so did book dealers' interest. People we had never met ordered the product in quantities we hadn't even dreamed of. Within a month, we doubled our projected sales, and sold out of our first issue before it appeared in August. And we realized we were in over our heads.

Dean and I are writers, creative types who pride ourselves on our lack of organization and our messy desks. (Dean, striving for perfection even in clutter, tends to have a *perfectly* messy desk.) We knew nothing about shipping, packing, or filing. We had enough work for the two of us, plus two more without trying to stay organized. If we had to be organized, we would be overloaded.

But to run a business of the size that Pulphouse had become in just a few short months, we needed to be organized or we would fail.

Enter Debra Gray Cook. Debb was a friend of Dean's who worked as a secretary/receptionist for a poster company. She took a half-time job at a video store because she was bored. She had been offering her assistance for months. We finally took her up on it.

Bringing in Debb was the second most intelligent thing we did.

Debb immediately organized us. Her job at the poster company had taught her about shipping. She spent a hot, dismal weekend with us (volunteering her labor—and we worked all night and into the next day) in Dean's unairconditioned second floor apartment shipping out Pulphouse's first issue. By the end of the marathon shipping session, we were all covered with sweat and styrofoam. Debb and I had rug burns from kneeling on the rough carpet, and shoving books into boxes. Dean had thrown out his back from carrying books up and down two flights of stairs (never do a shipping from the second floor), and Debb could barely move her arms from pulling the tape gun. We were too tired to celebrate.

But celebrate we eventually did. And we were well into Issue 2 by the time we saw that the reviews from the first issue were positive.

(Boy, was I relieved.) Pulphouse Publishing grew into an entity all its own. First Dean quit his day job. I followed, and Debb followed not long after that. We acquired Axolotl Press, started *Author's Choice Monthly*, and found an office. We hired help, most notably Mark Budz, who is now the editor of our Short Story Paperback Line. The office grew another story. At this writing, we have 14 employees, and more projects than I care to think about. Every time we announce something new, people tell us that we're crazy, that what we're trying is impossible. And we love proving them wrong.

But we never could have done this without the help and advice of Bill Trojan (skeptic book dealer with a heart of gold), Nina Kiriki Hoffman (typesetter/proofer/good friend *extraordinaire*), Phil Barnhart (former boss—a man who knows potential when he sees it [thank god]), Alan Bard Newcomer (computer/technical wizard), and Lynn Adams (whose creative touches have added more to the Pulphouse memorabilia line than anyone else's). These folks have been with us from the beginning. The other folks, whose contributions have been almost as significant, are listed on the acknowledgments page. These people have given more than we could ever hope for. We have a wonderful group of friends. They've supported us well.

As has the science fiction community. Issue 12, the last issue of the hardback, appeared this summer, and a number of people are sad to see it go. So are we. But the hardback served its time. We're moving on to larger, crazier projects with the potential for a larger audience. Dean Wesley Smith is now editing our flagship: *Pulphouse: A Weekly Magazine*. By the time you read this, he will already have more than 12 issues completed and shipped (in our air-conditioned shipping office on the first floor, thank you). It took the hardback three years to get that far. I hope that the Weekly will have as much success and acclaim. It already does, from my point of view.

I am pleased, though, that Gordon Van Gelder helped us do this book. Only 1250 copies of each issue of the hardback magazine exist. Although a number of the stories were reprinted in year's best anthologies, a number weren't. I wish we could find a paperback publisher for the entire run (even though I know I'm dreaming). But for every story included in this volume, there are five that I would have liked to have added. For every author, there are a dozen more I would have liked to include. Picking the stories for this volume was one of the most difficult tasks I've ever done.

So, if you get a chance, search out copies of the hardback magazine. Look up stories by newer writers, like Marina Fitch, Ken Wisman, and Kij Johnson. Keep your eyes open for stories of theirs; they'll be showing up in lots of publications. We weren't able to include stories by Damon Knight, Robert Sheckley, or Kate Wilhelm either. Please remember that what you have in your hand is just a sampling of what we have done in the hardback—and of what Pulphouse Publishing plans to do in the future. And above all, enjoy.

—KRISTINE KATHRYN RUSCH
Eugene, Oregon

While She Was Out

Edward Bryant

We approached Edward Bryant, award-winning writer, critic, and all-around good guy, at Norwescon in 1988. He promised us a story, and this one arrived just before our deadline closed for the first issue. Since then, he has written stories and essays for the hardback magazine, become a columnist for the Weekly, compiled an *Author's Choice Monthly* volume, and written two novellas (one in collaboration with Dan Simmons) for our Axolotl Press line.

Oh, yeah, and he's written for other publishers too.

"While She Was Out" opened that first issue of the hardback magazine. The story is tough, yet sensitive, just like we wanted the magazine to be.

It was what her husband said then that was the last straw.

"Christ," muttered Kenneth disgustedly from the family room. He grasped a Bud longneck in one red-knuckled hand, the cable remote tight in the other. This was the time of night when he generally fell into the largest number of stereotypes. "I swear to God you're on the rag three weeks out of every month. PMS, my ass."

Della Myers deliberately bit down on what she wanted to answer. PXMS, she thought. That's what the twins' teacher had called it last week over coffee after the parent-teacher conference Kenneth had skipped. Pre-holiday syndrome. It took a genuine effort not to pick up the cordless Northwestern Bell phone and brain Kenneth with one savage, cathartic swipe. "I'm going out."

"So?" said her husband. "This is Thursday. Can't be the auto mechanics made simple for wusses. Self defense?" He shook his head. "That's every other Tuesday. Something new, honey? Maybe a therapy group?"

"I'm going to Southeast Plaza. I need to pick up some things."

"Get the extra-absorbent ones," said her husband. He grinned and thumbed up the volume. ESPN was bringing in wide shots of something that looked vaguely like group tennis from some sweaty-looking third-world country.

"Wrapping paper," she said. "I'm getting some gift-wrap and ribbon." Were there fourth-world countries? she wondered. Would they accept political refugees from America? "Will you put the twins to bed by nine?"

"Stallone's on HBO at nine," Kenneth said. "I'll bag 'em out by half-past eight."

"Fine." She didn't argue.

"I'll give them a good bedtime story." He paused. "The Princess and the Pea."

"Fine." Della shrugged on her long down-filled coat. Any more, she did her best not to swallow the bait. "I told them they could each have a chocolate chip cookie with their milk."

"Christ, Della. Why the hell don't we just adopt the dentist? Maybe give him an automatic monthly debit from the checking account?"

"One cookie apiece," she said, implacable.

Kenneth shrugged, apparently resigned.

She picked up the keys to the Subaru. "I won't be long."

"Just be back by breakfast."

Della stared at him. What if I don't come back at all? She had actually said that once. Kenneth had smiled and asked whether she was going to run away with the gypsies, or maybe go off to join some pirates. It had been a temptation to say yes, dammit, yes, I'm going. But there were the twins. Della suspected pirates didn't take along their children. "Don't worry," she said. I've got nowhere else to go. But she didn't say that aloud.

Della turned and went upstairs to the twins' room to tell them good night. Naturally they both wanted to go with her to the mall. Each was afraid she wasn't going to get the hottest item in the Christmas doll department—the Little BeeDee Birth Defect Baby. There had been a run on the BeeDee, but Della had shopped for the twins early. "Daddy's going to tell you a story," she promised. The pair wasn't impressed.

"I want to see Santa," Terri said, with dogged, five-year-old insistence.

"You both saw Santa. Remember?"

"I forgot some things. An' I want to tell him again about BeeDee."

"Me, too," said Tammi. With Tammi, it was always "me too."

"Maybe this weekend," said Della.

"Will Daddy remember our cookies?" said Terri.

Before she exited the front door, Della took the chocolate chip cookies from the kitchen closet and set the sack on the stairstep where Kenneth could not fail to stumble over it.

"So long," she called.

"Bring me back something great from the mall," he said. His only other response was to heighten the crowd noise from Upper Zambo-somewhere-or-other.

Sleety snow was falling, the accumulation beginning to freeze on the streets. Della was glad she had the Subaru. So far this winter, she hadn't needed to use the four-wheel drive, but tonight the reality of having it reassured her.

Southeast Plaza was a mess. This close to Christmas, the normally spacious parking lots were jammed. Della took a chance and circled the row of spaces nearest to the mall entrances. If she were lucky, she'd be able to react instantly to someone's backup lights and snaffle a parking place within five seconds of its being vacated. That didn't happen. She cruised the second row, the third. Then—There! She reacted without thinking, seeing the vacant spot just beyond a metallic blue van. She swung the Subaru to the left.

And stamped down hard on the brake.

Some moron had parked an enormous barge of an ancient Plymouth so that it overlapped two diagonal spaces.

The Subaru slid to a stop with its nose about half an inch from the Plymouth's dinosaurian bumper. In the midst of her shock and sudden anger, Della saw the chrome was pocked with rust. The Subaru's headlights reflected back at her.

She said something unpleasant, the kind of language she usually only thought in dark silence. Then she backed her car out of the truncated space and resumed the search for parking. What Della eventually found was a free space on the extreme perimeter of the lot. She resigned herself to trudging a quarter mile through the slush. She hadn't worn boots. The icy water crept into her flats, soaked her toes.

"Shit," she said. "Shit shit shit."

Her shortest-distance-between-two-points course took her past the Plymouth hogging the two parking spots. Della stopped a moment, contemplating the darkened behemoth. It was a dirty gold with the remnants of a vinyl roof peeling away like the flaking of a scabrous scalp. In the glare of the mercury vapor lamp, she could see that the rocker panels were riddled with rust holes. Odd. So much corrosion didn't happen in the dry Colorado air. She glanced curiously at the rear license plate. It was obscured with dirty snow.

She stared at the huge old car and realized she was getting angry. Not just irritated. Real, honest-to-god, hardcore pissed off. What kind of imbeciles would take up two parking spaces on a rotten night just two weeks before Christmas?

Ones that drove a vintage, not-terribly-kept-up Plymouth, obviously.

Without even thinking about what she was doing, Della took out the spiral notebook from her handbag. She flipped to the blank page past tomorrow's grocery list and uncapped the fine-tip marker (it was supposed to write across anything—in this snow, it had *better*) and scrawled a message:

DEAR JERK, IT'S GREAT YOU COULD USE UP TWO PARKING SPACES ON A NIGHT LIKE THIS. EVER HEAR OF THE JOY OF SHARING?

She paused, considering; then appended:

—A CONCERNED FRIEND

Della folded the paper as many times as she could, to protect it from the wet, then slipped it under the driver's-side wiper blade.

It wouldn't do any good—she was sure this was the sort of driver who ordinarily would have parked illegally in the handicapped zone —but it made her feel better. Della walked on to the mall entrance and realized she was smiling.

She bought some rolls of foil wrapping paper for the adult gifts—assuming she actually gave Kenneth anything she'd bought for him—and an ample supply of Strawberry Shortcake pattern for the twins' presents. Della decided to splurge—she realized she was getting tired—and selected a package of pre-tied ribbon bows rather than simply taking a roll. She also bought a package of tampons.

Della wandered the mall for a little while, checking out the shoe stores, looking for something on sale in deep blue, a pair she could wear after Kenneth's office party for staff and spouses. What she *really* wanted were some new boots. Time enough for those after the holiday when the prices went down. Nothing appealed to her. Della knew she should be shopping for Kenneth's family in Nebraska. She couldn't wait forever to mail off their packages.

The hell with it. Della realized she was simply delaying returning home. Maybe she *did* need a therapy group, she thought. There was no relish to the thought of spending another night sleeping beside Kenneth, listening to the snoring that was interrupted only by the grinding of teeth. She thought that the sound of Kenneth's jaws moving against one another must be like hearing a speeded-up recording of continental drift.

She looked at her watch. A little after nine. No use waiting any longer. She did up the front of her coat and joined the flow of shoppers out into the snow.

Della realized, as she passed the rusted old Plymouth, that something wasn't the same. *What's wrong with this picture?* It was the note. It wasn't there. Probably it had slipped out from under the wiper blade with the wind and the water. Maybe the flimsy notebook paper had simply dissolved.

She no longer felt like writing another note. She dismissed the irritating lumber barge from her reality and walked on to her car.

Della let the Subaru warm up for thirty seconds (the consumer auto mechanics class had told her not to let the engine idle for the long minutes she had once believed necessary) and then slipped the shift into reverse.

The passenger compartment flooded with light.

She glanced into the rearview mirror and looked quickly away. A bright, glaring eye had stared back. Another quivered in the side mirror.

"Jesus Christ," she said under her breath. "The crazies are out tonight." She hit the clutch with one foot, the brake with the other, and waited for the car behind her to remove itself. Nothing happened. The headlights in the mirror flicked to bright. "Dammit." Della left the Subaru in neutral and got out of the car.

She shaded her eyes and squinted. The front of the car behind hers looked familiar. It was the gold Plymouth.

Two unseen car-doors clicked open and chunked shut again.

The lights abruptly went out and Della blinked, her eyes trying to adjust to the dim mercury vapor illumination from the pole a few car-lengths away.

She felt a cold thrill of unease in her belly and turned back toward the car.

"I've got a gun," said a voice. "Really." It sounded male and young. "I'll aim at your snatch first."

Someone else giggled, high and shrill.

Della froze in place. This couldn't be happening. It absolutely could not.

Her eyes were adjusting, the glare-phantoms drifting out to the limit of her peripheral vision and vanishing. She saw three figures in front of her, then a fourth. She didn't see a gun.

"Just what do you think you're doing?" she said.

"Not doing *nothin'*, yet." That, she saw, was the black one. He stood to the left of the white kid who had claimed to have a gun. The pair was bracketed by a boy who looked Chinese or Vietnamese and a young man with dark, Hispanic good looks. All four looked to be in their late teens or very early twenties. Four young men. Four ethnic groups represented. Della repressed a giggle she thought might be the first step toward hysteria.

"So what are you guys? Working on your merit badge in tolerance? Maybe selling magazine subscriptions?" Della immediately regretted saying that. Her husband was always riding her for smarting off.

"Funny lady," said the Hispanic. "We just happen to get along." He glanced to his left. "You laughing, Huey?"

The black shook his head. "Too cold. I'm shiverin' out here. I didn't bring no clothes for this."

"Easy way to fix that, man," said the white boy. To Della, he said, "Vinh, Tomas, Huey, me, we all got similar interests, you know?"

"Listen—" Della started to say.

"Chuckie," said the black Della now assumed was Huey, "Let's us just shag out of here, okay?"

"*Chuckie?*" said Della.

"Shut up!" said Chuckie. To Huey, he said, "Look, we came up here for a vacation, right? The word is fun." He said to Della, "Listen, we were having a good time until we saw you stick the note under the wiper." His eyes glistened in the vapor-lamp glow. "I don't like getting any static from some 'burb-bitch just 'cause she's on the rag."

"For God's sake," said Della disgustedly. She decided he didn't really have a gun. "Screw off!" The exhaust vapor from the Subaru spiraled up around her. "I'm leaving, boys."

"Any trouble here, Miss?" said a new voice. Everyone looked. It was one of the mall rent-a-cops, bulky in his fur trimmed jacket and Russian-styled cap. His hand lay casually across the unsnapped holster flap at his hip.

"Not if these underage creeps move their barge so I can back out," said Della.

"How about it, guys?" said the rent-a-cop.

Now there *was* a gun, a dark pistol, in Chuckie's hand, and he pointed it at the rent-a-cop's face. "Naw," Chuckie said. "This was gonna be a vacation, but what the heck. No witnesses, I reckon."

"For God's sake," said the rent-a-cop, starting to back away.

Chuckie grinned and glanced aside at his friends. "Remember the security guy at the mall in Tucson?" To Della, he said, "Most of these rent-a-pig companies don't give their guys any ammo. Liability laws and all that shit. Too bad." He lifted the gun purposefully.

The rent-a-cop went for his pistol anyway. Chuckie shot him in the face. Red pulp sprayed out the back of his skull and stained the slush as the man's body flopped back and forth, spasming.

"For chrissake," said Chuckie in exasperation. "Enough already. Relax, man." He leaned over his victim and deliberately aimed and fired, aimed and fired. The second shot entered the rent-a-cop's left eye. The third shattered his teeth.

Della's eyes recorded everything as though she were a movie camera. Everything was moving in slow motion and she was numb. She tried to make things speed up. Without thinking about the decision, she spun and made for her car door. She knew it was hopeless.

"Chuckie!"

"So? Where's she gonna go? We got her blocked. I'll just put one through her windshield and we can go out and pick up a couple of sixpacks, maybe hit the late show at some other mall."

Della heard him fire one more time. Nothing tore through the back of her skull. He was still blowing apart the rent-a-cop's head.

She slammed into the Subaru's driver seat and punched the door-lock switch, for all the good that would do. Della hit the four-wheel-drive switch. *That* was what Chuckie hadn't thought about. She jammed the gearshift into first, gunned the engine, and popped the clutch. The Subaru barely protested as the front tires clawed and bounced over the six-inch concrete row barrier. The barrier screeched along the underside of the frame. Then the rear wheels were over and the Subaru fishtailed momentarily.

Don't over-correct, she thought. It was a prayer.

The Subaru straightened out and Della was accelerating down the mall's outer perimeter service road, slush spraying to either side. Now what? she thought. People must have heard the shots. The lot would be crawling with cops.

But in the meantime—

The lights, bright and blinding, blasted against her mirrors.

Della stamped the accelerator to the floor.

This was crazy! This didn't happen to people—not to *real* people. The mall security man's blood in the snow had been real enough.

In the rearview, there was a sudden flash just above the left-side headlight, then another. It was a muzzle-blast, Della realized. They were shooting at her. It was just like on TV. The scalp on the back of her head itched. Would she feel it when the bullet crashed through?

The twins! Kenneth. She wanted to see them all, to be safely with them. Just be anywhere but here!

Della spun the wheel, ignoring the stop sign and realizing that the access road dead-ended. She could go right or left, so went right. She thought it was the direction of home. Not a good choice. The lights were all behind her now; she could see nothing but darkness ahead. Della tried to remember what lay beyond the mall on this side. There were housing developments, both completed and under construction.

There had to be a 7-Eleven, a filling station, *something*. Anything. But there wasn't, and then the pavement ended. At first the road was suddenly rougher, the potholes yawning deeper. Then the slush-marked asphalt stopped. The Subaru bounced across the gravel; within thirty yards, the gravel deteriorated to roughly graded dirt. The dirt surface more properly could be called mud.

A wooden barrier loomed ahead, the reflective stripes and lightly falling snow glittering in the headlights.

It *was* like on TV, Della thought. She gunned the engine and ducked sideways, even with the dash, as the Subaru plowed into the barrier. She heard a sickening *crack* and shattered windshield glass sprayed down around her. Della felt the car veer. She tried to sit upright again, but the auto was spinning too fast.

The Subaru swung a final time and smacked firm against a low grove of young pine. The engine coughed and stalled. Della hit the light switch. She smelled the overwhelming tang of crushed pine needles flooding with the snow through the space where the windshield had been. The engine groaned when she twisted the key, didn't start.

Della risked a quick look around. The Plymouth's lights were visible, but the car was farther back than she had dared hope. The size of the lights wasn't increasing and the beams pointed up at a steep angle. Probably the heavy Plymouth had slid in the slush, gone off the road, was stuck for good.

She tried the key, and again the engine didn't catch. She heard something else—voices getting closer. Della took the key out of the ignition and glanced around the dark passenger compartment. Was there anything she could use? Anything at all? Not in the glovebox. She knew there was nothing there but the owner's manual and a large pack of sugarless spearmint gum.

The voices neared.

Della reached under the dash and tugged the trunk release. Then she rolled down the window and slipped out into the darkness. She wasn't too stunned to forget that the overhead-light would go on if she opened the door.

At least one of the boys had a flashlight. The beam flickered and danced along the snow.

Della stumbled to the rear of the Subaru. By feel, she found the toolbox. With her other hand, she sought out the lug wrench. Then she moved away from the car.

She wished she had a gun. She wished she had learned to *use* a gun. That had been something tagged for a vague future when she'd finished her consumer mechanics course and the self defense workshop, and had some time again to take another night course. It wasn't, she had reminded herself, that she was paranoid. Della simply wanted to be better prepared for the exigencies of living in the city. The suburbs weren't *the city* to Kenneth, but if you were a girl from rural Montana, they were.

She hadn't expected *this*.

She hunched down. Her nose told her the shelter she had found was a hefty clump of sagebrush. She was perhaps twenty yards from the Subaru now. The boys were making no attempt at stealth. She heard them talking to each other as the flashlight beam bobbed around her stalled car.

"So, she in there chilled with her brains all over the wheel?" said Tomas, the Hispanic kid.

"You an optimist?" said Chuckie. He laughed, a high-pitched giggle. "No, she ain't here, you dumb shit. This one's a tough lady." Then he said, "Hey, lookie there!"

"What you doin'?" said Huey. "We ain't got time for that."

"Don't be too sure. Maybe we can use this."

What had he found? Della wondered.

"Now we do what?" said Vinh. He had a slight accent.

"This be the West," said Huey. "I guess now we're mountain men, just like in the movies."

"Right," said Chuckie. "Track her. There's mud. There's snow. How far can she get?"

"There's the trail," said Tomas. "Shine the light over there. She must be pretty close."

Della turned. Hugging the toolbox, trying not to let it clink or clatter, she fled into the night.

They cornered her a few minutes later.

Or it could have been an hour. There was no way she could read her watch. All Della knew was that she had run; she had run and she had attempted circling around to where she might have a shot at making it to the distant lights of the shopping mall. Along the way, she'd felt the brush clawing at her denim jeans and the mud and slush attempting to suck down her shoes. She tried to make out shapes in the clouded-over dark, evaluating every murky form as a potential hiding place.

"Hey, baby," said Huey from right in front of her.

Della recoiled, feinted to the side, collided painfully with a wooden fence. The boards gave only slightly. She felt a long splinter drive through the down coat and spear into her shoulder. When Della jerked away, she felt the splinter tear away from its board and then break off.

The flashlight snapped on, the beam at first blinding her, then lowering to focus on her upper body. From their voices, she knew all four were there. Della wanted to free a hand to pull the splinter loose from her shoulder. Instead she continued cradling the blue plastic toolbox.

"Hey," said Chuckie, "what's in that thing? Family treasure, maybe?"

Della remained mute. She'd already gotten into trouble enough, wising off.

"Let's see," said Chuckie. "Show us, Della-honey."

She stared at his invisible face.

Chuckie giggled. "Your driver's license, babe. In your purse. In the car."

Shit, she thought.

"Lousy picture." Chuckie. "I think maybe we're gonna make your face match it." Again, that ghastly laugh. "Meantime, let's see what's in the box, okay?"

"Jewels, you think?" said Vinh.

"Naw, I don't think," said his leader. "But maybe she was makin' the bank deposit or something." He addressed Della, "You got enough goodies for us, maybe we can be bought off."

No chance, she thought. They want everything. My money, my rings, my watch. She tried to swallow, but her throat was too dry. My life.

"Open the box," said Chuckie, voice mean now.

"Open the box," said Tomas. Huey echoed him. The four started chanting, "Open the box, open the box, open the box."

"All right," she almost screamed. "I'll do it." They stopped their chorus. Someone snickered. Her hands moving slowly, Della's brain raced. Do it, she thought. But be careful. So careful. She let the lug wrench rest across her palm below the toolbox. With her other hand, she unsnapped the catch and slid up the lid toward the four. She didn't think any of them could see in, though the flashlight beam was focused now on the toolbox lid.

Della reached inside, as deliberately as she could, trying to betray nothing of what she hoped to do. It all depended upon what lay on top. Her bare fingertips touched the cold steel of the crescent wrench. Her fingers curled around the handle.

"This is pretty dull," said Tomas. "Let's just rape her."

Now!

She withdrew the wrench, cocked her wrist back and hurled the tool about two feet above the flashlight's glare. Della snapped it just like her daddy had taught her to throw a hardball. She hadn't liked baseball all that much. But now—

The wrench crunched something and Chuckie screamed. The flashlight dropped to the snow.

Snapping shut the toolbox, Della sprinted between Chuckie and the one she guessed was Huey.

The black kid lunged for her and slipped in the muck, toppling face-first into the slush. Della had a peripheral glimpse of Tomas leaping toward her, but his leading foot came down on the back of Huey's head, grinding the boy's face into the mud. Huey's scream bubbled; Tomas cursed and tumbled forward, trying to stop himself with out-thrust arms.

All Della could think as she gained the darkness was, I should have grabbed the light.

She heard the one she thought was Vinh, laughing. "Cripes, guys, neat. Just like Moe and Curley and that other one."

"Shut up," said Chuckie's voice. It sounded pinched and in pain. "Shut the fuck up." The timbre squeaked and broke. "Get up, you dorks. Get the bitch."

Sticks and stones—Della thought. Was she getting hysterical? There was no good reason not to.

As she ran—and stumbled—across the nightscape, Della could feel the long splinter moving with the movement of the muscles in her shoulder. The feeling of it, not just the pain, but the sheer, physical sensation of intrusion, nauseated her.

I've got to stop, she thought. I've got to rest. I've got to think.

Della stumbled down the side of a shallow gulch and found she was splashing across a shallow, frigid stream. Water. It triggered something. Disregarding the cold soaking her flats and numbing her feet, she turned and started upstream, attempting to splash as a little as possible. This had worked, she seemed to recall, in *Uncle Tom's Cabin*, as well as a lot of bad prison escape movies.

The boys were hardly experienced mountain men. They weren't Indian trackers. This ought to take care of her trail.

After what she estimated to be at least a hundred yards, when her feet felt like blocks of wood and she felt she was losing her balance, Della clambered out of the stream and struggled up the side of the gulch. She found herself in groves of pine, much like the trees where her Subaru had ended its skid. At least the pungent evergreens supplied some shelter against the prairie wind that had started to rise.

She heard noise from down in the gulch. It was music. It made her think of the twins.

"What the *fuck* are you doing?" Chuckie's voice.

"It's a tribute, man. A gesture." Vinh. "It's his blaster."

Della recognized the tape. Rap music. Run DMC, the Beastie Boys, one of those groups.

"Christ, I didn't mean it." Tomas. "It's her fault."

"Well, he's dead," said Chuckie, "and that's it for him. Now turn that shit off. Somebody might hear."

"Who's going to hear?" said Vinh. "Nobody can hear out here. Just us, and her."

"That's the point. She can."

"So what?" said Tomas. "We got the gun, we got the light. She's got nothin' but that stupid box."

"We *had* Huey," said Chuckie. "Now we don't. Shut off the blaster, dammit."

"Okay." Vinh's voice sounded sullen. There was a loud click and the rap echo died.

Della huddled against the rough bark of a pine trunk, hugging the box and herself. The boy's dead, she thought. So? said her common sense. He would have killed you, maybe raped you, tortured you before pulling the trigger. The rest are going to have to die too.

No.

Yes, said her practical side. You have no choice. They started this.

I put the note under the wiper blade.

Get serious. That was harmless. These three are going to kill you. They will hurt you first, then they'll put the gun inside your mouth and—

Della wanted to cry, to scream. She knew she could not. It was absolutely necessary that she not break now.

Terri, she thought, Tammi. I love you. After a while, she remembered Kenneth. Even you. I love you too. Not much, but some.

"Let's look up above," came the voice from the gully. Chuckie. Della heard the wet scrabbling sounds as the trio scratched and pulled their way up from the stream-bed. As it caught the falling snow, the flashlight looked like the beam from a searchlight at a movie premiere.

Della edged back behind the pine and slowly moved to where the trees were closer together. Boughs laced together, screening her.

"Now what?" said Tomas.

"We split up." Chuckie gestured; the flashlight beam swung wide. "You go through the middle. Vinh and me'll take the sides."

"Then why don't you give me the light?" said Tomas.

"I stole the sucker. It's mine."

"Shit, I could just walk past her."

Chuckie laughed. "Get real, dude. You'll smell her, hear her, somethin'. Trust me."

Tomas said something Della couldn't make out, but the tone was unconvinced.

"Now *do* it," said Chuckie. The light moved off to Della's left. She heard the squelching of wet shoes moving toward her. Evidently Tomas had done some wading in the gully. Either that or the slush was taking its toll.

Tomas couldn't have done better with radar. He came straight for her.

Della guessed the boy was ten feet away from her, five feet, just the other side of the pine. The lug wrench was the spider type, in the shape of a cross. She clutched the black steel of the longest arm and brought her hand back. When she detected movement around the edge of the trunk, she swung with hysterical strength, aiming at his head.

Tomas staggered back. The sharp arm of the lug wrench had

caught him under the nose, driving the cartilage back up into his face. About a third of the steel was hidden in flesh. "Unh!" He tried to cry out, but all he could utter was, "Unh, unh!"

"Tomas?" Chuckie was yelling. "What the hell are you doing?"

The flashlight flickered across the grove. Della caught a momentary glimpse of Tomas lurching backward with the lug wrench impaled in his face as though he were wearing some hideous Halloween accessory.

"Unh!" said Tomas once more. He backed into a tree, then slid down the trunk until he was seated in the snow. The flashlight beam jerked across that part of the grove again and Della saw Tomas' eyes stare wide open, dark and blank. Blood was running off the ends of the perpendicular lug wrench arms.

"I see her!" someone yelled. "I think she got Tomas. She's a devil!" Vinh.

"So chill her!"

Della heard branches and brush crashing off to her side. She jerked open the plastic toolbox, but her fingers were frozen and the container crashed to the ground. She tried to catch the contents as they cascaded into the slush and the darkness. Her fingers closed on something, one thing.

The handle felt good. It was the wooden-hafted screwdriver, the sharp one with the slot head. Her auto mechanics teacher had approved. Insulated handle, he'd said. Good forged steel shaft. You could use this hummer to pry a tire off its rim.

She didn't even have time to lift it as Vinh crashed into her. His arms and legs wound around her like eels.

"Got her!" he screamed. "Chuckie, come here and shoot her."

They rolled in the viscid, muddy slush. Della worked an arm free. Her good arm. The one with the screwdriver.

There was no question of asking him nicely to let go, of giving warning, of simply aiming to disable. Her self defense teacher had drilled into all the students the basic dictum of do what you can, do what you have to do. No rules, no apologies.

With all her strength, Della drove the screwdriver up into the base of his skull. She thrust and twisted the tool until she felt her knuckles dig into his stiff hair. Vinh screamed, a high keening wail that cracked and shattered as blood spurted out of his nose and mouth, splattering against Della's neck. The Vietnamese boy's arms and legs tensed and then let go as his body vibrated spastically in some sort of fit.

Della pushed him away from her and staggered to her feet. Her nose was full of the odor she remembered from the twins' diaper pail.

She knew she should retrieve the screwdriver, grasp the handle tightly and twist it loose from Vinh's head. She couldn't. All she could do at this point was simply turn and run. Run again. And hope the survivor of the four boys didn't catch her.

But Chuckie had the light, and Chuckie had the gun. She had a feeling Chuckie was in no mood to give up. Chuckie would find her. He would make her pay for the loss of his friends.

But if she had to pay, Della thought, the price would be dear.

Prices, she soon discovered, were subject to change without warning.

With only one remaining pursuer, Della thought she ought to be able to get away. Maybe not easily, but now there was no crossfire of spying eyes, no ganging-up of assailants. There was just one boy left, even if he *was* a psychopath carrying a loaded pistol.

Della was shaking. It was fatigue, she realized. The endless epinephrine rush of flight and fight. Probably, too, the letdown from just having killed two other human beings. She didn't want to have to think about the momentary sight of blood flowing off the shining ends of the lug wrench, the sensation of how it *felt* when the slot-headed screwdriver drove up into Vinh's brain. But she couldn't order herself to forget these things. It was akin to someone telling her not, under any circumstances, to think about milking a purple cow.

Della tried. No, she thought. Don't think about it at all. She thought about dismembering the purple cow with a chainsaw. Then she heard Chuckie's voice. The boy was still distant, obviously casting around virtually at random in the pine groves. Della stiffened.

"They're cute, Della-honey. I'll give 'em that." He giggled. "Terri and Tammi. God, didn't you and your husband have any more imagination than that?"

No, Della thought. We each had too much imagination. Tammi and Terri were simply the names we finally could agree on. The names of compromise.

"You know something?" Chuckie raised his voice. "Now that I know where they live, I could drive over there in a while and say howdy. They wouldn't know a thing about what was going on, about what happened to their mom while she was out at the mall."

Oh God! thought Della.

"You want me to pass on any messages?"

"You little bastard!" She cried it out without thinking.

"Touchy, huh?" Chuckie slopped across the wet snow in her direction. "Come on out of the trees, Della-honey."

Della said nothing. She crouched behind a deadfall of brush and dead limbs. She was perfectly still.

Chuckie stood equally still, not more than twenty feet away. He stared directly at her hiding place, as though he could see through the night and brush. "Listen," he said. "This is getting real, you know, *boring*." He waited. "We could be out here all night, you know? All my buddies are gone now, and it's thanks to you, lady. Who the hell you think you are, Clint Eastwood?"

Della assumed that was a rhetorical question.

Chuckie hawked deep in his throat and spat on the ground. He rubbed the base of his throat gingerly with a free hand. "You hurt me, Della-honey. I think you busted my collarbone." He giggled. "But I don't hold grudges. In fact—" He paused contemplatively. "Listen now, I've got an idea. You know about droogs? You know, like in that movie?"

Clockwork Orange, she thought. Della didn't respond.

"Ending was stupid, but the start was pretty cool." Chuckie's personality seemed to have mutated into a manic stage. "Well, me droogs is all gone. I need a new gang, and you're real good, Della-honey. I want you should join me."

"Give me a break," said Della in the darkness.

"No, really," Chuckie said. "You're a born killer. I can tell. You and me, we'd be perfect. We'll blow this popsicle stand and have some real fun. Whaddaya say?"

He's serious, she thought. There was a ring of complete honesty in his voice. She floundered for some answer. "I've got kids," she said.

"We'll take 'em along," said Chuckie. "I like kids, always took care of my brothers and sisters." He paused. "Listen, I'll bet you're on the outs with your old man."

Della said nothing. It would be like running away to be a pirate. Wouldn't it?

Chuckie hawked and spat again. "Yeah, I figured. When we pick up your kids, we can waste him. You like that? I can do it, or you can. Your choice."

You're crazy, she thought. "*I* want to," she found herself saying aloud.

"So come out and we'll talk about it."

"You'll kill me."

"Hey," he said, "I'll kill you if you *don't* come out. I got the light and the gun, remember? This way we can learn to trust each other right from the start. I won't kill you. I won't do nothing. Just talk."

"Okay." Why not, she thought. Sooner or later, he'll find his way in here and put the gun in my mouth and— Della stood up. —but maybe, just maybe—Agony lanced through her knees.

Chuckie cocked his head, staring her way. "Leave the tools."

"I already did. The ones I didn't use."

"Yeah," said Chuckie. "The ones you used, you used real good." He lowered the beam of the flashlight. "Here you go. I don't want you stumbling and falling and maybe breaking your neck."

Della stepped around the deadfall and slowly walked toward him. His hands were at his sides. She couldn't see if he was holding the gun. She stopped when she was a few feet away.

"Hell of a night, huh?" said Chuckie. "It'll be really good to go inside where it's warm and get some coffee." He held the flashlight so that the beam speared into the sky between them.

Della could make out his thin, pain-pinched features. She imagined he could see hers. "I was only going out to the mall for a few things," she said.

Chuckie laughed. "Shit happens."

"What now?" Della said.

"Time for the horror show." His teeth showed ferally as his lips drew back in a smile. "Guess maybe I sort of fibbed." He brought up his hand, glinting of metal.

"That's what I thought," she said, feeling a cold and distant sense of loss. "Huey, there, going to help?" She nodded to a point past his shoulder.

"Huey?" Chuckie looked puzzled just for a second as he glanced to the side. "Huey's—"

Della leapt with all the spring left in her legs. Her fingers closed around his wrist and the hand with the gun. "Christ!" Chuckie screamed, as her shoulder crashed against the spongy place where his broken collarbone pushed out against the skin.

They tumbled on the December ground, Chuckie underneath, Della wrapping her legs around him as though pulling a lover tight. She burrowed her chin into the area of his collarbone and he screamed again. Kenneth had always joked about the sharpness of her chin.

The gun went off. The flash was blinding, the report hurt her ears. Wet snow plumped down from the overhanging pine branches, a large chunk plopping into Chuckie's wide-open mouth. He started to choke.

Then the pistol was in Della's hands. She pulled back from him, getting to her feet, back-pedaling furiously to get out of his reach. She stared down at him along the blued-steel barrel. The pirate captain struggled to his knees.

"Back to the original deal," he said. "Okay?"

I wish, she almost said. Della pulled the trigger. Again. And again.

"Where the hell have you been?" said Kenneth as she closed the front door behind her. "You've been gone for close to three hours." He inspected her more closely. "Della, honey, are you all right?"

"Don't call me that," she said. "Please." She had hoped she would look better, more normal. Unruffled. Once Della had pulled the Subaru up to the drive beside the house, she had spent several minutes using spit and Kleenex trying to fix her mascara. Such makeup as she'd had along was in her handbag, and she had no idea where that was. Probably the police had it; three cruisers with lights flashing had passed her, going the other way, as she was driving north of Southeast Plaza.

"Your clothes." Kenneth gestured. He stood where he was.

Della looked down at herself. She'd tried to wash off the mud, using snow and a rag from the trunk. There was blood too, some of it Chuckie's, the rest doubtless from Vinh and Tomas.

"Honey, was there an accident?"

She had looked at the driver's side of the Subaru for a long minute after getting home. At least the car drove; it must just have been flooded before. But the insurance company wouldn't be happy. The entire side would need a new paint job.

"Sort of," she said.

"Are you hurt?"

To top it all off, she had felt the slow stickiness between her legs as she'd come up the walk. Terrific. She could hardly wait for the cramps to intensify.

"Hurt?" She shook her head. No. "How are the twins?"

"Oh, they're in bed. I checked a half hour ago. They're asleep."

"Good." Della heard sirens in the distance, getting louder, nearing the neighborhood. Probably the police had found her driver's license in Chuckie's pocket. She'd forgotten that.

"So," said Kenneth. It was obvious to Della that he didn't know at this point whether to be angry, solicitous or funny. "What'd you bring me from the mall?"

Della's right hand was nestled in her jacket pocket. She felt the solid bulk, the cool grip of the pistol.

Outside, the volume of sirens increased.

She touched the trigger. She withdrew her hand from the pocket and aimed the pistol at Kenneth. He looked back at her strangely.

The sirens went past. Through the window, Della caught a glimpse of a speeding ambulance. The sound Dopplered down to a silence as distant as the dream that flashed through her head.

Della pulled the trigger and the *click* seemed to echo through the entire house.

Shocked, Kenneth stared at the barrel of the gun, then up at her eyes.

It was okay. She'd counted the shots. Just like in the movies.

"I think," Della said to her husband, "that we need to talk."

Foresight

Michael Swanwick

Michael Swanwick's story, "Foresight," arrived a few days too late for our first issue. No matter, I thought. We needed something strong for our second issue. And "Foresight" is strong.

Michael Swanwick's current novel, *Stations of the Tide*, is climbing the Nebula ballot. His other novels, *In the Drift* and *Vacuum Flowers*, have received great critical acclaim, as has his recent novella *Griffin's Egg*.

"Foresight" fits into a different category of *Pulphouse* story: the kind that challenges the perceptions.

He died.

They killed John Fox in the unlit parking lot behind an abandoned Safeway on the outskirts of the Altoona Reclamation Area. There were four of them, tall and slender in Italian suits. Two knelt on his arms, and another held his legs while the fourth injected a cardioparalytic into his heart.

He whited out for an instant as his head hit the tarmac, and when he came to, the pavement was gritty under his cheek, and he could see a flattened section of rusted tailpipe, the styrofoam sleeve from a

Coke bottle, and a galaxy of broken glass. A cigarette coal tumbled inches from his face, a tiny midnight sun. It was the cheery reddish-orange of Halloween pumpkins and midwinter bonfires. The wind puffed it away. Crickets chirped in the tangle of deadwood, chickweed and thistle at the verge of the lot.

There was a momentary thrill of horror as he looked down the narrowing tunnel of his life at the instant of approaching death. So near, and beyond it . . . blackness, mystery. It might be that all men die alike, but it was still awful to die in ignorance. "Why are you doing this?" he cried.

The three with the stiff, robotlike expressions of predeterminists went about their business as if he were about to say nothing—but the fourth smiled sadly, even fondly. He paused, the needle-case halfway out of his inner jacket pocket. "Who can say? The past is unknowable, and the future is fixed—only in the present moment can we act with grace. You are about to die well. Let that comfort you." He made a short, formal bow.

They were Chinese, all of them, corporate assassins from Neue Telefunken's Taiwanese division. They stepped from their stretch Cadillac smoothly, calmly. They knew he was about to die as well as he did. Their faces were white triangles, and they had shadows in place of their eyes. One rolled down his window to flick away his cigarette. The coal was knocked free.

Fox leaned against his car, trying to compose himself. All that was important now, as his assassin would soon say, was to die well. The Camaro was a ruin—a hole had been punched through the engine block by an illegal, but quite effective, Israeli combat laser.

The long, midnight-black limo whispered to a halt just ten yards behind him.

An hour before, Fox sat naked on a chair beside an unmade motel bed, alone. His trousers, belt still in the loops, lay at his feet, but he made no move to pick them up. He smoked a Marlboro slowly, thinking about his death. The killers must be on their way already. They probably had some kind of tracer on his car, because he wasn't going to notice anyone following him when he left. Then again—they were *going* to find him. They might not need a mechanism; maybe Fate would simply bring them to him when the time came.

The woman left. She picked up her handbag.

Lying on the bed, Fox watched her dress. Her suit was expensive: gray wool, cut-for-success, with a little corporate jacket and a single string of pearls so luminous they glowed on her neck. She wore an imported German *fikt-nicht* skirt, and authoritative mid-height heels. But under that were a black lace bra, silk panties so sheer her pubic triangle showed through, and a frilly garter belt to hold up those smoke-gray boardroom stockings. It was both luscious and impersonal watching this stranger dress, like viewing an erotic movie. He wondered who she was. A pickup? She wasn't a hooker—not with those clothes, that expensive three-color gold wedding band. (There was no ring on his hand, so probably he wasn't her husband.) Those were intimate underthings. Maybe they had meant a lot to each other. No one could tell.

The woman pulled her lingerie on quickly, discomforted by his presence, but too proud to ask him not to look. She wouldn't meet his eyes. Fox found her embarrassment and tension arousing. She was obviously wondering who he was, how deeply involved they were. Possibly she was thinking forward to her husband finding out. Her breasts were large and lovely. Fox had left bite-marks on one; the marks were red and angry, and when she put on the bra, it didn't cover them all.

They made love. There were occasional awkwardnesses, for they no longer knew each other's bodies or tastes. But his coming death, the knowledge that this was his last time with a woman, made Fox hot and desperate. The woman too—though he had no idea why. Maybe it would be a long time after this before her next good session in bed. When she took her clothes off, she paused briefly to give him the chance to look away politely. He didn't.

"We might as well get on with this," she said, touching the top button of her pewter silk blouse. She was blushing. "Since we're going to do it anyway."

"No," he had just said. "Whatever we do, let's not do it because we have to. For this one present moment, we're free to do whatever we wish. If we don't act that way, we might just as well be zombies."

He thought forward to his assassin, and wished he knew the man's name.

"Go with God then, Fox," Gingrich said. There were tears in his eyes.

A moment before he had asked, "You won't tell me how you're going to die?" and Fox had replied, "What would be the point?" It was time he left for his last meeting with Carolyn.

Gingrich's apartment had multicolored Aztec-cut carpeting, uncluttered walls, and a bachelor's fussy tidiness. Solemn music soothed the ear, and holographic abstracts played against the gently curving beige ceiling. It was new construction, a rarity in these days. There were few enough luxuries to go around, with nine-tenths of the world in virtual chaos and anarchy.

"I can't imagine how I ever got this job," Gingrich said. He ran a hand over his round, hairless head. "I'm too soft. It hurts me to see one of my boys walk out to die."

Unmoved, Fox had said nothing. A moment before Gingrich sighed and said, "You've got a good record, Fox—I'll read your files after you leave. A *very* good record, I—well, never mind. This is the last time we'll talk, and I still have to give you your recruitment pitch."

"Go ahead," Fox had said.

"John, there was a time—not too long ago, we think—when consciousness was . . . different. Memory extended not just a few seconds into the past, but all the way back to birth. And, if you can believe the records from that period, they could not remember any of their future. Not an instant." He shook his head. "Almost unimaginable. You know, it'll be said that life is like climbing a very long stairway, able to see from your feet to that closed door at the top, while the steps you've left behind crumble to nothing. I think life then must have been like climbing that same stairway backwards, able to see all the past, but none of what was about to happen to you." He'd paused for effect. "Then came the Event." Before this, he went on to describe the chaos that had followed the change of consciousness—if that was what the Event had been—and the rise of the Reclamation Authority, as would be reconstructed by scholars forty years hence. Then he had explained what the Authority had expected of Fox, what it had given him in return. Fox listened mechanically, his thoughts on Carolyn Mies. She was a hot number, whoever she was, and he liked her style. The speech was for the benefit of his earlier, younger self, and he presumed he'd have thought it over long before. If not—well, it was too late now.

An hour before, Gingrich greeted him with a slap on the shoulder and a firm handclasp. He ushered Fox into the apartment.

Standing in the hallway, overseen by a dozen mechanicals, Fox made a face. He disliked his superior's false camaraderie, that forced, jowly heartiness. A battered Sony bodycounter strapped to the wall by the door clicked softly. A Chase-Geigy genesniffer hummed to itself. Cameras telemetered his image in infrared, visual and ultraviolet to Central Accountability. He wouldn't let Gingrich see how he felt, though. It must be rough on the poor bastard, sending old friends out to die, and then knowing that he had as good as killed total strangers.

The night before, he and Carolyn met in a hotel built a century before the chaos. The building was old and shadowy, drenched in mystery and forgotten time. It was a good hour's drive from Pittsburgh, deep in dreamlogic Pennsylvania, and the desk clerk was a thin, pinched man with wirerims and the dusty-glass eyes of a predeterminist. He moved like an automaton—stiffly, impersonally—never quite focusing on Fox.

Fox paid with a large bill. Carolyn was already waiting in the car.

It was all so mechanical. What would happen if he yanked the bill back from the clerk? Probably the man's hand would close about empty air, transport nothing to the register, dole out change, slam the money drawer shut. I won't pay, Fox thought in sudden rebellion. I'll resist. But of course he would forget his resolve an instant after he made it.

The room was Victorian in proportion, small with high walls. The ceiling was molded plaster—fruit clusters, vines, cornucopias, all gone soft and vague from uncounted coats of paint. The wallpaper had been rubbed all but transparent by generations of feather-light touches, the pattern gone and indistinct shapes threatening to emerge from beneath. The thick wood door fit clumsily in its frame, and its brass knob was pitted with corrosion.

Carolyn's beeper lay neatly atop her folded clothing. They stood by the window, lights out, watching.

Directly across the street was a dark Rite-Aid. The Reclamation Authority had restored electricity as a prelude to opening a local office, and the red neon DRUGS sign sputtered and hissed. To one side of the Rite-Aid was a burned-out Florsheim's, and to the other, a 7–Eleven. Cold white light flared from the 7–Eleven, and occasionally people wandered in and out.

"No responsibility, no guilt, no conscience," Carolyn concluded.

"I suppose that, in our different ways, this is what each of us is fighting," Fox said.

A bonfire had been built in the middle of the street, and the locals were drawn to its light. A line of middle-class respectables had set up folding chairs at the flickering edge of light. A heavy woman with the jaw of a snapping turtle knitted.

Beside the fire a woman was pulling the train. She looked young because she was skinny and beautiful because she was naked and her hair was long and blonde, but a closer look revealed her as old and plain. The men standing in line for her looked considerably less interested than did the spectators.

Beside the turtle woman an old man in a John Deere cap, plaid shirt and gray chinos belted above the waist, stood, unzipped, and casually urinated. Nobody turned to look. The watchers gasped, and then a woman ran out of the darkness, seized one of the men in line and with a sudden wrench tumbled him into the fire. He leaped up, frantically beating down the flames in his hair. Fox saw that the hair was previously charred.

A nondescript man walked up to the fire, shook his head, walked away. He returned, shook his head, walked away again. And again. Once started, he was incapable of stopping, caught in a behavior-loop by his own sense of futility.

"Grotesque," Carolyn said. She nudged Fox, pointing off to the side. The desk clerk stood in the shadows, watching. There was a gleam of life in those taxidermy eyes, a sour, lascivious smile on those thin lips.

As they moved to the window, Fox wondered at his meeting Carolyn two nights in a row. Could her husband be away? Or had he—horrible possibility, but by now Fox barely knew the woman—agreed to this, as part of some mousetrap operation, some elaborate plot to snare him?

As if reading his mind, Carolyn had said, "Helmut is a zombie. It doesn't matter if he finds out—he won't do anything because he's not *going* to do anything. He just does whatever he knows he's going to do."

A dark flash of doubt had hit Fox. "That's all we do too—really. It's not as if we can change anything that's going to happen. So what's the difference between us and him?"

She'd laughed then, and said, "Intent."

The sheets were a sticky, crumpled mass hanging off the foot of the bed. Sometime during their hours of sex, the mattress had been all but kicked bare. Between bouts, their talk was as urgent and passionate as their lovemaking. By the time they first got intimate they were already half in love.

Taking off his shirt, Fox had said, "I know that you're going to turn me over to your assassins tomorrow."

"Oh yes?" She did not meet his eyes.

"I wrote myself a letter a year ago. When we first met. With a note to read it tomorrow morning." He talked rapidly, anxious to get it said while he still felt for her. "It says to tell you that it's all right, that I understand. That if I'd had a choice, I'd still have done everything we did."

"Only a year?" she'd said wistfully.

Checking in, with Carolyn waiting impatiently by the ancient Otis elevator—the black ironwork doors open, the interior walnut-paneled and erotically snug—he had a brief conversation with the desk clerk. "The Reclamation will be coming through here soon," he said. "I imagine you're excited about the changes that are coming."

"No, I'm not," the man had snapped. His eyes still focused somewhere beyond Fox. A hand touched the register. "You've been here off-and-on some dozen times, all with the same woman. Did you know that?"

"No."

"Well, I do. I write it down. I write down what happens on the street every night too. When they bring in their machines, their location meters, their policemen and their *orders*, that'll all end. The only pleasure those fuckers leave me will be reading the goddamned book."

On the way in, Fox realized that the man was angry because he was losing his position. Soon, he would be obeying orders. Then he would no longer be the detached observer and recorder, the omnipotent voyeur. He would no longer be God.

The Porsche eased out of the parking garage. Carcounters tagged it and automatically flashed holographic directional arrows onto his windshield. Fox followed their directions exactly. He assumed there was some good reason for their orders.

He was at a training seminar in the old Koppers Building. Behind the conference table, the mirror glass towers and soaring crenellations of PPG Place dominated the horizon. Most of the trainees were old, factory managers and economic analysts, about to ease into retirement and the senility of fatalism. But there was also a twenty-five-year-old, a victim of an impending industrial accident.

The table fed him a program. The only interesting item was number eight, Technology Creep Through Temporal Backfeed. He was sorry to have forgotten that. He also got a machine printout of his activities in the past week. Fox saw that he'd left the surveillance-net areas five times. There was a computer generated reprimand at the bottom of the page. It probably would've been stronger, he surmised, had he stayed in town. One thing he disliked about the new order was its latent puritanism; lust was too dreamlogic for the system to condone.

Gingrich closed with a little speech: "What was the collapse itself like—the time when the flow of memory abruptly and totally changed in nature and direction? Scholars will be able to tell us surprisingly little. The Event is like a black hole in history, surrounded by impenetrable mystery. It cannot even be dated. Records from that period are confusing and contradictory. Most likely the Event was a natural occurrence—we know so little about time or consciousness, it seems highly dubious the disaster was man-made."

While Gingrich preceded in a historical vein, Fox doodled on his notepad: long spiraling stairways that led nowhere and ended in whiteness. He tried to imagine experience and memory both running forward. He didn't think it would change much. Water would still run downhill. Modern times probably differed very little from ancient. Conversations were held backwards, but that was only a social convention, a polite means of those speaking retaining some understanding of what they were saying as the conversation unraveled beneath them.

"Our struggle is not entirely against the blind forces of ignorance and confusion, though," Gingrich concluded. "Speaking in complete confidence, many of the multinational corporations would like nothing better than to grab control of big chunks of real estate and create corporate states—the way they will in Italy and Japan. In addition to the work of reconstruction, we are engaged in an extended covert war for control of North America."

"Who's going to win?" someone had asked.

"We are." Gingrich squared up his notes even with the edge of the table. He wasn't going to glance at them once, so far. "Ultimately. Before I retire. But it'll be nip-and-tuck there for a time to come. We're lucky to have leverage over one of the major multinationals. Soon they'll be as good as in our pockets."

Oddly enough, Gingrich was looking directly at Fox when he said this. And smiling.

In the preceding months, Fox grew closer to Carolyn. They met more and more frequently, and he learned more than he wanted to know about Helmut Mies. Until finally, their first time in the dreamlogic hotel with the mad desk clerk, he had put the question to her directly, and Carolyn told him, "I married Helmut to get control of Telefunken-Amerika. I held eight percent of the stock and a seat on the board, and it was the only way to go any higher."

Just before that she began to cry. "No, I married him because I was going to. I hate the fat son of a bitch. It's like fucking a robot. What do I care about Telefunken-Amerika? Hell, it's only a regional, an out-colony of the real thing. Do you know what's going to happen to me?"

"No I don't," he'd said quietly.

"I'm going to grow extremely old and bitter, and I'll have nominal control over Telefunken-Amerika and I won't give a shit. It's your people who will be making the decisions anyway. When you're gone, all I have to look forward to is going predeterministic and then senile."

One of Gingrich's clever young men came and took the stacks of floppies away, hands cupped protectively about each load. The office was as fastidiously neat as Gingrich's apartment would be, with clear work surfaces and not so much as a spent staple on the cream shag rug. The heavy cranberry drapes were kept shut.

Gingrich unloaded the ostrich-hide briefcase slowly, examining the label of each floppy disk and piling them into short stacks. "This is beautiful," he chortled. "John, I don't believe you have any idea what you've got here."

In the coming year, Fox would learn to respect his boss, and even to like the man—though he suspected they had never actually been friends. "Samuel," he had said. "I don't want to ask her for these. Can you understand that? I love the woman, and if I could change *one* act of my life, it would be to not ask her to do this tomorrow." He slammed his fist into his leg, hard, with the knuckles down, and savored the pain.

Awkwardly, Gingrich put a hand on Fox's shoulder. It rested there like an inanimate object—a banana, or a box of cornmeal. Before a long silence, he said. "She's already given them to you. I think we can assume that—how else could you have gotten them? If you don't ask for them, then all the guilt rests on her alone, and none on you. If you love her, you'll be as eloquent and persuasive as you know how tomorrow."

Fox gave him the briefcase.

The hotel was right in the middle of town, with location meters in every hall, and genesniffer/bodycounter units over the doors. They weren't ashamed of their love, and they didn't care who knew about it.

It was late afternoon when Carolyn left, called away to an emergency session of Telefunken-Amerika's security people. She nodded to the briefcase on the way out and said, "Now we're even. I'm going to have you killed, and you've made me betray my husband, my career, everything I've worked for all my life." She was smiling as she said it.

"It must be a relief to have done with it," he'd said. "To forget. Now you'll never know who it was that sold you out."

"I don't want to forget a thing. But I suppose it's not my choice, is it?"

A slash of honey-colored sunlight knifed through the air form the gap between the drapes. It caressed Carolyn's naked cheeks as she struggled into her blouse, danced to her thighs, then leaped from her body as she reached for her panties.

The beeper went off and she slapped it silent.

A moment before they were sprawled lazily across the bed, legs tangled, skin slippery. "Do you keep a diary?" Carolyn asked.

"No," he'd said. "What would be the use?"

"I'm going to burn mine just before I betray you. So I won't remember that you ever existed. Do you understand that? If I can't have you, I don't want the least trace of you to survive."

"You're a romantic."

He'd gasped with pleasure on entering her. Having known all his life that it was going to be like this didn't spoil the present instant one bit.

Beneath her business suit Carolyn wore the same lacy underthings she would wear on their last night together . . . a bleak joke that made them both laugh.

"I'd do anything for you," she said. "You know that. I wish you wanted to do something filthy to me, I wish you wanted to hit me. I'd let you do that." In the elevator, her long red nails left love tracks down his back. She ran her hands up under his shirt, and a small white button went flying. He stroked her back, as if he could melt the silk of her blouse with the heat of his palms. They were only seconds away from lovemaking, and the memory of it aroused them both to feverish heat. Fox guessed that this would be their first time together. They stepped into the elevator. The door opened.

A few minutes earlier, they met for the first time.

The Moral Virologist

Greg Egan

By the end of our first year, I hadn't received a hard science fiction story—what some folks call a "rivets and robots" story—that satisfied my need for strong characterization. So I asked writers to send me hard sf stories with strong characters and a dangerous theme. "The Moral Virologist" met my challenge.

Greg Egan is an Australian writer whose work has just started appearing in the United States. In the past few years, he has been a regular in *Isaac Asimov's Science Fiction Magazine* and in year's best anthologies.

Out on the street, in the dazzling sunshine of a warm Atlanta morning, a dozen young children were playing. Chasing, wrestling, and hugging each other, laughing and yelling, crazy and jubilant for no other reason than being alive on such a day. Inside the gleaming white building, though, behind double-glazed windows, the air was slightly chilly—the way John Shawcross preferred it—and nothing could be heard but the air conditioning, and a faint electrical hum.

The schematic of the protein molecule trembled very slightly.

Shawcross grinned, already certain of success. As the pH displayed in the screen's top left crossed the critical value—the point at which, according to his calculations, the energy of conformation B should drop below that of conformation A—the protein suddenly convulsed and turned completely inside-out. It was exactly as he had predicted, and his binding studies had added strong support, but to *see* the transformation (however complex the algorithms that had led from reality to screen) was naturally the most satisfying proof.

He replayed the event, backwards and forwards several times, utterly captivated. This marvelous device would easily be worth the eight hundred thousand he'd paid for it. The salesperson had provided several impressive demonstrations, of course, but this was the first time Shawcross had used the machine for his own work. Images of proteins *in solution*! Normal X-ray diffraction could only work with crystalline samples, in which a molecule's configuration often bore little resemblance to its aqueous, biologically relevant, form. An ultrasonically stimulated semi-ordered liquid phase was the key, not to mention some major breakthroughs in computing; Shawcross couldn't follow all the details, but that was no impediment to using the machine. He charitably wished upon the inventor Nobel Prizes in chemistry, physics, and medicine, viewed the stunning results of his experiment once again, then stretched, rose to his feet, and went out in search of lunch.

On his way to the delicatessen, he passed *that* bookshop, as always. A lurid new poster in the window caught his eye, a naked young man stretched out on a bed in a state of post-coital languor, one corner of the sheet only just concealing his groin. Emblazoned across the top of the poster, in imitation of a glowing red neon sign, was the book's title: *A Hot Night's Safe Sex*. Shawcross shook his head in anger and disbelief. What was wrong with people? Hadn't they read his advertisement? Were they blind? Stupid? Arrogant? Safety lay *only* in the obedience of God's laws.

After eating, he called in at a newsagent that carried several foreign papers. The previous Saturday's editions had arrived, and his advertisement was in all of them, where necessary translated into the appropriate languages. Half a page in a major newspaper was not cheap anywhere in the world, but then, money had never been a problem.

ADULTERERS! SODOMITES!
REPENT AND BE SAVED!
ABANDON YOUR WICKEDNESS *NOW*
OR DIE AND BURN FOREVER!

He couldn't have put it more plainly, could he? Nobody could claim that they hadn't been warned.

In 1981, Matthew Shawcross bought a tiny, rundown cable TV station in the Bible belt, which until then had split its air time between scratchy black-and-white film clips of fifties gospel singers, and local novelty acts such as snake handlers (protected by their faith, not to mention the removal of their pets' venom glands) and epileptic children (encouraged by their parents' prayers, and a carefully timed withdrawal of medication, to let the spirit move them). Matthew Shawcross dragged the station into the nineteen eighties, spending a fortune on a thirty-second computer-animated station ID (a fleet of pirouetting, crenellated spaceships firing crucifix-shaped missiles into a relief map of the USA, chiseling out the station logo of Liberty, holding up, not a torch, but a cross), showing the latest, slickest gospel rock video clips, "Christian" soap operas and "Christian" game shows, and, above all, identifying issues—communism, depravity, godlessness in schools—which could serve as the themes for telethons to raise funds to expand the station, so that future telethons might be even more successful.

Ten years later, he owned one of the country's biggest cable TV networks.

John Shawcross was at college, on the verge of taking up paleontology, when AIDS first began to make the news in a big way. As the epidemic snowballed, and the spiritual celebrities he most admired (his father included) began proclaiming the disease to be God's will, he found himself increasingly obsessed by it. In an age where the word *miracle* belonged to medicine and science, here was a plague, straight out of the Old Testament, destroying the wicked and sparing the righteous (give or take some hemophiliacs and transfusion recipients), proving to Shawcross beyond any doubt that sinners could be punished in this life, as well as in the next. This was, he decided, valuable in at least two ways: not only would sinners to whom damnation had seemed a remote and unproven threat now have a powerful, worldly reason to reform, but the righteous would be strengthened in their resolve by this unarguable sign of heavenly support and approval.

In short, the mere existence of AIDS made John Shawcross feel *good*, and he gradually became convinced that some kind of personal involvement with HIV, the AIDS virus, would make him feel even better. He lay awake at night, pondering God's mysterious ways, and wondering how he could get in on the act. AIDS research would be aimed at a cure, so how could he possibly justify involving himself with *that*?

Then, in the early hours of one cold morning, he was woken by sounds from the room next to his. Giggling, grunting, and the squeaking of bedsprings. He wrapped his pillow around his ears and tried to go back to sleep, but the sounds could not be ignored—nor could the effect they wrought on his own fallible flesh. He masturbated for a while, on the pretext of trying to manually crush his unwanted erection, but stopped short of orgasm, and lay, shivering, in a state of heightened moral perception. It was a different woman every week; he'd seen them leaving in the morning. He'd tried to counsel his fellow student, but had been mocked for his troubles. Shawcross didn't blame the poor young man; was it any wonder people laughed at the truth, when every movie, every book, every magazine, every rock song, still sanctioned promiscuity and perversion, making them out to be normal and good? The fear of AIDS might have saved millions of sinners, but millions more still ignored it, absurdly convinced that *their* chosen partners could never be infected, or trusting in *condoms* to frustrate the will of God!

The trouble was, vast segments of the population *had*, in spite of their wantonness, remained uninfected, and the use of condoms, according to the studies he'd read, *did* seem to reduce the risk of transmission. These facts disturbed Shawcross a great deal. Why would an omnipotent God create an imperfect tool? Was it a matter of divine mercy? That was possible, he conceded, but it struck him as rather distasteful: sexual Russian roulette was hardly a fitting image of the Lord's capacity for forgiveness.

Or—Shawcross tingled all over as the possibility crystallized in his brain—might AIDS be no more than a mere prophetic shadow, hinting at a future plague a thousand times more terrible? A warning to the wicked to change their ways while they still had time? *An example to the righteous as to how they might do His will?*

Shawcross broke into a sweat. The sinners next door moaned as if already in Hell, the thin dividing wall vibrated, the wind rose up to shake the dark trees and rattle his window. What was this wild idea in his head? A true message from God, or the product of his own imperfect understanding? He needed guidance! He switched on his reading lamp and picked up his Bible from the bedside table. With his eyes closed, he opened the book at random.

He recognized the passage at the very first glance. He ought to have; he'd read it and reread it a hundred times, and knew it almost by heart. *The destruction of Sodom and Gomorrah.*

At first, he tried to deny his destiny: he was unworthy! A sinner himself! An ignorant child! But everyone was unworthy, everyone was a sinner, everyone was an ignorant child in God's eyes. It was pride, not humility, that spoke against God's choice of him.

By morning, not a trace of doubt remained.

Dropping paleontology was a great relief; defending Creationism with any conviction required a certain, very special, way of thinking, and he had never been quite sure that he could master it. Biochemistry, on the other hand, he mastered with ease (confirmation, if any was needed, that he'd made the right decision). He topped his classes every year, and went on to do a Ph.D in Molecular Biology at Harvard, then postdoctoral work at the NIH, and fellowships in Canada and France. He lived for his work, pushing himself mercilessly, but always taking care not to be too conspicuous in his achievements. He published very little, usually as a modest third or fourth co-author, and when at last he flew home from France, nobody in his field knew, or would have much cared, that John Shawcross had returned, ready to begin his real work.

Shawcross worked alone in the gleaming white building that served as both laboratory and home. He couldn't risk taking on employees, no matter how closely their beliefs might have matched his own. He hadn't even let his *parents* in on the secret; he told them he was engaged in theoretical molecular genetics, which was a lie of omission only—and he had no need to beg his father for money week by week, since for tax reasons, twenty-five percent of the Shawcross empire's massive profit was routinely paid into accounts in his name.

His lab was filled with shiny gray boxes, from which ribbon cables snaked to PCs; the latest generation, fully automated, synthesizers and sequencers of DNA, RNA, and proteins (all available off the shelf, to anyone with the money to buy them). Half a dozen robot arms did all the grunt work: pipetting and diluting reagents, labeling tubes, loading and unloading centrifuges.

At first Shawcross spent most of his time working with computers, searching databases for the sequence and structure information that would provide him with starting points, later buying time on a supercomputer to predict the shapes and interactions of molecules as yet unknown.

When aqueous X-ray diffraction became possible, his work sped up by a factor of ten; to synthesize and observe the actual proteins and nucleic acids was now both faster, and more reliable, than the hideously complex process (even with the best shortcuts, approximations, and tricks) of solving Schrödinger's equation for a molecule consisting of hundreds of thousands of atoms.

Base by base, gene by gene, the Shawcross virus grew.

As the woman removed the last of her clothes, Shawcross, sitting naked on the motel room's plastic bucket chair, said, "You must have had sexual intercourse with hundreds of men."

"Thousands. Don't you want to come closer, honey? Can you see okay from there?"

"I can see fine."

She lay back, still for a moment with her hands cupping her breasts, then she closed her eyes and began to slide her palms across her torso.

This was the two hundredth occasion on which Shawcross had paid a woman to tempt him. When he had begun the desensitizing process five years before, he had found it almost unbearable. Tonight he knew he would sit calmly and watch the woman achieve, or skillfully imitate, orgasm, without experiencing even a flicker of lust himself.

"You take precautions, I suppose."

She smiled, but kept her eyes closed. "Damn right I do. If a man won't wear a condom, he can take his business elsewhere. And *I* put it on, he doesn't do it himself. When I put it on, it stays on. Why, have you changed your mind?"

"No. Just curious."

Shawcross always paid in full, in advance, for the act he did not perform, and always explained to the woman, very clearly at the start, that at any time he might weaken, he might make the decision to rise from the chair and join her. No mere circumstantial impediment could take any credit for his inaction; nothing but his own free will stood between him and mortal sin.

Tonight, he wondered why he continued. The "temptation" had become a formal ritual, with no doubt whatsoever as to the outcome.

No doubt? Surely that was pride speaking, his wiliest and most persistent enemy. *Every* man and woman forever trod the edge of a precipice over the inferno, at risk more than ever of falling to those hungry flames when he or she least believed it possible.

Shawcross stood and walked over to the woman. Without hesitation, he placed one hand on her ankle. She opened her eyes and sat up, regarding him with amusement, then took hold of his wrist and began to drag his hand along her leg, pressing it hard against the warm, smooth skin.

Just above the knee, he began to panic—but it wasn't until his fingers struck moisture that he pulled free with a strangled mewling sound, and staggered back to the chair, breathless and shaking.

That was more like it.

The Shawcross virus was to be a masterful piece of biological clockwork (the likes of which William Paley could never have imagined—and which no godless evolutionist would dare attribute to the "blind watchmaker" of chance). Its single strand of RNA would describe, not one, but *four* potential organisms.

Shawcross virus A, SVA, the "anonymous" form, would be highly infectious, but utterly benign. It would reproduce within a variety of host cells in the skin and mucous membranes, without causing the least disruption to normal cellular functions. Its protein coat had been designed so that every exposed site mimicked some portion of a *naturally occurring* human protein; the immune system, being necessarily blind to these substances (to avoid attacking the body itself) would be equally blind to the invader.

Small numbers of SVA would make their way into the bloodstream, infecting T-lymphocytes, and triggering stage two of the virus's genetic program. A system of enzymes would make RNA copies of hundreds of genes from every chromosome of the host cell's DNA, and these copies would then be incorporated into the virus itself. So, the next generation of the virus would carry with it, in effect, *a genetic fingerprint* of the host in which it had come into being.

Shawcross called this second form SVC, the C standing for "customized" (since every individual's unique genetic profile would give rise to a unique strain of SVC), or "celibate" (because in a celibate person, only SVA and SVC would be present).

SVC would be able to survive only in blood, semen and vaginal fluids. Like SVA, it would be immunologically invisible, but with an added twist: its choice of camouflage would vary wildly from person to person, so that even if its disguise was imperfect, and antibodies to a dozen (or a hundred, or a thousand) *particular* strains could be produced, universal vaccination would remain impossible.

Like SVA, it would not alter the function of its hosts—with one minor exception. When infecting cells in the vaginal mucous membrane, the prostate, or the seminiferous epithelium, it would cause the manufacture and secretion from these cells of several dozen enzymes specifically designed to degrade varieties of rubber. The holes created by a brief exposure would be invisibly small—but from a viral point of view, they'd be enormous.

Upon reinfecting T cells, SVC would be capable of making an "informed decision" as to what the next generation would be. Like SVA, it would create a genetic fingerprint of its host cell. It would then compare this with its stored, ancestral copy. If the two fingerprints were identical—proving that the customized strain had remained within the body in which it had begun—its daughters would be, simply, more SVC.

However, if the fingerprints failed to match, implying that the strain had now crossed into another person's body (*and* if gender-specific markers showed that the two hosts were *not* of the same sex) the daughter virus would be a third variety, SVM, containing both fingerprints. The M stood for "monogamous," or "marriage certificate." Shawcross, a great romantic, found it almost unbearably sweet to think of two people's love for each other being expressed in this way, deep down at the subcellular level, and of man and wife, by the very act of making love, signing a contract of faithfulness until death, literally in their own blood.

SVM would be, externally, much like SVC. Of course; when it infected a T cell it would check the host's fingerprint against *both* stored copies, and if *either* one matched, all would be well, and more SVM would be produced.

Shawcross called the fourth form of the virus SVD. It could arise in two ways; from SVC directly, when the gender markers implied that a homosexual act had taken place, or from SVM, when the detection of a third genetic fingerprint suggested that the molecular marriage contract had been violated.

SVD forced its host cells to secrete enzymes that catalyzed the disintegration of vital structural proteins in blood vessel walls. Sufferers from an SVD infection would undergo massive hemorrhaging all over their bodies. Shawcross had found that mice died within two or three minutes of an injection of pre-infected lymphocytes, and rabbits within five or six minutes; the timing varied slightly, depending on the choice of injection site.

SVD was designed so that its protein coat would degrade in air, or in solutions outside a narrow range of temperature and pH, and its RNA alone was non-infectious. Catching SVD from a dying victim would be almost impossible. Because of the swiftness of death, an adulterer would have no time to infect an innocent spouse; the widow or widower would, of course, be sentenced to celibacy for the rest of their life, but Shawcross did not think this too harsh: it took two people to make a marriage, he reasoned, and some small share of blame could always be apportioned to the other partner.

Even assuming that the virus fulfilled its design goals precisely, Shawcross acknowledged a number of complications:

Blood transfusions would become impractical until a foolproof method of killing the virus *in vitro* was found. Five years ago this would have been tragic, but Shawcross was encouraged by the latest work in synthetic and cultured blood components, and had no doubt that his epidemic would cause more funds and manpower to be diverted into the area. Transplants were less easily dealt with, but Shawcross thought them somewhat frivolous anyway, an expensive and rarely justifiable use of scarce resources.

Doctors, nurses, dentists, paramedics, police, undertakers . . . well, in fact, *everyone* would have to take extreme precautions to avoid exposure to other people's blood. Shawcross was impressed, though of course not surprised, at God's foresight here: the rarer and less deadly AIDS virus had gone before, encouraging practices verging on the paranoid in dozens of professions, multiplying rubber glove sales by orders of magnitude. Now the overkill would all be justified, since *everyone* would be infected with, at the very least, SVC.

Rape of virgin by virgin would become a sort of biological shotgun wedding; any other kind would be murder and suicide. The death of the victim would be tragic, of course, but the near-certain death of the rapist would surely be an overwhelming deterrent. Shawcross decided that the crime would virtually disappear.

Homosexual incest between identical twins would escape punishment, since the virus would have no way of telling one from the other. This omission irritated Shawcross, especially since he was unable to find any published statistics that would allow him to judge the prevalence of such abominable behavior. In the end he decided that this minor flaw would constitute a necessary, token remnant—a kind of moral fossil—of man's inalienable potential to consciously choose evil.

It was in the northern summer of 2000 that the virus was completed, and tested as well as it could be in tissue culture experiments and on laboratory animals. Apart from establishing the fatality of SVD (created by test-tube simulations of human sins of the flesh), rats, mice, and rabbits were of little value, because so much of the virus's behavior was tied up in its interaction with the human genome. In the cultured human cell lines, though, the clockwork all seemed to unwind, exactly as far as, and never farther than, appropriate to the circumstances; generation after generation of SVA, SVC, and SVM remained stable and benign. Of course more experiments could have been done, more time put aside to ponder the consequences, but that would have been the case regardless.

It was time to act. The latest drugs meant that AIDS was now rarely fatal—at least, not to those who could afford the treatment. The third millennium was fast approaching, a symbolic opportunity not to be ignored. Shawcross was doing God's work; what need did he have for quality control? True, he was an imperfect human instrument in God's hands, and at every stage of the task he had blundered and failed a dozen times before achieving perfection, but that was in the laboratory, where mistakes could be discovered and rectified easily. Surely God would never permit anything less than an infallible virus, His will made RNA, out into the world.

So Shawcross visited a travel agent, then infected himself with SVA.

* * *

Shawcross went west, crossing the Pacific at once, saving his own continent for last. He stuck to large population centers: Tokyo, Beijing, Seoul, Bangkok, Manila, Sydney, New Delhi, Cairo. SVA could survive indefinitely, dormant but potentially infectious, on any surface that wasn't intentionally sterilized. The seats in a jet, the furniture in a hotel room, aren't autoclaved too often.

Shawcross didn't visit prostitutes; it was SVA that he wanted to spread, and SVA was not a venereal disease. Instead, he simply played the tourist, sight-seeing, shopping, catching public transport, swimming in hotel pools. He relaxed at a frantic pace, adopting a schedule of remorseless recreation that, he soon felt, only divine intervention sustained.

Not surprisingly, by the time he reached London he was a wreck, a suntanned zombie in a fading floral shirt, with eyes as glazed as the multicoated lens of his obligatory (if filmless) camera. Tiredness, jet lag, and endless changes of cuisine and surroundings (paradoxically made worse by an underlying, glutinous monotony to be found in food and cities alike), had all worked together to slowly drag him down into a muddy, dreamlike state of mind. He dreamt of airports and motels and jets, and woke in the same places, unable to distinguish between memories and dreams.

His faith held out through it all, of course, invulnerably axiomatic, but he worried nonetheless. High altitude jet travel meant extra exposure to cosmic rays; could he be certain that the virus's mechanisms for self checking and mutation repair were failsafe? God would be watching over all the trillions of replications, but still, he would feel better when he was home again, and could test the strain he'd been carrying for any evidence of defects.

Exhausted, he stayed in his hotel room for days, when he should have been out jostling Londoners, not to mention the crowds of international tourists making the best of the end of summer. News of his plague was only now beginning to grow beyond isolated items about mystery deaths; health authorities were investigating, but had had little time to assemble all the data, and were naturally reluctant to make premature announcements. It was too late, anyway; even if Shawcross had been found and quarantined at once, and all national frontiers sealed, people he had infected so far would already have taken SVA to every corner of the globe.

He missed his flight to Dublin. He missed his flight to Ontario. He ate and slept, and dreamt of eating, sleeping, and dreaming. *The Times* arrived each morning on his breakfast tray, each day devoting more and more space to proof of his success, but still lacking the special kind of headline he longed for: a black and white acknowledgement of the plague's divine purpose. Experts began declaring that all the signs pointed to a biological weapon run amok, with Libya and Iraq the prime suspects; sources in Israeli intelligence had confirmed that both countries had greatly expanded their research programs in recent years. If any epidemiologist had realized that only adulterers and homosexuals were dying, the idea had not yet filtered through to the press.

Eventually, Shawcross checked out of the hotel. There was no need for him to travel through Canada, the States, or central and South America; all the news showed that other travelers had long since done his job for him. He booked a flight home, but had nine hours to kill.

"I will do no such thing! Now take your money and get out."
"But—"
"*Straight sex*, it says in the foyer. Can't you read?"
"I don't want sex. I won't touch you. You don't understand. I want you to touch *yourself*. I only want to be *tempted*—"
"Well, walk down the street with both eyes open, that should be temptation enough." The woman glared at him, but Shawcross didn't budge. There was an important principle at stake. "I've *paid* you!" he whined.
She dropped the notes on his lap. "And now you have your money back. Good night."
He climbed to his feet. "God's going to punish you. You're going to die a horrible death, blood leaking out of all your veins—"
"There'll be blood leaking out of *you* if I have to call the lads to assist you off the premises."
"Haven't you read about the plague? Don't you realize what it is, what it means? It's God's punishment for fornicators—"
"Oh, get out, you blaspheming lunatic."
"*Blaspheming?*" Shawcross was stunned. "You don't know who you're talking to! I'm God's chosen instrument!"
She scowled at him. "You're the devil's own arsehole, that's what you are. Now clear off."

As Shawcross tried to stare her down, a peculiar dizziness took hold of him. *She was going to die, and he would be responsible.* For several seconds, this simple realization sat unchallenged in his brain, naked, awful, obscene in its clarity. He waited for the usual chorus of abstractions and rationalizations to rise up and conceal it.

And waited.

Finally he knew that he couldn't leave the room without doing his best to save her life.

"Listen to me! Take this money and let me talk, that's all. Let me talk for five minutes, then I'll go."

"Talk about what?"

"The plague. *Listen!* I know more about the plague than anyone else on the planet." The woman mimed disbelief and impatience. "It's true! I'm an expert virologist, I work for, ah, I work for the Centers for Disease Control, in Atlanta, Georgia. Everything I'm going to tell you will be made public in a couple of days, but I'm telling you *now*, because you're at risk from this job, and in a couple of days it might be too late."

He explained, in the simplest language he could manage, the four stages of the virus, the concept of a stored host fingerprint, the fatal consequences if a third person's SVM ever entered her blood. She sat through it all in silence.

"Do you understand what I've said?"

"Sure I do. That doesn't mean I believe it."

He leapt to his feet and shook her. "I'm deadly serious! I'm telling you the absolute truth! God is punishing adulterers! AIDS was just a warning; this time *no* sinner will escape! *No one!*"

She removed his hands. "Your God and my God don't have a lot in common."

"*Your God!*" he spat.

"Oh, and aren't I entitled to one? Excuse me. I thought they'd put it in some United Nations Charter: Everyone's issued with their own God at birth, though if you break Him or lose Him along the way there's no free replacement."

"Now who's blaspheming?"

She shrugged. "Well, my God's still functioning, but yours sounds a bit of a disaster. Mine might not cure all the problems of the world, but at least he doesn't bend over backwards to make them worse."

Shawcross was indignant. "A few people will die. A few sinners, it can't be helped. But think of what the world will be like when *the message finally gets through*! No unfaithfulness, no rape; every marriage lasting until death—"

She grimaced with distaste. "For all the wrong reasons."

"No! It might start out that way. People are weak, they need a reason, a selfish reason, to be good. But given time it will grow to be more than that; a habit, then a tradition, then part of human nature. The virus won't matter anymore. People will have *changed*."

"Well, maybe; if monogamy is inheritable, I suppose natural selection would eventually—"

Shawcross stared at her, wondering if he was losing his mind, then screamed, "*Stop it!* There is *no such thing* as 'natural selection'!" He'd never been lectured on Darwinism in any brothel back home, but then what could he expect in a country run by godless socialists? He calmed down slightly and added, "I *meant* a change in the spiritual values of the world culture."

The woman shrugged, unmoved by the outburst. "I know you don't give a damn what I think, but I'm going to tell you anyway. *You* are the saddest, most screwed-up man I've set eyes on all week. So, you've chosen a particular moral code to live by; that's your right, and good luck to you. But you have no real *faith* in what you're doing; you're so uncertain of your choice that you need God to pour down fire and brimstone on everyone who's chosen differently, just to prove to you that you're right. God fails to oblige, so you hunt through the natural disasters—earthquakes, floods, famines, epidemics—winnowing out examples of the 'punishment of sinners.' You think you're proving that God's on your side? All you're proving is your own insecurity."

She glanced at her watch. "Well, your five minutes are long gone, and I never talk theology for free. I've got one last question though, if you don't mind, since you're likely to be the last 'expert virologist' I run into for a while."

"Ask." She was going to die. He'd done his best to save her, and he'd failed. Well, hundreds of thousands would die with her. He had no choice but to accept that; his faith would keep him sane.

"This virus that your God's designed is only supposed to harm adulterers and gays? Right?"

"Yes. Haven't you listened? That's the whole point! The mechanism is ingenious, the DNA fingerprint—"

She spoke very slowly, opening her mouth extra wide, as if addressing a deaf or demented person. "Suppose some sweet, monogamous, married couple have sex. Suppose the woman becomes pregnant. The child won't have exactly the same set of genes as either parent. So what happens to it? What happens to the baby?"

Shawcross just stared at her. *What happens to the baby?* His mind was blank. He was tired, he was homesick . . . all the pressure, all the worries . . . he'd been through an *ordeal*—how could she expect him to think straight, how could she expect him to explain every tiny detail? *What happens to the baby?* What happens to the innocent, newly made child? He struggled to concentrate, to organize his thoughts, but the absolute horror of what she was suggesting tugged at his attention, like a tiny, cold, insistent hand, dragging him, inch by inch, toward madness.

Suddenly, he burst into laughter; he almost wept with relief. He shook his head at the stupid whore, and said, "You can't trick me like that! I thought of *babies* back in '94! At little Joel's christening —he's my cousin's boy." He grinned and shook his head again, giddy with happiness. "I fixed the problem: I added genes to SVC and SVM, for surface receptors to half a dozen fetal blood proteins; if any of the receptors are activated, the next generation of the virus is *pure* SVA. It's even safe to breast feed, for about a month, because the fetal proteins take a while to be replaced."

"For about a month," echoed the woman. Then, "What do you mean, you *added* genes . . . ?"

Shawcross was already bolting from the room.

He ran, aimlessly, until he was breathless and stumbling, then he limped through the streets, clutching his head, ignoring the stares and insults of passersby. A month wasn't long enough, he'd *known* that all along, but somehow he'd forgotten just what it was he'd intended to *do* about it. There'd been too many details, too many complications.

Already, children would be dying.

He came to a halt in a deserted side street, behind a row of tawdry nightclubs, and slumped to the ground. He sat against a cold brick wall, shivering and hugging himself. Muffled music reached him, thin and distorted.

Where had he gone wrong? Hadn't he taken his revelation of God's purpose in creating AIDS to its logical conclusion? Hadn't he devoted his whole life to perfecting a biological machine able to discern good from evil? If something so hideously complex, so painstakingly contrived as his virus, still couldn't do the job . . .

Waves of blackness moved across his vision.

What if he'd been wrong, from the start?

What if none of his work had been God's will, after all?

Shawcross contemplated this idea with a shell-shocked kind of tranquility. It was too late to halt the spread of the virus, but he could go to the authorities and arm them with the details that would otherwise take them years to discover. Once they knew about the fetal protein receptors, a protective drug exploiting that knowledge might be possible in a matter of months.

Such a drug would enable breast feeding, blood transfusions, and organ transplants. It would also allow adulterers to copulate, and homosexuals to practice their abominations. It would be utterly morally neutral, the negation of everything he'd lived for. He stared up at the blank sky, with a growing sense of panic. Could he do that? Tear himself down and start again? He had to! *Children were dying.* Somehow, he had to find the courage.

Then, it happened. Grace was restored. His faith flooded back like a ride of light, banishing his preposterous doubts. How could he have contemplated surrender, when the *real* solution was so obvious, so simple?

He staggered to his feet, then broke into a run again, reciting to himself, over and over, to be sure he'd get it right this time: "ADULTERERS! SODOMITES! MOTHERS BREAST FEEDING INFANTS OVER THE AGE OF FOUR WEEKS! REPENT AND BE SAVED. . . ."

Jamais Vu

Geoffrey A. Landis

"Jamais Vu" appeared in our final issue. The story is so subtle that I nearly asked for a rewrite the first time I read it. Then I reread it and understood what I had missed.

Geoffrey A. Landis's fiction often plays with time and perception. His Nebula-award-winning short story, "Ripples in the Dirac Sea," does both, as does this story. His first book, a collection of short stories, will appear in *Author's Choice Monthly* this fall.

Something distracts you—a noise, perhaps a branch tapping against a window—and when you look back you suddenly don't know where you are. Everything seems strange; you can't, for a moment, even remember what it was you were doing just a second ago.

And then everything snaps back into place. You are sitting in your own living room, in your favorite chair, and you chuckle to think how a place so familiar could seem strange, even for a moment. The French have a word for this experience, you think: *jamais vu*, the opposite of *déjà vu*.

A cup of coffee sits by your elbow, and sunlight is streaming in the window. It must be morning; you had better get hustling or you'll be late for work. You begin to stand up, then, with a sudden start, remember that you don't have to. The company you used to work for had been bought out by a conglomerate—was it really only last week? You were one of the whiz kids in research and development, but the conglomerate sold off the company's assets, and the whole R&D division was cut back. Your department, biology and pharmaceuticals, was shut down completely. Not that it was a loss to you personally. They'd let you go with a golden handshake, a separation settlement large enough to ensure that, if you wanted, you need never work again.

The day stretches out ahead of you, free and clear. There is nothing you have to do, no place you have to be. You are free of the tyranny of the timeclock.

And then, just as you start to relax, you realize there is nothing you particularly *want* to do, either. Remember? Your long-time lover walked away last month; the parting was cordial, but irrevocable. The idea of pick-ups and singles' bars always did nauseate you, and your old friends are scattered far away. You settle back, confused and puzzled.

Your eyes drop down to the table, and you see the book. You smile. Things are not all bad. The book is a new one by your favorite author. The book you'd heard so much about, but hadn't had time to read because your job kept you so busy. *A Sky of Shattered Diamonds*. Now you have time for it. The cover is worn; somehow you must have found a copy in the used book store. You sit down and flip it open. In an instant you're swept away.

The insistent ringing of the doorbell interrupts you. You come out of the novel slowly, reluctant to give up the vivid world of *Diamonds*. Your mind is still reeling from the book. The wonder of it, the incredible panaroma of experience! What an adventure!

You are struck by the blast of cold air as you open the door. Wasn't it just spring? But there is snow on the ground. Peculiar how time flies when you're not paying attention.

At the door is a pizza delivery boy, shivering slightly in the cold. He's come to the wrong house; you didn't order a pizza. But the name on the order slip is yours, and the pizza has all your favorite toppings. Suddenly you realize how hungry you are and just how good that pizza smells. You start to search for money to pay him, but the delivery boy smiles and says it's on your account.

You'd like to read as you eat, but hold yourself back. You want to stretch out the book as long as you can, savor it like a fine wine, rolling it over on your tongue. You wish the book, and the afternoon you'll spend reading it, would never end.

Instead, while eating you think back on your research. Your team was hot on the trail of a cure for Alzheimer's disease; another year and you might have had it. You'd mapped out the degradation mechanism, a subtle depolarization of the neural fibers; last week your team completed tests on a drug that would mimic the symptoms in chimpanzees. Now your cure will never be developed. These days there is no profit in developing new drugs; the time and expense of FDA approval and the potential for devastating lawsuits are far too high for any risk-conscious executive.

You shake your head at the folly of it all, eat the last piece of pizza, and return to a brighter, more vivid world.

It's evening by the time you finish. Tears stream down your cheeks, and your breath comes in short gasps. You're emotionally exhausted. Books like this are what makes life worth living. The book calls for a celebration, so you decide to go out for a steak dinner. You eat slowly, still half immersed in the intense reality of *Shattered Diamonds*. You head home feeling fat and satisfied. If only every day could be like this!

A tear leaks out of your eye. You'll reread it, of course, over and over, but never again with quite the same intensity or joy of discovery as today.

After dinner you go jogging, stretch your muscles after a long day. The wintery air feels good against your skin. When you get back, you head for the fridge. Ahead of you stretches the world of reality, day after pointless day, made even dimmer seen in the afterglow of *Diamonds*. But, today, nothing can shatter your good spirits.

In the refrigerator there is nothing to drink. It is packed from front to back with vials of clear fluid. They're quite familiar; you must have taken them from work your last day (funny you don't remember your last day of work. You'd think you ought to remember that). You look around, and, yes, there are the syringes. By the syringes is a notepad. In slightly faded felt-tip ink is a note in your own handwriting: "twenty-four hours: 0.41 cc."

The drug is familiar, yes. The one you helped develop, the one that creates one. of the symptoms of Alzheimers disease, selective removal of recent memory. What else could it be?

You pick up the phone to place the pizza order for tomorrow. When you hear the voice answer, you can faintly hear him shout to someone in the background "the usual."

All in all, you can't think of a thing you'd want to change.

How long had it been? A year? A decade? It doesn't matter. You make the injection and lie down to sleep, dreaming of shattered diamonds.

The Third Sex

Alan Brennert

"The Third Sex" introduced me to the work of Alan Brennert. Actually, I had encountered Alan's work before, on *Simon and Simon, China Beach*, and the new *Twilight Zone* T.V. series, but I had never seen anything in print. After we bought "The Third Sex," I went out and bought a copy of his novels, *Kindred Spirits* and *Time and Chance*. Now I give them away as Christmas presents.

"The Third Sex" lacks the hard edges of the earlier stories in this anthology. It represents another kind of *Pulphouse* story: a gentle fantasy on sexual themes.

I couldn't have been more than three years old, that night I wandered into my parents' bedroom; I'd had the dream again, the one where I was being crushed between floor and ceiling, unable to breathe or break free. Shaken, I raced down the hall, pushed open my parents' door—then stopped as I saw what they were doing.

Locked in a sweaty tangle of sheets, they were jerking back and forth, making short, breathless sounds; for a minute I thought maybe they were having the same bad dream I'd just had. Their arms were wrapped around one another, the two of them lying face-to-face, so close I couldn't tell where one began and the other left off. When they saw me, my mother called out my name, my father swore, they pulled apart with a wet, sucking sound . . . and as the sheets fell away I saw a thick, curved finger between my father's legs, and between my mother's, another pair of lips. I rushed up, fascinated, asking a million questions at once; my father just looked at my mother, sighed, and tried to answer my questions—what is that called? what is that *for*? —as completely and honestly as you can, to a three-year-old; and when I went to bed that night, I reached down under my pajamas and touched the smooth, unbroken skin between my thighs, and dreamed of the day—Daddy never mentioned it, but I knew it had to come— when my own penis or vagina would start to grow. But somehow, it never did.

I'd been a perfectly normal newborn infant in all other respects, though not the first of my kind to appear. At first no one had a clue what to put on the birth certificate, much less what to name me, so they equivocated and the name on the county records is Pat; Pat Jacquith. Later, of course, they realized I had to have some identity, and since they were hoping for a daughter, that's what I became . . . at least until that night in their bedroom. "You're Daddy's little girl," my father had always told me, but if I *was* a girl, why didn't I have what Mommy had, that second pair of lips, that bristly hair? All I had was a pee-hole; it hardly seemed fair. And in years to come, when Mommy would take me out, shopping for skirts, or dolls, or frilly bedclothes, I knew I wasn't *really* like Mommy, would never *be* like Mommy . . . and I felt ashamed. Ashamed to be seen in clothes I didn't belong in, pretending to be something I wasn't.

So I started picking fights, at school . . . jumping hedges, shinnying up hills, sliding down cliffs . . . anything to get my pretty dresses torn, or dirty. We lived in a woodsy suburb called Redmond, and between the ages of six and thirteen I could usually be found in t-shirt and jeans, hiking, bicycling, or swimming in Lake Washington. I was a bit taller than the average girl, a bit shorter than the average boy; my voice was pitched a little lower than most girls, a little higher than most boys, but with a scratchy quality that somehow made it acceptable for either sex. I had no curves to speak of, and as the girls had begun to blossom with puberty, I stayed pretty much the same, going on hikes or playing shortstop in sandlot baseball games; but even this new, tomboy role would start to feel wrong, in its own way, soon enough.

I was fourteen; it was summer; a dozen of us, guys and girls, were camping at Lake Sammamish. I was wearing a one-piece bathing suit, my only concession to femininity, and when I dressed in the bushes I was careful, as always, to keep my distance from the others. To my left, Melissa Camry was suiting up behind a stand of bushes; to my right, my friend Davy Foster—a tall, loping blond who'd been my best pal for years—was stripping off his clothes in back of a tall tree. I caught a glimpse of Davy's genitals, and a peek at Melissa's impressively large breasts, and I felt an erotic tingle, but for which one, I didn't know; and then they were dressed and into the water, and swimming between them I continued to feel excited, but confused, as well.

Afterward, Davy and I went hiking, our trail coming to an end at the crest of a low, but steep, cliff. The rockface was intimidating; neither of us could resist the challenge. We descended carefully, finding ample foot and handholds for the first ten feet; then, midway down the bluff, Davy flailed about, looking for a foothold, not finding any: the cliff was sheer granite for the next ten feet. Davy called up to me, "Hard way down," and, propelling himself away from the cliff, plummeted into the bushes below. In moments I was faced with the same choice, and so, feeling almost like a parachutist, I followed his lead. We found ourselves lying tangled, ass-over-teakettle, in shrubbery. We looked at one another, splayed at weird angles, our legs looped through each other's, and started giggling. And couldn't stop. The harder we tried to untangle ourselves, the harder we giggled; we'd grab at a branch, trying to haul ourselves up, only to have the branch snap off as we fell deeper into the bramble. Davy leaned down to help me, his cheek grazing mine—

And then, somehow, we were kissing. I wasn't feeling the same kind of tingle I had earlier, but it still felt nice; the wonderful pressure of lips against mine, our tongues meeting, licking . . . Before I knew it Davy had his hand under my shirt (withdrawing it when he found that my tits were no larger than his); I slid my panties down around my thighs, part of me knowing I shouldn't, knowing there was nothing down there for him to enter, but not caring. Davy's penis was stiff, the tip of it was flushed red; he guided it awkwardly toward my crotch—

And then he saw.

He stopped and drew back, eyes wide with shock and disbelief. "What—" he started to say, and by then I knew I'd made a mistake, a bad one; but some part of me tried to pretend it would all be all right, and I reached out to him, imploring, "Please . . . Davy, please—" There was fear, now, in his eyes, but I didn't want to see it. "We don't have to. We can just keep on touching, can't we, we can keep on kissing—"

I tried to draw him closer to me, but he jerked back, jumping to his feet, swaying as he sought to keep his balance amid the thick bramble. Wordlessly he pulled up his pants, and despite my pleas, staggered out of the underbrush and ran like hell out of sight.

I cried for half an hour before getting up the courage to head back to camp, certain that I'd return to have them all staring at me, whispering about me behind my back; but Davy not only never told anyone else, he never said another word about it to me, either . . . because when we all graduated to high school the next year, Davy somehow managed to transfer to a different school . . .

I never wanted to see again what I saw in his eyes, that afternoon; never wanted to feel so *different*, ever again. And so, two months before my fifteenth birthday, I simply decided to deny it. All of it.

Overnight, I was no longer Pat, but Patty. Out went the jeans and sneakers; now, to my parents' shock, I wanted dresses, and nylons, and makeup—I became obsessed with learning everything there was to learn about putting on foundation, blusher, and eyeshadow. Mother was eager and willing to teach me, and my first hour in front of her dressing mirror I was amazed and delighted as my boyish features were transformed, through the miracle of Helena Rubenstein, into a soft, feminine face. My eyes, which had always seemed a bland brown, now looked almost exotic—hooded and sophisticated—with a touch of mascara and Lancôme; and as I carefully applied a coat of coral lip gloss, the image was complete. I stared at the girl in the mirror, so feminine, so pretty . . . and cried with joy and relief as I realized that the girl was *me*. Mother held me, relieved herself that she finally had a daughter again; that perhaps things might work out, after all.

Once I'd had a taste of what I could become, there was no stopping me: I had my ears pierced, and came to love the feeling when I shook my hair out and felt my hoop earrings jiggling to and fro; I even loved the sound my porcelain nails made when I drummed them impatiently on my desk in class. By the end of my freshman summer I convinced my parents to let me color my hair, and so I began the new year as a blonde, flirtatious sophomore, thrilled that boys would open doors for me, or light my cigarettes for me—each ritual confirming my own femininity.

I dated around, saw lots of boys, but knew I could take the role only so far. The dates would often end up in a boy's car, parked at a romantic lookout, with the two of us necking hot and heavily, his hands roaming my body; my breasts were still nonexistent, but now, taken in the context of my new look, the boys didn't seem to mind. But the petting always stopped short of one point: when the boy's hand reached for my panties. I'd let him masturbate against them, or bring him off myself, but that was all. They couldn't know it was as frustrating for me as for them. They at least could masturbate, but all I knew was the pleasure of touching, of caressing, of kissing. I read about orgasms, listened to my girlfriends talk endlessly about them; the more I listened, the more envious I became. And so I kept searching, hoping that someday, the right boy, the right touch, might bring me that release, that . . . fulfillment . . . everyone else seemed capable of. Most of the boys I dated didn't see me more than once or twice before dismissing me as a tease; but that reputation worked to my advantage, too, because there was always a ready supply of boys who saw me as a challenge, a prize to be won, and I was more than willing to let them try.

It was in my last semester of high school that my parents unexpectedly whisked me away for a rare day trip into Seattle. At first they tried to pass it off as a whim, but as the white brick buildings of the university medical center swung into view, they dropped the pretense; they seemed excited and enthused, and I became more than a little afraid at the whisper of zealousness in their tones. I could tell the extent of their preoccupation because when, nervously, I lit up a cigarette, neither of them gave me any grief about my smoking. Whatever this was about, it was important.

They wanted to be with me when I saw the doctor—a surgeon named Salzman, a balding, gentle man in his early fifties—but Dr. Salzman insisted on seeing me alone. My heart pounding for no reason that I knew, I sat in his comfortable office, in front of his expansive desk; I took a pack of Virginia Slims from my purse, then hesitated, but Dr. Salzman just pushed a heavy crystal ashtray toward me and I lit up, feeling a bit more relaxed, but certain that this amiable man was going to tell me I had three days to live.

"You've grown up to be quite a lovely young lady," he said approvingly. "I imagine you don't remember the last time I saw you?"

I smiled, shook my head. "I'm afraid not. Was I very small?"

He nodded. "Seven months." He leaned forward a bit in his chair, saw my nervousness, then laughed, putting me immediately at ease. "Don't look so worried. There's nothing wrong with you, at least nothing you don't already know about." He paused a moment, then, in a slightly more sober tone: "When did your parents tell you? About your—condition?"

It felt so strange, talking about this with someone other than my parents, but there was nothing threatening about this man. "They said it was a . . . a birth defect."

Salzman nodded to himself. "Yes, that about covers it as well as a child could understand. But you're no longer a child, are you?"

Suddenly it was a welcome relief just to have someone to talk to, someone who wouldn't cringe in fear. "It's called—androgyny, isn't it? I looked it up. But that's just something out of mythology, isn't it? How can I be—I mean, why—?"

Salzman stood, paced a little behind his desk. "It *used* to be something out of mythology. Your case, eighteen years ago, was the first on the West Coast, but before that there was one in Denver, two in New York, a few in the Midwest . . . the incidences are still rare, less than one hundredth of one percent, but . . ." He circled round and sat on the edge of his desk. "You were lucky; the first few cases attracted the most attention. Lived most of their youth under a microscope, and for all that we still don't know anything about the causes. Your parents wanted you to have as normal a life as possible, so we restricted ourselves to periodic exams. There was nothing we could do until you reached maturity, anyway."

I sat up, snubbing out the cigarette in the crystal ashtray. "Do? You mean there's something—"

"Slow down, now," Salzman cautioned. "What you are, you are; you have a . . . different chromosome, not X, not Y, something entirely new . . . and no one can change your genetic makeup. But we *can* give you a closer cosmetic resemblance to a normal female. We can start you on a course of hormone therapy to facilitate breast and hip development, augmented with silicone implants . . ."

I was leaning forward in my seat, my heart racing, barely able to contain my excitement. Dr. Salzman went on, "Now, as to sex organs, we can make a surgical incision in your—please tell me if this is getting too clinical—in your groin; then place a sort of plastic sac just inside the skin, and fashion a vagina and clitoris out of skin taken from elsewhere on your body. This is similar to what we do for male-to-female transsexuals, and it may require a follow-up operation to make sure the vagina remains open, but—"

"Oh, Doctor, *thank* you," I said, tears starting to well up in my eyes; "You don't know how often I've dreamed about—"

He held up a hand. "Don't thank me yet. There *are* limits. Like a transsexual, you won't, of course, be able to conceive children; but unlike a transsexual, whose vaginal lining is made of penile tissue, yours will be relatively insensate . . . no more sensitive to pleasure than any other part of your body. Do you understand?"

My hopes plummeted. "Why not?" I asked, voice low.

He looked at me with sadness and sympathy. "Because, child, you don't have any sex organs, and no tissue of the same sensitivity as a penis, or a clitoris. Perhaps the estrogen will give you some sensitivity in your breasts; perhaps not. This will be *cosmetic* change only . . . but won't that still go a long ways to relieving your gender discomfort?"

I thought about it a moment, my reservations melting away. I could go to bed with a man . . . get married . . . live something approaching a normal life. What did the rest matter, really? "Yes. Of course," I said. I stood, and couldn't help but hug him in gratitude. "When can I have the surgery?"

"We'll want to do a routine exam on you now, and if everything's satisfactory, we can do it whenever I can schedule an OR. Within the week, if you like."

When I left the office my parents saw at once the happiness in my eyes, and the three of us embraced, and laughed, and cried. All the way back they talked about how long they had been waiting for this day; how happy they were that their daughter was going to have a normal, healthy life. That night, there was laughter from their bedroom for the first time in years. The week until surgery passed quickly. And then, the night before I was to go to the medical center, I told my parents I was going out to meet friends, got into the flame-red Datsun my father had bought me for my seventeenth birthday, and I ran away from home.

I left a note, saying how sorry I was, explaining why I had to leave, and how I knew I couldn't live with their disappointment and betrayal. But I simply couldn't go through with it.

Oh, at first I was thrilled; I lay awake in bed, that first night, dreaming about being a girl, a real girl, for the first time. I had a date the next night, a new boy named Charles: good-looking, studious, and a little nervous. We ended up at the lookout outside town, but as we sat there, necking and petting, I realized nothing was happening— not even the whisper of anticipation I usually felt with a new boy, wondering if this, maybe, were the one who would be *different*—and as his hand reached under my blouse, I pushed him away with a little shove. "Charles, please *don't*. Let's go back to town." To prevent any further moves, I lit a cigarette and used it as a subtle shield between us. Charles turned slowly away, started the car, and headed back.

I caught a glimpse of myself in the rearview mirror and, reflexively, began to primp, more concerned with my own appearance than Charles beside me. It wasn't until he dropped me off that I saw the hurt and anger in his eyes, and by then it was too late; he was gone before I could apologize. He hadn't even been in danger of discovering my secret; I'd just become bored, and used the same coquettish tone I always did to end the scene, without any thought to him. My God, I thought; what kind of selfish, manipulative little bitch am I turning into?

That night, I undressed in front of the full-length mirror on the inside of my closet door, and stood staring at my reflection, taken aback at what I saw. I saw a girl's face, immaculately made up—pink lipstick, blue eyeshadow, a hint of blusher along the cheekbones— framed by strawberry-blonde hair. A girl's face, sitting atop a boyish body . . . not muscular enough to *be* a boy's, but too contourless to be a girl's, either. The juxtaposition seemed suddenly, and painfully, ridiculous. Looking at the head of a *Cosmo* girl sitting atop a neutered body, I *knew* for the first time that I was neither boy nor girl, but— something else.

I slept badly that night, and the next morning could barely bring myself to apply my makeup. As the days wore on, as the date of surgery approached, the operation seemed less like a deliverance than a . . . a mutilation. A plastic sac inside my groin? The thought made me shiver. And if I did go through with it, then what? I'd still have no sex organs, no orgasms; would I make the best of it, get a job, fall in love and marry? Or would I continue to search, irrationally, for that one man who *might* bring me complete satisfaction, in the process hurting how many others who failed to make the grade?

I looked at the fickle blonde in my makeup mirror, and knew which path *she* would take. I left her behind in Redmond that night I drove away; I stopped at a mini-mall on Route 22 and picked up a suitcase full of unisex clothing—jeans, shirts, sweaters. At the nearest salon I had my blonde mane trimmed short, in a style of indeterminate sex; when the blonde grew out, I returned to my natural brown. I drove as far from Redmond as I could manage, with no particular destination, no purpose beyond discovering just who, and what, I really was.

A stranger, looking at me, had little clue to whether I was a man or a woman; depending on the pitch of my voice at any given time, I could be either one. It wasn't unusual for me to sit at the counter of a roadside diner, and for the waitress to ask, "What can I get you, sir?"; only to have the person at the cash register hand me my change with a friendly, "Have a nice day, ma'am." I became a chameleon, my gender determined as much by the observer's biases as by anything physical; and the further I drove, the freer I felt, a living Rorschach test with no demands put upon me to be one sex or the other.

I worked my way cross-country, waiting on tables, clerking in stores, delivering packages. I gave my name as Pat, which was both true and ambiguous. I'd never overtly state my sex unless it was absolutely necessary—on a job application, or if I was pulled over for a traffic ticket—and then only check "female" out of expediency, since that's what all my IDs read. But such instances were rare. It's amazing how much gender identification is really just in the eye of the beholder; I gave no cues, but each person I met brought his or her own lens to the focus of my identity. If I was driving fast, or aggressively, other drivers treated me like a man; if I was looking in a shop window displaying women's fashions, passersby would assume I was a woman. I could, with impunity, enter either a men's or a ladies' room; context, I discovered, was everything.

For the first time, too, I was free to follow my sexual feelings without playing a role. Working in a record store in Wyoming, I let myself experience, finally, the attraction I felt for women as well as men; I slept with a female co-worker, keeping the lights dim, and in lieu of intercourse I spent hours caressing her, holding her, massaging her clitoris with my tongue and fingers. She told me later she'd never really liked sex all that much, but this time was different; this time she was starting to see what it was all about. When a lonely, middle-aged man in a diner made a pass at me, I assumed he thought me a woman; but as we talked, it became apparent he took me for a young gay male. In his hotel room, I performed fellatio on him, and then— careful to roll my underwear down only as far as necessary, explaining it was a minor fetish—let him have anal sex with me; then we just held one another for a long while. And as I lay there, both times, feeling warm and happy, I realized with a start I had given no thought to that all-important "culmination" I had been in search of, so desperately, for so long.

Kansas City, Boston, Fayetteville, New York . . . my odyssey took me across the country and halfway back again. Sometimes I settled in various cities for months at a time, taking college-credit courses in psychology and sociology; but it was impossible to maintain gender ambiguity when you settled in one place for long, and eventually I'd get restless with being either man or woman, anxious to be perceived simply as *me*, and I'd be on the road again, searching.

One thing became clear: with more and more of these cases cropping up, the medical establishment could no longer dismiss them as genetic quirks. And a few times I even got to meet my kindred. In Fayetteville I met a 22-year-old living as a male, his full beard and hairy arms a testament to testosterone; an Army brat, he'd spent a good deal of time under the eye of military doctors, and it seemed to me his macho, swaggering pose was just that—a pose to satisfy his family and government, forcing them to leave him in peace. In New York I was shocked to find another androgyne who'd set up shop as a hooker, catering to any and all sexual persuasions, willing to be either man or woman, stud or harlot; he/she had a collection of wigs, toupees, strap-on dildoes and sponge rubber vaginas, and his/her arms were riddled with track marks. I got out of there, fast, feeling sick and sad. And in Miami I met a young "woman" with long auburn hair, dazzling eyes made up exactly right, full breasts peeping out of a low-cut dress, long red fingernails; the surgeons had done an amazing job on her. We sat in an open-air café as she flirted with every man who passed, preening in her compact mirror, yet if I asked her about her past, what it was like growing up, she found a way to change the subject, a dweller in an eternal, and ephemeral, present.

In Tennessee I finally met someone who'd taken the same path as I: Alex, slender, sandy-haired, living neither as a male nor a female, shunned by family, working as a teller in an S&L. We were astonishingly similar in our outlooks, in the decision we'd both come to, and both of us longed for that same unimaginably distant thing: a sense of belonging, of being loved and needed and necessary. We came together, in desperation more than want, and made love—as best as two neuters, two neither-nors, could make love. There were no sex organs to stimulate, but in our travels we each had learned much about touching, and caressing, and the sensitivities of the flesh; we could appreciate, as well as anybody, the gentle brush of lips along the nape of a neck, the sensuous massage of fingers kneading buttocks, the lick of a tongue inside the rim of an ear. It was very tender, and very loving, but when it was over . . .

When it was over, Alex stroked my cheek and said, almost sadly, "We're much alike. Aren't we?"

I nodded, wordlessly.

"I always thought when I found someone like myself, I'd be truly happy," Alex said, in a soft Tennessee drawl.

"So did I," I said, quietly.

Alex held me, then gave an affectionate peck on my cheek. "I'm sorry, Pat."

We were alike; too alike. Even our sexual responses were nearly identical. It wasn't just the lack of orgasm, it was . . . like making love to yourself; narcissistic, somehow. Patty, the strawberry blonde, would probably have liked it, but I felt only vaguely depressed by it. Both of us knew, instinctively, that the answer to our problem—if there was an answer—lay not in each other, but somewhere else.

My search, my quest for identity and purpose, was unraveling before my eyes. There *was* no purpose. There *was* no identity. I was neither man nor woman, yin nor yang; I was the line, the invisible, impossible-to-measure demarcation *between* yin and yang, as impossible to define as the smallest possible fraction, as elusive as the value of *pi*. I was neither, I was no one, I was nothing.

Not knowing what else to do . . . I went home.

* * *

I'd kept in touch with my parents, over the years; letters, post-cards, a phone call on Christmas or Thanksgiving. At first they were furious, even hung up the first time I called; eventually though they forgave me, and lately they'd written of how much they wanted to see me again. They were growing old, and I was afraid that if I didn't go now, I might never get the chance; so I headed west, to Washington, to Redmond, and home.

But the closer home I got, the faster my heart raced, the weaker my grip on the steering wheel; finally, somewhere between Bellevue and Kirkland, I lost my nerve and pulled into a motel off 405. It was well past eleven, and after checking in I headed down to the all-night coffee shop in the lobby. Exhausted, hungry, and nervous, I sat at a corner table, ordered a sandwich, and began chatting with a man at an adjoining table; he had the smooth, charming sheen of a salesman, and as he flirted with me, I found myself unconsciously changing the way I sat, the way I crossed my legs, even the way I held my glass of iced tea. I leaned forward, my now very feminine body language belying my androgynous appearance. It all came back so quickly, so easily. Before he could make a proposition, I realized what was happening and hurried off, feigning a stomachache; I hadn't come this far to lapse back into old patterns.

I slept badly, and wasted most of the next day window-shopping in a Kirkland mall, putting off the inevitable as long as I could. I was eating lunch when I looked up to find a man staring at me from a table across the room; this time I fought off the reflex that had overtaken me last night and simply glanced away, but when I looked up again the man was standing in front of me, a quizzical look on his face . . . a face I suddenly recognized.

"Pat?"

It was Davy. For a moment I was stunned that anyone here would recognize me, looking as I now did, but of course Davy had always known Pat, not Patty. The embarrassment of that day in the woods came rushing back; I must have looked terrified as I jumped to my feet, spilling coffee all over the table, and started to hurry away, but Davy rushed after. "Pat—wait—"

Outside he took me by the arm, but it was the gentle look on his face, and the softness of his voice, that brought me to a stop. "It's okay," he said quietly. "I'm not going to . . . I mean, that was a long time ago, right?"

He was only in his twenties, and already his blond hair was thinning, but his eyes were still a bright blue, and now they seemed to be looking straight through me. Part of me wanted to run; thank God, I didn't. He let go of my arm, smiling apologetically. "Been a while," he said.

It took me a moment to collect my thoughts.

"I've been—away," I said. "Traveling."

"Back for a visit, or to stay?"

I wished I knew. "A visit. I was going to head over to Redmond later and see my parents."

We stood there, awkwardly, for several moments, before he said, haltingly, "Look. If you've . . . got an hour to spare, I'd . . . like to talk with you. Let me call my office, okay?"

"I really should be getting—"

"Please?" What was that intensity, that desperation, I read in his eyes? "Just an hour?"

We skirted the edge of Lake Washington in his Jeep, a gray mist obscuring the few sailboats out on this drizzly day. We chatted innocuously for the first half hour, pointing out familiar sights, the snowy caps of nearby mountains, but finally, as we stood at a deserted lookout over the lake, Davy worked up the nerve to say what had been on his mind all afternoon.

"I'm sorry, Pat," he said, quietly.

I looked up at him. "Sorry for what?"

"For running," he said, glancing away uneasily. "For cutting you off like that. But I couldn't handle it. You were the first girl—" He stopped, momentarily panicked that he'd used the wrong word, but when I didn't react negatively he went on, hesitantly, "—that I was ever really . . . attracted to. I mean, you have no idea how many times I thought about it, about you, and me . . . when we were out hiking, or swimming, or in school—"

I couldn't help smiling. "Really?" I said. "I thought you just thought I was just, you know, one of the guys."

"Yeah, well, that's the hell of it. Even though I knew—thought—you were a girl, I couldn't shake this weird feeling that you *were* a guy . . . that being attracted to you was wrong, somehow. So there we are, the perfect situation, and I figure, okay, I'll prove to myself she's just like any other girl, that it's okay for me to want her—"

"Oh, God," I said, realizing. "And instead you found—"

"Yeah," he said. "Talk about gender confusion. I freaked. And for a while, I wasn't even sure what *I* was, much less you." He looked away. "Later, I did a lot of reading, found out about . . . people like you . . . and when I was in college, I saw a therapist who helped me out. Then I met Lyn. But all during high school. . . ."

I put a hand on his; now it was my turn to feel guilty. "Oh, God, Davy, I'm so sorry. I was so shaken up by it myself, I guess I never gave a thought to what it must've been like for you—your first sexual experience and it's so . . . so *bizarre* . . ."

He put his other hand on top of mine, and the warmth of it was familiar and comforting. "It's okay. I came out of it okay. But I wanted to apologize. For not—" His voice caught. "For not being a friend."

I couldn't think of anything to say, so I hugged him, trying to release some of that guilt which had been dogging him all these years; as we stood there the light drizzle became heavier, and when we separated the sky was darker, the ground turning muddy as a gray slanting rain pebbled the surface of the lake. "I'd better get a move on," I said, glancing at the thunderheads on the horizon.

"Rotten weather to be driving in. Why don't you come home and have dinner with Lyn and me?"

The idea frightened me, I'm not sure why; perhaps it was the warmth of Davy's body, still with me after our embrace. "No, I better not," I said, and in my haste to get back to the car I took the muddy embankment a bit too quickly, my foot sliced sideways, I felt a *pop* in my ankle as I tumbled down the small incline. I yelled, swore, but Davy was right behind me, pulling me up with a strong arm; though the damage, damn it, had already been done. "Take it easy," he said, helping me hobble up the embankment to the road. The pain in my foot was overshadowed, briefly, by the feel of his arm around my waist, but I thought of the last time something like this had happened, the blind alleys it had led us both to for so many years, and I resolved it would not happen again. "I'm all right," I protested, his grip loosening as I moved away—but the moment I took a step without his help all my weight fell on my twisted ankle and a stabbing pain shot up through my knee and into my thigh. I buckled, and Davy was there again to catch me.

"Come on. We'll fix you up back at my place."

I was hardly in a position to argue. We climbed into his Jeep, the rain drumming on its canvas roof as we headed down the road, and I cursed myself, wondering if I hadn't done this on purpose . . .

We were dripping wet, our shoes muddied, when we entered Davy's tract home in Kirkland, but Davy led me unhesitatingly to a dining room chair, carefully propped my ankle up on a second chair, and headed for the kitchen. "I'll get some ice," he said, and as the kitchen door swung shut behind him I saw the flash of headlights outside the dining room window, then heard the hurried slap of footsteps on the wet sidewalk leading to the house. Oh, great, I thought. I looked around for Davy, thinking that this was going to be an awkward introduction at best, but without him here—

The door opened and, along with a spray of rain, a petite blonde in a damp gray suit entered, at first so intent on closing her umbrella she didn't notice me. Then she looked up, stopped in mid-stride, and stared at me, her face contorting into an almost comical look of apprehension.

"Oh, God," she said, in a fast Eastern cadence. "You're not a burglar, are you? I left Chicago after the third burglary. Please tell me you're not a burglar."

I had to smile, but before I could say anything Davy entered with the ice pack, introducing me as an old schoolmate; I couldn't tell from the look on Lyn's face whether Davy had told her anything more about me, but as soon as she saw my ankle she came over, wincing as she touched my foot, lightly. "Ouch. Hold on, I think we've got an Ace bandage in the bathroom." Within minutes she was wrapping a long, slightly ragged bandage around my ankle, as Davy took off the icepack. "Mud," she said with a sardonic grin. "There should be mud miners up here, you know, providing the rest of the country with our unending supply. Mud and rain, rain and mud—"

She finished wrapping, secured the bandage with a butterfly clip, then let Davy wrap the icepack around the ankle again. "There. That should keep the swelling down." She stood, and for the first time I noticed the disparity in height between her and Davy; she stood on tiptoe, kissed him affectionately on the lips. "Guess what, dear heart," she said.

Davy looked apprehensive. "My turn to cook?"

She nodded. Davy sighed, picked up his raincoat from the chair he'd draped it over, looked at me. "You like Chinese?"

"Sure."

"Back in a flash." He was out the door and gone in a shot. Lyn turned, grinned. "Never fails. My turn to cook, I feel this obligation to make veal scallopini; his turn to cook, he goes out for Szechwan. Would you like some Tylenol for that foot?"

"Thanks."

With the Tylenol came hot coffee and a dry sweater; we shifted my ankle to the coffee table in front of the sectional sofa, and Lyn and I dried out in front of the gas logs, as we waited for the mu shu pork and kung pao chicken. I asked her what kind of work she did.

"Loan manager. B of A. You?"

"Retail sales," I hedged. "I've been on the road for quite a while."

"Back to visit your family?"

"Yes. Right."

She took out a pack of Salems, offered me one; and as she lit it for me, over the flame of the lighter I thought I could see her staring at me, oddly, trying to figure me out—not muscular enough for a man, not round enough for a woman. Was I live, or was I Memorex? Or was it just my own paranoia?

"I actually quit," she said, taking a deep drag on the cigarette, "back when I thought I was pregnant." At my puzzled look she explained, "False alarm. Or 'hysterical pregnancy' as they put it. If it happened to men, you *know* they'd call it something like 'stress-induced symptomatic replication,' but women, we're *hysterical*, right? Like, 'Oh, my God, I burned the roast, and—' " She looked down at her stomach in mock-surprise. " 'Whoops! Honey, do I look *pregnant* to you?' " We laughed, and that led to a general discussion of the peculiarities of men in general . . . and as I listened to Lyn's good-natured but very funny catalog of male excesses, not so different from the catalog of female excesses I'd listened to from men, something occurred to me, something crystallized after all these years.

All my life I'd felt like a member of a different race, human but not-human; similar but separate. And now I realized that this was, to some degree, how men and women viewed each other, at times—like members of a different species entirely. I saw it even more clearly over dinner, because even though Davy and Lyn had a good, loving relationship, there were the inevitable rough edges. Toward the end of the evening they got into a heated argument, as they were showing me around the soon-to-be-renovated basement, over what color tile would be used; Davy kept insisting it would be red, while Lyn said that wasn't it at all, more like terra-cotta, and they went on like that for almost a minute before I stepped into the breach with:

"Uh . . . Davy? When you say *red*, you mean like a fire-engine?"

"No, no, darker than that, more like—like—"

"Brick?"

"Yeah! Yeah, like brick."

"That's terra-cotta," Lyn said, exasperated.

"Well how the hell am I supposed to know that?"

After a moment, both Davy and Lyn loosened up and Lyn even suggested I should stick around and interpret while they were redecorating the house. We went upstairs, had some wine, watched a little cable . . . me stealing glances at Dave and Lyn, snuggled up together . . . and slowly my mood darkened. I liked them, liked them both; Davy's steady presence, Lyn's manic energy. I could fantasize myself falling in love with or marrying either one. Everyone in the world, it seemed, could look forward to that—male, female, gay, lesbian, they could all find a partner. Everyone except me. I was grateful when the movie ended and I could retire, alone, to the sofabed in the living room.

Lying there under a thick, warm quilt, listening to the tattoo of rain-drops on the roof, I drifted asleep . . . and had a nightmare I hadn't had in years, the one that had plagued me so often as a child, the one that drove me to my parent's bedroom years before.

I looked up to see the ceiling was dropping toward me, as, beneath me, the floor was rushing up. It happened too fast to do anything but shut my eyes against the coming collision; but when I hit, I didn't hit hard but *soft*, as though both floor and ceiling had turned to feather-down and were now smothering me between them. Out of the corner of my eyes I could see a thin wedge of light on either side, kept there only by the obstruction of my own body between floor and ceiling; then the wedge shrank to a slit, then a line, then a series of small pinpoints. I fought against the pressure but it was useless, the pinpoints of light vanishing one after another; I tried to take a breath but couldn't, my chest in a vise, unable to expand or contract; I was dying, I was defeated, I was—

"*Pat!* Pat, *wake up!*"

I was in the vise, and I was being held by my shoulders by Davy; my eyes were open, but I was in both places. He shook me, and the vise opened a crack; shook me again, and it fell away. I was in the living room, and I was awake; but I was still terrified. I broke down, as I hadn't in years—not since that day in the woods—but instead of shame and humiliation I felt pain, and loneliness; only the sense of apartness was the same. I held desperately onto Davy, tears running down my cheeks, trying to hold sleep at bay. Davy held me, and stroked my back, and after I'd finished he looked at me, put a hand to my cheek, and said in a soft, sad voice: "I think it's time I made it up to you," and then he was kissing me, tenderly. Part of me wanted to stay like that for the rest of my life, pretending to be what he wanted and needed, suspended forever in illusion; but I drew back, shook my head, tried to pull away. "Davy, *no*—your wife, I can't—"

And then there was a hand on my shoulder; a small hand, not very heavy, and I could feel the tips of her fingers on my skin. I turned. Lyn sat in her nightgown on the edge of the bed, looking not at all angry or disturbed; I started to say something, but she just shook her head, said, "Sshh, sshh," and leaned in, her lips brushing the nape of my neck, her breath moving slowly along the curve of my neck to my face, my mouth . . .

She knew. All along, she *must* have known . . .

Lyn gently pushed me back onto the bed, just as I became aware of a pleasant tickle on my legs; I looked down to see Davy, his hands stroking the knotted muscles of my calves, his lips moving slowly up my legs, covering them with tiny kisses.

Lyn took my face in her hands, put her mouth to mine, and our tongues met and danced round one another in greeting . . .

And then I felt something I had never felt before—a mounting pressure, a thrilling tension, as though every nerve ending in my body were about to burst, but didn't, just kept building and building in intensity—a pleasure I had never known, never imagined I *could* know. And it was then that I realized: the doctors had been wrong; all of them. Very wrong. I wasn't lacking in erogenous tissue. My whole *body* was erogenous tissue.

All it needed was the proper stimulation.

* * *

I finally worked up the nerve to see my parents; when Mother opened the door there was a moment's shock at my appearance—so different from the flirty blonde teenager who'd run away years before —but then she reached out and embraced me, holding me as though I might blow away on the wind. Then Daddy stepped up out of the shadows of the living room and did something odd and touching: he reached out and shook my hand, the way he might greet a son coming home from college; and then kissed me on the cheek, as he might a daughter. It was his way, I think, of acknowledging I was both, and neither; his way of telling me that they didn't love a daughter, they didn't love a son . . . they loved a child.

Funny; for years I thought of myself as a freak, a useless throwback to another time—but despite all the psych courses I'd taken, all the books I'd read, I never really thought about that time, eons before recorded history, when my kind shared the earth with men and women. Why we vanished, or died out, may never be known; but the real question is, why were we there in the first place? It wasn't until Lyn, and Davy, that I began wondering . . . thinking about how, in the millennia since, men and women had had such difficulty understanding one another, seeing the other's side . . . as though something were— missing, somehow. A balance; a harmonizing element; the third side of a triangle. Maybe *that* was the natural order of things, and what's come since is the deviation. All along I'd been thinking of my kind as throwbacks, when perhaps we're just the opposite; perhaps we're more like . . . precursors.

The basement's been converted, not into a recreation room as once planned, but into extra living quarters; I have a bedroom, for when Davy and Lyn want to be alone, and a small library/den where I can study. So far, no one's been scandalized by the arrangement; lots of people room together to save rent or mortgage payments, after all. I've enrolled at the University of Washington, aiming first for my Master's, then my Ph.D., in psychology . . . because now, finally, I think I know what that purpose is I was seeking for so many years. If the statistics are right, our numbers will be doubling every ten months; thousands more like me, going through the same identity crises, the same doubt and fear and loneliness . . . and who better to help them than a psychologist who truly understands their problems?

Lyn's quit smoking again, but this time, happily, the pregnancy

isn't a—what did she call it?—"stress-induced symptomatic replication." And I can't help but feel that after so many false starts,
maybe, somehow, it was me who tipped the scales—gave them that
extra little push they needed. After all, who's to say life can't be
transmitted just as easily in saliva or sweat as it is in semen or ova?
We only have one problem now: the nagging suspicion that when it
comes time to buy baby clothes, neither pink nor blue may be appropriate. Green? Yellow? Violet? Take my word for it: there's big money
to be made here for some enterprising manufacturer, one ready to tap
an expanding market. Wait and see; wait and see.

The Two-Headed Man

Nancy A. Collins

"The Two-Headed Man" has a strange history. Alice K. Turner at *Playboy* bought and paid for the story, then had to reject it at the request of her publisher who thought the story too "odd" for that market. Nancy Collins contacted *Pulphouse* next because we had a reputation for publishing the bizarre. "The Two-Headed Man" was exactly the kind of story we were looking for.

Nancy Collins rose to prominence just a few years ago with her Stoker-award-winning novel, *Sunglasses After Dark*. She followed that book with several short stories and a new novel, *Tempter*.

Reviewers have called "The Two-Headed Man" realistic fiction, with no fantastic element whatsoever. I, on the other hand, believe that the story belongs to that realm of fantasy that we call wish fulfillment.

It was going on midnight when the two-headed man walked into Kelly's Stop.

The short order cook glanced up when the burst of cold air rifled the newspaper spread across the formica serving counter. The man stood in the diner's doorway, the fur-fringed hood of the parka casting his face in deep shadow. He tugged off his mittens and stuffed them into one pocket, flexing his fingers like a pianist before a recital.

"You're in luck, buddy," said the cook, refolding the newspaper. "We was just about ready to call it an early night."

The'waitress stabbed out a cigarette and pivoted on her stool to get a better look at the stranger. She tugged at her blouse waist, causing her name, LOUISE, to twitch over her heart.

"Car had a flat . . . up the road . . ." came a voice from inside the shadow of the parka's hood. "We don't . . . have a spare . . ."

The cook shrugged, his back to the stranger. "Can't help you there, bub. Mike Keckhaver runs the Shell station down the road a piece, but he don't open up till tomorrow morning."

"Then we'll . . . have to wait."

"We?" Louise moved to the front window and peered out between the neon Miller Hi-Life and Schlitz signs. The gravel parking lot fronting the diner was empty. "You got somebody with you, mister?"

"Yes . . . you could say that," answered the stranger as he unzipped the parka and tossed back the hood.

Louise gasped and clamped a hand over her mouth, smearing lipstick against her palm. The cook spun around to see what was going on, butcher knife in hand: late-night truck-stop robberies were not uncommon along Highway 65.

The stranger had two heads. One was where heads are supposed to be. And a damn fine one at that. It was the handsomest head Louise had seen this side of a TV screen. The stranger's hair was longish and curly and the color of winter wheat. It framed a face designed for a movie star; straight nose, strong and beardless chin, high cheekbones, and eyes bluer than Paul Newman's.

The second head looked over the stranger's left shoulder, perched on his collarbone like a parrot. It wasn't a deformed or even an unsightly head—just average. But its extreme proximity to such masculine perfection made it seem . . . repulsive. The second head was dark where the other was fair, brown-eyed where the first was blue. It regarded Louise with a distant, oddly disturbing intelligence, then turned so its lips moved against its fellow's left ear. The stranger laughed without much humor.

"Yeah, guess I *did* scare 'em some . . ." The stranger shrugged off his coat. "Sorry, didn't mean to startle you like that."

Now that the parka was all the way off they could see that the stranger really didn't have two heads. A padded leather harness, like those worn by professional hitchhikers, was strapped to his shoulders and midsection. But instead of a bed roll and an army surplus duffle-bag, he carried a little man on his back.

The stranger seated himself on one of the stools, leaning slightly forward under the weight of his burden.

"What is he? A dwarf or somethin'?" The cook ignored the look Louise shot him.

The man did not seem at all insulted. "Nope. Human Worm."

"Huh?"

"Carl's got no arms . . . or legs."

"That so? Was he in Viet Nam?"

"No. Just born that way."

"How about that. Don't see that everyday."

"No, you don't," he agreed amiably. The Human Worm leaned closer and whispered into his ear again. The stranger nodded. "Okay. Why not, long as we're here. We'll have two orders of bacon and eggs . . . one scrambled . . . one sunny-side up . . . two orders of toast . . . and two coffees. Got that?" The stranger pulled a cloth hankie out of his pants pocket and draped it over his left shoulder.

"Uh, yeah. Sure. Comin' right up."

"Name's Gary. This here's Carl," the stranger jerked a thumb to indicate his piggyback passenger.

"Pleased t'meetcha," the cook grunted.

Carl bobbed his head in silent acknowledgement.

Louise stood near the end of the serving counter, debating on whether she should try to talk to the handsome stranger with the freak tied to his back.

Talking to the various strangers that found their way into Kelly's Stop was one of the few perks the job had to offer. The trouble with the locals was that she knew what they were going to say before they even opened their mouths. She hated living in a pissant little town like Seven Devils.

She envied the strangers she met; travelers from somewhere on their way to someplace. She like to pretend that maybe one of them would be her long-awaited Dream Prince and take her away from Kelly's Stop—just like Ronald Coleman rescued Bette Davis in *Petrified Forest*. But if her Prince was going to put in an appearance, it was going to have to be pretty damn soon. Her tits were starting to sag and the laugh-lines at the corners of her eyes were threatening to become crow's feet.

She studied the two men as they waited to be served. It was sure as hell a *weird* set-up. But that face . . . Gary's face . . . was the one she'd pictured in her fantasies. It was the face of the Prince who would deliver her from a lifetime of bunions, corn plasters, varicose veins and cheap beer.

The more she thought about it, he wasn't really *that* strange. It was kind of sweet, really, the way he carried the crippled guy on his back. It wasn't that much different than pushing a wheelchair.

The cook plopped the eggs and bacon onto the grill, slammed twin slices of bread into the toaster and returned his attention to the spitting bacon.

"Louise! Get th' man his coffee, willya?" The command made her jump and she scurried over to the Mr. Coffee machine.

"How you like it?" she asked, hoping she didn't sound shrill. Her hands were shaking. She took a deep breath before she poured.

"Black. Cream and sugar."

She slid the cups across the counter and located a sugar dispenser. She felt his gaze on her as she moved to get the cream from the cooler, but she wasn't sure which one was doing the looking.

Gary picked up the cup of black coffee with his left, blew on it a couple times, then lifted it over his shoulder. Carl lowered his head and noisily sipped from the lip of the cup while Gary stirred his coffee with his right hand.

"Wow. Neat trick." She kicked herself the minute she said it. What a *hick* thing to say.

Gary shrugged, causing Carl to bounce slightly. "Helps if you're ambidextrous."

"Ambiwhat?"

"Carl says that's being good with both hands," he explained, gesturing with a piece of bacon. Carl leaned forward, grasping the proffered strip with surprisingly white, even teeth before bolting it down like a lizard.

Louise watched as Gary fed himself and his rider, both hands moving with unthinking grace. He acted as if it was as natural for him as breathing. Carl wiped his mouth and chin, shiny with grease and butter, on the napkin draped over his companion's shoulder. His eyes met Louise's and she hastily looked away.

There was something hot and alive in those eyes; something hungry and all too familiar. Her cheeks burned and she dropped a bouquet of clean flatware onto the floor.

"Look, mister, I'm gonna be closin' shop real soon. Like I said, the Shell station don't open till seven or eight. There's a motel up the road a bit, the Driftwood Inn. You shouldn't have no trouble findin' a place there. They're right off th' highway, so they're open all night. I'd give you a lift but, uh, my car's in the shop an' I live in town, so . . ." The cook fell silent and returned to cleaning the grill.

The two-headed man sat and drank coffee while Louise and her boss busied themselves with the ritual of closing. Louise mopped the floor faster than usual, trying not to look at the stranger and his freakish papoose.

"Well, lights out, folks," the cook announced with a forced smile. The two-headed man stood up and began shouldering themselves back into the parka. "Uh, look, Louise. . . . Why don't you lock up for me, huh? Laurie's waitin' up on me and you know how she gets."

Louise certainly did. Laurie had had enough of waiting up for her husband three years back and joined the others who'd abandoned Seven Devils, Arkansas. She nodded and watched him flee the diner for the safety of a nonexistent wife.

Gary pulled the parka's hood over his head and zipped up. All she could see was his face—that achingly handsome face—with its baby-smooth jaw and electric blue eyes.

It was bitterly cold outside, their breath wreathing their heads. The hard frost had turned the highway into a strip of polished onyx. Gary stuffed his hands into his mittens, gave Louise a nod and a half-wave and began to walk away, the parking lot's gravel crunching under his boots heels. The lump under his parka stirred.

Do something, girl! Say something! Don't just let him walk off!

"Hey, mister . . . er, misters!"

He turned to smile at her. She felt her bravado slip. *Dear God, what am I getting myself into?* But it was two in the morning and everyone in Choctaw County was asleep except for her and the blue-eyed stranger . . . and his traveling companion.

"I've got a place 'round back. It's not much, but it's warm. You're welcome to stay . . . I hate to think of you walking all the way to the motel and then it turn out to be full-up."

Gary stood there for a moment, his hands in his pockets and his head cocked to one side as if he was listening to something. Then he smiled.

"We'd be delighted."

* * *

The frozen grass crunched gently under their feet. The dark bulk of Louise's trailer loomed ahead of them, resting on its bed of cinderblocks.

"Where are we . . . exactly? We've no real idea . . ."

"You're in Choctaw County."

"That's the name of this place?"

"No. Not really. This here's Seven Devils. Or its outskirts, at least. Not much to it, except that it's th' county seat. This used to be a railroad town, back before the war. But now that everything's shipped by trucks, there ain't a whole lot left. What makes you want to drive around in this part of Arkansas in the first place? There's nothing down here but rice fields, bayous and broke farmers."

"We like the old highways . . . we meet much nicer people that way . . ."

Louise stopped to glance over her shoulder as she dug the housekey from her coat pocket. Had it been Gary's voice she'd heard that time? All she could see was shadow inside the parka's hood. She stood on the cinder block that served as her front stoop and fussed with her keychain. She could hear him breathing at her elbow.

"Welcome to my humble abode! It ain't much, but it's home. It used to belong to the boss. I keep an eye on the place for him."

Why was she so anxious? He certainly wasn't the first man she'd invited back to her trailer. She'd known her share of truckers, salesmen, and hitchhikers tricked out in their elaborate backpacks. Some of them she'd even deluded herself into thinking might be her Prince in disguise.

Each time there had been the meeting of tongues, the grunts in the dark as loins slapped together, and the cool evaporation of sweat on naked flesh. Each time she woke up alone. Sometimes there'd be money on the dresser.

She flicked on the lights and she entered the trailer. The tiny kitchen and shoebox-sized den emerged from the darkness.

"Like I said; it ain't much."

He stood on the threshold, one hand on the doorknob. "It's nice, Louise."

She shivered at the sound of her name in his mouth. She moved into the living room, hoping for a chance to compose herself. She needed to think.

"Close the door! You're lettin' the cold air in!" Her voice was unnaturally chirpy.

Gary closed the door behind him. She felt a bit more secure, but she couldn't help but notice how worn and tacky everything looked: the sofa, the dinette set, the easy chair. . . . For a fleeting second she was overwhelmed by a desire to cry.

Gary removed his parka, carefully draping it over the back of the easy chair. He was wearing faded denims and a flannel shirt and he was so beautiful it scared her to look at him. He was so perfect she could almost ignore the Human Worm strapped to his back.

"Get you a drink?"

"That would be . . . nice."

She hurried past him and back into the kitchen. She retrieved her bottle of Evan Williams and a couple of highball glasses. She poured herself two fingers, knocked it back, then poured another two before preparing a drink for her guest. She returned to the living room—he was standing in the exact same spot—and handed Gary the glass.

"Skoal."

"Cheers," he replied, lifting the glass to Carl's lips.

While his partner drank, Gary's eyes met and held hers. "We know why you invited us here, Louise . . ."

Her heart began to beat funny, as if she'd been given a powerful but dangerous drug. She wanted this man, this gorgeous stranger. She wanted to feel his weight on her, pressing her into the mattress of her bed.

". . . but there's one thing you ought to know before we get started . . . and that's Carl's got to go first."

She stood perfectly still for a second before the words her Dream Prince had spoken sank in. She was keenly aware of Carl's eyes watching her. Her face burned and her stomach balled itself into a fist. She felt as if she'd awakened from a dream to find herself trapped in the punchline of a dirty joke.

"What kind of *pervert* do you think I am?" The tightness in her throat pitched her voice even higher.

"I don't think you're a pervert, Louise. I think you're a very sweet, very special lady. I didn't mean to hurt you." There was no cynicism in his voice. His tone was that of a child confused by the irrationality of adults.

She felt her anger fade. She gulped down the rest of her drink, hoping it would fan the fires of her indignation. "I expected *something* kinky out of you—like maybe letting th' little guy *watch* . . . but not, y'know . . ."

"I see."

Gary moved to retrieve his parka. Before she realized what she was doing, she grabbed his arm. She was astonished by the intensity of her reaction.

"No! Don't leave! Please . . . it's so lonely here . . ."

"Yes, it *is* lonely," he whispered. His eyes would not meet hers. "Go stand over there. By the sofa. Where we can see you."

Louise did as she was told. Everything seemed so far away, as if she were watching a movie through the wrong end of a pair of binoculars. Her arms and legs felt so fragile they might have been made of light and glass.

Carl whispered into Gary's ear. His eyes had grown sharp and alive while Gary's seemed to lose their focus.

"Take off your blouse. Please." The words came from someplace far away.

She hesitated, then her hands moved to the throat of her blouse. The buttons seemed cold and alien, designed to frustrate her fingers. One by one they surrendered until her shirtfront fell open, revealing pale flesh. She shrugged her shoulders and the blouse fell to the floor.

Carl once more whispered something to Gary, never taking his eyes off Louise. "The skirt. Take it off."

Her hands found the fastener at her waist. Plastic teeth purred on plastic zipper and her skirt dropped to the floor, a dark puddle at her ankles. She took a step forward, abandoning her clothes.

Carl murmured into Gary's ear. She unhooked her bra, revealing her breasts. Her skin was milky white and decorated by dark aureoles. Her nipples were as hard as corn kernels.

On Carl's relayed command she skinned herself free of her panty-hose. When the cool air struck her damp pubic patch, her clitoris stirred.

Gary moved toward her, bringing Carl with him.

She gasped aloud when Gary's hands touched her breasts. His thumbs flicked expertly over her nipples, sending shudders of pleasure through her. Then one hand was between her legs, teasing and gently massaging her.

Louise felt her knees buckle and she grabbed hold of Gary's shoulders to keep from falling backwards. Her eyes opened and she found herself staring into Carl's dark, intense eyes. She felt a brief surge of shame that her orgasm had become a spectator event, then Gary worked a finger past her labia and sank it to the second joint. Louise groaned aloud and all thoughts of shame disappeared.

He moved swiftly and quietly, wrapping her in his powerful arms and lifting her bodily. She felt a different form of pleasure now, as if she was once more within her father's safe embrace. He moved down the narrow hall, past the cramped bathroom alcove and into the tiny bedroom at the back of the trailer. He lowered her trembling body onto the bed, draping her legs over the edge of the mattress.

His left hand continued to trace delicate patterns along her exposed flesh while his right loosened the harness that held Carl in place. He only halted his exploration of her body when he moved to free his burden.

Louise saw that Carl was dressed in a flannel shirt identical to Gary's, except that the empty sleeves had been pinned up and the shirt tail folded back on itself and fastened shut, just like a diaper. Gary removed the shirt and Louise swore out loud.

Even on a normal man's body Carl's penis would have been unusually large. It stood red and erect against the thick dark hair of his belly. Louise was so taken aback she scarcely noticed the smooth lumps of flesh that should have been Carl's arms and legs.

Gary positioned Carl's naked torso between her spread thighs. His gaze met and held her own so intently Louise almost forgot the absurd perversity of what they were doing.

"We love you," said Gary and shoved Carl on top of her.

Louise cried out as Carl penetrated her. It had been a long time since she'd been with a man, and she had never known one of such proportions. She involuntarily contracted her hips, taking him in deeper. Gary's right hand kneaded the flesh of her breasts. His left hand helped Carl move. She could also feel something warm and damp just below her breasts. She suddenly realized it was Carl's face.

Gary's face was closer to hers now, his eyes mirroring her heat. She snared a handful of his hair, drawing him closer. His mouth was warm and wet as he clumsily returned the kiss. She felt the quivering that signalled the approach of orgasm and her moans became cries, giving voice to an exquisite wounding. Her hips bucked wildly with each spasm, but Carl refused to be unseated. As she lay dazed and gasping in her own sweat, she was dimly aware of him still working between her legs. Then there was a deep groan, muffled by her own flesh, and she felt him stiffen and then relax.

Louise rarely experienced orgasms during intercourse. She had been unprepared for such intensity; it was if Gary had stuck his finger in her brain and swirled everything around so she was no longer sure what she thought or knew.

No. Not Gary. Carl.

The thought made her catch her breath and she raised herself onto her elbows, staring down at the thing cradled between her thighs. Carl's face was still buried in her breast. She touched his hair and felt him start from the unexpected contact. It was the first time since their strange rut had begun that she'd acknowledged his presence.

She felt Gary watching her as she moved back farther onto the bed. Carl remained curled at the foot of the mattress, his eyes fixed on her. Gary stood in the narrow space between the bed and the dresser, his hands at his sides.

"What about you? Aren't you interested?" Her voice was hoarse.

Gary did not meet her gaze as he shifted his weight from foot to foot.

"What's the matter? Is it me?"

His head jerked up. "No! It's not you. You're fine. It's just. . . ." He fell silent and looked to Carl, who nodded slightly.

Gary took a deep breath and loosened his belt buckle. His manner had changed completely. His movements had lost their previous grace. Biting his lower lip and tensing as if in anticipation of a blow, he dropped his pants.

Gary's sex organs were the size of a two-year-old child's. They lay exposed like fragile spring blossoms, his pubic area as smooth and hairless as his face. His eyes remained cast down.

Louis's lips twisted into a wry smile. She had willingly serviced a freak in order to please her long-awaited Prince, only to find him gelded. Yet all she could feel for the handsome near-man was sorrow.

"You poor thing. You poor, poor thing." She reached out and touched his hand, drawing him into the warmth of her arms. Surprised, Gary eagerly returned her embrace. To her own surprise, she reached down to pull Carl toward her. The three of them lay together on the bed like a nest of snakes, Louise gently caressing her lovers. After awhile Gary began to talk.

"I've known Carl since we were kids. My mama used to cook and clean for his folks and I kept Carl company. His mama and daddy were real rich; that's how they could afford to keep him home. At least his mama wanted him home. Carl's daddy drank a lot and used to say how it wasn't *his* fault in front of Carl. I knew how he felt. About having your daddy hate you because of the way you was born. Maybe that's why me and Carl made such good friends. You see, I can't read so good. And I'm really bad with math and things like that. My daddy got mad at my mama when they found out what was wrong with me and he ran away. I never really went to school. When Carl was five, his daddy got real mad and started kickin' him. And Carl hadn't even done anything bad! He kicked Carl in the throat and they took him to the hospital. That's why Carl can't talk too good. But he's real smart! Smarter than most people with arms and legs! He knows a lot about history and math and important stuff like that. Carl tells me what to say and how to act and what to do so people don't know I've got something wrong with me. If people ever knew I wasn't smart they'd be even meaner to us." He exchanged a warm, brotherly smile with the silent man and squeezed him where his shoulder should have been. "Carl looks after me. I'm his arms and legs and voice and he's my brain and, you know." He blushed.

"You're lucky. Both of you. Not everyone is as . . . whole."

"But we're not!" He folded her hands inside his own. "Not really. That's why we've been traveling. We've been trying to find the last part of us. The part that *will* make us whole."

Louise did not know what to say to this, so she simply kissed him. Sometime later they fell asleep, Carl's torso curled between them like a dozing pet.

The alarm went off at eight-thirty, jarring Louise from a dreamless sleep. She lay there for a moment, staring at Gary then Carl. She should have felt soiled, but there was no indignation inside her. She gently shook Gary's beautiful naked shoulder.

"It's morning already. The filling station must be open by now. You can get your tire fixed."

"Yes." His voice sounded strangely hollow.

She got out of the rumpled bed, careful to keep from kicking

Carl, and put on a housecoat. Now that it was daylight she felt embarrassed to be naked. She hurried into the kitchen and made coffee.

Gary emerged from the bedroom, dressed, with Carl once more harnessed to his back. She handed him two mugs, one black and one with cream and sugar, and watched, a faint smile on her lips, as they repeated their one-as-two act.

After they finished, Gary picked his parka up and laid it across one arm. He glanced first at her then angled his head so that he was as close to face-to-face with his passenger as possible. After a moment's silent communion, he once more turned to look at her, and his eyes lost their focus. Carl's lips moved at his ear and Louise could hear the faint rasping of his ruined voice.

Gary spoke, like a man reading back dictation.

"Louise . . . you're a wonderful woman . . . I know you're not attracted to me, that's understandable . . . but I see something in you that might, someday . . . respond to *me* too . . ."

As Gary continued his halting recitation, Louise's gaze moved from his face to Carl's. For the first time since she'd met them, she really looked at *him*. She studied his plain, everyday face and his brown eyes. As she listened, the voice she heard was Carl's and she felt something inside her change.

"We'll stop back after we get the tire repaired. . . . It's up to you. . . . We shouldn't be more than an hour at the most. Please think about it."

Gary began to put his parka on, but before the jacket hid Carl completely she darted forward and kissed both of them. First Gary, and then, with great care, Carl. They paused for a second and then smiled.

Louise stood in the middle of the trailer, hugging herself against the morning cold, as she watched her lovers leave. Funny. She'd always imagined her Prince having blue eyes . . .

Bits and Pieces

Lisa Tuttle

Lisa Tuttle's work has appeared since 1980. She has published three novels (*Windhaven* with George R. R. Martin; *Familiar Spirit,* and *Gabriel*) and two short story collections (*A Nest of Nightmares* and *Spaceship Built of Stone*). In addition, she has also written nonfiction and edited a highly acclaimed volume of women's fiction, *Skin of the Soul.*

"Bits and Pieces" works on a number of levels: as an examination of love and male/female relations, as metaphor, and as a cautionary tale. But most of all, it works.

On the morning after Ralph left her, Fay found a foot in her bed.

It was Ralph's foot, but how could he have left it behind? What did it mean? She sat on the edge of the bed holding it in her hand, examining it. It was a long, pale, narrow, rather elegant foot. At the top, where you would expect it to grow into an ankle, the foot ended in a slight, skin-covered concavity. There was no sign of blood or severed flesh or bone or scar tissue, nor were there any corns or bunions, over-long nails or dirt. Ralph was a man who looked after his feet.

Lying there in her hand it felt as alive as a motionless foot ever feels; impossible as it seemed, she believed it was real. Ralph wasn't a practical joker, and yet—a foot wasn't something you left behind without noticing. She wondered how he was managing to get around on just one foot. Was it a message? Some obscure consolation for her feeling that, losing him, she had lost a piece of herself?

He had made it clear he no longer wanted to be involved with her. His goodbye had sounded final. But maybe he would get in touch when he realized she still had something of his. Although she knew she ought to be trying to forget him, she felt oddly grateful for this unexpected gift. She wrapped the foot in a silk scarf and put it in the bottom dresser drawer, to keep for him.

Two days later, tidying the bedroom, she found his other foot under the bed. She had to check the drawer to make sure it wasn't the same one, gone wandering. But it was still there, one right foot, and she was holding the left one. She wrapped the two of them together in the white silk scarf and put them away.

Time passed and Ralph did not get in touch. Fay knew from friends that he was still around, and as she never heard any suggestion that he was now crippled, she began to wonder if the feet had been some sort of hallucination. She kept meaning to look in the bottom drawer, but she kept forgetting.

The relationship with Ralph, while it lasted, had been a serious, deeply meaningful one for them both, she thought; she knew from the start there was no hope with Freddy. Fay was a responsible person who believed the act of sex should be accompanied by love and a certain degree of commitment; she detested the very idea of "casual sex"—but she'd been six months without a man in her bed, and Freddy was irresistible.

He was warm and cuddly and friendly, the perfect teddy bear. Within minutes of meeting him she was thinking about sleeping with him—although it was the comfort and coziness of bed he brought to mind rather than passion. As passive as a teddy bear, he would let himself be pursued. She met him with friends in a pub, and he offered to walk her home. Outside her door he hugged her. There was no kissing or groping; he just wrapped her in a warm, friendly embrace, where she clung to him longer and tighter than friendship required.

"Mmmm," he said, appreciatively, smiling down at her, his eyes button-bright, "I could do this all night."

"What a good idea," she said.

After they had made love she decided he was less a teddy bear than a cat. Like a cat in the sensual way he moved and rubbed his body against hers and responded to her touch: she could almost hear him purr. Other cat-like qualities, apparent after she had known him a little longer, were less appealing. Like a cat he was self-centered, basically lazy, and although she continued to enjoy him in bed, she did wish sometimes he would pay more attention to *her* pleasure instead of assuming that his was enough for them both. He seemed to expect her to be pleased no matter what time he turned up for dinner, even if he fell asleep in front of the fire immediately after. And, like many cats, he had more than one home.

Finding out about his other home—hearing that other woman's tear-clogged voice on the phone—decided her to end it. It wasn't— or so she told him—that she wanted to have him all to herself. But she wouldn't be responsible for another woman's sorrow.

He understood her feelings. He was wrong, and she was right. He was remorseful, apologetic, and quite incapable of changing. But he would miss her very much. He gave her a friendly hug before they parted, but once they started hugging it was hard to stop, and they tumbled into bed again.

That had to be the last time. She knew she could be firmer with him on the phone than in person, so she told him he was not to visit unless she first invited him. Sadly, he agreed.

And that was that. Going back into the bedroom she saw the duvet rucked up as if there was someone still in the bed. It made her shiver. If she hadn't just seen him out the door, and closed it behind him, she might have thought . . . Determined to put an end to such mournful nonsense she flung the duvet aside, and there he was.

Well, part of him.

Lying on the bed was a headless, neckless, armless, legless, torso. Or at least the back side of one. As with Ralph's feet there was nothing unpleasant about it, no blood or gaping wounds. If you could ignore the sheer impossibility of it, there was nothing wrong with Freddy's back at all. It looked just like the body she had been embracing a few minutes before, and felt. . . .

Tentatively, she reached out and touched it. It was warm and smooth, with the firm, elastic give of live flesh. She could not resist stroking it the way she knew he liked, teasing with her nails to make the skin prickle into goose-bumps, running her fingers all the way from the top of the spine to the base, and over the curve of the buttocks where the body ended.

She drew her hand back, shocked. What *was* this? It seemed so much like Freddy, but how could it be when she had seen him, minutes before, walking out the door, fully equipped with all his body parts? Was it possible that there was nothing, now, but air filling out his jumper and jeans?

She sat down, took hold of the torso where the shoulders ended in smooth, fleshy hollows, and heaved it over. The chest was as she remembered, babyishly pink nipples peeking out of a scumble of ginger hair, but below the flat stomach only more flatness. His genitals were missing, as utterly and completely gone as if they had never been thought of. Her stomach twisted in shock and horror although, a moment later, she had to ask herself why that particular lack should matter so much more than the absence of his head—which she had accepted remarkably calmly. After all, this wasn't the real Freddy, only some sort of partial memory of his body inexplicably made flesh.

She went over to the dresser and crouched before the bottom drawer. Yes, they were still there. They didn't appear to have decayed or faded or changed in any way. Letting the silk scarf fall away she gazed at the naked feet and realized that she felt differently about Ralph. She had been unhappy when he left, but she had also been, without admitting it even to herself, furiously angry with him. And the anger had passed. The bitterness was gone, and she felt only affection now as she caressed his feet and remembered the good times. Eventually, with a sigh that mingled fondness and regret, she wrapped them up and put them away. Then she returned to her current problem: what to do with the part Freddy had left behind.

For a moment she thought of leaving it in the bed. He'd always been *so* nice to sleep with . . . But no. She had to finish what she had begun; she couldn't continue sleeping with part of Freddy all the time when all of Freddy part of the time had not been enough for her. She would never be able to get on with her life, she would never dare to bring anyone new home with her.

It would have to go in the wardrobe. The only other option was the hall closet which was cold and smelled slightly of damp. So, wrapping it in her best silken dressing gown, securing it with a tie around the waist, she stored Freddy's torso in the wardrobe behind her clothes.

Freddy phoned next week. He didn't mention missing anything but her, and she almost told him about finding his torso in her bed. But how could she? If she told him, he'd insist on coming over to see it, and if he came over she'd be back to having an affair with him. That wasn't what she was after, was it? She hesitated, and then asked if he was still living with Matilda.

"Oh, more or less," he said. "Yes."

So she didn't tell him. She tried to forget him, and hoped to meet someone else, someone who would occupy the man-sized empty space in her life.

Meanwhile, Freddy continued to phone her once a week—friendly calls, because he wanted to stay friends. After a while she realized, from comments he let drop, that he was seeing another woman; that once again he had two homes. As always, she resisted the temptation she felt to invite him over, but she felt wretchedly lonely that evening.

For the first time since she had stored it away, she took out his body. Trembling a little, ashamed of herself, she took it to bed. She so wanted someone to hold. The body felt just like Freddy, warm and solid and smooth in the same way; it even smelled like him, although now with the faint overlay of her own perfume from her clothes. She held it for awhile, but the lack of arms and head was too peculiar. She found that if she lay with her back against his and tucked her legs up so she couldn't feel his missing legs, it was almost like being in bed with Freddy.

She slept well that night, better than she had for weeks. "My teddy bear," she murmured as she packed him away again in the morning. It was like having a secret weapon. The comfort of a warm body in bed with her at night relaxed her, and made her more self-confident. She no longer felt any need to invite Freddy over, and when he called it was easy to talk to him without getting more involved, as if they'd always been just friends. And now that she wasn't looking, there seemed to be more men around.

One of them, Paul, who worked for the same company in a different department, asked her out. Lately she had kept running into him, and he seemed to have a lot of business which took him to her part of the building, but it didn't register on her that this was no coincidence until he asked if she was doing anything that Saturday night. After that, his interest in her seemed so obvious that she couldn't imagine why she hadn't noticed earlier.

The most likely reason she hadn't noticed was that she didn't care. She felt instinctively that he wasn't her type; they had little in common. But his unexpected interest flattered her, and made him seem more attractive, and so she agreed to go out with him.

It was a mistake, she thought, uneasily, when Saturday night came around and Paul took her to a very expensive restaurant. He was not unintelligent, certainly not bad-looking, but there was something a little too glossy and humorless about him. He was interested in money, and cars, and computers—and her. He dressed well, and he knew the right things to say, but she imagined he had learned them out of a book. He was awfully single-minded, and seemed intent on seduction, which made her nervous, and she spent too much of the evening trying to think of some way of getting out of inviting him in for coffee when he took her home. It was no good; when the time came, he invited himself in.

She knew it wasn't fair to make comparisons, but Paul was the complete opposite of Freddy. Where Freddy sat back and waited calmly to be stroked, Paul kept edging closer, trying to crawl into her lap. And his hands were everywhere. From the very start of the evening he had stood and walked too close to her, and she didn't like the way he had of touching her, as if casually making a point, staking a physical claim to her.

For the next hour she fended him off. It was a wordless battle which neither of them would admit to. When he left, she lacked the energy to refuse a return match, the following weekend.

They went to the theatre, and afterwards to his place—he said he wanted to show her his computer. She expected another battle, but he was a perfect gentleman. Feeling safer, she agreed to a third date, and then drank too much; the drink loosened her inhibitions, she was too tired to resist his persistent pressure when they arrived at her home, and finally took him into her bed.

The sex was not entirely a success—for her, anyway—but it would doubtless get better as they got to know each other, she thought, and she was just allowing herself a few modest fantasies about the future, concentrating on the things she thought she liked about him, when he said he had to go.

The man who had been hotly all over her was suddenly distant and cool, almost rude in his haste to leave. She tried to find excuses for him, but when he had gone, and she discovered his hands were still in her bed, she knew he did not mean to return.

The hands were nestling beneath a pillow like a couple of soft-shelled crabs. She shuddered at the sight of them; shouted and threw her shoes at them. The left hand twitched when struck, but otherwise they didn't move.

How dare he leave his hands! She didn't *want* anything to remember him by! She certainly hadn't been in love with him.

Fay looked around for something else to throw, and then felt ashamed of herself. Paul was a creep, but it wasn't fair to take it out on his hands. They hadn't hurt her; they had done their best to give her pleasure—they might have succeeded if she'd liked their owner more.

But she didn't like their owner—she had to admit she wasn't really sorry he wouldn't be back—so why was she stuck with his hands? She could hardly give them back. She could already guess how he would avoid her at work, and she wasn't about to add to his inflated ego by pursuing him. But it didn't seem possible to throw them out, either.

She found a shoe box to put them in—she didn't bother about wrapping them—and then put the box away out of sight on the highest shelf of the kitchen cupboard, among the cracked plates, odd saucers and empty jars which she'd kept because they might someday be useful.

The hands made her think a little differently about what had happened. She had been in love with Ralph and also, for all her attempts to rationalize her feelings, with Freddy—she hadn't wanted either of them to go. It made a kind of sense for her to fantasize that they'd left bits of themselves behind, but that didn't apply to her feelings for Paul. She absolutely refused to believe that her subconscious was responsible for the hands in the kitchen cupboard.

So if not her subconscious, then what? Was it the bed? She stood in the bedroom and looked at it, trying to perceive some sorcery in the brand-name mattress or the pine frame. She had bought the bed for Ralph, really; he had complained so about the futon she had when they met, declaring that it was not only too short, but also bad for his back. He had told her that pine beds were good and also cheap, and although she didn't agree with his assessment of the price, she had bought one. It was the most expensive thing she owned. Was it also haunted?

She could test it; invite friends to stay. . . . Would any man who made love in this bed leave a part of himself behind, or only those who made love to her? Only for the last time? But how did it know? How could it, before she herself knew a relationship was over? What if she lured Paul back—would some other body part appear when he left? Or would the hands disappear?

Once she had thought of this, she knew she had to find out. She tried to forget the idea but could not. Days passed, and Paul did not get in touch—he avoided her at work, as she had guessed he would —and she told herself to let him go. Good riddance. To pursue him would be humiliating. It wasn't even as if she were in love with him, after all.

She told herself not to be a fool, but chance and business kept taking her to his part of the building. When forced to acknowledge her his voice was polite and he did not stand too close; he spoke as if they'd never met outside working hours; as if he'd never really noticed her as a woman. She saw him, an hour later, leaning confidentially over one of the newer secretaries, his hand touching her hip.

She felt a stab of jealous frustration. No wonder she couldn't attract his attention; he had already moved on to fresh prey.

Another week went by, but she would not accept defeat. She phoned him up and invited him to dinner. He said his weekends were awfully busy just now. She suggested a week night. He hesitated— surprised by her persistence? Contemptuous? Flattered?—and then said he was involved with someone, actually. Despising herself, Fay said lightly that of course she understood. She said that in fact she herself was involved in a long-standing relationship, but her fellow had been abroad for the past few months, and she got bored and lonely in the evenings. She'd enjoyed herself so much with Paul that she had hoped they'd be able to get together again sometime; that was all.

That changed the temperature. He said he was afraid he couldn't manage dinner, but if she liked, he could drop by later one evening —maybe tomorrow, around ten?

He was on her as soon as he was through the door. She tried to fend him off with offers of drink, but he didn't seem to hear. His hands were everywhere, grabbing, fondling, probing, as undeniably real as they'd ever been.

"Wait, wait." she said, laughing but not amused. "Can't we . . . talk?"

He paused, holding her around the waist, and looked down at her. He was bigger than she remembered. "We could have talked on the phone."

"I know, but . . ."

"Is there something we need to talk about?"

"Well, no, nothing specific, but . . ."

"Did you invite me over here to talk? Did I misunderstand?"

"No."

"All right." His mouth came down, wet and devouring, on hers, and she gave in.

But not on the couch, she thought, a few minutes later. "Bed," she gasped, breaking away. "In the bedroom."

"Good idea."

But it no longer seemed like a good idea to her. As she watched him strip off his clothes she thought this was probably the worst idea she'd ever had. She didn't want him in her bed again; she didn't want sex with him. How could she have thought, for even a minute, that she could have sex for such a cold-blooded, ulterior motive?

"I thought you were in a hurry," he said. "Get your clothes off." Naked he reached for her.

She backed away. "I'm sorry, I shouldn't have called you, I'm sorry—"

"Don't apologize. It's very sexy when a woman knows what she wants and asks for it." He'd unbuttoned her blouse and unhooked her bra earlier, and now tried to remove them. She tried to stop him, and he pinioned her wrists.

"This is a mistake, I don't want this, you have to go."

"Like hell."

"I'm sorry, Paul, but I mean it."

He smiled humorlessly. "You mean you want me to force you."

"No!"

He pushed her down on the bed, got her skirt off despite her struggles, then ripped her tights.

"Stop it!"

"I wouldn't have thought you liked this sort of thing," he mused.

"I don't, I'm telling the truth, I don't want to have sex, I want you to leave." Her voice wobbled all over the place. "Look, I'm sorry,

I'm really sorry, but I can't, not now." Tears leaked out of her eyes. "Please. You don't understand. This isn't a game." She was completely naked now and he was naked on top of her.

"This *is* a game," he said calmly. "And I do understand. You've been chasing me for weeks. I know what you want. A minute ago, you were begging me to take you to bed. Now you're embarrassed. You want me to force you. I don't want to force you, but if I have to, I will."

"No."

"It's up to you," he said. "You can give, or I can take. That simple."

She had never thought rape could be that simple. She bit one of the arms that held her down. He slapped her hard.

"I told you," he said. "You can give, or I can take. It's that simple. It's your choice."

Frightened by his strength, seeing no choice at all, she gave in.

Afterwards, she was not surprised when she discovered what he had left in her bed. What else should it be? It was just what she deserved.

It was ugly, yet there was something oddly appealing in the sight of it nestling in a fold of the duvet; she was reminded of her teenage passion for collecting bean-bag creatures. She used to line them up across her bed. This could have been one of them: maybe a squashy elephant's head with a fat nose. She went on staring at it for a long time, lying on her side on the bed, emotionally numbed and physically exhausted, unable either to get up or to go to sleep. She told herself she should get rid of it, that she could take her aggressions out on it, cut it up, at least throw it, and the pair of hands, out with the rest of her unwanted garbage. But it was hard to connect this bean-bag creature with Paul and what he had done to her. She realized she had scarcely more than glimpsed his genitals; no wonder she couldn't believe this floppy creature could have had anything to do with her rape. The longer she looked at it, the less she could believe it was that horrible man's. It, too, had been abused by him. And it wasn't his now, it was hers. Okay, Paul had been the catalyst, somehow, but this set of genitalia had been born from the bed and her own desire; it was an entirely new thing.

Eventually she fell asleep, still gazing at it. When she opened her eyes in the morning it was like seeing an old friend. She wouldn't get rid of it. She put it in a pillowcase and stashed the parcel among the scarves, shawls and sweaters on the shelf at the top of the wardrobe.

She decided to put the past behind her. She didn't think about Paul or Ralph or even Freddy. Although most nights she slept with Freddy's body, that was a decision made on the same basis, and with no more emotion, as whether she slept with the duvet or the electric blanket. Freddy's body wasn't Freddy's anymore; it was hers.

The only men in her life now were friends. She wasn't looking for romance, and she seldom thought about sex. If she wanted male companionship there was Christopher, a platonic friend from school, or Marcus, her next-door neighbor, or Freddy. They still talked on the phone frequently, and very occasionally met in town for a drink or a meal, but she had never invited him over since their break-up, so it was a shock one evening to answer the door and discover him standing outside.

He looked sheepish. "I'm sorry," he said. "I know I should have called first, but I couldn't find a working phone, and . . . I hope you don't mind. I need somebody to talk to. Matilda's thrown me out."

And not only Matilda, but also the latest other woman. He poured out his woes, and she made dinner, and they drank wine and talked for hours.

"Do you have somewhere to stay?" she asked at last.

"I could go to my sister's. I stay there a lot anyway. She's got a spare room—I've even got my own key. But—" he gave her his old look, desirous but undemanding. "Actually, Fay, I was hoping I could stay with you tonight."

She discovered he was still irresistible.

Her last thought before she fell asleep, was how strange it was to sleep with someone who had arms and legs.

In the morning she woke enough to feel him kiss her, but she didn't realize it was a kiss goodbye, for she could still feel his legs entwined with her own.

But the rest of him was gone, and probably for good this time, she discovered when she woke up completely. For a man with such a smooth-skinned body he had extremely hairy legs, she thought, sitting on the bed and staring at the unattached limbs. And for a woman who had just been used and left again, she felt awfully cheerful.

She got Ralph's feet out of the drawer—thinking how much thinner and more elegant they were than Freddy's—and giggling to herself, pressed the right foot to the bottom of the right leg just to see how it looked.

It looked as if it was growing there and always had been. When she tried to pull it away, it wouldn't come. She couldn't even see a join. Anyone else might have thought it was perfectly natural; it probably looked odd to her because she knew it wasn't. When she did the same thing with the left foot and left leg, the same thing happened.

So then, feeling daring, she took Freddy's torso out of the wardrobe and laid it down on the bed just above the legs. She pushed the legs up close, so they looked as if they were growing out of the torso—and then they were. She sat it up, finding that it was as flexible and responsive as a real, live person, not at all a dead weight, and she sat on the edge of the bed beside it and looked down at its empty lap.

"Don't go away; I have just the thing for Sir," she said.

The genitals were really the wrong size and skin-tone for Freddy's long, pale body, but they nestled gratefully into his crotch, obviously happy in their new home.

The body was happy, too. There was new life in it—not Freddy's, not Paul's, not Ralph's, but a new being created out of their old parts. She wasn't imagining it. Not propped up, it was sitting beside her, holding itself up, alert and waiting. When she leaned closer she could feel a heart beating within the chest, sending the blood coursing through a network of veins and arteries. She reached out to stroke the little elephant-head slumbering between the legs, and as she touched it, it stirred and sat up.

She was sexually excited, too, and at the same time, horrified. There had to be something wrong with her to want to have sex with this incomplete collection of body parts. All right, it wasn't dead, so at least what she felt wasn't necrophilia, but what was it? A man without arms was merely disabled, but was a man without a head a man at all? Whatever had happened to her belief in the importance of relationships? They couldn't even communicate, except by touch, and then only at her initiative. All he could do was respond to her will. She thought of Paul's hands, how she had been groped, forced, slapped, and held down by them, and was just as glad they remained unattached, safely removed to the kitchen cupboard. Safe sex, she thought, and giggled. In response to the vibration, the body listed a little in her direction.

She got off the bed and moved away, then stood and watched it swaying indecisively. She felt a little sorry for it, being so utterly dependent on her, and that cooled her ardor. It wasn't right, she couldn't use it as a kind of live sex-aid—not as it was. She was going to have to find it a head, or forget about it.

She wrapped the body in a sheet to keep the dust off and stored it under the bed. She couldn't sleep with it anymore. In its headless state it was too disturbing. "Don't worry," she said, although it couldn't hear her. "This isn't forever."

She started her head hunt. She knew it might take some time, but she was going to be careful; she didn't want another bad experience. It wouldn't be worth it. Something good had come out of the Paul experience, but heads—or faces, anyway—were so much harder to depersonalize. If it looked like Freddy or Paul in the face, she knew she would respond to it as Freddy or Paul, and what was the point of that? She wanted to find someone new, someone she didn't know, but also someone she liked; someone she could find attractive, go to bed with, and be parted from without the traumas of love or hate. She hoped it wasn't an impossible paradox.

She asked friends for introductions, she signed up for classes, joined clubs, went to parties, talked to men in supermarkets and on buses, answered personal ads. And then Marcus dropped by one evening, and asked if she wanted to go to a movie with him.

Marcus was her next-door neighbor. They had seen a lot of movies and shared a fair number of pizzas over the past two years, but although she liked him, she knew very little about him. She didn't even know for sure that he was heterosexual. She occasionally saw him with other women, but the relationships seemed to be platonic. Because he was younger than she was, delicate-looking and with a penchant for what she thought of as "arty" clothes, because he didn't talk about sex, and had never touched her, the idea of having sex with him had never crossed her mind. Now, seeing his clean-shaven, rather pretty face as if for the first time, it did.

"What a good idea," she said.

After the movie, after the pizza and a lot of wine, after he'd said he probably should be going, Fay put her hand on his leg and suggested he stay. He seemed keen enough—if surprised—but after she got him into bed he quickly lost his erection and nothing either of them did made any difference.

"It's not your fault," he said anxiously. It had not occurred to her that it could be. "Oh, God, this is awful," he went on. "If you only knew how I've dreamed of this . . . only I never thought, never dared to hope, that you could want me too, and now . . . you're so wonderful, and kind, and beautiful, and you deserve so much, and you must think I'm completely useless."

"I think it's probably the wine," she said. "We both had too much to drink. Maybe you should go on home. . . . I think we'd both sleep better in our own beds, alone."

"Oh, God, you don't hate me, do you? You will give me another chance, won't you, Fay? Please?"

"Don't worry about it. Yes, Marcus, yes, of course I will. Now, goodnight."

She found nothing in her bed afterwards; she hadn't expected to. But neither did she expect the flowers that arrived the next day, and the day after that.

He took her out to dinner on Friday night—not pizza this time —and afterwards, in her house, in her bed, they did what they had come together to do. She fell asleep, supremely satisfied, in his arms. In the morning he was eager to make love again, and Fay might have been interested—he had proved himself to be a very tender and skillful lover—but she was too impatient. She had only wanted him for one thing, and the sooner he left her, the sooner she would get it.

"I think you'd better go, Marcus, let's not drag this out," she said.

"What do you mean?"

"I mean this was a mistake, we shouldn't have made love, we're really just friends who had too much to drink, so . . ."

He looked pale, even against the pale linen. "But I love you."

There was a time when such a statement, in such circumstances, would have made her happy, but the Fay who had loved, and expected to be loved in return by the men she took to bed, seemed like another person now.

"But I don't love you."

"Then why did you—"

"Look, I don't want to argue. I don't want to say something that might hurt you. I want us to be friends, that's all, the way we used to be." She got up, since he still hadn't moved, and put on her robe.

"Are you saying you never want to see me again?"

She looked down at him. He really did have a nice face, and the

pain that was on it now—that she had put there—made her look away
hastily in shame. "Of course I do. You've been a good neighbor and
a good friend. I hope we can go on being that. Only . . ." she tried
to remember what someone had said to her once, was it Ralph? "Only
I can't be what you want me to be. I still care about you, of course.
But I don't love you in that way. So we'd better part. You'll see it's
for the best, in time. You'll find someone else."

"You mean you will."

Startled, she looked back at him. Wasn't that what she had said
to Ralph? She couldn't think how to answer him. But Marcus was out
of bed, getting dressed, and didn't seem to expect an answer.

"I'll go," he said. "Because you ask me to. But I meant what I
said. I love you. You know where I live. If you want me . . . if you
change your mind . . ."

"Yes, of course. Goodbye, Marcus, I'm sorry."

She walked him to the door, saw him out, and locked the door
behind him. Now! She scurried back to the bedroom, but halted in
the doorway as she had a sudden, nasty thought. What if it hadn't
worked? What if, instead of a pretty face, as she found, say, another
pair of feet in her bed?

Then I'll do it again, she decided, and again and again until I
get my man.

She stepped forward, grasped the edge of the duvet, and threw
it aside with a conjurer's flourish.

There was nothing on the bare expanse of pale blue sheet; nothing
but a few stray pubic hairs.

She picked up the pillows, each in turn, and shook them. She
shook out the duvet, unfastening the cover to make sure there was
nothing inside. She peered beneath the bed and poked around the
sheet-wrapped body, even pulled the bed away from the wall, in case
something had caught behind the headboard. Finally she crawled
across the bed on her belly, nose to the sheet, examining every inch.

Nothing. He had left nothing.

But why? How?

They left parts because they weren't willing to give all. The bed
preserved bits and pieces of men who wanted only pieces of her time,
pieces of her body, for which they could pay only with pieces of their
own.

Marcus wanted more than that. He wanted, and offered, everything. But she had refused him, so now she had nothing.

No, not nothing. She crouched down and pulled the sheet-wrapped form from beneath the bed, unwrapped it and reassured herself that the headless, armless body was still warm, still alive, still male, still hers. She felt the comforting stir of sexual desire in her own body as she aroused it in his, and she vowed she would not be defeated.

It would take thought and careful planning, but surely she could make one more lover leave her?

She spent the morning making preparations, and at about lunchtime she phoned Marcus and asked him to come over that evening.

"Did you really mean it when you said you loved me?"

"Yes."

"Because I want to ask you to do something for me, and I don't think you will."

"Fay, anything, what is it?"

"I'll have to tell you in person."

"I'll come over now."

She fell into his arms when he came in, and kissed him passionately. She felt his body respond, and when she looked at his face she saw the hurt had gone and a wondering joy replaced it.

"Let's go in the bedroom," she said. "I'm going to tell you everything; I'm going to tell you the truth about what I want, and you won't like it, I know."

"How can you know? How can you possibly know?" He stroked her back, smiling at her.

"Because it's not normal. It's a sexual thing."

"Try me."

They were in the bedroom now. She drew a deep breath. "Can I tie you to the bed?"

"Well." He laughed a little. "I've never done that before, but I don't see anything wrong with it. If it makes you happy."

"Can I do it?"

"Yes, why not."

"Now, I mean." Shielding the bedside cabinet with her body, she pulled out the ropes she had put there earlier. "Lie down."

He did as she said. "You don't want me to undress first?"

She shook her head, busily tying him to the bedposts.

"And what do I do now?" He strained upwards against the ropes, demonstrating how little he was capable of doing.

"Now you give me your head."

"What?"

"Other men have given me other parts; I want your head."

It was obvious he didn't know what she meant. She tried to remember how she had planned to explain; what, exactly, she wanted him to do. Should she show him the body under the bed? Would he understand then?

"Your head," she said again, and then she remembered the words. "It's simple. You can give it to me, or I can take it. It's your choice."

He still stared at her as if it wasn't simple at all. She got the knife out of the bedside cabinet, and held it so he could see. "You give, or I take. It's your choice."

Savage Breasts

Nina Kiriki Hoffman

"Savage Breasts" was an underground classic long before it appeared in print. Students used to sneak into the Clarion archives at Michigan State University to read the story. Editors loved it and told each other about it, but were hesitant to purchase it.

At the time, Nina Kiriki Hoffman was herself a bit of an underground classic. Readers who had discovered her work in *Amazing Stories*, *Isaac Asimov's Science Fiction Magazine*, *Shadows*, and a number of other horror anthologies loved everything they read. She became one of those authors familiar to people in the know.

Now Nina's work is more accessible. Her first short story collection, *Legacy of Fire*, appeared last year in *Author's Choice Monthly*. Her second short story collection will be published by Wildside Press this year.

And "Savage Breasts" has gained a wider following. In many ways, it is a perfect Pulphouse story: the kind that no one but we were willing to take a chance on. Perhaps other underground classics are out there, waiting to be discovered . . .

I was only a lonely leftover on the table of Life. No one seemed interested in sampling me.

I was alone that day in the company cafeteria when I made the fateful decision which changed my life. If Gladys, the other secretary in my boss's office and my usual lunch companion, had been there, it might never have happened, but she had a dentist appointment. Alone with the day's entree, Spaghetti-O's, I sought company in a magazine I found on the table.

In the first blazing burst of inspiration I ever experienced, I cut out an ad on the back of the Wonder Woman comic book. "The Insult that Made a Woman Out of Wilma," it read. It showed a hipless, flat-chested girl being buried in the sand and abandoned by her date, who left her alone with the crabs as he followed a bosomy blonde off the page. Wilma eventually excavated herself, went home, kicked a chair, and sent away for Charlotte Atlas's pamphlet, "From Beanpole to Buxom in 20 days or your money back." Wilma read the pamphlet and developed breasts the size of breadboxes. She retrieved her boy-friend and rendered him acutely jealous by picking up a few hundred other men.

I emulated Wilma's example and sent away for the pamphlet and the equipment that came with it.

When my pamphlet and my powder-pink exerciser arrived, I felt a vague sense of unease. Some of the ink in the pamphlet was blurry. A few pages were repeated. Others were missing. Sensing that my uncharacteristic spurt of enthusiasm would dry up if I took the time to send for a replacement, I plunged into the exercises in the book (those I could decipher) and performed them faithfully for the requisite twenty days. My breasts blossomed. Men on the streets whistled. Guys at the office looked up when I jiggled past.

I felt like a palm tree hand-pollinated for the first time. I began to have clusters of dates. I was pawed, pleasured, and played with. I experienced lots of stuff I had only read about before, and I mostly loved it after the first few times. The desert I'd spent my life in vanished; everything I touched here in the center of the mirage seemed real, intense, throbbing with life. I exercised harder, hoping to make the reality realler.

Then parts of me began to fight back.

I reclined on Maxwell's couch, my hands behind my head, as he unbuttoned my shirt, unhooked my new, enormous, front-hook bra, and opened both wide. He kissed my stomach. He feathered kisses up my body. Suddenly my left breast flexed and punched him in the face. He was surprised. He looked at me suspiciously. I was surprised myself. I studied my left breast. It lay there gently bobbing like a Japanese glass float on a quiet sea. Innocent. Waiting.

Maxwell stared at my face. Then he shook his head. He eyed my breasts. Slowly he leaned closer. His lips drew back in a pucker. I waited, tingling, for them to flutter on my abdomen again. No such luck. Both breasts surged up and gave him a double whammy.

It took me an hour to wake him up. Once I got him conscious, he told me to get out! Out! And take my unnatural equipment with me. I collected my purse and coat and, with a last look at him as he lay there on the floor by the couch, I left.

In the elevator my breasts punched a man who was smoking a cigar. He coughed, choked, and called me unladylike. A woman told me I had done the right thing.

When I got home I took off my clothes and looked at myself in the mirror. What beautiful breasts. Pendulous. Centerfold quality. Heavy as water balloons. Firm as paperweights. I would be sorry to say goodbye to them. I sighed, and they bobbled. "Well, guys, no more exercise for you," I said. I would have to let them go. I couldn't let my breasts become a Menace to Mankind. I would rather be noble and suffer a bunch.

I took a shower and went to bed.

That night I had wild dreams. Something was chasing me, and I was chasing something else. I thought maybe I was chasing myself, and that scared me silly. I kept trying to wake up, but to no avail. When I finally woke, exhausted and sweaty, in the morning, I discovered my sheets twisted around my legs. My powder-pink exerciser lay beside me in the bed. My upper arms ached the way they did after a good workout.

At work, my breasts interfered with my typing. The minute I looked away from my typewriter keyboard to glance at my steno pad, my breasts pushed between my hands, monopolizing the keys and driving my Selectric to distraction. After an hour of trying to cope with this I told my boss I had a sick headache. He didn't want me to go home. "Mae June, you're such an ornament to the office these days," he said. "Can't you just sit out there and look pretty and suffering? More and more of my clients have remarked on how you spruce up the decor. If that clackety-clacking bothers your pretty little head, why, I'll get Gladys to take your work and hers and type in the closet."

"Thank you, sir," I said. I went back out in the front room and sat far away from everything my breasts could knock over. Gladys sent me vicious looks as she flat-chestedly crouched over her early-model IBM and worked twice as hard as usual.

For a while I was happy enough just to rest. After all that nocturnal exertion, I was tired. My chair wasn't comfortable, but my body didn't care. Then I started feeling rotten. I watched Gladys. She had scruffy hair that kept falling out of its bobby pins and into her face. She kept her fingernails short and unpolished and she didn't seem to care how carelessly she chose her clothes. She reminded me of the way I had looked two months earlier, before men started getting interested in me and giving me advice on what to wear and what to do with my hair. Gladys and I no longer went to lunch together. These days I usually took the boss's clients to lunch.

"Why don't you tell the boss you have a sick headache too?" I asked. "There's nothing here that can't wait until tomorrow."

. "He'd fire me, you fool. I can't waggle my femininity in his face like you can. Mae June, you're a cheater."

"I didn't mean to cheat," I said. "I can't help it." I looked at her face to see if she remembered how we used to talk at lunch. "Watch this, Gladys." I turned back to my typewriter and pulled off the cover. The instant I inserted paper, my breasts reached up and parked on the typewriter keys. I leaned back, straightening up, then tried to type the date in the upper right-hand corner of the page. Plomp plomp. No dice. I looked at Gladys. She had that kind of look that says eyoo, ick, that's creepy, show it to me again.

I opened my mouth to explain about Wilma's insult and Charlotte Atlas when my breasts firmed up. I found myself leaning back to display me at an advantage. One of the boss's clients had walked in.

"Mae June, my nymphlet," said this guy, Burl Weaver. I had been to lunch with him before. I kind of liked him.

Gladys touched the intercom. "Sir, Mr. Weaver is here."

"Aw, Gladys," said Burl, one of the few men who had learned her name as well as mine, "why'd you haveta spoil it? I didn't come here for business."

"Burl?" the boss asked over the intercom. "What does he want?"

Burl strode over to my desk and pushed my transmit button. "I'd like to borrow your secretary for the afternoon, Otis. Any objections?"

"Why no, Burl, none at all." Burl is one of our biggest accounts.

We produce the plastic for the records his company produces. "Mae June, you be good to Burl now."

Burl pressed my transmit button for me. I leaned as near to my speaker as I could get. "Yes, sir," I said. With tons of trepidation, I rose to my feet. My previous acquaintance with Burl had gone further than my acquaintance with Maxwell yesterday. Now that my breasts were seceding from my body, how could I be sure I'd be nice to Burl? What if I lost the company our biggest account?

With my breasts thrust out before me like dogs hot on a scent, I followed Burl out of the office, giving Gladys a misery-laden glance as I closed the door behind me. She gave me a suffering nod in return. At least there was somebody on my side, I thought, as Burl and I got on the elevator. I tried to cross my arms over my breasts, but they pushed my arms away. A familiar feeling of helplessness, one I knew well from before I sent away for that pamphlet, washed over me. Except this time I didn't feel my fate lay on the knees of the gods. No. My life was in the hands of my breasts, and they seemed determined to throw it away.

Burl waited until the elevator got midway between floors, then hit the stop button. "Just think, Mae June, here we are, suspended in mid-air," he said. "Think we can hump hard enough to make this thing drop? Wanna try? Think we'll even notice when she hits bottom?" With each sentence he got closer to me, until at last he was pulling the zip down the back of my dress.

I smiled at Burl and wondered what would happen next. I felt like an interested spectator at a sports event. Burl pulled my dress down around my waist.

"You sure look nice today, Mae June," he said, staring at my front, then at my lips. My breasts bobbled obligingly, and he looked down at them again. "Like you got little joy machines inside," he said, gently unhooking my bra.

Joy buzzers, I thought. Jolt city.

"You like me, don't you, Mae June? I can be real nice." He stroked me.

"Sure I like you, Burl."

"Would you like to work for me? I sure like you, Mae June. I'd like to put you in a nice little apartment on the top story of a real tall building with an elevator in it." As he talked, he kneaded at me like a kitten. "An express elevator. It would only stop at your floor and the basement. We could lock it from the inside. We could ride it. Up. Down. Up. Down. Hell, we could put a double bed in it. You'd like that, wouldn't you, Mae June?"

"Yes, Burl." When would my mammaries make their move?

He bent his head forward to pull down his own zipper, and they conked him. "Wha?" he said as he recoiled and collapsed gracefully to the floor. "How the heck did you do that, Mae June?"

I decided Burl had a harder head than Maxwell.

"Your hands are all snarled up in your dress. You been taking aikido or something?"

"No, Burl."

"Jeepers, if you didn't like me, you shoulda said something. I woulda left you alone."

"But I *do* like you, Burl. It's my breasts. They make their own decisions."

He lay on the floor and looked up at me. "That's the dumbest-assed thing I ever heard," he said. He rolled over and got to his feet. Then he came over, leaned toward me, and glared at my breasts. The left one flexed. He jumped back just in time. "Mae June, are you possessed?"

"Yes!" That must be it. The devil was in my breasts. I wondered what I had done to deserve such a fate. I wasn't even religious.

Burl made the sign of the cross over my breasts. Nothing happened. "That's not it," he said. "Maybe it's your subconscious. You hate men. Something like that. So how come this didn't happen last time, huh?" He began pacing.

"They were waiting to get strong enough. Oh, Burl, what am I going to do?"

"Get dressed. I think you better see a doctor, Mae June. Maybe we can get 'em tranquilized or something. I don't like the way they're sitting there, watching me."

I managed to hook my bra without too much trouble. Burl zipped me up and turned the elevator operational again. "Do you hate me?" I asked him on the way down.

"Course I don't hate you," he said, shifting a step further away from me. "You're real pretty, Mae June. Just as soon as you get yourself under control, you're gonna make somebody a real nice little something. I just don't want to take too many chances. Suppose what you've got is contagious? Suppose some of my body parts decide they don't like women? Let's be rational about this, huh?"

"I mean—you won't drop the contract with IPP, will you?"

"Shoot no. You worried about job security? I like that in a woman. You got sense. I won't complain. But I hope you got Blue Cross. You may have to get those knockers psychoanalyzed or something."

He offered to drive me to a doctor or the hospital. I told him I'd take the bus. He tried to get me to change my mind. He failed. I watched him drive away. Then I went home.

I picked up the powder-pink exerciser and took it to the window. My apartment was on the tenth floor. I was just going to drop the exerciser out the window when I looked down and saw Gladys's red coat wrapped around Gladys. My doorbell rang. I buzzed her into the building.

By the time she arrived at my front door I had collapsed on the couch, still holding the exerciser. "It's open," I called when she knocked. My arms were pumping the exerciser as I lay there. I thought about trying to stop exercising, but decided it was too much effort. "How'd you know I'd be home?" I asked Gladys as she came in and took off her coat.

"Burl stopped by the office."

"Did he say what happened?"

"No. He said he was worried about you. What *did* happen?"

"They punched him." I pumped the exerciser harder. "What am I going to do? I can't type, and now I can't even do lunch." I glared at my breasts. "You want us to starve?"

They were doing push-ups and didn't answer.

Gladys sat on a chair across from me and leaned forward, her gaze fixed on my new features. Her mouth was open.

My arms stopped pumping without me having anything to say about it. My left arm handed the exerciser to her. Her gaze still locked on my breasts, Gladys gripped the powder-pink exerciser and went to work.

"Don't," I said, sitting up. Startled, she fell against the chairback. "Do you want this to happen to you?"

"I—I—" She gulped and dropped the exerciser.

"I don't know what they want!" I stared at them with loathing. "It won't be long before the boss realizes I'm not an asset. Then what am I going to do?"

"You . . . you have a lot of career choices," said Gladys. "Like—have you ever considered mud wrestling?"

"What?"

"Exotic dancing?" She blinked. She licked her upper lip. "You could join the FBI, I bet. 'My breasts punched out spies for God and country.' You could sell your story to the *Enquirer*. 'Double-breasted Death.' Sounds like a slick detective movie from the Thirties. You could—"

"Stop," I said, "I don't want to hear any more."

"I'm sorry," she said after a minute. She got up and made tea.

We were sitting there sipping it when she had another brainstorm. "What do they want? You've been asking that yourself. What are breasts for, anyway?"

"Sex and babies," I said.

We looked at each other. We looked away. All those lunches and we had never talked about it. I bet she only knew what she read in books too.

She stared at the braided rug on the floor. "Were you . . . protected?"

I stared at the floor too. "I don't think so."

"They have tests you can do at home now."

I thought it was Burl's, so my breasts and I went to visit him. "You talk to them," I said. "If they think you're the father, maybe they won't beat you up anymore. Maybe they're just fending off all other comers."

Between the three of them they reached an arrangement. I moved into that penthouse apartment.

I shudder to think what they'll do when the baby comes.

Willie of the Jungle

Steve Perry

Somewhere along the way, Steve Perry got into the habit of sending *Pulphouse* his "wild hair" stories. Steve defines a wild hair story as one the author had to write, even though a market may not exist for it.

Nowadays, Steve has the luxury of writing more wild hair stories. Novels comprise the bulk of his work. He has written a of lot them, the most recent being *The Albino Knife*. He has also written a lot of screenplays and non-fiction articles and books.

More than any other story Steve has sold us, "Willie of the Jungle" seemed to strike a chord with our readers —especially our male readers. I think the story is particularly well-suited to follow the female fantasy of "Savage Breasts."

Bits and pieces, that's all Willie had, scattered chunks, half-seen fragments, but there was something he was supposed to do. Some place he was supposed to get to. Somehow. What? Where? How? Well. That was another game, Willie didn't have those rules: what he had was weird flashes coming out of nowhere once in a while. Confusing as hell, but there was *some*thing. What was it?

Willie shrugged and leaned his pale naked body against the paler bark of the fat alder tree. Being Lord of the Jungle had its problems sometimes.

He was forty feet above the spongy green mat of the rain-forest's floor and he looked down upon sprawling, crawly-thick ferns, young Douglas fir and hemlock and the decayed guck of a thousand moldy years—the last busily and damply smoldering its way to valuable petroleum tar. So far, the guck had only rotted as far as green-brown humus, weren't any dead dinosaurs to help it along this time. Young pre-oil down there had a ways to go, it did, maybe another fifty million years and a climate change or three, whatever.

Now how did he know that? And—was it important?

Willie leaned against the rough bark. Nah. Worry about it later—

Hello? Looky down there, Willie.

Willie looked. Treecutters! Oh, ho.

Willie became one with the forest, he steeled himself into a statue that was as much tree as any branch, but he figured the two white men probably wouldn't see him up here if he jumped up and down and waved like crazy. White men in the forest were generally blind, pretty much deaf and for sure stupid, as he remembered. He thought he remembered. They sure couldn't smell him, likely they couldn't smell a tub full of snake-shit over the stink of their gasoline-powered chain saws. White men. Gah.

Willie had a vagrant thought, something about white men, something he could not quite get his mind around . . .

Well. It didn't matter. What *mattered* were the two cutters down there, white men with their mechanical beavers, come fucking around in *Willie's* forest. Scaring his rabbits and trees and bears. Big men, dressed in short-legged and loose pants held up by wide suspenders, caulk boots with spikes that dug into the soft ground, bright plaid shirts and baseball caps that said Perennial Rye Grass and Caterpillar. Lumber jack-offs, come to slay Willie's trees.

Willie smiled. *That* will be the day.

The men passed directly under Willie's perch. Blindly, deafly and stupidly. They stomped along, human tanks, shoving saplings aside, tromping mushrooms, crushing delicate ferns under their heavy boots. Ecological nitwits, both of them. Christ.

Willie let them pass. Only when the two men were a hundred yards away, hidden by heavy, old growth timber, did Willie come down. Down, and the wind rushed past him as he dropped the last five feet, sank into the springy ground and felt the cushion of the thick, moist humus under his bare feet. Right. That was how it went.

He raised from the crouch, stood tall in his rugged manhood, put his hands along the sides of his mouth, and took a deep breath. Then he did the yell: "Uhhhh-ahuhahuh-ah-uh-ahuhah-uh!"

It was a sort of sing-song yodel, but it was loud in the quiet woods, a chilling, goose-flesh producing cry. It always impressed the hell out of the rabbits and trees and bears, Willie knew, just as he knew it would also scare the living shit out of the white men.

Of course, almost everything scared the shit out of white men. As a rule.

Willie bent and picked up his stick. The stick was an arm-long, arm-thick chunk of slightly curved hardwood. The cutters had walked right past it, blindly-deafly-and-stupidly, no surprise there. Willie hefted the heavy wood, got a good grip on it and said, "What say, stick, you want to take a little trip?"

The stick allowed as how it wouldn't mind, so Willie thought. You could never be too sure with sticks.

Willie started running. He couldn't see them and they couldn't see him, but in a few seconds he would be right on top of the two cutters.

He ran lightly, one with his forest, his blood rumbling in his ears, his breath singing hah-hah-hah-hah in tune with his quick steps. He dodged his way through a thick stand of fifty-year-old almost-ripe evergreens and came smack into the little clearing where the two cutters stood nailed stock-still, listening for the yell again.

Even blind, deaf and stupid, they couldn't miss him now. They saw Willie. Finally.

"Mother*fucker*!" one of them said.

"Gawd-damn!" the other one said.

Regular pair of anglo-saxon geniuses, these two.

The first cutter, that was Motherfucker, dropped his heavy chain saw and turned to run. Willie read the man's mind by the way his legs pumped. Feet, do your stuff!

Willie was on him before he got two yards. He swung the club and caught the man between the neck and shoulder. Whack!

Good shot, Willie, the stick seemed to say.

Why, thank you, stick.

Motherfucker fell, screaming. "Mama-oh shit-daddy!"

Strange relationship his parents must have had, Willie thought. He turned. The second cutter had dropped his saw, too, but he wasn't running. He shambled instead toward Willie, his arms lifted, his big hands clutched into white-knuckled fists. His young face was cornered-rat desperate.

Willie admired bravery in an enemy, but Gawd Damn lost big points for dumb, there was more than normal white man stupidity going on here. This fool would dare to attack *him*, Willie, the Lord of the Jungle? Jesus, would they never learn?

Willie ran for the cutter, ducked the awkward, panicked round-house punch the man threw and slammed his club into the man's belly. Gawd Damn went, "Uh-hoo!" and doubled up. He fell forward onto the damp ground, forehead first. Willie admired the noise when the cutter hit the soft ground, it was kind of a whumpish thump. Or maybe a thumpish whump.

Willie lowered his club. Enough. The Lord of the Jungle fought clean. The Lord of the Jungle didn't hit 'em when they were down. The Lord of the Jungle didn't kill 'em unless he absolutely had to. They'd live and they'd leave and they'd spread the word not to fuck around in Willie's forest, by God.

Willie took a deep breath, and the sound of his yell bounced once again through the forest, and, naturally, impressed the hell out of all the rabbits and trees and bears who heard it. The yell summed it all up, more or less, into "I'm-Willie-the-Lord-of-the-Jungle-and-I've-just-saved-all-your-asses-from-the-evil-white-men-tree-cutters." More or less.

The rabbits and the trees and the bears would be grateful, Willie knew. It was his job to protect them, their jobs to be grateful. It evened out.

With those thoughts filling his head, Willie loped easily off into the trees. He glanced back once and saw the man with the broken collarbone sit up and moan.

"Mother*fucker*," the man said softly.

Later, Willie slept soundly in the the cradle of a three hundred year old Douglas fir branch, eighty feet up. It was the sleep of a man good at his work, and as he'd drifted into it, he knew he'd earned it.

* * *

"—crew can clean it all out in six months, the goddamned union doesn't call a strike." The speaker was a tall, spindly man with a salt-and-pepper beard—no mustache—and exophthalmically bulged eyes. Ichabod Crane in middle age, but named Leroy Haskins; he was the manager of the Callam Bay office.

"What about the Indians?" the second man asked. He was William Parkhurst, and he fiddled with his tie; it was silk, with regimental stripes he'd never earned. He walked to the window and looked out through the dirty glass. Raining again. So what else was new? God, he wasn't cut out for this kind of pressure.

"No problem," Haskins said. "They're still hassling with King over their shut-down. The tribal council isn't going to risk pissing— ah—irritating the only paper company still hiring. Too many men out of work as it is."

Parkhurst nodded. "It would make us look very good to develop a positive cash-flow, Leroy. Atlanta would be pleased. But the risks have to be considered. What was that number you came up with?"

"Six million nine," Haskins said. "Counting the Japanese log exports and the pulp deal with Greach."

Parkhurst stroked his tie, thinking about that. Almost seven million dollars. My. With every other division of Multinational Paper currently losing money ass over teakettle, the boys on the fourteenth floor in Atlanta would be very pleased. They'd line up to kiss Parkhurst's cheeks. Both sets.

But.

One had to be cautious, always. Never run when you could walk, never walk when you could crawl, never crawl when you could grovel. That was the basis of Parkhurst's personal and corporate policy and it had served him well for years, it had kept him alive in the shark-infested waters. He hated making decisions. Direct action was so . . . unsettling. There needed to be a committee, a sub-committee, an executive board, feints, subterfuges, and some general beating-around-the-bush. To spread the blame around when—God forbid—the shit hit the fan as it was sometimes wont to do. It ought to be taught in every business school in America: Cover-Your-Ass 101.

Parkhurst blinked and stared at Haskins. "What about the environmentalists?"

"Bates is handling that, no problem. A few loose nuts and bolts will protest like always, but the Washington State Legislature knows which side of the bread is buttered. We've been cutting trees here for twenty-nine years; every log truck on the road means dollar signs for the state and they know it."

Parkhurst nodded absently. It would be a simple deal, technically. Almost a straight swap, all that lovely old-growth timber for some useless scenic-view property out by Sekiu.

Six million nine.

Parkhurst sighed. He had the power to do it, all on his own, a quick scrawl of the pen, zip, it was in the works.

But.

If there was a screw-up, anywhere, for any reason, it was his ass. On the other hand . . .

MacArdle's red face with its Freud-like beard popped into Parkhurst's mind. How could you trust a psychiatrist named MacArdle? Still, the man was the second most expensive analyst in Seattle, highly regarded and sought after. He'd been Parkhurst's shrink for four years.

"Now, Bill, why is it you don't feel comfortable today?"

"Christ, you're the doctor, Art, you tell me."

"Ah. Avoiding responsibility again, I see. You know you have to take care of your own problems, eventually."

Parkhurst sighed. He knew. Decisions, all the time, decisions. Why couldn't he be a fucking housewife like Marsha? Lie around all day, watching the tube, getting fatter—life wasn't fair.

"It isn't—"

"—fair," MacArdle finished for him. "Come on, let's not do that again, Bill. It's your head, so it's your problem. Or, as we like to say, the Frankenstein Concept of psychoanalysis: you created it, you take care of it." MacArdle smiled.

The son-of-a-bitch—

"—see them?" Haskins said, interrupting Parkhurst's flashback.

The VP blinked. "Uh, yeah. Work up the numbers for me on a graph, use colored pens, and I'll take it back to Seattle."

Well. He could do that much. But should he make a presentation to the boys on the fourteenth floor? Or maybe delegate somebody else to do it? Or should he just spring it on them? Decisions, all the fucking time! There had to be some way to weasel out of it—

* * *

Willie shifted on the thick branch and his sense of balance took over. He awoke in plenty of time to keep from rolling ass-first out into empty air. Not even close.

It was cool and dark, a nice late-spring evening. No rain today, that was unusual. Willie settled himself back onto the limb and faded slowly back to sleep. He was master of all he could see and hear and smell. Protector of the rabbits and trees and bears. It was a good feeling.

"Come on, Barry, what are you and Jimmy using in those tobacco tins? Not Copenhagen, not with a story like that."

"I'm telling you, Leroy, that's the way it happened!" Barry Lotz was tall, heavy-set, young and mean. He'd once laid out four men in a bar in Forks for laughing too loud; another time, he'd spun his pickup over the side of Dead Car's Curve and totalled it, only to come up without a scratch, carrying a forty-pound chain saw in each hand and cursing. Barry was nobody's play toy, no sir.

Right now, though, Barry looked like six miles of dirt road after two days of hard rain and log tricks. Pale as a toadstool bottom. *Scared.*

"He was a short, stubby dude, he had a spare tire around his middle and he was as naked as a fuckin' jaybird. And old, too. He had gray hair all over his crotch—" Barry pronounced it "crouch"— "and he had to be at least fifty."

Barry was twenty-three. Leroy was fifty and he didn't much care for the old man label on somebody his age. "And he came running out of the trees carrying a baseball bat and took you and Jimmy out, bap, just like that? This fat, gray, *old* man?"

"He was fast, Leroy! Before I could do much more than get a look, he whacked Jimmy and came back at me. I went to deck him and he let me have it in the gut with that stick. He bounced around like a goddamned deer! I couldn't breathe for five minutes."

"It's true, Leroy." That was Jimmy Henderson. He sat on a padded black table while the short nurse practitioner put a figure-eight brace over his bare back and shoulders. "Just like Barry said. We heard this awful yell—ow, shit, lady!"

"Sorry," the NP said, pulling the strap tighter. She might be a small woman, but she was strong enough to cinch a broken collarbone into place. And she didn't look sorry.

"He yelled, you said," Leroy prompted.

"Just like fucking Tarzan in the movies. After he finished bashing on us, he did it again. Scared the shit out of me."

Haskins shook his head. That was all he needed. Some loon running around in the woods playing a apeman, kicking the piss out of his loggers. Ah, Jesus.

"Did he look like anybody you know?"

Both Jimmy and Barry shook their heads.

"So what we have is a fat old man with no clothes on."

"Well," Barry said, "he was wearing something."

"Oh?"

"Yeah, around his waist. A piece of cloth with stripes on it, the stripes ran like this." He made slashes into the air at a forty-five degree angle.

Leroy shook his head again. Brother.

The receptionist for the NP came into the room. "Telephone, Leroy." It didn't matter that he was the Resident Manager, there was no formality in a town of three hundred people. Haskins went to the phone.

"Haskins? This is Dupuis, in Atlanta."

Leroy sucked in a sudden breath. Fuck, it was old man Doopwee himself! "Sir?"

"Where is William Parkhurst? Seattle says he's still up there in the woods with you. I need to talk to him."

Haskins was surprised. His goggle eyes got a little more so. "No, sir, he left, day before yesterday."

"The hell he did. His plane is still parked at the airport in Port Angeles."

"He left here Tuesday morning in his Continental, Mr. Dupuis, sir, I saw him pull out. He said he was going straight to the airport."

"Has he got a woman out there somewhere?"

Well, yes, there was Becky, but she was working, so that didn't count. "Uh, not that I know of, sir."

"Well, if he doesn't, he didn't make it to the airport for some other reason. Stir up the local law and find him."

"Yes sir, right away Mr. Dupuis sir."

After he cradled the receiver, Haskins stared at the white plastic phone. Oh, Christ, what a mess! First, some kook in the woods, now this. It was not going to be his day.

Suddenly, a flash lit Haskins' brain. It made no sense, at first.

He got an image of his boss, Parkhurst, playing with his silk tie. With his striped silk tie. With the strips that ran like *this*.

He got another image, of Barry slashing in the air.

Like this.

Oh, my. Oh, no. It couldn't be.

Even as he thought about how impossible it was, Haskins had another thought: he'd just lied to the President of the Company. Parkhurst *was* still here.

In the woods.

A short, fat, gray man, naked except for a striped piece of cloth around his middle. Like that cloth was a regimentally striped tie, maybe?

Oh, Jesus Fucking Christ.

Willie chewed on the root and watched the three deer. He shook his head to clear away the sudden hot lance of thought which impaled his skull. William Hollis Parkhurst, sir, corporate Vice-President, Wood Products Division, Multinational Paper?

No. He wasn't forty-eight years old with gray hair—what was left of it—with thirty pounds of flab that ballooned his body, lapped over his expensive belt and tailored trousers and gave him high blood pressure and low backaches. And *Semi-erectus hardus* for the last three damned years. No way! That was a dream. A nightmare.

The vision faded. Good. He took another bite of the root. It was tough, starchy, and slightly bitter. Didn't matter. He could eat something else. Maybe he could even get one of the deer. Or did they come under his protection? The rabbits and trees and bears did, of course, but deer? Hmm. He'd have to think about that one.

Well, the root was better than the mushrooms, with their dank, dirty-wet taste. Those had been nasty. When had he eaten them? Ah, yes, he remembered. Just after the other bad dream. He'd dreamed he'd been inside a metal-and-glass cage, zooming over a hard path, when the path collapsed. He'd bounced and jostled and jolted inside the cage down the side of a hill, through thin trees until he'd been knocked stupid. When he woke up, it was dark and he was lost. And tired and cold and hungry and it was raining and he was . . . frightened.

Willie laughed aloud at that memory. Frightened! In *his* woods? Ha!

But he had been hungry, in the dream, so he'd tried some of the pale brown mushrooms he found growing up from a pile of stinky, cow-pie-like mud. Gah.

Things had gotten very strange in the dream after that.

Still, the bad dream had faded and Willie got back to the business of being who he was: Willie, Lord of the Jungle. Things got clear, a lot of things. All about the white men who were out to cut his forest and machines and dangers and all like that. So Willie took to the trees, naturally, where he felt right at home.

Willie sniffed and caught the scent of a black bear turd. He stood and caught the lowest branch of the alder tree. The bear, being one of his charges, wouldn't bother him, of course, but there might be a male and a female and he didn't want to scare them away, in case they wanted to mate or something. He could watch.

Climbing seemed harder than he remembered and his muscles were sore, but Willie tried to ignore these things. He was after all, the Lord of the Jungle and such things went with the job.

Something was bothering him, though, he couldn't quite put his finger on it. No matter. It would come to him later, he was sure.

The deputy was an ugly man. He looked a lot like a 1940s movie character called the Creeper. Rondo somebody or other. He said, "Jeez, Leroy, what do you want me to do?"

"What I want you to do, Burt, is find our missing Vice-President. And bring him back. Carefully. He must have hit his head or something, he wasn't anywhere around the wrecked car, so maybe he has amnesia or something."

"He sounds like a dangerous fruit-loop to me."

"Now what makes you think that, Burt?"

"Word gets around."

Haskins smiled, but it was to cover his anger. Dammit! Somebody let it out. If Burt knew, everybody in the fucking town must know by now. Half the people in the state. Probably Channel Four and Dan Fucking Rather knew by now. Ah, Jesus, why do you hate me? What'd I ever do to you?

"Look, you can take some of the crew with you, as many as you need. If anything happens to Parkhurst, my tail will be chopped liver. They bring in a new President Manager, where will that leave your cedar scrounging operation?"

The deputy nodded. "Okay, okay. We'll find him, Leroy."

"Carefully, Burt, carefully. Bring him back very carefully."

With all the cunning of the jungle, Willie knew they were after him. Eight, no, nine of them. They bungled their way into his forest, making a racket which would raise a dead slug. Nine men—

Whups. Hold it. Willie sniffed. What was—was that what he thought it was—? He circled around, downwind of them, and sniffed again. Yes! There was no mistake about *that* odor!

One of the nine was a woman.

Willie knew immediately this was a Good Thing. He had no woman and he certainly needed one. The rabbits had mates, the bears had mates—the trees didn't need any—but he, Willie, had none. Which was wrong, since Lords of the Jungle always had mates. As a rule.

He worked his way carefully through the woods, inching quietly through the vines and brush. Not that they could hear him; they wouldn't have heard a bomb with all the noise they were making. Laughing, talking, stomping about.

"—Jimmy and Barry must have been nipping away at a pint—"

"—rain again, don't it? That's all we need—"

"—fast for you, Becky? I'll be happy to carry you—"

"—walk you into the ground, buddy-boy—"

The last voice was that of the woman. She was dressed like the others, in loose shirt and pants and boots, but her smell left no doubt in Willie's mind. He crept closer.

The problem was simple: he was Willie, Lord of the Jungle, but he wasn't invincible. Or stupid. Eight-to-one, on the ground, straight up, that might be more than even Willie could handle.

He looked around. There was a hand-sized rock half-buried in a clump of electric-green moss by his foot. He dug the rock out. He aimed at a tree to the left of the men and threw, hard. The rock sailed true and smacked into the tree, chunk.

Everybody looked that way.

Everybody except Willie. He leaped up behind the woman, caught her around the waist with one arm, covered her mouth with his other hand, and pulled her back into the cover of the brush.

The others were already running toward the rock he'd thrown. Good old stupid-blind-deaf white men, they did it every time.

"Mmmmuuhh!" The woman struggled, but Willie had her. He could feel her tight, muscular buttocks working against him. She kicked and tried to twist away, but she was wasting her time against the strength of Willie.

Against the hardness of Willie . . .

"Where the hell is Becky?"

"I don't know, she was right here—"

"Becky!"

"Oh, damn—"

The woman struggled briefly at the beginning, but Willie was persistent. Very persistent.

Four times already he had persisted.

She was a slippery, hot, strong woman, and it was a little awkward on the narrow tree branch eighty feet up, but all in all, it was fine. When her smell told Willie she was ready again, he reached over and touched her. Willie was ready, Willie was rampant, Willie was tempered steel, which was as it should be.

"Oh," she said, as she reached her peak for the fifth time. "Oh, yes!"

She looked much better without her clothes, Willie saw. A natural blonde, too, he saw.

Afterwards this time, she smiled. "It wasn't *any*thing like this before, Mr. Parkhurst. You been taking vitamins, or what?"

"Willie," Willie said, touching his chest.

"Well, I hope you remember that I'm Becky and that we've done this before, only not anything at *all* like this."

Willie nodded. Somehow, that didn't seem quite how it was supposed to go, but it was close enough, he guessed. He didn't remember exactly how it was supposed to go, anyhow. But he knew where this thing down between his legs went. He reached for her.

"You ought to be in a circus," she said. But she giggled and held him tightly.

When he finished this time, Willie leaned back and cupped his hands around his mouth and did the yell. "Uhhh-ahuhahuh-ah-uh-ahuhah-uh!" This translated loosely to, "Six times, everybody!"

The rabbits and trees and bears all stopped what they were doing.

Those with heads shook them, impressed as hell. Those with bark and leaves just smiled inwardly as only they can, but all in all, everyone was pretty much blown away.

Half a mile into the forest, eight white men suddenly had the shit scared out of them.

"Gone? What the fuck do you mean, 'Gone'?" Haskins's eyes looked ready to pop from his head and drop onto his desk top—a thing which would have given truth to many a malapropism, but it didn't happen.

"Uh . . ."

"Dammit, man—!"

"We—uh—found her clothes," somebody said.

Haskins stared at the deputy, who looked uglier than ever. "Jesus Christ, man, I send you to find Parkhurst and you fucking *lose* my only woman forester?" EEO would scream, he could already hear them. Another case of blatant discrimination. Why couldn't Parkhurst be queer? Nobody would miss a logger, they were like fleas, but his only woman . . .

"We figure Parkhurst has got her, she is okay, probably."

Haskins wanted to scream. "Stark naked in the woods with a crazy man who thinks he is fucking *Tarzan* and *you* think she's okay? You fucking moron!"

Haskins reached for his phone. His plans of retiring as a respected corporate officer were rapidly going down the toilet. He knew when he was out of his depth.

He called Seattle.

Normally, corporate wheels ground slowly, but not this time. No, this time, they ground like the Indy 500. This time, the Flash would have had trouble keeping up. In six hours, there were people swarming all over the Callam Bay office. There arrived: the second highest paid psychiatrist in Seattle; a pair of big-game hunters from Canada; a primate expert from the San Diego Zoo, by way of Tarzana; and twenty Washington state troopers.

Multinational already had an image problem, what with all the scalped hills they'd clearcut in the last few years. If the news media found out about this so many heads would roll they'd have to import a herd of guillotine just to keep up. It was a bad day at black rock here. It was break out the lifeboats and hope they'd float on a sea of shit time.

A special assistant to President Dupuis had even flown up from Atlanta, no mean feat in six hours, and he stood around like something from a Haitian cemetery. Haskins couldn't be sure, but he thought he'd seen fangs when the man smiled, the one time he'd moved his lips.

It was dark, but first thing in the morning, all those people were, by God, going out to find Mr. Parkhurst and Rebecca Lea Copes. And bring them back alive.

Becky snuggled closer to Willie and smiled in her sleep. Under the moon's ghostly gleam, Willie himself was having trouble sleeping Damned dreams again.

"—process cannot be delegated on this level—"
"—cost-risk is good, save for the foreign—"
"—excuses! Make a decision and stick to it—"
"—no drive, no guts, you have to get tough—"
"—parameters of the overall scenario show—"
"—marketing research indicates—"
"—can't see how—"
"—no, I—"
"—Willie!"

Willie jerked awake and stared out from the safety of the tree—

Safety of the tree? What the hell was he doing in a tree?
The sudden surge passed. Only a dream, Willie, he told himself. Whoee.
Sometimes it wasn't easy being Lord of the Jungle.

He heard them just after sunrise, coming through the woods, a lot of them. Willie nudged Becky awake.

"Huh? What is it? I—oh, God!" She stared at empty space and suddenly latched onto Willie's leg. It took a few seconds to remember.

"Got to go," Willie said, begrudging the words. "Men coming."

Becky yawned. She scratched her left breast; the nipple stood up. "Um. Okay, honey, this is your show."

She climbed pretty well, Willie noticed, as he looked up and watched Becky come down. And looked very good from this angle right beneath her, too.

No time for that now, Willie, get moving.

But—why? Another bad dream reached out and nailed Willie. He looked down and saw his paunch, his bare body, scraped in a dozen places by branches and rough tree bark. And his dick, that was red and sore, too. My God, what was he doing here? Who was this naked woman smiling at him? Oh, yeah, right, Becky something, the forester he'd slept with a couple of times, but . . . where were his clothes? Was this something kinky she'd cooked up or what?

There was a mental jumble; his thoughts bounced and rolled and smacked into each other, and, mercifully, the dream faded.

"Come on," Willie said, taking his woman's hand.

They ran.

"Tracks, eh?" one of the Canadian hunters said.

"Fresh, eh?" the other Canadian said. He had the arm and shoulder of a competition curler, which he was. And the brain of a curling stone, too, Haskins thought.

The psychiatrist, dressed in bush khaki from Abercrombie & Fitch, smiled. He spoke briefly into a small recorder he carried. All material for the next book.

The primate expert poked at a dropping near the base of the big alder tree. "Feces," he said.

Haskins stared at the primate expert. "I brought you all the way out here from San Diego so you could tell me that stinking pile there is shit? Jesus, man—"

"I hate to interrupt your scatalogical research," President Dupuis's assistant said in a voice that would freeze molten steel, "but it looks as if they went that way. Shall we?"

Haskins was sure the man had fangs, look at them! but he wasn't going to point that out to anybody. He knew who had the vulnerable throat here. He nodded. They all went in that direction.

Willie was moving much slower than he wanted. Becky wasn't used to running barefoot and bare-assed through the woods.

"Can't we take a rest, Willie?"

Willie didn't think that was a good idea, but he could see she was tired. So they stopped.

Becky flopped down onto a mat of fir needles. She came up just as fast. "Ouch, crap! I wish you'd let me keep my pants!" She rubbed her rear, then plucked something long and skinny from her pubic thatch.

Willie smiled. She would learn. Once she'd been in the jungle as long as he had—

His brain rumbled and quaked. As long as you have been in the jungle? Listen up, Ace, you've only been here for three days.

Willie shook his head. Something wrong here. He was Willie, Lord of the Jungle, he'd been here his whole life—

Dummy! You're William Parkhurst, Vice-President, Multinational Paper, Wood Products, timber, like that. And weasel. Crawfish. Waffle. Old, let's-decide-later Bill, remember?

No! Willie shook his head harder. I'm the Lord of the Jungle! Wait. Listen to this: he raised his hands, cupped them around his mouth, took a deep breath. "Uh—" that was as far as he got. His great cry, the yell which always blew the rabbits and trees and bears away, the sound which scared the shit out of white men, sputtered into a hacking cough.

"Willie?"

Willie looked at Becky.

William Parkhurst's eyes opened wide.

Willie started to reassure his new mate.

William Parkhurst's voice took over. "My God!"

The sounds of the men tromping through the trees reached them. Willie felt a stab of alarm. William Parkhurst felt a surge of relief.

The dichotomy of minds twirled and the single body ached trying to pull the two together. Which was the dream and which was real? God, William Parkhurst thought, what the hell is going on here? Wrongness, Willie thought. Bad things here.

Twirling and swirling, the two minds banged against each other, fighting to survive, clawing at each other like starved animals in a cage.

Something had to give.

Something did.

The group of men charged into the clearing. Becky stared at Willie. It was a slow-motion film, a morning mired in molasses.

And when the thing going on within the mind of the naked man with the tie around his waist finally stopped, he became something different from what he had been.

He *fused.*

"Mr. Parkhurst?" Leroy Haskins said.

"Bill?" the psychiatrist said.

"Just call me Willie," Willie said. Not that he was Willie of the Jungle anymore. Somebody else would have to protect the rabbits and trees and bears from now on, now that Willie understood who he really was. No more namby-pamby shifting for him, No more weasel or crawfish or later-Bill, no way. He knew who he was, now. He knew.

He grinned a wide and happy grin. He was going to be scaring the shit out of a lot of white men directly. They didn't have a chance.

He was Willie of the *Corporate* Jungle now, and he had bigger fish to fry.

The boys in Atlanta were in for a little surprise, they were.

Uhhh-ahuhahuh-ah-uh-ahuhah-uh, Willie thought.

But he kept it to himself.

For now.

Honeymouth

Harry Turtledove

I used to decry stories with unicorns, fairies, and elves. Then Harry Turtledove (and Janet Kagan, in her story "Naked Wish-Fulfillment" which is, unfortunately, too long to reprint here) showed me what someone with a bit of an imagination can do with these traditional creatures. Now I'm fond of strange unicorn stories.

Harry Turtledove has published a dozen sf and fantasy novels. He has also sold about 80 pieces of short fiction. He has two fantasy novels appearing this year, and he is currently working on another science fiction novel.

The charge of unicorn cavalry would be the most deadly tool of war, if not for one small difficulty.

The Emperors of the East try to get round the problem by mounting eunuchs on their special steeds, but western knights reckon this company is lacking in courage. "No balls," they say, and laugh at their own wit.

Yet the westerners' efforts to use unicorns to their best advantage are makeshifts too. The Duke of Hispalis used to maintain a Stripling

Squadron, a hundred youths aged fourteen to seventeen. They did well enough, but lacked the experience (and often the bulk) that would have ensured success against seasoned troops on more ordinary mounts. And, youths fourteen to seventeen being what they are, the Duke often found the unicorns would not let half of them ride when they set out on campaign.

For a while the Kings of Gothia raised an Amazon Corps, but it suffered from the same problems of size and inexperience as the Stripling Squadron. Further, should anyone think women immune to the calls of the flesh, let him examine the rosters of the Amazon Corps year by year.

In every generation arose one or two warrior-saints who genuinely were immune to sensual allure, but unicorns bear such more gladly than princes. Armored in righteousness, they obeyed only their own consciences, and so hardly made pleasant company for the usual run of ruler. They also had the unfortunate habit of telling the truth as they saw it.

That unfortunate habit was one of the two things they had in common with Coradin the mercenary, called Honeymouth. Coradin was a warrior, but no saint he. His every third word was an oath, foul enough to account for his ironic nickname. When he was not swearing, he was mostly drinking. He betrayed whomever he pleased, whenever he pleased. Like too many such rogues, he had more than his share of luck with women. They fell all over him, and he did nothing to discourage them.

This Coradin rode a unicorn.

"Are you sure it's Coradin, my lord?" Milo the seneschal of the County of Iveria asked without much hope when his suzerain summoned him to the audience hall one fine spring morning. He was a big, dark, stolid man with wide shoulders and a slow walk.

Count Rupen, by contrast, was short, lean, handsome in a foxy way, and red-headed to boot. He also had a waspish temper. He scorched Milo with a glare as he paced quickly up and down the hall. "Who tethers a unicorn outside a whorehouse?"

"Coradin," Milo said. His head started to ache. Sometimes he wished his father had been a serf; he would have inherited a simpler calling. He suspected this was going to be one of those times.

"Huzzah," Rupen said sourly. He rubbed his little chin-beard. After a bit, he went on in a musing tone, "Milo, I have a task for you."

Milo had a bad feeling he knew what the task was going to be. "Sir?" was all he said. He might have been wrong.

He wasn't. "Get yourself down to that brothel and find out how this cursed Coradin can wench and wench without a thought in the world past his prick and keep a unicorn, where everyone else loses the beast with his cherry. If I can learn his secret and pass it to my knights, then let my neighbors beware." Rupen's eyes were foxy too, the exact shade of amber; they had a greedy gleam in them, like a fox's when he spots a henroost.

Knowing it would not help, Milo protested, "People have been trying to learn Coradin's secret for a dozen years now. No one has yet. What makes you think I'll have better luck than the wisest—to say nothing of the sneakiest—men in the western realms?"

"Because I told you to," Rupen snapped. "Do whatever you have to. Hire him into the army, bribe him—pay as much as he asks."

Milo's bushy eyebrows rose. Rupen was serious—he squeezed every piece of bronze till the copper and tin separated. The seneschal, however, was unhappily aware that richer treasuries than Iveria's had opened for Coradin. With characteristic skill, the mercenary had collected from several of them—and kept his secret.

Milo sighed. "Which crib is he at?"

"The Jadeflower."

"Can't fault his taste." The Jadeflower was the best—and the most expensive—joyhouse Iveria boasted. Milo sighed again. "All right, I'll see what I can do."

"Just do what I told you," Rupen said, but he was talking to the seneschal's back.

"Make way! Make way, there!" Milo elbowed through the milling crowd in front of the Jadeflower.

"Watch it!" someone snarled, whirling angrily. When he saw who was behind him, his face cleared. "Oops—sorry, sir." The fellow raised his voice. "It's the lord count's seneschal."

That helped clear the path; if not widely loved, Milo had earned solid respect in Iveria. He squeezed up to the Jadeflower's hitching rail and gaped with the rest of the throng at the unicorn.

He had seen the magnificent beasts only two or three times; Rupen did not keep a squadron of them. To find one tied in front of a whorehouse was like finding a nightingale singing from a dungheap.

Snow, milk: those were the comparisons that sprang into the seneschal's mind. He gave them up. The unicorn was past comparison. It was simply *white*. It gazed at Milo with absolute unconcern for its surroundings. The man it had chosen was somewhere near, and that sufficed.

The crowd whooped when Milo, tearing himself away from the unicorn's perfection, strode up the broad marble steps toward the Jadeflower's door. Someone shouted, "Rupen's bumped his pay!"

Several people made it into a chant: "Bump, bump, bump!" Milo felt his ears grow hot. He was happily married, and not given to straying.

The door swung open on silent hinges. When it closed behind the seneschal, the ribald noise outside vanished as if it had never been. Standing in the vestibule waiting for him was the Jadeflower's proprietress. Her name, he knew, was Lavira. She was plump now, and her hair silver, but it was easy to see that she was once a famous beauty not so many years ago.

"What an unexpected pleasure," she said with the slightest hint of malice. She knew he was faithful, then.

He covered his discomfiture with brusqueness. "Where's Coradin?"

"Why, upstairs, of course." Lavira's manner changed subtly; this was business too, but of a different sort. "Come into the parlor and wait, if you care to. He's paid enough not to be disturbed." She held the brocaded curtain wide in invitation.

The Jadeflower's reception chamber lived up to the place's reputation. Panes of gold-and rose-colored glass gave the entering light the texture of thick velvet. The paintings on the wall were erotic without being blatant. A lutanist better than the one at Rupen's castle sat on a tall stool in one corner of the room, playing softly. Even the bouncer bathed. And when Milo picked a chair, he thought the soft goosedown cushions would swallow him up.

A few seconds later, a servant appeared at his elbow with a goblet of wine. The goblet was cut crystal. At the first taste of the wine, his eyebrows shot up. "Rincian!" Maybe every other year, a handful of bottles of the precious stuff reached Iveria.

The banister of the stairway that led up to the girls' rooms had to be polished brass, he decided. It could not be gold . . . could it? That he wondered showed how much the place intimidated him.

A door closed upstairs, with a slam that rattled the stained-glass windows. Someone howled out a snatch of bawdy song in an off-key bass voice. That sounded like the kind of racket Coradin might make. Milo mouthed the name, looked a question to the lute-player, who nodded. The seneschal rose expectantly.

Coradin appeared at the head of the stairs, a blond giant of a man, even bigger than Milo, and at the moment mightily rumpled. The seneschal hardly gave him a glance—he was not alone up there. No fewer than three of Lavira's choicest girls were seeing him off. Transparent silk that displayed rather than hid the softly rounded flesh beneath held Milo transfixed. He was happily married, but a long way from blind.

Three—! And every one of them gazed at Coradin with a satisfied languor that was a million miles from the hard, bright professional smiles of their trade.

Milo ground his teeth. He had expected to dislike the mercenary, but not to hate him on sight.

Coradin kissed the girls thoroughly, gave them a pat or two, and started down the stairs. He noticed Milo staring up at him. "Do you want something with me, you vinegar-faced bastard? Gods, in a place like this how can a man look like he's just had a live crab pounded up his arse?"

Milo's first impulse was to find out how good Coradin was with the sword that swung at his belt—but then he would have to explain to Rupen. That did not bear thinking about.

Instead, he drew himself up to his full height. Voice icily formal, he proclaimed, "Coradin Honeymouth"—he could not resist that much of a gibe; the girls at the top of the stair giggled—"I am charged by Rupen, lord of Iveria, to offer you employment with the County's army at a rate to be set by mutual agreement, and further to offer you a reward of your own choosing for the secret of your ability to ride the unicorn currently outside this establishment."

Coradin was close enough for the seneschal to smell the wine on his breath, but he turned alert even so. "Another snoopy bugger, eh?" Mischief kindled in his eyes, which were almost as blue as his mount's.

"I tell you what—we can dicker later, but I'll solve the mystery for you now, for free."

Milo waited, sure it was not going to be that easy. "What's this?" Coradin said in mock surprise. "You don't want the secret after all?"

"Tell me," the seneschal said wearily. As well have the foolishness over with, he thought, so we can get to serious haggling.

"All right, then, though you don't sound much interested." Coradin struck a pose. "You know not what bribes I've declined for this shameful secret out of my darkest past." His voice sank to a dramatic whisper. "You see, I'm a virgin."

He laughed so hard he almost fell over the banister. Above him, the courtesans clung to each other while tears of mirth ran down their cheeks. The lutanist missed a note.

Milo swore in disgust. "If you're quite through, let's head for my lord Rupen's hall. I told him he was giving me a sleeveless errand, but he still wants you to fight for him."

"So you can keep prying, of course," Coradin said.

Milo looked at him. "Of course."

"Maybe he is a virgin," the seneschal said a couple weeks later. "He's never left any byblows behind that I've been able to track down."

Count Rupen stared at him as if he were an idiot. "By the gods, it's not from lack of effort. There's not a tavern-wench in town hasn't had her skirts rucked up or her bodice torn. He's not shy about getting 'em alone, either. And the worst part is, they love it. Honeymouth, Honeymouth, Honeymouth—it's all you hear in the bloody town these days." That infuriated Rupen as much as it had Milo; the count snarled every time he saw Coradin riding through the streets on his unicorn.

"He'd best be good at more than friking, if he's to earn what you're giving him."

Rupen snarled all over again. Coradin was profane and drunken, but drunk or sober he knew to the half-copper what his services were worth. "Pay what I ask or go piss yourself," he'd said. "It doesn't matter a fart to me. If you don't, plenty of others will." Rupen had paid.

The count brought himself back to the business at hand. "That's why you're going along, to make sure he earns it and doesn't decide to pick old Gui's side instead." Rupen and Gui had been quarreling about their border for years. With Coradin available, the count of Iveria had chosen direct action.

As Rupen's war party rode south, Milo marveled anew at the unicorn. It paced the knights' brawny horses with effortless ease. The seneschal was sure it could have left them in the dust as easily, though Coradin was as heavily accoutered as any of the warriors.

Milo soon saw the mercenary was in his element on campaign. Coradin swapped rough jokes with Rupen's troopers, and howled with laughter at the few he hadn't heard. When they camped that night, he produced a lute from his saddlebag and led the men in a series of songs that started foul and ended fouler. His playing wasn't up to the standard of the lutanist at the Jadeflower, but he was far from bad, and his big bass voice covered a lot of fluffs. The knights took to him without reservation. Milo kept his own counsel.

Somehow Gui heard Rupen was about to have a go at the valley they both claimed. Arches shot at the war party from ambush as it splashed through the little creek that, Gui claimed, marked the rightful boundary. They hit two horses and a man. Arrows flew all around Coradin but, with what Milo was beginning to think of as his customary luck, he escaped unscathed.

Lances couched, the knights thundered into the brush after the bowmen. They flushed three snipers and rode them down. That must have been the lot, for the shooting stopped. But Rupen's warriors had little chance to rejoice. Coming from the other side of the valley was a band of knights at least as big as theirs, all wearing Gui's dark green surcoats.

Milo quickly re-formed his own troop. They spurred to face the foe. Out of the corner of his eye the seneschal saw Coradin dart ahead of the battle line, but he had no time to spare for the mercenary. All his attention was on one knight in the line rumbling at them, a knight whose gleaming lancehead pointed straight at his own chest. He brought his own lance down.

They met with a crash like an accident in a smithy. The enemy knight's lance shivered against Milo's shield. His own stroke was better aimed. Gui's man flew over his horse's tail and thudded to the ground. He lay there, out cold.

The first impact between the two lines expended the momentum of their charge. The fight became a wild mêlée, knights on both sides hacking away at one another with swords and warhammers and swinging broken lances club-fashion. Unhorsed men, those who could, clambered to their feet and did their best to help their comrades. The ones who could not rise were soon trampled under the iron-shod hooves of the knights' war-horses.

In the mêlée Coradin truly came into his own. He slid away from the blows of Gui's men as if he were made of shadow, and struck his own from places where he had no right to be. Foes tumbled from their mounts like ninepins. The unicorn was so much faster and more agile than the knights' snorting chargers that they might as well have been riding oxen.

But the unicorn was not faster than a flung stone. One of Gui's men hurled a fist-sized rock at Coradin from behind. Stunned, he crashed to the ground, sword flying from nerveless fingers.

The unicorn screamed, a high, keening sound like a woman in pain. The anguished cry was all but drowned by the triumphant roar from Gui's knights. Three of them closed in to finish Coradin. The unicorn attacked furiously, but not even its speed and gleaming horn could hold off three knights for long.

Milo was charging to the mercenary's rescue before he wondered why. His instinct, or so he would have thought, would have been to say good riddance to Coradin. But there was the matter of Rupen's temper, and something more. A thoroughly stubborn man, he was still working away at the puzzle Coradin posed, and could hardly expect to solve it with him killed.

The seneschal's sword crunched into a hauberk. The iron rings kept the blade from his opponent's flesh, but the fellow grimaced and went white all the same; the force of the blow was enough to break ribs. Gui's knight wheeled his horse and fled. The unicorn routed a second enemy, goring him in the thigh and his mount in the flank. Wild with pain, the horse bucketed away, out of the fight.

But the third knight was on Coradin, who groggily tried to rise. He lurched away from a swordstroke that would have taken his head; luckily, Gui's trooper had shattered his lance, or he would have pinned the mercenary to the ground like a bug. Then Milo and the unicorn attacked the knight together. The fellow was a good swordsman. He matched Milo blow for blow. But the added threat of the unicorn distracted him. Milo felt the jar all the way to his shoulder as his sword made a bloody mask of his opponent's face. Gui's knight died before his feet slid from the stirrups.

That was enough to send his comrades, already wavering, into headlong retreat. Rupen's men chased them a little way, then let them go. Milo turned back to see how Coradin was. The unicorn was anxiously nuzzling its master, who did not seem badly hurt. "The father and mother of all headaches, but I'll live," he told the seneschal. He watched Gui's warriors disappear. "We won, eh? Good. Now to serious business—where do we celebrate?"

The disputed valley held a small village: a few houses, a smithy, a mill, a three-story tavern that was much the most impressive structure there. The villagers gave Rupen's troops a warm welcome—for a while, at least, they would only pay taxes to one overlord, not two. Coradin's unicorn didn't hurt, either. No one remembered the last time the village had seen such a beast. Children shyly stroked it; their parents wished they could.

The tavern served bad wine and surprisingly good ale. The knights filled the taproom to overflowing. A good half of them sat outside on the steps or in the street, which had only a little less grass in it than the meadow where the cows grazed back of the village.

Milo climbed to the two little attic rooms to see if he could spot Gui's men—and to make sure they were not trying to return stealthily and take revenge on his troopers while they roistered. A long way away, the setting sun glinted from chainmail. Trimming fingernails he had broken in the fighting, Milo grunted in satisfaction. He took a long pull at the jack of ale beside him, went downstairs again. The steps seemed to wobble under his feet: it was not the first jack he'd had.

Down below, Rupen's followers were giving Coradin his due. Not even Milo begrudged him that; his work with the unicorn had done a lot to beat Gui's warriors. The knights brought him round after round, and cheered when he made what was obviously going to be a successful play for the tavern's prettiest serving-girl.

As the evening wore along, some of the knights who had been drinking hard fell asleep in their chairs. Others stretched out on bedrolls outside. Milo thought he would join them. On a fine mild night like this, sleeping indoors held no appeal for him.

He broke another nail, this one on the buckle of the belt that held his bedroll closed. He reached down to his belt for his dagger to pare it, and discovered the scabbard was empty. He could have borrowed anyone else's, but by then his ale-soaked wits had room for only one thought at a time: nothing would do but his own. He wearily climbed the stairs to the attic again, and fuzzily wondered why the job seemed so much harder than it had the last time.

He had forgotten to bring along a candle, and had also forgotten which room he'd been in. Searching on hands and knees, at last he found the dagger. "There!" he said, and carefully trimmed the broken nail. He started to get up, but rolled over and fell asleep instead.

The noise of someone shutting the door to the other attic room did not wake him, but Coradin's voice did. It pierced the thin wall as if that were made of gauze: "Here we are, my pretty, all the privacy we need—"

Other noises followed, rustlings and wrestlings and thumps and squeals of delight. Milo made a noise of his own, a groan; his head was already beginning to pound. The pair in the other room ignored it.

The amatory racket went on and on. Milo had not intended to listen, did not want to listen, but had little choice but to listen. After a while he sat bolt upright (sending a spear of pain through his skull) and exclaimed, "So that's it!" Being a cautious sort, he added, "I think."

Exclamation and addition passed unnoticed on the far side of the wall. The seneschal did not care. He did not think Rupen could use the answer, but he didn't care about that either. He had it. Racket or no, he lay down and went back to sleep.

Milo woke the next morning feeling exactly like death. When he went downstairs for hot porridge, he found Coradin already there, looking much less crapulent than he should have. Even so, the seneschal gazed at him with something approaching benevolence.

Coradin noticed. "What's *your* problem?" he demanded.

"None at all, except for too much ale last night. I own I could use some fresh air, though. Shall we wander outside?"

"Mm." The mercenary packed a world of suspicion into a grunt. He lifted his cup, tossed down what was left in it. "Why not?"

The unicorn gave a happy whicker as its master came out of the tavern. He fed it a dried apple. It licked his fingers, looking for more. "Later," he chuckled. The beast's feelings mattered much more to him than Milo's did.

Coradin and the seneschal wandered out of the village and down a twisting lane. After a minute, Coradin said, "This is charming and all, but piss or get off the pot."

So much for benevolence, Milo thought. He came back bluntly, "I have your precious secret."

The mercenary laughed in his face. "If I got a goldpiece for every time I've heard that, I'd be too rich to fight. What's *your* version?"

"Just what you told me at the Jadeflower: you're a virgin—in a matter of speaking, anyway."

Coradin was still laughing. "Go ask Vylla back there—she'll sing you a different tune."

"I don't need to ask her. Truly I hadn't intended to spy that way, but you weren't as private as you thought last night." He told the mercenary what he'd heard, and what it meant. From the way Coradin scowled, he knew he had it right. "One way or another, that's all you do, eh?"

"Yes, curse you." Coradin turned purple, because the seneschal had started to laugh. "What's so funny, you beetle-headed black-guard?"

A little vindictiveness went a long way with Milo. "Sorry," he said. "It just now hit me."

"What did?" Coradin looked as if he wanted to hit Milo himself.

"Now I know why they really call you Honeymouth."

On A Phantom Tide

William F. Wu

William F. Wu has had a story in almost every issue of the hardback magazine. Most stories dealt with Jack Hong, a man who spends his life following the *kei-lun*, the Chinese unicorn.

Bill, a multiple award nominee, has published stories in every major market, and has had one story, "Wong's Lost and Found Emporium," done as a teleplay on the *Twilight Zone* T.V. series. He has completed the Second Book of Chaos, and he has also started the young adult series *Isaac Asimov's Robots in Time*, a six-volume series that he is writing in its entirety.

The Jack Hong stories deal with Chinese American issues, many of them historical, from across the nation. "On A Phantom Tide," a stand-alone story, comes in the middle of the series. It appeared in the first issue of *Pulphouse*.

I was standing on the rich Iowa turf by a highway in the middle of nowhere. All night, I had shivered in the back of a pickup truck in a thunderstorm, huddled in a heavy canvas tarp. Now, in the earliest hint of dawn, I was cold and dizzy with exhaustion.

The *kei-lun* had been here, though—the Chinese unicorn. I had only seen a flash of it, as always, but that was enough. With horses' hooves, a fleshy horn, and all the different colors on its back, it was hard to mistake for anything else.

I started to walk.

The sky was clear now and I hiked, soaked and shivering, into a little town. It was the kind with a main drag on six blocks of highway and a four-way blinking red light in the center. I could hear rainwater running in the sewers. The residential area was big, though, and old. It seemed rich, in a 1930s sort of way.

The early sun was bright, and it seemed too hot for an early midwestern June this far north. At least it was drying me off.

The town was still asleep. Everything was still wet and a sparkling haze hung in the air. Squinting in the bright light, I looked over a Gulf station casually, like I wanted a restroom. It was a small, tight place with no service area, just gas pumps and the office. The restrooms and pop machines and all the empty bottles were inside. I used the side of the building for effect, in case anyone was watching.

I reached a Standard station a block farther up. Their wooden racks of empties were stacked outside by the back door. I picked up two full racks, all I could carry easily, and circled around to the front. It wasn't my best scam, but it was easy and pretty safe. I didn't feel up to much. Since I hadn't eaten for a while, the bottles were heavy. I sat down across the street on the porch of a bank where the steps were dry and yawned for a while.

Traffic picked up. A tall skinny guy in white work clothes and a light blue baseball cap came to open the Standard station. I went over with the bottles and set them down in front of the pop machine with bottles. Another one had cans. The guy ran around opening doors and wheeling racks of new tires out of the bays into the driveway.

One bay had a huge chopper in it, the kind I occasionally saw ridden in packs on the highway. I watched him through a ring of white sparkles on the edges of my vision.

"Help ya," he said, switching his baseball cap for a Standard one. The name "Marc" was stitched in cursive on his shirt pocket in red thread. His brown hair looked slimy.

I waved at the bottles. "How much?"

He glanced down and frowned. "Register's empty, 'cept for the change I'll need. Sorry." He started back into the service area.

"I'll wait for some business."

He shrugged without stopping and went on in to clang things around.

I went out and sat on the step by the door where the sun was warm. Traffic was still light. I yawned twice. The rain had kept me from sleeping all night. I had gone about twenty hours without it, and none of them relaxing.

Marc came out and leaned on the doorframe. "It'll be a while, yet."

"Nothing but time." I slapped my face once, but it didn't help.

He looked down at me and put his hands in his pockets. "You're Chinese, ain'tcha?"

"Somebody was," I said. He didn't understand that, but he pretended to. I meant my ancestors, some four generations back, but I didn't feel like helping him with it.

"Where's your friend?"

At first I thought he meant the somebody. Then I wasn't sure. "You got me," I said, which was certainly true.

He went back inside to bang around some more.

A couple of cars rolled in for gas. I started counting them. A sort of white haze in my eyes kept obscuring them unless I blinked it away. I figured if just a few customers paid cash, he'd pay me for the bottles to get rid of me. He kept getting credit cards, though.

Chasing the *kei-lun* was a ridiculous occupation. I had seen it one night and just run off after it. I told other people I was just a drifter, but I was sure the *kei-lun* was leading me somewhere. Every so often, I glimpsed it waiting. When I changed direction to follow it, it vanished again.

The other Chinese guy came along about a minute later.

He was about five feet five, thin, with braces and heavy glasses. I guessed he was about sixteen. He had a nervous, shy look. Only he wasn't Chinese, really; he was as American as I was.

He stopped dead when he saw me and looked around a little too anxiously, with a jerky smile.

"He's in there," I said, yanking a thumb toward the bays.

The new guy looked in but stayed where he was, fidgeting.

I stood up, feeling fidgety now myself. He looked up at me expectantly.

"I'm Jack Hong," I said, holding out my hand.

He lifted a limp hand, grinning. "Helmut Han," he said.

I suppressed a wince. Another Mandarin surname after a stupid first name. Or at least, I didn't like it. I could see the type. He looked like a doormat on legs, and would be a bookworm and a class-A wimp. Mandarin background, I guessed, and first generation.

"Hi," I said, letting go of his paw. He had a puppy's eyes and did everything else but wag his tail. I imitated the station guy's Iowa accent. "You're Chinese, ain'tcha?"

He didn't get it, of course, having just come in. I didn't care.

"Yeah," he said, with a kind of goofy grin.

I looked into the service area. Marc was polishing the chrome on the chopper with a towel and flicking off lint with a snap. He'd left it in the bay all night; it didn't need any polishing.

"Go get him," I said. "He doesn't know you're here."

Helmut shrugged and blinked a couple of times slowly, squinting behind his glasses. "I'll just wait."

I went and banged on the glass door to the service area and then opened it. "Got a guy here."

Marc came in and looked down at Helmut with distaste. "Yeah?"

"Uh, I can't get the money here. There's no place to wire it to. But I can't take my car back on the highway, either."

Marc ran his fingers through his greasy hair and adjusted his cap. "Hell." He shrugged and started back.

Helmut looked uncomfortable, but he didn't say anything.

"What is it?" I asked, loud enough to stop Marc. I looked at Helmut. "You got a car?"

"Yeah, a brown Pinto with a broken thermostat. It overheats every—"

I looked at Marc. "You can't fix it, eh?"

Marc looked annoyed. " 'Course I can fix it. I can fix anything I got parts for, and I got parts for that. He can't pay for it. Not my—"

"Lemme see." I held out my hand to Helmut.

"What?"

"Your wallet."

He chuckled nervously and handed it to me. I flipped through the contents fast, while Helmut watched carefully. Of course, he was too polite to show real disgust. He had one ten-dollar traveler's check, bank cards, and a bunch of gasoline credit cards, but none Standard took. "There," I said, tapping a Gulf card. "Use that."

"Not here." Marc sneered and started away.

I put a hand on the door handle in front of him. "Rig it with the place up the street. Any classy place can." I gave the card to him and returned Helmut's wallet.

Marc looked at me hard with an unfriendly half-smile. Then he looked up and moved his cap with one hand. I expected something to crawl out of the crud in his hair.

"What do you mean, bud?"

"Take it up the street and let 'em look over the card. They'll guarantee you payment when his money comes in through the Gulf card."

"Yeah?" Marc looked at the card as though it said something important. He couldn't think of an objection. "Hell." He stomped to the phone and dialed.

I glanced at Helmut, who was grinning at me happily. He was starting to scare me. I shushed him, even though he wasn't saying anything.

"Okay," said Marc, hanging up. "I read 'em the number and they okayed it. I didn't know places did that." He looked angry, though. "I just work here," he muttered.

Helmut's brown Pinto was parked in the station driveway where he'd brought it the night before. He drove it into one of the bays and got out. We waited while Marc pumped gas to a customer.

"How'd you get here?" I asked Helmut.

"Huh? Oh, I had to pull off yesterday when it overheated. I came real slowly along these little highways before I found a town. Then I had to stay in this old little motel, you know, the sign said 'Auto Court.' It was a real dump." He laughed a little.

"I spent the night in the back of a moving pickup truck," I said, grinning. "Trade you, next time."

Marc came back, looking mean. "I can start on it, but I have to pump gas, too. Can't work on it steady till another guy comes in, about ten. Understand?" He was hoping we'd get discouraged.

"Well, sure," said Helmut. "That's fine." He looked at me. "Have you eaten? I'll buy you breakfast." He made a face. "When I'm hungry, I *eat*. I hate to wait."

"Sure," I said, figuring that a high school kid with a car and credit cards could afford me. "There's a roadside place down there a mile or so." I inclined my head in the direction I had hiked in from.

"A mile?" Helmut blinked slowly. "I don't want to walk that far—"

"We don't have to walk at this hour. C'mon." I led him out to the side of the road.

Helmut chuckled nervously as I glanced up the road for cars.

"Sit down," I said, yawning.

"Huh?"

"Might as well sit. If it takes a while, you can stand and I'll sit." A car appeared over a little rise up the street and I stuck my right arm out straight, thumb up. The car went by.

"*Ding hao*," said Helmut, grinning.

"What?"

"*Ding hao*. It means, like, 'real good' in Mandarin. 'Just right.' You never heard that?"

"Nope."

"In World War II, they used to say it in China. With Americans. It meant 'thumbs up,' like that."

I looked at my thumb and finally got it. "Oh. *Ding hao*."

Helmut smiled, looking pleased that he had taught me something.

I watched him for a moment. "You, uh . . . know there was a legend about a Chinese unicorn?"

"Really?" He laughed. "No . . . I'm interested in real stuff."

He was normal—not like me. I yawned. I'd be better off making conversation. "You know this World War II stuff? Your family come here in '49, then?"

"Well, to Taiwan, first. Then here. But I studied it in college, too."

College?

A roar of machinery down the street caused me to turn. It was a big guy in brown leather and a red helmet coming in fast on a huge bike whose noise drowned out everything else. He swung suddenly into the station, forcing Helmut and me to dive clear.

I rolled over on the grass and squinted after the guy. Some friend of Marc's, apparently. My head was spinning. Now that I was horizontal, I wanted to stay that way and go to sleep. But I really needed food.

Helmut grinned. "Guess he didn't see us."

I got up very slowly. "Sure he did. He just thought he'd have some fun." Helmut knew that. I looked toward the station. Marc was pointing toward us and laughing with his friend.

College, Helmut had said.

"How old are you?" I dusted myself off.

"Twenty-two."

"I'm twenty-four," I said, for something to say. I looked at him again. He could be twenty-two, all right; I'd just made the same mistake that others made about me all the time. And his braces threw me.

I looked back at Marc, talking and shrugging and gesturing at us. His friend took off his helmet and looked, too. I got it, then; as soon as the other employee came to work, Marc had planned to sneak off with his biker buddy, but now he had Helmut's car to fix.

"Put your thumb out," I said, over my shoulder, as I started back to the station.

They didn't see me coming. Both had turned and gone into the bays. When I got there, they were squatting down by the engine and poking at it and grinning. I went into the service area through the station room.

For a moment I stood just inside, watching them play around across the way. The new guy had carefully hung his jacket and helmet on a wall hook meant for tools. He was wearing a ragged turquoise t-shirt and I could see elaborate dark blue tattoos on his powerful arms. His hair was long, straggly, and blond under the filth. He had a short full brown beard. Although he looked like a good guy and a fine drinkin' buddy to his friends, I didn't suppose I qualified.

Since they didn't seem to have noticed me, I wandered over and they both looked up over their shoulders.

"Yeah?" the new guy sneered.

"C'mon, Lee," said Marc, but he was laughing.

"Just thought I'd ask about the car," I said as firmly as I dared.

"I'll get to it," growled Marc. He sounded tougher, now that his friend was watching. "Finish it, maybe after lunch."

"Yeah, sure," I said.

Lee stood up, a gigantic hairy bulk that stunk with old sweat and leather. His face was shiny and he wiped it on his short sleeve. I backed up a little.

" 'Yeah, sure,' " Lee whined, mimicking me. He laughed. "Get lost." He started making nasal noises he thought sounded like Chinese.

My judgment was lacking, from no sleep. "So long, fatso," I said, turning.

A fist hit me in the back of the head so hard that I stumbled forward. Before I fell, a boot kicked me in the rear hard enough to straighten me up. I managed to keep my balance, and skipped out of the station to the hooting laughter behind me. They didn't follow me; I was lucky they were in a good mood.

When I stumbled out of the station, Helmut had a car stopped on the street with a teenaged guy at the wheel. I was amazed, but found the energy to run, clumsily, to catch them. The green grass ahead of me swam lazily in my vision, but I stayed upright and jumped into the front seat next to Helmut. He grinned proudly at getting us a ride.

The little roadside place had just a few customers. We slid into a booth with tan vinyl seats repaired with wide, ragged red plastic tape. Helmut flipped through the selections on the little silver jukebox, but my eyes stung when I tried to read the song titles. The waitress was a smiling high school girl with long brown hair, wearing a tight white plastic uniform. I drooled over the menu.

"Orange juice," I said, picking at random. "Hot tea. Ice water. Vegetable soup. The number two breakfast, eggs over easy. Cinnamon toast. Tomato juice, too. Reuben sandwich. How 'bout a Coke? Tossed salad with Italian dressing. Uh . . ."

Helmut looked up at the waitress, grinning. "I'll have the same." He caught my eye and we both started laughing.

"Okay . . ." She sang amiably, giggling as she walked away.

"I'm thirsty," I explained, feeling silly.

"That's okay. Hey, listen. Did you know . . ." Helmut earnestly launched into a whirl of historical facts about Chinese immigrants over a century ago. I guessed he'd learned it in college. Teaching me made him feel good. I was too tired to concentrate and let most of it go by until he got to white ship captains sneaking illegal Chinese immigrants into San Francisco on their ships.

"Yeah, man," he said, just as the food began arriving. "They were packed in like on slave ships, and all of 'em chained together."

"What?"

"Chained together, so they couldn't get away and cause trouble on board to get better treatment." He grinned. "Listen, if the ship captains were about to be caught by the authorities, they'd just chuck 'em all overboard, chains and all—let 'em sink." He chuckled nervously and looked in surprise at the amount of food placed in front of him. "They were treated just like inanimate cargo, or animals."

"Huh." I started eating, with visions of starving and chained Chinamen drowning in my soup. Helmut went on talking while we ate, but the white haze around my head seemed to fog out everything except my food and the splashing of chains and flailing bodies in my mind.

When I finally finished, my stuffed stomach hurt with the unaccustomed intake. I leaned back in the booth and looked up. Helmut was talking about Chinese junks in San Francisco Bay.

"Jack London wrote about 'em there. So did other people. They used to catch shrimp and carry cargo and all kinds of stuff. Only you never hear about them now. It's like they never existed, even though they did."

"What happened to them?" I felt guilty for not listening while I had been eating. Helmut had more substance than I had thought.

He shrugged. "Sank, I guess." He laughed. "Sank, burned, I don't know."

I nodded. "Interesting. I never knew this stuff."

"Really?" He looked pleased. "Hey, when the car's fixed, I'll take you around. You wanna?"

"Sure." I grinned. "We can watch all the Asian women with white guys." I laughed looking away and he laughed and then I caught his eye and we both laughed. I laughed a lot. I laughed at him for appreciating it and I laughed at myself for knowing what would make him laugh. Then I laughed at myself for laughing. The only thing I didn't laugh at was all the Asian women with white guys.

I was starting to like the slob.

"How come you helped me?"

"Huh?" I hesitated, surprised.

"I really appreciate it."

"Oh . . . yeah, sure." I avoided looking at him. I wasn't sure why I had helped, except that he hadn't seemed capable of helping himself. More important, though, was the *kei-lun*. It had come this way, led me here. Its appearance was auspicious; good events occurred where it went.

Helmut paid the check and I staggered outside, so drowsy I could hardly walk. I could hear Helmut following me, but I was too weary to consider him. We went out onto the grass near the highway and I crumpled to the earth. "I gotta sleep," I muttered, by way of apology.

Falling asleep on him just gave me more to feel guilty about, but

I had no choice. Besides, I was too tired to feel guilt, or anything else. My body was finally taking control, after I had abused it through sheer will. Anyway, Helmut's car wouldn't be ready for hours.

The grass was cool and green, the ground hard and flat. Yet I sank into it all, descending from sunlight, from traffic, from bugs. Helmut and my tight belt and boots and all the hassles of the road stayed somewhere on the surface of my mind, left far behind. I flowed downward, falling slowly through a sea of green shapes and blue shadows. Choking, waterlogged, bug-eyed yellow faces came whirling lazily down past me in brightly lit water, limbs kicking and stroking in a frantic slow-motion dance. Their trailing black queues swirled and flipped like sleepy kite-tails and the chains shackling their ankles and wrists clanked dully in the water, pulling the prisoners steadily downward. They left me behind and darkness fell over a dreamless sleep.

The heat woke me up. My clothes were soaked in sweat and I was groggy from sleeping in the muggy June afternoon. Even so, I had slept for hours, judging by the sun.

I rolled over, wiped my face on my sleeve, and looked around. The sun was bright. A car went by.

Helmut was gone. Taking a deep breath, I pushed myself erect and started back to the little restaurant. Standing up in the breeze was cool. The sleep helped a lot, but not enough. One afternoon in the heat was not very restful.

Still waking up, I walked a crooked line to the door and went inside to collapse on a booth. Helmut wasn't there, either. Now that I was in the air conditioning, my mind began to clear.

The same waitress came up. "Your friend left a message. I promised to tell you he's gone back to the station?" She turned it into a question at the end, like she wasn't sure she had it right.

"Okay. Could I have some ice water?"

"Sure."

While I sat staring still glassy-eyed at the far wall, another question occurred to me. I was yawning when she came back with the water, but I motioned for her to wait till I finished. "I was, uh, wondering if you know how he went back into town. Did he walk?"

"Oh, no. I saw him out the window. He hitchhiked."

"Thanks." I finished the water quickly and asked for more. Altogether I drank four glasses fast and another one slowly. I was vaguely pleased that Helmut had had the guts to thumb alone. Nothing would happen to him at this short distance in mid-day.

Chuckling at this new protective concern, I went out to the little highway and stood waiting. After ten minutes and only four cars, I started walking. By the time I finally got a ride, I had already covered all but a hundred yards of the trip, but every little ride helps. I found Helmut sitting on the same bank porch where I had sat across the street from the station.

Helmut grinned as I came up the steps. The sunlight flashed on his braces. "Did you have a nice nap?"

"I guess." I sat down. I hadn't thought of collapsing exhausted on the earth and lying uncovered outside as a nap, exactly. "Say, aren't they done yet?"

Helmut shrugged, blinking nervously at the station across the street. His bravery was coming one step at a time. "The truck came in a while ago."

Not much of an answer. I sighed. "Okay."

I got up and started across the street. By this time, I was fully awake and feeling my lunch and my sleep. I could hear Helmut following me.

A semi with a gray trailer and green lettering was angled across the doors to the bays. The empty cab was up and steam issued from its insides. Only an emergency would bring a big rig into a little station like this. Marc walked around in circles in the bays, nodding, with the trucker following him jabbering into his ear.

Helmut's Pinto was in one of the bays with the hood down. Lee was leaning against it, monkeying around in a tool chest. I waited outside, watching as Marc picked up a length of rope and started coiling it. The trucker was getting more excited. Finally Marc followed him out to the truck and started tinkering around. The new guy was pumping gas to a customer and wiping the windshield. We'd have to wait for Marc, on account of the weird credit arrangement.

I didn't want to interrupt an angry trucker and confronting Lee would be worse. Folding my arms, I leaned against the back of the semi. Helmut joined me. I wasn't any braver than he was, at the moment.

"I think it's done," I said. Marc had had plenty of time. The clock in the station said it was 6:30 P.M.

"That'd be nice." Helmut went to stand behind Marc and his greasy hair.

I stood there doing nothing, just looking around, and heard Marc say that the truck just had a broken hose clamp that he could fix right away. When he started back for the station, Helmut caught up with him. Marc nodded as they entered and I relaxed a little. I also figured out why nothing disgusting had crawled out of Marc's hair. Even vermin died in it.

Marc had dropped his coil of rope over a rack of new tires. One end hung from the rack, swinging very slightly. It was quarter-inch orange plastic rope and it started me thinking.

Helmut came up grinning. "All set. Wanna go?"

I looked into the service area where Lee was walking around and messing with his bike. "Go on up the hill about a block," I told him. "Keep the engine running and my door open."

"Just go on," I said, smiling confidently. It reassured him.

I waited a long time. First I waited for Lee to leave the bays, which he finally did to join Marc working on the truck. I took the coil of rope and started looping the ends. My timing would have to be just right.

When Marc had finished with the truck, the cab went down and the driver walked into the station with Marc and Lee. I tensed, waiting to see if Lee would kill the scheme by returning to his bike. He didn't, so I scooted in through an open bay door and looped one end of the rope over the big handlebars of Lee's bike—not Marc's. I ducked out quickly and wound the other end of the rope around one big handle of the doors at the back of the truck. Everything depended on them, which was a lousy way to plan anything.

A few more minutes passed and I knew Helmut would be worrying and wanting to come back. I was sure he wouldn't, though, since I'd told him to wait. He could do me a real favor this time, instead of lecturing me.

The trucker mounted his cab and fired up. Lee and Marc started into the service area but didn't notice the rope right away. They did when the truck started forward, though, and the rope tightened.

I hopped on the ledge at the back of the moving truck and watched as the motorcycle was pulled over on its side and dragged out the open door of the bay, screeching and tearing on the concrete. Lee ran out screaming while Marc skipped alongside the bike trying to grab the rope off the handlebars. It was too taut.

I caught Lee's eye and blew him a kiss. He ran after the truck yelling every insult at his command—about two. Pounding his fists against the air over his head, he screamed red-faced and horrible, still chasing me as the truck picked up speed.

Suddenly the driver slowed, looking back out of the cab window to see what the noise was about. I jumped off and ran for my life.

I didn't look back for Lee, but a guy like him can worship his machine and Lee seemed ready to kill for it. Breathing hard, I charged up the hill toward the open door of the Pinto wondering if I'd miscalculated my energy. The rear of the Pinto bounced and blurred in my eyes as I ran and the foggy white faces appeared on either side of me, staring as I ran a corridor between them. But this time they were laughing, too, and they all wore long transparent queues flying behind them. Then I heard Lee's footsteps and struggling breath closing in.

The Pinto suddenly lurched forward away from me, swung into a tight U-turn toward us with a squeal of tires, and came down the hill. This kid was okay after all. Helmut slammed on the brakes and I leaped into the car with Lee's hands clawing and tugging at my shirt. He couldn't get a grip, though, and Helmut launched the car with a roar and a jerk that swung the door shut behind me. I slammed back against the seat, laughing.

For a while I watched out the rear window to see if Lee would appear behind us on Marc's bike, but he didn't. Finally I settled into my seat and told Helmut about it. He laughed nervously but his grin had that same puppy-eyed awe that made me feel strange.

"You know where we're goin'?" I asked him, to change the subject.

"Oh, yeah. The guy at the station told me how to get to I-35. It'll take a while, but it's real simple. We just—"

"Which guy? The one there this morning?"

"Uh, yeah."

"Mm." I didn't like having Marc know our short-term destination. "Well, just keep driving," I said. "We have a good lead."

"Good."

I gazed out the window without seeing anything. I had not seen the *kei-lun* since just before dawn and was afraid that I was losing its trail. Still, it would reveal itself again when it wished, I was sure. Cars and bikers and highways seemed like an odd world for a Chinese unicorn, but I believed in it—I had seen it, more than once.

I decided I could do nothing at the moment. Gradually, the rhythm of the car began lulling me to sleep. I curled up in my seat and closed my eyes.

"You ever hit anybody?"

"What?" I opened my eyes and sat up.

Helmut laughed. "People walk all over me. I've, well, never done anything that took any guts. You're really a, you know, a hero type."

I grimaced. "What I did was pretty stupid. That guy wants to kill both of us, I'm sure. Staying alive is more important. Really."

"*You* can say that." Helmut looked over at me and dropped the nervous laughter. "I wish I'd done what you did. In fact, I wish I'd done practically anything. I've never even stood up for myself, let alone anyone else. You just stepped right in."

"Glad to help," I said lamely. I curled up in my seat again and closed my eyes. Soon I was asleep again.

I woke up in darkness, alone. The car was stopped and felt cold, like it had been parked for a while. I sat up and rubbed my face with the heel of one hand. Forcing myself to wake up quickly was becoming tiresome. So to speak. Well, since it was dark, we were well away from that particular little town and its gas station.

I opened the car door slowly and climbed out. A little roadside restaurant faced me. The light from it cast a dim glow over the nearly deserted parking lot. Helmut was just having dinner without me.

The air was pleasantly cool. I walked around a little to get the blood moving and then stopped suddenly. We weren't on any interstate. A little highway ran past the restaurant, the same one we had taken out of that little town, according to the sign near the streetlight. What had Helmut said before breakfast? When he's hungry, he *eats*.

Trying to sort it out, I realized that if we'd been stopped for long, Helmut would be finished soon. Instead of rushing to haul him out, I decided to stay where I was and watch for Lee—or rather, listen for a chopper in the distance. I stayed well away from the Pinto, in the shadows by the highway.

Nothing happened, but I stayed alert, adrenalin flowing. Lee had loved his bike too much not to try catching us, and he could have borrowed Marc's. I had been too careless of Helmut's innocence when I assumed that he would know better than to stop before the interstate, where we could lose ourselves. I wondered if those weird pale faces were watching—and what they were.

Then, just up the highway, I saw it—not the big motorcycle, but a pale equine shape standing in profile, switching its tail. The horn on its head stood out clearly for just a moment. Then it turned and cantered soundlessly up the highway, to disappear in the darkness.

A flash of light behind me made me jump. The restaurant door had opened. It was Helmut, but he hadn't seen me right away. I started toward him and then the roar of a huge motorcycle thundered from the darkness along one side of the restaurant. Lee had just been waiting to get us both on foot at once.

"Get in the car!" I screamed, but Helmut turned from it and ran toward me as Lee circled around the few other cars in the lot. *"C'mon! C'mon!"* I waved frantically, running away toward the highway myself. Lee seemed to be alone, probably because he was hurried.

Lee's shadow had one heavy booted leg cocked to get us as he passed. As Lee's great dark metal monster closed in, I tackled Helmut and threw us both on the shoulder of the road. We were on the grass now, away from the lights of the little restaurant. I leaped up, dragging Helmut back toward the faint light of the parking lot. Lee circled and cut us off, so we had to run back again.

This time, as we ran, he singled me out. Light from his bike caught me like a stage spot and stayed on me, no matter how I dodged, as he roared toward me. I hurdled the roadside ditch, fell, and turned wide-eyed to watch him come.

As the big white headlight grew gigantic, Helmut flung himself at me in probably the only tackle he had ever tried. He was blindsided by the chopper and never touched me. The collision was horrible, a thump and a shriek of metal against the asphalt of the road as the cycle skidded and Lee fell spinning to one side. I half-crawled, half-ran into a clump of bushes and trees.

Helmut was dead when the cycle hit him and dead again when he slammed neck-snapping into a tree. Lee got up painfully, forcing the bike into control again with sheer muscle. He swept the trees and bushes with his headlight, knowing he'd left a witness. I was out of sight, though, acting dead.

Lee yelled something at me, but the rumble of his machine

drowned it out. Then he turned and sped down the highway into the night. I stood and watched his headlight shrink in the distance.

Helmut had found his courage at the wrong moment—for himself. I had never owed my life to anyone before, especially for their single reckless, gutsy move. This time someone had actually done something for me—something important. I felt tears coming, but not only from sorrow.

I turned away into the darkness of the trees, taking deep breaths. Trees in Iowa, I thought idiotically. I thought this was prairie country.

The appearance of the *kei-lun* was auspicious. My meeting up with Helmut would have been good—if not for the choice he had just made. Or perhaps the *kei-lun* knew better than I.

I heard wood creaking loudly above me. Still stunned, I looked up, smelling the sharp salt breeze of an ocean. A huge white ship, splintered and blasted, hovered over us in the night blackness—a Chinese junk with its mast broken and the top section hanging bent toward me, tatters of sail trailing in the wind. Bits of board hung from holes ripped out of the hull and frayed rope swung from the swaying top section of the mast and over the sides of the junk. The hull was crusted with barnacles and smeared with the slime of the deep, gathered before this phantom was raised to the star-splashed sky.

The ship wasn't the worst of it.

Faces crowded the railing of the hull. Figures hung from the broken mast and the torn rigging. Wraiths in rags, skeletons in rotted clothing, grinning skulls yet with long, braided queues all packed the pale wispy craft. Every one of them was chained together.

As I watched, they threw something down—a glowing translucent chain that clanked as it sailed through the air. The end of it touched down at the lifeless body on the ground and when the silent figures on the junk began to pull up the chain, a limp human form dangled and swayed from the end of it.

As fleshless fingers hoisted the sagging shape aboard, one white face turned and looked at me, dark eye sockets locking to mine. His queue waved in the wind. A great-great grandfather, maybe. Or a great-great-great uncle. He knew me and I got it. He knew everything I had ever been, everything I had ever done. He knew my dusty roads and my lonely soul. He knew the *kei-lun* that had led me here.

The empty black eyes held my gaze as the junk drifted away on a phantom tide, fading and floating into the darkness of the sky, the one face still staring. I watched until it was gone.

If there was a body lying near me, I didn't want to see it, because what if it wasn't there.

I started to move, but my wrists were locked—only for a moment. I felt the cold damp press of century-old irons binding my hands together, stinking of rotting seaweed. Then it was gone.

Slowly, I brought my eyes down all the way to my feet. I was standing on the rich Iowa turf in the middle of nowhere. The air was cool. A car hummed faintly in the distance. I stepped out of the trees and went slowly to the edge of the highway. When the headlights hit me, I extended my arm and stuck up my thumb. *Ding hao*.

Illusions in Relief

Kathe Koja

Kathe Koja's career has risen dramatically in the past few years. Known for her stunning short stories, Kathe has also received acclaim for her first novel, *The Cipher*. The novel is the lead title in Dell's new Abyss line; it is a rarity to have a first novel as the featured book.

"Illusions in Relief" displays Kathe's startling style to great effect. The story examines the nature of both art and obsession, as does most of Kathe's work. This piece, however, requires an added touch of concentration—the story and its message are very subtle.

Little boy at the basement window, his gray tongue slack on the glass, small ugly face one big shiver of delight as Joseph, seeing him, rose, shivering himself, to readjust the makeshift paper curtain. Firm ripping noise of the duct tape no cover for the boy's sad grunt, his mother's snarl, curse and beseechment all in a word. Joseph's hand ached as he picked up the X-acto knife, silently slit one black-cheeked harlequin from the old magazine page on the table before him, added the harlequin to the larger distortion behind him: his latest work. It had brought the boy and his mother; a fat white man with no hair and many boils; an old couple, ailment not casually apparent, who with the grim humor of wolves had stationed themselves just at the end of his driveway: we'll get you, sooner or later. They probably would, too.

Joseph dissected another harlequin, carefully poised its torso, doppelgänger, beside the first—no. No, not there, steady fingers tremored just a little by someone's voice, not the boy's or his mother but definitely one of the new ones, very close to the window.

"Please," just above his head, intimate and sick, "I want to *talk* to you, I only want to *talk* to you," as he placed the harlequin, studied it or tried to, "please talk to me, *talk* to me, *talk to me*," a groan, near-orgasmic entreaty, he imagined a mouth rubbing wide against the glass, drier than the boy's lips, scaly with a kind of saucy poison, the words it made unimportant beside the tone, the timbre and reek of that voice and his hand was on the knife, he had cut and placed another piece without realizing: the first harlequin's head was now that of a lion, bald and nearly earless, eyes old with the limitless deceits of those promised to show it mercy; the second harlequin's torso issued, limp and smug, from the lion's bony mouth. The voice had stopped. Joseph set the knife down; he was very tired.

Upstairs, closed blinds, the unfresh smell of a house shut tight too long; if only he could open a window, one fucking window, was that to much to ask. Reaching for a beer he noticed with dull dismay that the refrigerator was almost empty, he would be forced to go shopping again. He hated shopping: they followed him around the grocery store, blocked his desperate cart with their empty ones. Hey, aren't you? I just want. Please, for my boy, my sister, my dad.

Can't shop, can't get gas, people following him home, inexplicably convinced of the help he could not give. Letters and notes and pictures, the pictures were the worst, jammed in the mailbox before they stole it. People rolling on the grass, digging it up—if he looked out there right now he was sure to see them, somebody was always digging up the grass. There was even a guy who was counting it; he wrote the day's tally on the sidewalk and threw a fit if anyone walked on it. Chipping pieces off the front porch, creeping around the back yard with lighted candles, leaving love offerings: food, porno magazines, obscure religious tracts. Once he had kicked open the back door, scattering them a moment, and "I'm not Jesus," he had screamed, "I can't help you, why don't you mother-fuckers go home?" and that of course had only made it worse. No wonder the neighbors hated him.

Empty beer already. He opened another one, stood drinking in the cool air of the open refrigerator, wishing he could get drunk and go to bed. Simple pleasures. No rest for the fucking wicked, though, or even the merely cursed. *God* they were fierce out there tonight, if he didn't get right back to work he was going to start seeing things and oh boy how he hated that. Oh boy oh boy. Snakes' heads in the shower, a face flying large around the kitchen, the severed limbs of bloodless fetuses lying scattered in the basement steps—*keep* your fucking brain tumors, your cancers and crotch rot and lost kids and lost minds, I'm losing mine too but there was no stopping, no, and he knew it, welcomed it too; he would not have stopped for the world, would not in fact have healed them if he could; ugly, selfish, true. He had never in his life done work like this and it was worth everything, all the waste and sorrow they shit on him, every holy dollop, every crusty squirt. Everything. And the pair of too-large eyes blinking solemn semaphore, just inches from his own, assured him with match-less conviction that this in fact was simply so.

He woke in his chair with a headache and wet pants: spilled beer, almost a canful, and he reached in angry terror for the collage, had he spilled on it, fucked it up?

No. "God," he said, a soft statement of fact. It was even titled: "Working by the Light of Burning Human Bodies." He turned on the gooseneck lamp to examine it more closely. "Jesus God," he said.

Nothing was waiting for him in the shower. He watched the *Today* show while he ate, the dregs of a box of Rice Krispies, all powder and grit. Somebody from a local talk show called. He didn't even bother to sneer at the message; his machine was full of them. Back downstairs to look, again, at the collage. Shivering, he turned it on the stack so it faced away from him.

It was always like this when a piece was finished: a kind of listlessness, a feeling of waiting for the next thing. Of course for sheer drastic grotesquerie he could always try a trip to the grocery store, in fact would have to and to hell with the cover of darkness, it never did him any good anyway.

It was always nerve-wracking, that first crack of the front door. Keys out and ready, face composed into a mask less indifference than sheer brick wall: go.

Heads, turning, and hands already out—more of them today, maybe thirty. Ignore them all. Somebody was rubbing at his calf, someone else grabbing for the sleeve of his jacket. He wrenched his arm away, kicked out his leg, small polka of revulsion, get *off* me and maybe he even said it out loud because somebody sighed, somebody else said please and oh Jesus it was the magic word, pleasepleaseplease like a swarm of insects. He slammed the car door without even wondering if hands were there. Screw them. Something else he couldn't cure.

He spent the ride home worrying about the money he had spent. Very soon he would have to choose between food and the gas bill, and after that, what? The house? Stop it, he told himself, maybe it won't come to that, maybe it'll stop and they'll go away. Yeah, and maybe one day they'll break in and *eat* you, oh boy, and he had to laugh at that.

He knew with a dry certainty that he could have sold the collages. Anybody crazy enough to camp out in his back yard for weeks on end would surely be crazy enough to pay large sums of money for what they thought was a cure. He would sooner burn them, every one. Bad enough that this inexorable craziness had rushed into his home, his very life, worse yet that his reactions to the visions their sickness sent had gone beyond merely shaping to dominate his work; he would not commit the final act. A voyeur, yes; without trying but it was still the truth. But he was not a whore. They sent things to him, he made art from them, a closed loop and that was that, final.

Halfway down the street, almost home when he saw with despairing clarity that the crowd had doubled at least; word was out, then, that the hermit had emerged. Now he would have to fight his way in, with groceries yet. Rage made his head pound, he felt like running them over, all of them, human bowling pins, whee! Stop it, he said, you're crazier than they are, but the image would not leave him and he had to laugh. Welcome to nirvana.

As it was he could only manage two bags. Investigating the contents he was depressed to find S.O.S. pads, tomato sauce, pepper and paper towels, a hearty ragout, you bet. "Son of a *bitch*," and back he went, get the rest or die trying.

He was halfway up the porch again, grim elbows-out death march, when a woman in a red jogging suit fastened on him and would not, would *not*, let go. He was actually dragging her along and she was no lightweight, he was losing breath, slowing down when out of the bubble of faces sharp muddy-brown eyes, no rapture there, meeting his and all at once the woman let out a mighty howl and dropped from him, yelling, "He punched me in the *tit*!" and in the sudden grateful lightness Joseph gained the door and slammed inside, sagged to the floor with the bags and laughing in breathless bursts.

The cold of the basement, why was it always so damp, what the hell was he doing down here anyway. Half-asleep, and in the corner of his midnight bedroom some dog, graceful bas-relief ballet, paws hanging broken and the bones of its throat hideously warped, warping still under an incredible inner pressure until the head blew free like geysering water, hounding him, ha ha, all the way down the stairs, whispering half-heard prophecy until he threw an empty bottle at it just to shut it up.

The bottle shattered on the wall, glass sparkling across the sheaf of collages; he sat down, sighing, to work. Was working. Had been, how long, who knew. Assembled before him a picture of a scalpel, of a little girl, of a fat woman masturbating, of a bottle of 1890's patent medicine. Never Fails to Bring Relief. I've heard that about a lot of things, he thought, and started to cry, a dull monotonous sound, huh-huh-huh like air squeezed in bursts from his chest, heard above the noise his name. Someone saying his name.

[Joseph]

Who was out there tonight, looking brown-eyed at the house, at him, standing bareheaded and serene in the dark, a warm peculiar itching on a forearm, just above the ancient mottled wrist.

[Joseph let me in]

"Fuck you," he whispered, "fuck you to death," warm snot on his lips, too sick to wipe it away, too tired. Nothing is worth this, nothing.

[Joseph]

The back door curtains, pinned shut for your protection, the porch light hadn't worked since he bought the house. Opening the door, no tears but still that endless chuffing sound, he stared out at the diehards, a part of him remarking Shit you look even crazier than they do, and an old man, brittle and fine as an antique weapon, scratching at his arm as he stepped up to the door like a step in a dance, raising one forearm and the sleeve of one forearm to display with silent assurance—surely this will interest you—an irregular coin-shaped patch, the skin a rich and deadly green.

"Joseph," the same voice in and out of his head, and he grabbed the old man by the other arm and dragged him in.

"Cures anything," the old man said, lifting his beer.

"Cheers," Joseph said. He was possessed of a marvelous lightness, a full and expansive drunkenness that was less a state than a symptom; he felt better than he had for months. "Who're you,"drinking, "Santa Claus?" and he laughed again; it seemed he had done nothing but laugh since the old man came in.

"Who gives a shit what my name is." The old man drank again, let out a thin scentless belch. "Watch this," and up with the sleeve again, poured a few drops of beer on the green spot. Joseph leaned forward to see the beer foam up like raw acid, sink back into the skin. The spot. The old man looked at his face and laughed.

"I knew you'd like it."

"I can't," leaning back, far back, "I can't do anything about that."

"Oh yes you can."

"I said I can't fix that."

"Who wants it fixed?"

Morning, Joseph waking to a half-stale cooking smell and bounding up, in terror that he had somehow left something on the stove, was the house burning, or—Ah. Memory. The old man sat at the kitchen table, eating the last of a piece of wheat toast.

"You sure got a shitload of food," he said.

"I buy in bulk." There was coffee. Joseph sat across from the old man, who promptly hauled up his sleeve: the green spot had easily doubled. "Just being in the house helps," he said to Joseph.

Joseph rubbed at his face. "Things are getting too weird even for me."

"Don't start," said the old man impatiently. He took a beer from the refrigerator. "We went through all this last night."

"I don't remember that. I don't even know why I let you in." He didn't either.

The old man stared at him over the rim of the can, slow slide of Adam's apple in the veiny tube of throat: not unhappy, or hysterical, or worshipful or greedy, not wanting.

"Everybody gets what they don't want," he said. "The trick is to find a way to want it. But that's not your problem, is it?"

Joseph said nothing.

"Your problem is, and stop me if I'm wrong (but I'm not): you don't want to go where it wants to take you. Like me. But I got over that. All I want now," tapping his arm, "is for this to go on."

"And you want me to help you."

"I want you to work. You get where you're going the way you're meant to get there. If you don't jerk yourself off with a lot of shit about guilt. Save your own fucking soul, you know?"

"Jesus. Philosophy."

"Jesus *is* philosophy." The old man finished off the beer, hollow aluminum thump on the tabletop. "Let's go."

Joseph thought he would feel like an asshole, did as he sat down, supremely conscious of the old man, like a column, behind him. Turning green. "Fucking *A*," Joseph said, and started in again on the dog collage. Scalpel and little girl, fat woman, the patent medicine dripping, running, long voluptuous stream like a waterfall, infinite relief, infinite cure, peace is flowing like a river. His busy hands warm at the palms, cool the tips of his fingers. Sweat on his back. Yes. The little girl, daisy-faced and hair a river too, the fat woman's cum a river, the scalpel splitting skin to make the biggest river of all. It all wound into a road leading into darkest peace, a vortex not black but green, a deep wet green.

Joseph raised his head, smiling, took a long happy breath and saw the old man move, just a little to the left; he had taken off his shirt and was staring as happily at his arm, which was green to the shoulder.

"Just look!" the old man said, and waved his arm like a trophy, then bent to examine the collage. "Pretty good," he said. "Better than anything those other fucks ever sent you."

That night they had an amazing drunk, all the beer in the house, watching the greening of the old man. Joseph told him everything, everything that had happened since the first time, that original supplicant, his first vision or dream: "I thought I was going crazy," Joseph said.

"I bet you did." The old man drank. "I bet you were."

"I called the police," shaking his head, tired amazement still at his own naiveté. "They told me I'd have to press charges, you know, for trespass. Okay. Fine, for the first one or two. Or ten. But after that, shit." Slow sluice of Pabst Blue Ribbon. "They tried to make out it was my own fault, attractive nuisance, like I had too many Christmas lights or something. The traffic was *incredible*." and incredibly he laughed, and the old man laughed too. It *was* funny in a way. A weird way.

"Open another one of those for me," the old man said.

"You got it." Snap pop off comes the top, drink it on down and we'll never stop. He told the old man about the reporters, the tabloids and minicams, the failed attempts to make it stranger than it was which had to fail because there was no way, no *way* it could be: the shared hysteria of ten, twenty, fifty people, faces changing all the time, chasing their terrified messiah who wanted only to be left alone.

"Pictures," he told the old man bitterly. "Of babies. With no arms. Pictures of old people with big fucking tumors, *close-ups* of tumors. Dead wives or missing kids or who the hell knows what. They taped 'em to the window. Facing in. That was when I used to try to open the drapes." More beer. "*Why*, you know? Why do they think I can help them? It wasn't me made them crazy." And the visions, more certain with each one that he was going madder, working under their pernicious influence and waking to find grotesquerie, and beauty, beyond anything he had ever hoped to do: a power so harsh he was helpless before his own talent, magnified by their need, by the pain they carried like the seeds of some rich disease. Manna in reverse. The multitude feeding him.

"How can I say no to it?" wild, spilling his beer, head pointed to the ceiling, compass of grief revealed. "I don't want them to be hurt, but I can't help them anyway, and they keep *giving* me this stuff, how can I turn it down? How can I do that? I can't do that."

The old man opened another beer for them both, drank with lips green at the corners. "Come on," a gentle hand on Joseph's. "Back to work."

Waking in darkness. The old man, long swath of color in the metal folding chair. Joseph had to piss something terrible. On his way back from the bathroom he chanced a look outside: they were still there.

"Hey," second day, third? Who knew. He had done six new pieces. "Hey. What the hell's happening to you anyway?"

The old man's luminous smile; his teeth were as falsely white as ever. "Feels great," he said. "Riding the current usually does."

Eighteen, nineteen new pieces, they poured out of him like water. The old man was totally green now but insisted there was more to come, wait, just wait a little longer.

"Wait for what," said Joseph, but mildly. He felt better, oh God how much better he felt. He hadn't had a vision, a hallucination, since the old man came, except of course (of course) for the ones the old man carried, but those, oh those were different. Because they actually did something. For someone else, someone besides Joseph. Although they left him with an aftertaste, a restlessness that was perhaps a curve in the circle begun by the old man, instigated by the offering of his willful mutation, a cycle that nourished them and itself: more art equals more change equals more art, infinite cure, yes. Never Fails to Bring Relief.

The people outside did not leave but no new ones came. Joseph, pointing at the collages, told the old man. "Then these must all be for you."

"Not really," he said.

Palms to cheeks, a long yawn, Joseph rubbed his eyes to consider this last piece: the pristine alien beauty of wasps in promenade, long black streamers like cries of wonder from the skeleton children beneath, their skeleton mothers askip in their own inimitable waltz. He turned, to display it to the old man, hey look at this.

"Hey, look at this," he said, turning all the way in his chair. Nothing. "Hey," louder. He got up, still holding the collage, walked all around the basement. He realized he didn't even know the old man's name. He went upstairs, searched the house collage in hand, "Hey!"

The front door was unlocked.

He sat in the chair nearest the door to consider this. The collage was still in his hand. Someone knocked at the door and he opened it. It was a girl, young girl, with a mild case of acne and no right hand.

"Here," he said, and gave her the collage. As it left his hand and touched hers one of his fingers blossomed a bright and ineffable green.

Boat People

Joyce Thompson

Joyce Thompson is best known as a mainstream writer with an off-beat perspective. She has written innumerable short stories, and has published a number of novels, the most recent being *Bones*.

Despite the fact that "Boat People" has not overt sf, fantasy, or horrific element, it made *Locus Magazine*'s Recommended Reading list for 1990. Deservedly so. This subtle story finds its horror in everyday human relations and the horror is so powerful that I don't care what genre it's categorized as.

When my mother calls them "boat people," I have to bite my tongue to keep from reminding her her own none-too-distant relations reached American soil by the same means of transport. The stories she likes best to tell feature my Swedish grandmother in her lady phase, straight-spined, her white gloves spotless, every tortoiseshell hairpin in its place beneath a flowered straw hat, at home among the silver-plated splendors of Frederick and Nelson's tearoom when visiting the city, the woman rural neighbors applied to in time of want or sickness, when babies needed assistance entering this world or elders were ready to depart it. About the sixteen-year-old girl who landed all by herself at Ellis Island and somehow made it to Montana with little money and less English, my mother keeps resounding silence, whether from ignorance or through discretion, I do not know.

My mother calls Medicare with a question, hangs up without an answer. She splutters, then shrugs. "I got a boat person."

My mother goes to the neighborhood market, wanting artichoke hearts, and comes home empty-handed. "Boat people," she says.

New graffiti blossoms in black and red on the brick walls of Rainier Valley buildings, spray-paint calligraphy, a chaos of Chinese characters my mother can't understand. She is sure the message is hostile, that the pictographs speak of her, unkindly.

My mother detested Douglas MacArthur and his imperialism; in 1961, she joined the NAACP; she wrote her congressman to protest the bombing of Hanoi. Now lithe bronze teenage boys with stiff black buzz cuts and slanted almond eyes skateboard through her neighborhood. On hot summer nights, throngs of black-haired barefoot children play tag in the dusty blacktop parking lots of cheap two-story apartment buildings, their cries incomprehensible to her, and the local Safeway carries bok choy and ginger root, tofu and wonton wrappers, six different brands of soy sauce.

"Too much," my mother says. "I want to move."

Part of me wants to correct her myopia, part to excuse it. "Most Southeast Asians came by plane," I say, or else remind her that the Mayflower was originally a boat, and not a fleet of eighteen-wheelers. "We're all immigrants," I say, "except the Indians," realizing even as I do how sanctimonious that sounds. When my mother was born, people lighted their houses with kerosene and cooked with wood, they rode in buggies. Seventy-five years of changes have eclipsed her tolerance for change.

At nineteen, I wanted to be president. I would have fired Henry Kissinger, I would have stopped the war, mandated free, fair public elections in a unified Vietnam, elections I had no doubt that Ho Chi Minh would win. One night in 1968 I flew the red-eye from Seattle to New York. I was the only female on the plane except the stewardesses, the only civilian. The rest of the passengers were soldiers, on the third leg of a drunken journey home. At first a corporal from Vermont sat down beside me but his sergeant ordered him to move and took the

seat himself. He was drinking Jack Daniels, straight. The sergeant
was burly and half bald, his tan face seamed with a cheek-long scar.
After the third shot of Jack, he pulled a skinning knife from the sheath
on his belt and caressed the blade with the calloused pad of his thumb.

"Feel this," he said. "Feel how sharp." His voice was deep and
hoarse, as damaged as his dried-kelp skin. I pretended to be asleep.
He thrust the knife in front of my face, just inches from my nose.
"Feel it, I said."

I opened my eyes and told him I didn't want to.

The knife moved closer to my nose. "Feel it."

Being young and righteous, I was more angry than afraid. "I'm
not in the army," I said. "I don't take orders."

"You're one of those protesters, aren't you? One of those snot-
nose smartass rich kids."

The whites of his eyes were yellow, webbed with red. The irises
looked furry at the edges. "Yes," I said.

His fingers were stubby, I remember, fleshed with something that
looked tougher than human skin, strong when they bit into my shoulder.
The knife approached my throat. He held it steady, two inches from
the skin. "I use this knife to scalp gooks," he said. His words came
clothed in the commingled smell of alcohol and rotting teeth. "Thirty-
seven gooks," he said. "There's something real satisfying in the first
cut. It makes a noise, not like anything else you ever heard."

"I wish you'd put your knife away," I said. I spoke slowly, with
no inflection.

"You think I'm crazy," the sergeant said. "Don't you?"

When I didn't answer, his fingers tightened on my shoulder.
"Don't you?"

"Yes," I said.

He laughed. "You're right. War makes you crazy. Especially war
with gooks." Laughed again, a gust of stink. "I love this war."

I knew he was telling the truth. The steel blade of the skinning
knife touched my throat, whispered when he flicked it against the skin.
How calm I was surprised me. It was my lesson in the difference
between fear and terror. "Would you please turn on my reading light?"
I asked him. "I want to see your knife."

The request surprised him. He squinted at the overhead panel,
and I felt his grip slacken a little on my shoulder.

"The red button," I said.

He hesitated. "You want to see my knife?"

"Please."

With his right hand, he kept the knife poised at my throat, but his left released my shoulder. He used his middle finger to stab the red button. No light came on. He jabbed again.

"It must be broken," I said.

"Tough luck," he said. "Now I'm going to show you how to skin a gook." The sergeant inched forward on his seat, swiveled to face me, so the breath-stench came full strength. His left hand pinned my shoulder to the seat back. The blade edge teased my throat, not breaking skin. We were like that when the stewardess came.

She wasn't much older than I was. I watched her eyes, shocked, then opaque. "You start right under the hairline," he told me. "Sometimes I cut the ears off first. When they dry up, they look like prunes," he said.

"Excuse me, Captain," the stewardess said. She was blonde, with a long, high-tied ponytail.

Without releasing me, he looked up at her. "Forget the glasses," he told her. "Just bring the bottle."

"The young lady needs to go to the bathroom," the stewardess said. Her voice was admirably level.

"I'm not done," he said. "I'm teaching her about war."

"I really do need to go to the bathroom," I said. "Bad."

Confusion softened his face, slacking the scar-seam. The stewardess said, "Just put your knife away and let her get out of her seat."

The sergeant looked from her to me, from her to me, from her to me. I imagined I could hear the slow grind of his synapses.

"No more drinks for you," the stewardess said, "until you let her go."

"I want the bottle," he said.

"Let her go."

Slowly he lowered the knife.

"Put it away," she said.

Slowly, he did.

"Now let her stand up."

Slowly, his hand retreated from my shoulder.

Slowly, I stood. The stewardess stepped back to let me out into the aisle. My legs had no feeling in them, and I wondered if I remembered how to walk. She gave me a gentle shove, propelling me toward the rear of the airplane. When we got to the galley, we hugged each other. "Thank you," I said. It was as much as I saw of that war.

A new job maps new routes. First day, almost late, I wheel-squeal into the tiny parking lot of a neighborhood market still bravely withstanding the offensive of the namebrand chains. Inside, it does what it can to mimic a 7-11: coffee urn here, slushies and donuts there, sad zap-fried chicken slowly drying in a lighted display case. My mind's already at the office, befriending the secretary, calculating the relative merits of claiming my dependents, all or none, on yet another W-2. The coffee smells promising and is not too translucent in its white cup. I lid it and join the line to pay. If I'm lucky, my new boss will oversleep today.

"Two packs of Merits, please."

They appear on the counter before me. The four bills I push forward return as assorted coins. It's not until I ask for matches too please that I look up. The most evident thing about the woman behind the counter is how much she doesn't want to be there, the second, how beautiful she is. Used but lovely, her skin the color of fine brass lightly tarnished, the eyes surprising, round as olives and as black. They study me closely, taking stock of my hair, my dress, without revealing how they judge. Her lips are full, pouting, and painted siren red. The fingernails match, two broken ones with ragged white edges, the rest perfectly soignée. She wears a silk blouse, narrow stripes of black and dulled gold, cut low for evening, safety-pinned chaste by day.

I thank her for the matches.

A thin worried man in a white shirt appears beside her, scolding in Vietnamese. She does not answer him, but lifts her head until it blooms alert, queenly, on her slim brass stem of neck, and she raises her eyes to mine. A smile both utterly mechanical and wholly charming lifts her red lips from their pout.

"You have nice day now." The syllables taste sour, I can tell; defiance abrades a melodious voice. Beside her, the worrier nags on. Because I have no right to tell him to back off, I hold her gaze, trying to invest particularity in the ritual reply. "Thanks. You, too."

On the freeway, I speed toward work, but my new boss fades into a cartoon shadow, Portland dissolves and with it, twenty years. It is Saigon, a humid night. The bar is dim and blinking neon reddens the resinous haze. Music, raw male guffaws, the sibilant giggles of girls. The woman from the market wears a black silk sheath and the heat of the night polishes her brass skin shiny. The chirp of cracking ice cubes amuses her. Her smile is real.

What did it cost me personally, that war? A couple of friends, pieces of more, boys I drank beer with, kissed on summer nights but never would have married. It was, be honest, a conflict that institutionalized class. Our leaders were willing to sacrifice a quantity of young Americans, but the draft was a winnow. The sons of the successful, the professional, the rich were safe unless they kamikazied out of the safety net themselves.

The friends I lost: a full-blooded Suquamish Indian named Jim, whose father was a commercial fisherman; Ray, who stocked shelves at Thriftway; Bill, who hated school and wanted war—he was a helicopter pilot, re-upped three times himself. Doug lost his hearing in the upper ranges when a bomb went off too close; he dresses like Rambo but holds a steady job. A grenade blew off half of Carl's left leg; he is a college professor now and skis one-legged. Flat feet and good grades kept my cousins home.

When the boy I loved in 1970 drew number nine in the draft lottery, he went out to his father's garage on Sunday afternoon and chainsawed off two fingers. He wanted to be a doctor, so expatriation and jail were not choices. Lacking the manual dexterity to practice surgery, he became a psychiatrist instead.

The war cost me any lingering illusions about American righteousness, but having grown up left, there wasn't much to lose. Protests curtailed my college classes three springs running, so that I'm left with odd gaps in my knowledge of esoteric things, but that was a small price to pay for the self-righteous exhilaration of protesting. It opened a dossier I hope by now is fat and made me wish, for the first and only time in my life, I was a man, so that my choices would be hard and meaningful. I have always believed that I would have gone to jail, but that conviction remains necessarily untested.

The price of dissent, my penance for self-righteousness has been exacted late and in a strange way. I am a writer and teach writing. I do this in the west. Starting ten years ago, the manuscripts began arriving in my life, the stories of the men who went, bad novels, mostly, too poorly structured and crudely written for me to coach or counsel them into public acts, yet each one an absolute necessity, each one, no matter how artless or awkward, an utterly authentic human act. These men find me in community college classes, at writing conferences, sometimes through friends of friends of friends, they give me their nightmares in cardboard boxes.

I never refuse them. Our part of the country is vast, much uninhabited. The ratio of published writers to square western miles overwhelmingly favors the land. If a story finds me, I embrace it. The need to tell is a healthy impulse. Telling can shrive, can save, and story wants an audience. Sometimes I am the only one. I read, every word and every page of every book. I cherish the illusion, before I read, that the definitive novel of my generation's war has just passed into my hands, that it will fall to me to recognize genius and speed it on its way. At the same time, I know it doesn't matter.

Stan came from a big family in a small coastal Oregon town. Geographical placement and his own good grades won him a four year free ride at Yale and a solid gold exemption from the draft, but it didn't seem right to him that the system should value him above the guys he played football with at Seaside High School. Besides, it was *his* war, and he didn't want to miss it. As soon as he graduated from college, he joined the Marines. In Vietnam, he was a lieutenant. He spent two years in combat, five years writing about it. Except for their names, he and his protagonist are the same man.

This man went to war to test his mettle. He wanted to learn firsthand about adrenaline, about courage and cowardice, to know how men act and what they feel when what's at stake is life. One day, under enemy fire on a mountaintop his troops were charged with holding, against great odds and to no particular strategic purpose, in his eagerness to be a hero, he shot and killed his best friend. It was an accident of timing, the miscalculation of a few seconds and a few inches, it was a small mistake and a gigantic crime. Stan never told anyone and he never forgave himself until he handed me his thousand page confession.

Reading Stan's book, I cried. My son, a baby then, was playing on the floor at my feet. I gathered him in my lap and held him close, swore on his soft spot I would die before I let my government send my son to war. Later, when we met to talk, Stan cried. He had needed to cry for a long time.

* * *

Every day now, I stop at the Thurman Market for my morning coffee and cigarettes. The thin worried man has a thin worried wife. They dress alike in white shirts, black trousers, tennis shoes. My beauty is someone's sister, hers, I think. She has a second silk blouse, white flowers parading on a navy field, which she wears on alternating days. Those times she is out from behind the counter, stacking soup cans on the shelves or rearranging popsicles, I can see her black stockings with their straight seams, her short straight skirt and high spike heels. The man and his wife are fond of correcting and directing her. She absorbs their criticisms without expression. They expect her to be grateful, I think.

Slowly, my morning visits build familiarity, shrinking her wide performance smile to one of friendly shyness. She produces my cigarettes, then asks, "Merit, please, they are strong?"

"Medium, I guess. Not the strongest, not the weakest."

"I smoke Merit, too," she tells me.

It becomes a bond between us, thin but durable. One morning she's alone in the store and looks upset when I come in. She reaches across the counter to touch my arm with one red nail. "You help me?"

"Sure."

She hands me an open copy of the *National Enquirer*, points to a picture in the lower left hand corner of the page. "Please, what is the matter with her?"

The photograph shows a disheveled blonde, eyes wide with fear or loathing, face streaked with grime. The caption tells me she is Leigh Taylor-Hunt, a star of *Knotts Landing*, shown here in her role as an Australian miner's daughter, in a soon-to-be-released film.

"She's okay. She's an actress, playing a part."

Concern persists, depressing her eyebrows.

"It's a movie. It's pretend. She'll get paid a lot of money for pretending."

"A movie? Oh." With the oh, her face clears, then brightens. Nodding, she takes the paper from my hands. "A movie." Now she laughs, a sound that has the random happy clarity of windchimes or a small stream, rising over small stones.

She is about my age, I think, about forty. I want to know everything that has happened in her life.

* * *

My own stories are small, domestic, civilian; their politics is the politics of the heart. When human hardships were divided up by sex, women got childbirth, men got war, one cataclysm each. Sometimes, when my universe seems too small, I make up new worlds, new beings. Writing of war, I would feel illegitimate. Besides, I'm superstitious, half-believing the admonition. "Beware what you imagine, lest imagination make it so."

I write as a woman, but I dream of war. I have been in the jungle so long the flesh of my feet turned soft and gray. My arms and legs have been covered with leeches and I have seen the work of tigers, men with their throats ripped open and their bowels spilling out. I have been in the paddies when the bombs rained down. I know what it smells like when napalm melts human flesh. I have been ordered to burn villages and to shoot children. I have been so frightened I shat and pissed my pants, so homesick it gnawed like hunger, so angry I thought I would go mad. I have patrolled dark trails on moonless nights, afraid of every sound. I have machine gunned the wind in the leaves. My radio has crapped out on me. I have waited dying on the bald tops of mountains for the helicopters to come save me. I have screwed black-haired black-eyed Vietnamese teenage whores despite the stories of syphilis and how they keep razor blades deep up inside them. I have smoked the best hash and shot the best heroin. I hate my sergeant and my president. I have knifed old men in the back. I have thought it would never stop raining. I have killed my best friend.

So much horror, so much pain. Perhaps if I were trained as psychiatrist or priest I would know how to hold it lightly, how to touch the flame without burning, but the men who bring me their stories have turned not to counseling nor to religion for absolution, but to art itself. Art arises from life and then transforms it. I am made into a warrior, grieving for my dead comrades, sick with my sins.

The definitive novel of the Vietnam war will most likely be authored by a man who stayed home and studied writing. This seems unfair.

It is a Saturday morning, and my son comes with me to the Thurman Market. He browses the bins of candy, seeking the treat I've promised, thoughtfully examining each box and bar before he finally chooses a grape lollipop. My arms are loaded with weekend needs—paper towels, milk, a loaf of bread. I drop my purchases on the counter and call to my son. "It's time to pay now."

The counter is tall and my son is short. He stands on tiptoe to add to his treat to the pile. When my beauty, waiting, sees him there, her whole face blossoms. She points at my son. "Is yours?"

"Yes." I claim him, smiling.

"Mommy," my son says, "I can't see."

I lift him up to sit on the counter and he watches the woman push cash register buttons, tallying our bill.

"How old?" she asks me. "Four?"

My son says, "You're right. I'm four."

The woman reaches out to touch his short gold hair. My son, who has always appreciated beautiful women, beams back at her. He says, "Do you have any little boys?"

"You wait," she tells him, and ducks down behind the counter, retrieves a patent leather purse, takes out a wallet of red leather, from this extracts a battered snapshot. Our three heads almost touching, we study the photograph of a black-haired, big-eyed boy about the same age as mine. "My son," she says. "His father is American."

"Can I play with him sometime?" my own son asks.

The woman tucks the photograph back in its plastic sleeve. "He would be a teenager now," she says. "But he is dead."

My son did not expect this. It takes him a moment to process the information. I know he is reviewing all he knows of death. At last he says, "My grandpa's dead, too. I miss him." He runs the palm of his hand across his close-cropped hair. "What did he die of?" he asks.

"In the war," she says. Her big black eyes take refuge in the numbers on the cash register. "Eight sixty-five please."

To say I'm sorry is to say nothing. I hand her a ten dollar bill. The woman counts out my change.

"Strange music, strange writing, strange food," my mother says. "I've lived in this neighborhood for twenty-five years. Now it feels like a foreign country."

My mother blames the boat people. Myself, I don't know whom to blame.

A Traveler at Passover

Lisa Goldstein

"A Traveler at Passover" also deals with human relationships. This story, written especially for our holiday issue, focuses on the intricacies of the family.

Lisa Goldstein won the American Book Award for her first novel, *The Red Magician*. She has since written three others, the most recent being *Tourists*. Her short story collection, *Daily Voices*, appeared in *Author's Choice Monthly* last year.

The phone rang the minute Emily got home from work. She hung up her coat and yelled for Heather—"You home, kid?"—and finally answered it on the fourth ring.

"Hello?" the person at the other end said, as if uncertain she had reached the right number. And for a moment Emily didn't recognize the voice, it had been that long.

"Hello," she said.

"Emily." She heard relief in her mother's voice, but something more as well—trepidation, probably. "I was wondering—well, we'd like to know—that is, Passover starts next week." She was silent, waiting for Emily's reply. When it didn't come she said, "Well, we'd like it if you came over for the first night."

"We?" Emily said. "Or you?"

"Please. He misses you."

"Does he? He's got a funny way of showing it. Why can't he tell me so himself?"

"It's hard for him, you know that—"

"Actually I don't know it. I never noticed that it was hard getting him to talk. The problem was always shutting him up."

She heard her mother's in-drawn breath, and then the sound of static on the line. She'd gone too far. Or maybe not—how far were you allowed to go if your father had more or less disowned you? It was an interesting question. Probably the etiquette books didn't cover it.

"I called to ask you to dinner," her mother said. "Heather deserves to get to know her grandparents."

"And whose fault is it that she doesn't?" Emily said. Anger and resentment flared up so strongly she shook as she said it.

"I thought that for Heather's sake—"

Somehow her mother had hit on the only argument that would carry any weight at all. She had never been so good at getting her own way when Emily was growing up. Her father had been the one Emily had had to watch out for. What else had changed in six years?

Emily forced her anger away. She owed it to Heather to try to lay aside old wounds, old scores. "All right," she said reluctantly.

"And please—don't argue with him."

That was the way she remembered her mother. It had been so easy to disobey her as a child, almost a game. "Did you ask him not to argue with me?"

"He never starts it—"

"He *does*. He's just cleverer about it than I am. Watch him if you don't believe me."

"All right, I'll ask him."

For a moment Emily felt sorry for her mother, for the way she and her father had used her as a game-piece in their skirmishes. "Okay, I'll be there," she said. "Should I bring something?"

"Oh, no." Her mother sounded hurt. If Emily brought anything it would mean that her mother had been lacking in some way, that all bounty did not flow from her mother's kitchen. She was remembering all the ways her family interacted now, and she sighed. What had she gotten herself into? Would Heather be able to hold her own? "We're looking forward to seeing you," her mother said.

Emily sat by the phone for a while after she had hung up, thinking about her family. She was fourteen, and had brought home a boy from school. She had thought about this boy every day for the past month and having him so close to her now made her breath hurt. Everything seemed sharper, more filled with meaning, around him, so that she felt that she had never really noticed anything until this moment. And her father had laughed and joked with him, and told him a story about being captured by gypsies as a child.

"Your father is so great," the boy had said. "I wish mine was like that."

She couldn't describe what she felt until much later. It was jealousy, pure and simple. Jealousy, and anger that someone she loved had spent two hours talking to her father when he should have been paying attention to her. "You know that nothing he said was true," she said.

"So what?" the boy said.

She was eighteen, and the family car she had been driving had been hit by a van which had then driven off before she could get the license number. She arrived home shaking, terror at what had nearly happened to her mingling with anger at whoever had hit her. And her father, instead of comforting her, instead of saying that she was fine and that was the important thing, had told her a story about being a truck driver, and the strange people he had met on the road.

Over the years she had learned that very few of his stories were true. The process had been slow and painful, like coming to terms with a chronic but non-fatal illness. He might have been a construction worker and a truck driver, and maybe he had ridden the rails as a young man, but everything else had been elaborations, fantasies. In place of the conversations most kids had with their fathers she had gotten stories. Endless stories.

But the stories had ended when she'd married Andy, who wasn't Jewish. Tales of carnivals and princesses and magicians and pirates had given place to silence. And she wasn't at all sure that the silence hadn't been welcome, a space in which she could sort out who she really was, what was true and what was lies.

She and Andy had gotten divorced six months ago. It had been a friendly divorce; they still talked on the phone and she had met him for lunch once when his business took him close by. How typical of her parents that they called after the divorce, that now she was their daughter again. But her anger had gone for good; she wondered only how she would survive an evening with her family.

At first, as she stepped into the entryway with Heather, she thought that nothing had changed. The house still smelled of tea and chicken. The bulky furniture of her childhood, the hi-fi cabinet and end tables and coffee tables, stood in their old places. The same worn trail on the rug led from the living room to the kitchen.

Her mother, coming forward shyly to kiss her, as if entertaining royalty, seemed the same too: small and worried and smelling of cosmetic creams and dish detergent. But when she moved back Emily saw the lines in her mother's face and the thickness of her new glasses. She'd changed the color of her hair, too; it was redder now. "Hello, Emily," she said. "I'm so glad you came. Your father's out in back."

Of course, Emily thought. I've got to go to him. I wonder if he set it up that way.

"Heather!" her mother said. "I didn't see you at first. Look at how you've grown."

Heather had never been shy. "Yes, I have," she said gravely.

"You were only two years old the last time I saw you. I bet you don't recognize me, do you?"

"Sure I do."

Emily wondered if that was true. She still remembered the time her mother had stopped by the house, furtively, as if scouting out enemy terrain. There had been an argument about, of all things, whether she could have Sinclair the dog. "He's *my* dog!" Emily had screamed as her mother hurried toward her car. "I raised him. He's not yours. Or Dad's either!" The entire block must have heard her. Since then they had communicated through Emily's brother David.

"Just leave Heather with me," her mother said. "We have a lot to catch up on. Your father's looking forward to seeing you."

Was that true? Emily made her way down the hall and past her parents' bedroom. Her old room was at the back of the house but she didn't look inside. From the kitchen she heard laughter: David and his wife and their two children.

The light was going from the sky as she stepped out onto the back porch. Her father looked up from his weeding. He had always been a stocky, vital man, with powerful shoulders and black eyes and curly black hair. It came as a shock to see that his hair had turned almost pure white. But when she got closer she noticed that aside from his hair he had not changed at all. Just for a moment she had hoped he had become smaller, shrunken. But she couldn't wish that of anyone, even him. And he would stay the same until he died; he was too stubborn for anything else.

Why hadn't she stayed in the house? She couldn't think of anything to say to him. Or maybe she had too much to say, and no way to manage it. Why didn't you visit for six years? Are your stupid principles more important than your daughter, your grandchild?

Just as he filled any space he entered he filled her silence with words. Anyone watching wouldn't have guessed that six years had passed since they'd last seen each other. "Emily! I hope you brought Heather. She'll have to ask the Four Questions, your brother's boys are older than she is. We've got eight people here tonight—that's the largest Passover we've had since Aunt Phyllis and Uncle Moe moved away. Your mother's been cooking all week."

"Sure, Heather's a great reader," Emily said. You'll like her, she wanted to add, but she didn't know if that was true. He hadn't even visited when she was born, she thought, and, suddenly angry, she nearly said something she would regret. I won't argue if he doesn't, she thought, remembering the promise she had given her mother. "How've you been?"

"Fine, just fine. Your mother wants to go to Canada to see Phyl and Moe, and we're going to visit Quebec while we're there. I've always wanted to go someplace they speak French. I took a class at the local college. *Comment allez-vous?*"

She didn't understand him. "Listen, I think I hear Ma. I'd better go see if she needs any help."

He waved at her and returned to his weeds. Going inside felt like surrender, but she didn't think she could stay outside another minute. What did I expect? she thought. An apology?

In the house she helped set the table with David's wife Janet. "This is so great," Janet said. "My family never celebrated Passover when I was growing up."

"Wait till it's over before you say anything," Emily said.

Janet looked at her oddly. She wondered what her brother David had been saying about her. Did they think of her as the black sheep of the family, the one who had never fit in?

She went back into the kitchen to see what else needed to be done. David and his two sons had gone out to the backyard and the family was now divided the way she remembered it from her childhood: the men standing and talking, the women working in the kitchen. Heather watched while her grandmother lifted a platter from the oven. Wonderful, Emily thought. What terrific role models we're showing her. The kitchen windows had steamed over from all the cooking.

"I think we're done here," her mother said. "Oh—Elijah's cup. Could you reach it, Emily? It's on the top cupboard there. Heather, go tell your grandfather we're ready."

Emily would have wanted to be there when Heather met her father but she thought that her daughter could take care of herself. And maybe it would work out better this way; she knew she could hardly act neutral around him. Carefully she took down the goblet of cut crystal and filled it with wine.

She had been fascinated by the cup as a child, that something so weighty could be fashioned into such airy beauty. She remembered how the candlelight would shine from its facets. And sometime during the evening the wine in the goblet would disappear. Her father would tell her and David that Elijah had come, that they had missed him again this year. She had been eight or nine when she realized that her father had been the one to drink the wine, and then she'd felt angry and embarrassed, as if she'd been taken in by a confidence trick.

She took Elijah's cup to the table and set it in front of Heather. If her daughter got bored by the service at least she would have something to look at. Everyone except her father was already sitting down at the table: the chair at the head was empty. Finally he came into the room. He had washed and changed but Emily could see the dirt beneath his fingernails.

Her father looked at the family with great satisfaction and made the blessing over the wine. "The youngest child reads the Four Questions," he said when he had finished. "Bob read them last year and Mike the year before, and now it's Heather's turn."

Emily showed Heather the Four Questions in the Haggadah. She looked nervous but pleased by everyone's attention. "Why is this night di—diff—"

"Different," Emily said.

"Different. Different from all other nights." Her voice, which had started out breathy, grew louder, more confident.

"Very good," Emily said when she had done.

"You have asked me the Four Questions and now I will answer you," her father said solemnly, exactly as he had said to her and her brother twenty and thirty years before. He began to read from the Haggadah in his sing-song old-fashioned Hebrew. "*Avadim hayenu l'Paro b'Mizraim.*" We were slaves of Pharaoh in Egypt. . . .

She barely listened as her father told the story of Passover. The plagues sent to Pharaoh. The flight of the Jews in the night. The parting of the Red Sea. Manna in the desert. Stories and miracles; no wonder her father enjoyed Passover so much. It was rooted in his blood and stretched back thousands of years. But no more; it would end here, with her and Heather. Heather would not be raised on this superstitious nonsense.

She watched Heather and wondered what her daughter made of it all. She couldn't be following it very well, even in the English translation printed alongside the Hebrew in the Haggadah. But Heather wasn't even trying to understand. She was watching her father as he read, a look of wonder on her face.

Damn! Emily thought. He's doing it to her, just like he used to do it to all my friends. She's fascinated by him, she's under his spell. What on earth did he say to her outside? I'd better set her straight about him before it's too late. It was Andy her grandfather had snubbed, after all. We're only here because of the divorce—I'll have to tell her that. And even then he didn't even have the courage to invite me back—he had to get my mother to do it.

She was so angry she didn't notice her father had stopped reading. That was quick—they must have shortened the ceremony considerably during the years she'd missed. The shorter the better, as far as she was concerned. She had to get Heather home and tell her a few things, the difference between truth and lies, for one.

Her mother and Janet got up and went into the kitchen for the food. Her father had embarked on one of his stories. She had missed the beginning; he was somewhere in Prague, arguing with someone. She would bet any amount of money he had never been to Prague. He had been too young for World War II and too old for Korea; he had probably never left the country in his life.

"So I said to the rabbi, I said, I know you have him there, up in your attic. And the rabbi says no, but he's smiling, so I think, you know, he's not telling me everything. I've heard the stories, I tell him, I know there's a golem in the attic in this synagogue in Prague. You know what a golem is?"

Bob and Mike and Heather watched him closely, as if he might turn into something magical and strange before their eyes. Their mouths were half-open. "A golem is a man made out of clay. A wise man had made this particular golem, the golem of Prague, and he put a verse from the Bible in its mouth, and the clay man got up and walked. And then the wise man put another verse in his own mouth and he could fly."

"Which verse?" David asked.

"How do I know which verse? If I knew that I'd do it myself."

"People can't fly," Heather said.

Good for you, Emily thought.

Her father looked at Heather. Emily remembered that look from her childhood; it was as if he'd chosen you for something special. It felt terrifying and exhilarating at once. To her credit Heather looked back at him, unblinking.

"How do you know that, young lady?"

"Well, they can't. If you want to fly you have to get in a plane. I have to take a plane to visit my father."

"It's just a story," David said.

"That's the point," Emily said. "When you're a kid you don't know that. I don't want Heather growing up to believe all this mystical nonsense."

"But she knows what's real and what isn't. You heard her. She's not stupid."

"She doesn't know. That's why she had to say something, to make sure. He's confusing her." And now I'm talking about my child in the third person, something I swore I'd never do, Emily thought.

"Oh, come on, Emily. We knew, when we were kids."

"No, we didn't. We *believed* it. You don't remember."

"Maybe you believed it. I didn't."

She knew he was wrong. He had forgotten it all; he thought their childhood had been idyllic because he had been the pampered one, the son. Sometimes she wished she could talk to him about growing up, wished they could compare maps of the country of their childhood. She thought she might like getting to know him. But it was probably too late: he had had six years of hearing their father recreate their past just as he had fabricated his own. David was beyond knowing what had happened and what hadn't. The gulf between them was too great for her to cross.

Her mother and Janet came in with the last two plates, piled high with chicken and salad and potatoes, and the family started to eat. As always her mother waited until everyone else had started before she would begin. "Emily," she said. "Please don't argue."

"I—" Emily said.

"You either, David," her mother said. She had learned a few things over the years.

Heather reached out in front of her to play with Elijah's cup. "Uh uh, don't touch that, young lady," her father said. "Do you know whose glass that is?"

"No," Heather said.

"That's Elijah's glass. Do you know who Elijah is?"

Heather shook her head.

"A prophet," Mike said.

"That's right, a prophet. But more than that. When the Messiah comes, Elijah will come before him, announcing him. And tonight he visits every Jewish house in the world, drinking from the glasses we set out for him. What do you think of that? He must get awfully drunk, don't you think?"

Bob and Mike laughed. Heather, more serious, said, "Have you ever seen Elijah, Grandfather?" Emily thought she might be trying to get at the truth of this story too.

"Me? No. But my grandfather, your great-great-grandfather, he saw him once, when he was a small child."

Bob and Mike put down their forks, intrigued, hoping for another story. All around the table the rest of the family stopped eating and looked up expectantly. Satisfied that he had everyone's attention her father took a sip of his wine and began.

"My grandfather lived in Russia, a long time ago. They didn't treat the Jews very well in Russia, you know, they were very anti-Semitic. Do you know what that means?"

Heather shook her head. Emily remembered her father explaining the word to her when she was young, remembered the same tinge of sadness in his voice, so that she knew that whatever the word meant it was bad, very bad.

"It means they didn't like the Jews. Every so often they would sweep through a Jewish village and beat people, and steal things, and smash everything that was left. And when we celebrated Passover they would tell each other that we drank the blood of Christian babies, and then they would break into our houses and kill a few people.

"This particular Passover, the father of the house came back from the synagogue with a stranger, an old man. 'He's traveling by himself and he doesn't have anyone to celebrate with,' he said to his wife. 'I told him he was welcome at our house.'

" 'Of course,' the mother said, even though they were very poor and hardly had enough food for themselves.

"So they put another chair at the table and sat down, and just as they'd started the service they heard a knock at the door. The father opened the door but there was no one there. The flames of the candles nearly blew out in a sudden gust of wind. The father looked down and saw a young boy slumped on the doorstep. He looked closer and saw that the boy was dead.

"Sometimes, you see, the Russians would kill children, Christian children, and leave them on the doorsteps of Jewish homes. And then they would come by and look for this child, and the whole family would be blamed. They'd be arrested, or worse. So the father felt frightened, terribly frightened. He didn't know what to do. There was no time to bury the boy, or take him away. The mother was saying, 'Who is it?' and he stepped in front of the body so she wouldn't see it.

"But the stranger had come up behind him, and he knew what to do. 'Quick!' he said. 'This boy is about the same size as your youngest.' That was my grandfather. 'Dress him in his clothes and seat him at the table. When they come looking we'll say this boy is one of your children.' "

Her father took another sip of wine. Emily looked at Heather and wondered what she would make of all this. Whenever her family got together they would tell stories of atrocities against the Jews. She felt they were showing her little training films, and the lesson she had to learn was that to be Jewish was to suffer. But she had never encountered any anti-Semitism in her life, though she knew her father had. Did she want Heather to grow up knowing this long and bloody history?

Her father continued the story.

"The father didn't like that, but he could see he had no choice.

So they carried the boy inside and dressed him in my grandfather's clothes, and they sat him at the table, his head down. And no sooner had they done this there was another knock on the door.

"The father went to answer it, and another gust of wind came inside and shook the candle-flames. Five or six soldiers stood outside on the doorstep. 'A woman reported her boy missing,' one of them said. 'We're checking all the houses in the area.'

"Well, the father couldn't say anything, but the stranger waved them in. 'Of course, of course,' he said. 'Anything we can do to help.' He showed them around the house, which was very small, only three or four rooms. 'As you can see, the boy isn't here. I hope you find him.' And he led the soldiers back to the door.

"But one of them stopped and looked at the dead child, sitting face down at the table. 'He's been ill,' the stranger said. 'We didn't want to wake him for the service.'

" 'He looks like the one reported missing,' the soldier said.

"The father watched as he moved toward the table. He couldn't move, couldn't do anything. What would they do when they discovered the dead boy? His family, his children, would all be killed. He knew how the mother of this boy must feel. It's a dreadful thing to lose a child, the worst thing in the world."

Her father looked at Emily as he spoke. There it was again, that intense black gaze, the feeling of being singled out. He wanted her to understand something.

"The stranger went to the table. 'Rise, my child,' the stranger said. 'The time has come to say the Four Questions.' "

No one at the table spoke. They had forgotten to breathe. And suddenly Emily knew what it was her father wanted her to understand, though it had taken her a lifetime to learn it. He had never told her how he felt because he couldn't; the only way he knew was to tell stories. When he'd talked about losing a child he'd meant her. That was the only apology she would ever get for six years of silence, but it was enough. More than enough.

"There was silence in the room," her father said, finishing the story. "Some silences are terrible. Then the boy stood, and in a clear voice he said, 'Why is this night different from all other nights?' "

Everyone at the table sighed at the same time, a pent-up breath of relief. "The traveler, the old man," her father said. "That was Elijah."

"Was that a true story, Grandfather?" Heather asked.

"True?" her father said, looking at Emily. She nodded to show she understood. Some silences are terrible. "That's the way my grandfather told it to me, and I believed it. Not that I don't believe it now, on the first night of Passover, when everything is possible."

—to Amy and Alex Galas

Offerings

Susan Palwick

Susan Palwick has made a name for herself on short fiction and poetry. Although her output is slight, it is always of the highest quality. Since 1985, her work has appeared in *Isaac Asimov's Science Fiction Magazine*, *Amazing Stories*, *Pulphouse: A Weekly Magazine*, four year's best collections, and *Nebula Awards 22*. Word is already getting around that her first novel, coming next year, is a knockout.

"Offerings" shows Susan at her best. Like many fabulous tales, this story takes familiar fairy tale themes and makes them new. The saddest part of all may be the Same Old Story we always hear: just about every major magazine rejected "Offerings" before we published it.

"The little people feed on anything that's evil," Matthew's mother told him when he was very young. "They're like the spiders in the garden, Matthew, which look ugly but are really good, because they eat the bugs which kill the flowers."

Matthew didn't like spiders, and he didn't like Mother's description of the little people, who smelled like old leaves and had small teeth as sharp as razors. "They really aren't that different from Nutmeg," Mother always said, but she made Matthew bathe the dog once a week and screamed whenever she found another dead squirrel in the kitchen, so he guessed that she wasn't as fond of smells and teeth as she claimed. Nutmeg redeemed herself by fetching sticks and sleeping in a warm heap at the foot of Matthew's bed every night, but he knew from his mother's stories that the little people were neither playful nor comforting.

"They saved your grandfather's life," she told Matthew. She'd tell him the story when he was helping her bake cookies in the kitchen, or when she was knitting sweaters for him to wear to school, or on wet days when he couldn't play outside. "It was when I was a little girl. He used to drink all the time and he'd turned bad, oh so bad, Matthew. He was running around with other women, and one night my mother tried to kick him out and he broke all her best dishes, the set from England that was decorated with real gold leaf—just took them down off the shelves and started smashing them on the floor. She tried to stop him and he hit her, and then he tried to hit me too but she got between us. She was a big woman. So she hit *him* and he fell and knocked his head against the table—maybe he passed out then, I don't know, but anyhow she dragged him outside and left him there and locked the door. It was raining. I made her go back out and turn him on his side instead of on his back, so he wouldn't drown from the water running in his nose . . . oh, I was scared. I thought he was going to die, and Mother kept saying, 'Your real daddy died a long time ago; your real daddy was loving and faithful and didn't break things. The whiskey killed him, Miriam. Don't cry for that mean drunk out there.'

"But I did anyway. I went to bed and cried myself to sleep, and in the middle of the night I woke up because he'd started screaming, out there in the rain. He kept screaming, 'Go away, go away! Stop hurting me!' I ran into my mother's room and got under the covers with her, and she said, 'Don't be scared. Nobody's hurting him but his own demons,' and finally we heard him say, 'All right, all right, I'll stop, I promise,' and then he stopped screaming. Mother got up and let him back in—oh, he was scared, white as a sheet and shaking like a leaf. He told us how the little people had come up to him in the dark and bitten him, bitten him all over with their sharp little teeth. There were too many of them to count, he said; they gnawed at his fingers and toes and nibbled on his legs and chewed on his nose, and they drank his blood the way he drank whiskey. He knew he was going to die and he promised that if they didn't kill him he'd stop drinking and fooling around and hitting us—and the minute he said that all the wounds healed up like they'd never been there at all, and all the little people went away, because he wasn't evil anymore. And he kept that promise, too: he never touched a drop after that, and he got a good job and bought my mother new dishes and never looked at anybody else. He was a wonderful man after that, loving and faithful just like my mother had said, and whenever anybody asked him what had made him change he said, 'It was the little people. I thought they were going to kill me, but they really saved my life.' "

Matthew was fascinated by the story; Matthew's father hated it. "It's crazy nonsense, Miriam! Matthew, your grandfather was having DTs and seeing things, that's all. That's why the bite marks healed up like they'd never been there: they hadn't! You've never seen one of these critters, have you?"

"Have you ever seen a germ?" his mother countered. "No, of course not. But they still make you sick, just like the little people made my father well."

Germs smelled like Listerine and the little people smelled like dead leaves. These invisibilities were every bit as real to Matthew as Mother herself, who smelled like warm cookies, or Miss Summersong at school, who smelled like lavender and gave him special books to read, or Daddy, who smelled like gin.

As Matthew grew taller Nutmeg became progressively better at killing squirrels, and the books Miss Summersong gave Matthew became more difficult. Daddy smelled like gin more and more often, and Mother like cookies less and less. They fought in the evenings when Matthew was supposed to be sleeping, as he lay in bed with Nutmeg curled heavily on his feet, chasing squirrels in her sleep; to escape the words Mother and Daddy hurled at each other Matthew thought about Miss Summersong's books, some of which were about magical kingdoms and some of which were about science.

Matthew believed as completely in both as he still did in the little people. He knew from the rustlings and scamperings he heard at night that they lived in the woods just beyond the house; sometimes, during a lull in his parents' fighting, he heard soft chewing noises outside and imagined the little people feasting on evil, but he could no longer tell if they were a protection or a threat.

"Squirrels," Daddy said once when Matthew described the noises, but it couldn't be squirrels. Nutmeg, who could hear a squirrel from three miles away through a thunderstorm, always slept soundly through these disturbances.

"You see?" Mother said. "Nutmeg isn't scared of them and neither should you be, Matthew. Your father, on the other hand—"

"Raccoons," Daddy said, refilling his orange juice glass with gin. "Muskrats. Maybe a bunch of bunny rabbits are having an orgy and the dog isn't interested because their tails aren't long enough, okay? Jesus, Miriam! You'll have the kid believing in flying saucers if you keep this up."

"You're disgusting," she said. "Eat some breakfast like a decent—"

"I'm not decent and I don't want breakfast; I want a drink."

"I hope they come and nibble you bare as a corncob and take all your bottles—"

"And do what? Pour them down the sink the way you do? Hey, Matt, the little critters actually live in the plumbing, didja know that? Your mother's been treating them to a party every night, or else she likes 'em a lot less than she says she does and she's trying to drown them. But it doesn't matter. There's enough for all of us. Here, kid —try some."

Matthew's mother started screaming at Daddy then, but Daddy only laughed. "I'd better go wait for the bus," Matthew said, ignoring the proffered glass and giving his last piece of bacon to Nutmeg. His stomach ached, as it always did at breakfast. He knew he'd feel better as soon as he got on the school bus.

One morning when Matthew was ten the bus didn't come. There had been a heavy snowstorm the night before, and when Matthew had been waiting in front of the house for an hour, Mother came to fetch him back inside.

"The bus isn't coming, Matthew; they just said so on the radio. The roads are too bad. There won't be any school today."

Matthew followed her into the house along the narrow path he'd shoveled for himself earlier that morning. Daddy sat in the kitchen, his hands clenched around a mug which held nothing but coffee. Mother must have emptied his bottles the night before, although Matthew wasn't sure when she'd had time. The fighting from his parents' bedroom had gone on until dawn, long past Matthew's ability to block it out by thinking about schoolwork. He hadn't even been able to hear the little people over the din.

"Look what you're doing to Matthew," Mother had yelled, and Daddy had answered just as loudly, "Matthew's fine, nothing's wrong with him, what's Matthew got to do with it anyway?"

"I want to go to school," Matthew told them, his stomach clenching. He didn't want to have anything to do with it. He wanted to be with Miss Summersong with her silver braided hair, Miss Summersong who had been giving him books since he was five, who could make him forget about the drinking and the fighting and living in the woods so far from everyone else. "Why can't I go to school?"

"Because of the roads," Mother said.

Daddy let go of the coffee mug and pressed his hands flat on the table to keep them from shaking. It didn't work. "Matthew, if you really want to go I'll drive you. Get in the truck."

"No! You're in no shape to drive, or the truck to be driven, or the roads to be driven on. The school's probably closed, anyway. Matthew, take your coat off."

Daddy clenched his hands into fists and jammed them into his pockets. "The radio said it was open. You heard it, Miriam."

"Well, I'm sure Miss Summersong won't be there."

"Miss Summersong's always there," Matthew told her.

"Matthew, he doesn't really want to take you to school! He's just looking for an excuse to go to town and buy more liquor. Don't you understand?"

He understood, but he didn't care. His father would go to town anyway, and if anything was moving toward the schoolhouse Matthew wanted to be in it. The truck was aged and rusting, the roads nearly impassable; Daddy cursed and clutched the steering wheel while Matthew prayed and clutched his books. He prayed to Miss Summersong and to the little people, both of whom were much closer than God.

His prayer to Miss Summersong was simple: please be there. He asked more complex things of the little people, things he knew they probably couldn't grant, things he didn't know if they'd be able to understand because he wasn't sure he understood them himself. Please don't say I'm evil, he prayed, please don't call me evil for wanting to go to school and giving Daddy an excuse to go to town, please stay outside the house, please leave me alone and leave Mother and Daddy alone too, don't eat us, I don't want to be eaten and I don't want them to be eaten because then where would I live? I'll give you anything you want, but leave the three of us alone.

He prayed all the way to school, but he didn't know if his supplications were appeasing the little people or only catching their attention. As Matthew walked into the schoolroom that morning it seemed as if the little people must be very close and very hungry, and not even the sight of Miss Summersong waiting for him, smiling because he was the only one of her fifteen students who'd managed the trip through the snow, could make him feel less afraid.

"I won't give you regular work today, Matthew, because the other children aren't here. We'll just do special things." So they talked about the books she'd given him, about the Arabian Nights and Oz and the biology book which had pictures of a man's body stripped of its skin, of its muscles, finally even of its organs, so that just the bones were left; they talked about rocks and stars and animals, but through all of it Matthew kept thinking about Daddy driving in the snowstorm and the little people in the woods. Finally Miss Summersong said, "Matthew, what's the matter? You seem unhappy today."

"Nothing's the matter," Matthew told her. It was too complicated, and if he told her what had happened she might be angry at him for coming to school at all. He wondered if she could tell he was lying.

But she only sighed and said, "I have something to show you—I'd meant to save it until the others were here too, but I think maybe today would be a good day for it. Wait here."

She went to the closet at the back of the room and came back with a microscope. Matthew had only seen microscopes in books, being used in clean, orderly rooms by people who wore white coats and wise expressions. Microscopes were as foreign and incomprehensible as banks and satellites, and it had never occurred to Matthew that he might one day be allowed to handle such a thing.

The slides Miss Summersong showed him, of bits of flowers and seeds like battleships under the lens and tiny insects' eyes grown into faceted jewels, managed to make him forget about the snow and his parents for a little while. He looked at a speck of dust and saw a mountain; he examined a downy feather and saw filaments as rough and gigantic as a monster's tentacles. But as he was putting away the most beautiful slide, a fragment of butterfly wing as intricate as some distant city, it slipped from his hand the same way the road had slid under the wheels of the truck, and shattered to shards on the schoolroom floor.

Matthew cried out and bent to retrieve the pieces, but they were too small; even had he been able to gather them all up again he never would have been able to reassemble them. "I'm sorry, Miss Summersong, I'm so sorry, I didn't mean to do it, really I didn't—"

She frowned at him and said, "Of course you didn't, Matthew. It's all right. We'll clean it up."

He watched her sweep up the bits of glass with a broom and dustpan and pour them into the trashcan, and he knew he never should have been allowed to touch the microscope at all. She was still frowning and the windows rattled as if someone were trying to get in, and for a moment Matthew heard the soft, wet noises of the little people licking their lips. "I'll do extra homework if you want me to, Miss Summersong. I'll pay for it—"

"It was an accident, Matthew. You don't have to do anything." Her frown deepened, and Matthew stared at the floor, wondering if she'd stop giving him books, now that she knew he couldn't be trusted with anything. But she only said, very gently, "Matthew, look at me. Do you like yourself?"

He stared at her, bewildered. He could easily have answered questions about fractions or muscles or flying carpets, but this one defeated him. Miss Summersong watched him steadily, as if he were a slide under the microscope. He didn't know what she wanted him to say. If it hadn't been for the storm and the little people in the woods, he'd have turned and run outside.

His father's horn honked from the road, and for once Matthew welcomed the sound. "I have to go now, Miss Summersong."

"Saved," she said, and Matthew wondered why she sounded sad. "Well, Matthew, I guess I'll see you tomorrow."

"Are you going to give me any homework?"

She looked thoughtful for a moment. "Yes—yes, I am. Tomorrow morning I want you to tell me three things you like about yourself."

He blinked at her, feeling lost. "That's my homework? No reading?"

"No reading. Reading's gotten too easy for you. My job's to challenge you, Matthew." She smiled then, but she didn't look happy.

The trip home was worse than the trip to school had been. The minute Matthew got into the truck he knew that Daddy hadn't gone home at all, but instead had spent the entire day in town drinking gin. The inside of the car reeked of it; a half empty bottle sloshed on the dashboard, and a full case slid in the back of the truck. "Stocked up," said his father, remarkably coherent. "Got lots this time. She'll never find it all. Did you have a good time at school?"

"I broke a butterfly slide," Matthew said.

"Yeah? So? Have some gin, kid. You'll feel better."

"No. I don't want to." That was the money for groceries, he thought. For milk and bacon and dog food. They won't do anything but fight once we get home, and there won't be anything to eat for dinner, and Mother will blame it all on me because I wanted to go to school.

His mother met them at the door, crying as he had known she would be. "Matthew—Matthew, sweetheart, come inside—"

"What about me, Miriam? Do I get to come inside too?"

"Do whatever you want," she said, tugging Matthew into the house, and he knew that something was very wrong. Something terrible must have happened, for her not to start screaming because Daddy was drunk.

"Matthew," she said, "sweetheart, I'm afraid—"

"Where's Nutmeg?" The dog always threw herself on Matthew the minute he got home. The house felt empty, and too quiet. "What happened to Nutmeg?"

"I—" His mother twisted her hands and turned away from him. "She—this afternoon she started barking the way she does when there's a squirrel, you know. I didn't want to let her out because of the snow but she kept barking and scratching at the door, so finally I did and off she runs into the woods and—"

"Oh Christ," Daddy said. "Is that all? The dog isn't back yet and it's a national calamity? What's for dinner?"

"Leftovers. You spent the grocery money on liquor; do you think I don't know you by now? Matthew, I went out and called her and I even looked for her in the woods, but she didn't come back—"

"It was the little people," Matthew said, remembering his prayer on the way to school. I'll give you anything you want, but leave the three of us alone. "The little people took her." Three, he'd prayed, three and not four: he should have said four. How could he have forgotten about Nutmeg? And now she was gone, vanished into the snow, made into a meal for horrible creatures with teeth sharper than hers.

"Nobody took her," Daddy said. "She ran off after a squirrel, that's all. She'll be back. Everybody calm down."

Matthew shook his head. "If she's not back by now she's not coming. She never stays out so long. She's dead. They ate her—"

"Matthew, it was a squirrel! A squirrel, all right? You heard what your mother said, how she was barking and all. Aren't you the one who says she doesn't bark at these pixies? She ran outside after something real, and she'll come back when she's caught it. Let's eat dinner!"

"I can't eat," Matthew said. "I feel sick."

His mother knelt beside him and felt his forehead. "Matthew, why would the little people—"

"There aren't any little people! Miriam, can't you see what these stories have—"

"Shut up! Matthew, why would they take Nutmeg?"

Because he had promised her to them without knowing it; but if he told Mother that he'd have to tell her about his prayer, how terrified he was that everyone in the house would be eaten for being evil, how he lay awake at night listening to the fighting. Even if he'd been able to tell his mother that he thought she was evil, he'd have been too ashamed to admit that he'd forgotten Nutmeg in his prayers.

So he lied. "She—she pooped in my bed the other night and I cleaned it up but maybe the little people took her because she was bad—"

"No," his mother said gently. "Matthew, she's a good dog. Having an accident doesn't make you evil, and the little people only eat evil things, harmful things. That's why your grandfather was such a good man after—"

"Miriam, cut it out! Stop feeding him this garbage and feed me some supper."

"No! Why should I? You should have bought food and you didn't. You bought liquor instead—fine, so make that your dinner! I don't care anymore! They should come for you, the little ones should—oh, you'd make a lovely meal for them!"

Matthew clutched at her hand. She was undoing his prayer of safekeeping, inviting the little people into the house to feed on Daddy, and if that happened Nutmeg would have died for nothing. Daddy hated them so much he wouldn't believe in them even if he saw them. He'd think he was just imagining things even when they were devouring him, and he'd die too. "Mother, stop it! Don't say that. The little people will hear you—"

"Matthew," Daddy said, very quiet now, "there's no one to hear

her. The little people don't exist; that's just a scare story . . . let's fix
those leftovers, eh? Nutmeg's playing in the snow. She'll be back
soon."

But he was wrong. As anxiously as Matthew waited through the
evening, Nutmeg didn't come back. The little people came instead,
to claim the meal Mother had promised them.

Matthew awoke to find his room perfectly illuminated with moonlight reflected from the snow outside. "It's sunlight, Matthew," Miss
Summersong had said that day, "all light is sunlight, moonlight too,
which stops somewhere else on its way from the sun before it reaches
us;" but whatever heat this light had taken from the sun had been lost
long ago. The room was icy in a draft from the hall, and the blankets
on Matthew's bed did nothing to warm him without the familiar weight
on his feet. He got up, shivering, to close whatever window had been
left open.

Halfway down the hall to his parents' room he began to smell a
stench of rotting leaves and dead things far too vile to belong to Nutmeg.
The bedroom door was open, and Matthew saw the little people climbing in through the open window which was causing the draft.

They crept in one by one, as silent as cats, to gather around the
bed where Matthew's parents slept, oblivious, his father unconscious
from gin and his mother from despair. They looked incredibly old,
those little ones, standing no higher than Matthew's knee and dressed
in tattered clothing woven from moss and twigs and bits of shredded
fabric they must have found in the woods. Their faces were as wrinkled
as raisins around gleaming eyes and teeth which shone like needles
in the moonlight. And they were thin: skeleton-gaunt, bones like twigs
poking through their decaying garments. For all the times Matthew
had heard them feasting, they looked as if they'd starved for centuries.

Nearly gagging from the smell, Matthew crouched in the hallway
just outside the door. He was too afraid of drawing attention to himself
to call out, "He's not evil, not always, some things about him are
good!" How could he explain to the little people how parts of his father
could be loving and other parts so horrible, when he couldn't understand it himself?

They kept climbing in the window; it looked as if there were
hundreds of them now, swarming around the bed, clambering onto
each other's shoulders. Matthew imagined them taking Daddy apart

like the man in the biology book, stripping away first the skin and then the muscles and organs, until they found the part of him that was evil. Maybe they only wanted his liver; Miss Summersong said that the liver took poisons out of the blood, and the doctor that Daddy's liver was swollen. Matthew remembered, too, a fairy tale about a witch who stole people's livers to make magic with. But even if the little people only took Daddy's liver, he'd still be dead. Could Matthew somehow convince them to take something which could grow back— a strand of hair, a fingernail, a cell?

And then he remembered the biology book again, which told him that he'd grown from two cells, one from each of his parents, and he knew those cells must have been bad ones. Daddy was evil for drinking and Mother was evil for summoning the little people, but Matthew had helped his father get out of the house to buy liquor, and he'd called the little people before Mother had. He'd prayed that they wouldn't think he was evil, but even the prayer had only proven how bad he was, because he'd forgotten to include Nutmeg. The little people didn't want Daddy at all: Matthew was the one they'd come for.

He turned to run, knowing he was not only wicked but a coward, and the little people saw him at last and scampered to surround him before he could move. They began making a low, horrible sound, a cross between a chuckle and an idling motor, as their eyes and teeth caught glints of moonlight. The smell was unbearable. As they crowded closer Matthew tried frantically to think of some charm or spell, some magic which would drive them away, but all he could remember was his homework assignment.

"Tell me three things you like about yourself," Miss Summersong had said. Three was a number which could make powerful magic, according to any story Matthew had ever read; perhaps Miss Summersong, who knew everything else, had known that the little people would come, and had given him that odd riddle as a weapon against them.

"I like myself because Miss Summersong thinks I'm smart," Matthew whispered as the little people pressed against him. Their eyes brightened, and the chuckling grew louder.

"I like myself because I took good care of Nutmeg and didn't mean to hurt her," Matthew said desperately, shrinking away from them and thinking as hard as he could of the smell of lavender. Accidents weren't evil, Mother had said, and he'd left Nutmeg out of his prayer by accident. He'd been thinking too hard about his parents, but that couldn't be evil, could it? Could trying to protect people be evil?

One more and he might be safe, if the magic worked, if it were strong enough—what, what? He squeezed his eyes shut, trembling, certain he'd feel those teeth tearing into his flesh at any moment, and cried, "I like myself because I love Mother and Daddy!"

There was a gust of wind and stabbing cold. When he opened his eyes the little people were gone, having taken their stench and their uncanny laughter with them. In the pool of moonlight which bathed his parents' bed Mother muttered something in a dream, and Daddy began snoring very softly.

It was years before he understood what had happened. Nothing changed after that night. His father kept drinking and his mother kept nagging; the fights were as loud as ever, and Miss Summersong's books even more alluring. Nutmeg never came back, and Matthew never saw the little people again. In time, he came to believe that their visit had been nothing but a nightmare inspired by his mother's vivid, gruesome stories.

He moved away to go to college, and never moved back. He studied biology and chemistry and chose a career in research, becoming one of the wise, solitary men in white coats he had admired so as a child. He traveled to many cities and never ceased finding them beautiful and comforting; wilderness unnerved him, although he could not have said why. Nor could he have explained fully why he neither prayed nor drank, why he handled lab equipment with a care considered extraordinary even by his colleagues, why he married a woman whom he had first noticed because she smelled like lavender.

He was successful in his work and happy in his marriage. He and Molly bought a spacious house in a suburb luxurious with lawns and swimming pools, and had a daughter who grew livelier and more inquisitive with each passing year. He gave Katie the books he had loved as a child, but he wasn't displeased when she spent more time ice-skating and playing softball than doing homework. Her ability to make friends awed him. Because his daughter's childhood was happier than his own, he believed himself safe.

When Katie was sixteen she began coming home from parties later than she should have, her eyes glassy and her breath smelling of beer. Molly talked to her, gently; Matthew tried to be gentle, and failed. When Katie's grades slipped he screamed at her, and saw her withdrawing from him. When she began stealing small amounts of money he retaliated by searching her room; preoccupied with his daughter, he became careless at work. He dropped a culture dish on the lab floor one day, and couldn't understand why it took him an hour to stop shaking.

One Saturday afternoon in May when Katie had stormed out of the house, hurling curses over her shoulder, Matthew went on another search and destroy mission. He found two cans of beer stashed inside Katie's winter boots and carried them, as if they were live grenades, to the kitchen sink. His stomach clenched at the noise the liquid made running into the drain.

"No," he heard behind him, and turned to find Molly standing in the kitchen doorway. "Matthew, that won't work. She's just out buying more; you know she is. Or getting someone to buy it for her." She took a few steps closer and put a hand on his arm. "Matthew—you're doing what your mother did. You know it didn't do any good. Don't you remember?"

He pulled away from her; he didn't want to remember. For a brief, bitter moment he regretted having ever described his parents to his wife. When he spoke, his own voice sounded foreign to him. "What should I do, then?"

"Talk to me," Molly said, and he noticed for the first time how dark the circles had grown under her eyes. "You never talk anymore. Here: come here. Sit down."

She led him to the kitchen table as if he were blind. "You're scared," she said. "I'm scared. Your father died from drinking and now Katie's doing it and you can't save her any more than you could save him, and it isn't fair. But destroying yourself won't change anything. I love you as much as I love her, Matthew, and I don't know which of you is harder to live with anymore. Do you understand?"

"Don't lecture me," he said, and it was that stranger with the hoarse voice talking again, not himself at all. "I don't know what we did wrong, but I'm not going to stand by and watch her—"

"For God's sake, Matthew! We're better parents than most, and of course you're standing by and watching her. That's all you've been doing for months. Watching and yelling."

"Now you're blaming me," he said.

"No, I'm not! You're blaming yourself. You think she inherited the tendency from you and that means you have to do something about it. Well, you can't do a damn thing. Nothing you've tried has worked."

Matthew rubbed a hand over his eyes. His palms smelled of beer, and suddenly he felt ill. All those years of work, of study, of success; the beautiful home in the beautiful place, the family vacations, the piano lessons. Molly was right: he'd done everything he could think of to protect Katie, and it hadn't worked. It hadn't been good enough. He'd failed.

A breeze smelling of warm, wet earth blew in through the kitchen window, and he thought he heard a throaty chuckling noise outside. Silly, he told himself. There are no forests for miles, and it was just a dream. But suddenly his tongue tasted of garbage and rotting leaves, and he was cold despite the warmth of the day.

"Matt?" Molly said. "What's wrong?"

He couldn't look at her. He stared at his fingers, remembering the sharp pieces of butterfly slide on the schoolroom floor, the gleam of moonlight on pointed teeth. Could trying to protect people be evil? If he'd let the little people feast on his father, that winter night, would Katie have been safe?

"Matthew, your hands are shaking. What is it?"

He swallowed. "Did I ever tell you about that nightmare I had when I was a kid?" He knew he hadn't; he'd never told anyone. Why should he? He'd outgrown his mother's superstitions. It had only been a dream.

"No," Molly said. "Tell me now."

So he did, trying to laugh as he told her about his mother's stories, about Miss Summersong and Nutmeg and the freezing midwinter night when the little people had come to claim the evil in the house. "It was just a dream," he said when he was finished; and then, smelling her perfume across the table, "I think I fell in love with you because you reminded me of Miss Summersong."

"Thank you," she said gravely, and smiled. "I fell in love with you because you were the first man I'd ever met who admired bacteria and remembered the titles of all the Narnia books. Matthew, what if the little people were real?"

"If they were, it didn't do any good." The taste of garbage was gone; all he could smell now was honeysuckle. He got up and went to the window. The front yard stretched smooth and vibrant and empty to the road; a red sportscar sped by, too fast, filled with shouting teenagers. Katie, Matthew thought, his fear returning. "I drove them away with Miss Summersong's charm. I didn't let them have anything evil because I was afraid they'd hurt us. I was afraid my father wouldn't believe in them even when he saw them there, and that they'd kill him."

"I think you're wrong," she said. "I think they went away because you fed them."

"Then why didn't anything change? Why didn't the evil stop?"

"Because it wasn't evil at all, but illness and ignorance. Because the only evil you can give away is your own. Look—your grandfather gave up the behavior that was hurting him and his family, right? Well, maybe what you fed the little people that night was your *belief* that you were evil. Maybe that's what was hurting you most. Does that make sense?"

"No," he said, and heard chuckling again. He gripped the windowsill and peered outside, into the beginnings of dusk. No one was there. Go away, he thought. Go away and leave me alone. "If I gave it to them, why do I still have it?"

"Because it grew back," Molly said softly. "Like a fingernail, or a strand of hair." She came up behind him and held him for a long time, her arms around his waist and her face pressed against his shoulder. He allowed himself to be enveloped by the familiar smell of lavender, and finally he turned and kissed her.

"There's a meeting at the high school in half an hour," she said into the hollow of his breastbone. "For parents who are scared about drugs." She laughed, sounding embarrassed, and Matthew realized how hard she was working to keep her voice steady. "You know— what to look for, where to get help, that kind of thing. Do you want to come with me?"

"No," he said. He couldn't face it in public, not yet. "Come back and tell me about it."

"All right." She pulled away from him and gathered up her purse and keys. "Try not to yell at Katie if she comes home."

He nodded numbly and went back to stand, unseeing, at the kitchen window. He wondered if he could still remember the titles of all the Narnia chronicles, and found that he could. I like myself because I like good books, he thought. I like myself because I'm a good scientist. I like myself because I've been as good a parent as I knew how to be, even if I wasn't enough, even if I made too many mistakes.

It occurred to him that maybe he had loved Katie too much, been too proud of her, jinxed her somehow. "Take whatever bad stuff you want," he said aloud, speaking quietly because he felt foolish. He wondered if the neighbors could hear him through the open window. "Take away as much garbage as you can carry, but leave me what I love. Give me back what I love and I'll never ask you for anything again."

All he could smell was honeysuckle. And what good would it do, even if they were real? What could they return to him? His parents were dead, and at last he realized, aching, that Molly was right: Katie belonged only to herself. She'd have to make her own offerings.

He was very tired. He closed his eyes, leaning against the windowsill, and breathed in the smell of flowers. A dog barked in the distance, and when Matthew opened his eyes again he saw Nutmeg, as spry as she'd been on the day she vanished, trotting across the tranquil twilit lawn with a squirrel in her mouth.

Sendings

Robert Frazier

"Sendings" appeared in our twelfth issue, which I loosely called the "death and dying" issue. Most of the stories dealt with death. A number of them, including "Sendings," stressed the warmth and life-affirming aspects of that common yet tragic experience.

Robert Frazier first became known for his excellent science fiction poetry. He then turned to short fiction, publishing stories in *The Twilight Zone Magazine, Amazing Stories, Isaac Asimov's Science Fiction Magazine*, and many other magazines.

A string of Canadian geese angled over the roof line of the house and trailed toward the south shore as Andrew Fortune rested from his exertions at the sawhorse: fist locked about the saw handle, feet planted in the snow drifts, his body shaking with anger. He steadied the bow over the blade with his other hand and ripped through the log again, establishing a rhythm in the push and pull of his arms, the rocking of his shoulders. The smell of wild cherry rose out of where the sharp teeth shaved and dragged wood grains from the cut. The grains dribbled on the cross-supports of the sawhorse. They peppered his sneakers.

Scattered in a fan over the skim of white that blanketed the yard. The icy wind plastered them on his jeans and on the shirt front inside his coat, since he'd neglected to zip it before slamming his way out the front door. Andy felt much older than fifteen: just as ground down, just as wind-blown as the sawdust. He didn't care about the cold against his chest or the numb feeling in his hands. He just wanted to vent himself on the firewood until his mother finished lunch and left for work.

Andy stopped for another breather and leaned into the saw. The geese were gone from sight, but a short-eared owl drifted over the neighbor's field, dipping at each suspicious movement in the tall broomsage, then riding an updraft. A thin flurry dusted the roof again with big flakes. Long icicles hung from the gutter, looking like the wicked teeth of dinosaurs where the wind shaped their growth into curves. Andy liked to be outside in winter. He discovered something new with each rest stop in the sawing of a log. Some detail that kept his mind occupied. He could forget. In his imagination, he could drift mind-to-mind with the owl. He didn't have to think about Gramps, and the sendings the old man made while he dreamed.

The temperature of my veins runs higher than the surfaces of super novae. The heat. Burning me up.

"Andy." He heard the stern tone that underpinned the call. "Andy! Time to feed your grandfather."

Andy felt relieved that she'd interrupted the old man's sending. After he hung the saw over a four-footer sticking out from the big log pile, he stacked the cut wood into the crook of his left arm, balancing one too many and shifting it to a load for two arms. He stood straight and walked quickly. The snow packed with a crunch under Andy's feet as he plodded around the end of the house to the door. Sleez waited by the jam, her black fur fluffing about her and her tail swishing lazily. He dropped the heavy wood next to her in a jumble, but Sleez didn't jump away. The cat showed more poise than he. He flinched at everything these days. When, like this morning, Mom awoke tired and cranky and desperate to find a way out of her troubles without marrying another empty-hearted man. When she ranted about the late loan payments or yelled at him for the littlest offense. Or when, as of late, his grandfather's health took a turn for the worse, and the sendings grew powerful as a hurricane, almost overwhelming him with garble from the old man's head. As with his mother's angers, he knew that he wasn't the real focus of the frustrations and fears and sadness that twisted up into horrible images in Gramps' reveries. Nightmares, really. But he felt just as torn, just as skewered by them. Bricked in like the poor jerk in the Poe story he'd done a book report on last week. The guy who just wanted a taste of sweet Amontillado wine. A taste of the good life. He'd always wanted to share Gramps' power to communicate with the mind.

He had, and now he couldn't escape it.

Andy sucked in a cold deep breath, exhaled. The moisture frosted the glass of the storm door with fine clear beads. He thumbed the latch, propped it open against his knee, and bent to pick up two logs. An arm reached from inside and tugged his shoulder, setting him off balance. He dropped one log, missing Sleez as she bounded between his legs and into the hallway, but he managed to hold onto the smaller one as his mother pulled him inside.

"Hurry, Andy. I can't stir the soup any longer. I have to get to the office early."

"But, Mom . . ."

"No buts. Gramps is hungry despite a touch of fever. He can smell the peas."

She pecked him on the mouth with a kiss, which embarrassed him. Martha Fortune . . . at thirty-four, she possessed an ageless good looks that Andy envied. His same bold hair, yes, but cut at shoulder length. A restrained flare with make-up. Her trim figure that looked exceptional in contemporary fashions, or some wild bathing suit, or in a tee shirt. It was hard to believe she had two decades on him, and not a hint of the power to send had shown up in her yet. He envied that too. Just maybe.

"Sorry about the fight we had. And put that cat out. You know she lives in the barn. I left a note about putting rice on to boil at three o'clock. There are things I need done in the horse stalls, too."

As she stood on the bricks in the hall and pulled on her black wool coat, she verbally continued to list what the note on the refrigerator already listed for Andy to do. He blocked it out. He needed to shrug off the cold from outside. He needed to lift the lid on the pot-bellied heating stove in the kitchen and drop in a fat log on the coals. He needed nothing new to think about. What he truly needed to do was find some breathing space.

"Yes, Mom," he called to her at last. He stirred the green soup base laced with onions and half moons of carrot. "I'll get them done. Could you stop at the Hub and pick me up a *Sports Illustrated*?"

She was already in the driver's seat, though, fishtailing out the driveway in her little blue Volkswagen. She seemed to be headed toward a troubled zone, for in the distance and to the North, clouds gathered in a dark band. Beneath them angled fine threads of grey like the tentacles of a jellyfish trailing in the ocean currents. Andy felt a chill along his spine as he stood at the window and watched them close off the sky above town, and over Nantucket Sound. He turned and backed up close to the woodstove.

Gramps tasted the pea soup with a smack of his lips, eagerly ate several spoonfuls, then lost his appetite. Andy tried to spoon more into him, but he begged off with a complaint of discomfort in the bowels. They worked at getting him comfortable, plumping the pillows and lifting him back to the head of the bed so that his feet weren't hanging off the bottom, caught in a painful tangle in the sheets and covers. This tired Gramps, who answered fewer and fewer of Andy's inquiries. He looked flushed. Andy sat by his bed and allowed him to doze.

I'm guilty. I'm guilty. Ringing high in the belfry of my skull. Guilt. I should never have let poor Martha and Andy bear the burden of this. It's burning them up. Jesse was a good woman. Jesse would never have allowed this. Never . . .

His grandfather's head lolled to the side, and the skin inside his nose wattled and vibrated. A slow pulse throbbed through a big vein exposed in the hollows of his neck. Age lines formed a crackled glaze over his grandfather's features, but though the flesh bunched about his eye sockets under his glasses and purse-stringed at the lips, the skin now stretched taut on his cheeks and forehead and sunk in at his temples. He'd been losing weight for many months; the doctors were baffled. The tests showed nothing. A stay in the hospital revealed nothing as well, save that doctors were slow at making conclusions and fast at sending bills. So Andy returned from school at lunch and made up for his sixth and seventh period classes with studies in the evenings, and some tutoring on weekends. That way his mother was free to work afternoons and into the night, with time off for dinner.

Gramps had to be covered at all times—a simple equation. Andy even moved his bed into Gramps' room, so that he could be there in case of emergencies. So that his mother could get her extra hour of beauty sleep while he got Gramps cleaned and fed a hearty meal in the morning. So she'd be fresh for the insured customers who filled out homeowners applications or claims forms for accidents in their automobiles at the office. When Gramps was awake, he often chuckled about it, and he said she'd always slept late as a kid. He'd compare Martha to her mother, Jesse. He liked to tell stories about their early years together on Nantucket, and when he did, he turned his ring about his skeletal ring finger, the gold one with a buttery cat's-eye agate carved into a lion's head. Andy would watch the lion spin, and he'd drift off with the old man as he dozed, lost in the drone of his fever.

Ringing high and furious as black bees. Bees. Swarms crudely marked with sulfur yellow skeletal masks. Like those in the barn. Jesse's horse barn. Their faces angry . . .

The clouds that had swept over the moors after lunch began to separate back in the direction of town, allowing blue sky to peek between them. Fingers of illumination touched the tops of the pines nearby, and a beam of pure sunlight shone through the picture window that looked over the wire-fenced pastures and the frozen swamp beyond. This ray illuminated Gramps, setting the edge of the sheet beneath his chin aglow. It seemed like such a pure omen, such a hopeful one, that for a moment he felt uplifted, assured that Gramps would recover and the burdens of his dreams might ease for Andy. But the light shifted. Gramps moaned without awakening. It was painful to watch his grandfather, knowing that it took more than bright signs to change the inevitable, yet he continued to find it meaningful to stay in the room.

My head's twisted with gibberish. My heart with bitterness . . .

These were moments that Andy spent gladly with him, awake or sharing his sleep, and they both understood they would never share anything like this again. He touched Gramps' hand, placing his palm over the ring and the knobby knuckles on the back of his hand. Gramps opened his eyes for a minute, smiled wanly, then fell back to a dreamless sleep. Andy remembered the rice for the casserole Mom had planned for dinner, and he left the room on tiptoes to work downstairs in the kitchen. And then on the list of outdoor chores she left for him.

Andy felt elated to walk out on the back roads that afternoon after cleaning the old hay and manure from the stalls in the barn. The air crackled with sounds that seemed sharper and crisper than the muffled backdrop of, say, a foggy day. His breath rasped. Sparrows and finches flittered through the Japanese pines, knocking clods of snow onto the ground and chattering across the road. The ice that skimmed the shallow wheel ruts shattered with a satisfying crunch when he stepped on it. He could even hear the whinnying of the horses back in the fields. He'd returned once to lower the heat under the cooking pot and check in with Gramps, but found things as quiet as he'd expected. One of the ladies who boarded her horse with them in the barn had stopped at the house to chat, but she didn't need help. He'd covered his bases, so on this walk he extended his range into the less familiar parts of the forest off Burnt Swamp Lane, and found a narrow deer trail snaking through high brush.

A light snow began to angle in on the wind that had shifted around from the northwest, and the sky grew darker. Andy followed the trail slowly, enjoying a magical feeling that grew inside him. The deer trail wound into a hidden depression and around a tiny, seasonal pond frozen over by the recent cold snap. He skated figure eights on invisible blades across the surface. With a stick and a quahog shell abandoned—no doubt—by a sea gull, he pretended that he played hockey for the Bruins like Gramps had, before the injury to his head and a career in sports writing. A twist of overhanging branches, whose tips were anchored in the ice, acted as a goal, and Andy became adept at sweeping the puck through the center and at slap shots under the arch from tough angles. He cheered when he scored, moaned when the shell bounced off the edges of the goal. Time skipped away from him, blown aloft by increasingly powerful air currents that whistled over the depression. The earth appeared to spin about him with violent turbulence, carrying him off as well, locking him away in an arena where the cares of the world did not impinge on him. He stopped when the ice cracked beneath him, arresting his heart for a moment. In the silence that followed, he heard the bleating horn of his mother's car.

Andy ran all out in the direction of the sound.

His mother stood in the hallway between the kitchen and the front door, her arms crossed, eyes focused intently on him. Her bottom lip curled up under her top row of teeth. It was bleeding slightly where she'd bit it.

"You were supposed to stay here."

Andy hung his head. He hadn't removed his coat yet, and he tried to catch his breath. His chest ached.

"I just took a walk. It's snowing."

"I'm not blind. And I'm not blind to the fact you're lying. You'd have smelled the food burning if you'd left a few minutes ago."

Andy detected a distinct odor of carbon coming from the kitchen.

"I just needed to get out of the house. Gramps was sleeping."

"Your grandfather collapsed trying to reach the bathroom. That's how I found him when I called the doctor."

"I didn't know."

"You didn't know, did you? You didn't know." Her voice raised to a shrill pitch, flooded with sarcasm. "You didn't care. That's what. The doctor's come and gone. You just didn't care!"

That got to Andy. "Don't talk about who cares. You don't. That's for sure. You have a couple stupid hours in the morning with him. I spend all the rest."

"Andy! That's enough."

"Yeah. But when's it enough for you. You've got me doing all my work around here and yours too. And you're never satisfied. Always yelling at me. You're on me like flies on a crap."

His mother backhanded him with a slap that stung his cheek like a thousand needles. She grabbed the collar of his coat and shook him.

"I work so we've got a roof over our heads, and food on the table. Don't you ever forget that."

Mom started up the stairs, and though Andy wanted to say something, to apologize, he didn't know how. He knew that he'd failed her, and the trust of his grandfather. Andy didn't move, didn't say anything. He stood in the hallway and stared at his feet as the snow melted off the toes of his boots and seeped down between the bricks. Gramps was dreaming.

My time peels. Time, this raw element. All the time and memories entwined like the hairs in a lion's mane. Oh, Martha. Andy . . .

He could hear the fire roaring in the stove in the kitchen, and it distracted him. Outside, the wind increased, making the insulating plastic over the windows breathe as it pushed into the tiny leaks in the window casings. The storm door rattled in its frame. Andy pushed himself to send back a wave of reassurance.

It's okay, Gramps. It's okay.

He looked back into the kitchen and saw the snow falling in a blinding sheet against the windows. They were due for a hard blizzard. Just another thing to entrap him. He felt miserable. If he hadn't seen the cat in the kitchen, and gone in to pet her and sit in the rocker by the warm stove, hadn't been forced to move, he'd still have been standing in the hall when his mother descended the stairs an hour later, at dusk. He'd still have been succumbing to Gramps' sendings.

She loomed over him where he sat in the dark. Andy didn't meet her stare. He stroked Sleez and rocked and whistled under his breath with the howling at the eves.

"Andy. It's done."

He looked up. A rush of panic flooded him with adrenalin. His face burned, especially where she'd slapped him.

"Gramps is gone," she said.

"No! He would have told me. He would have sent . . . ah, called for me."

His mother looked puzzled. "He didn't want to see the doctor again. And he didn't want you to see him so bad off. I shared it with him. It was my place."

"You're just messing with me." Andy stood, and Sleez bounced from his lap. He stepped by his mother, meaning to run upstairs, or maybe outside. "He isn't dead. He would have sent to me. I would have shared it, really shared it!"

She grabbed his coat sleeve. She was gentle, though, and he didn't resist.

"He told me how good you were with him. How much it meant to him, and how much I didn't give you the credit you deserved for all you've done. I'm sorry, Andy." She paused a moment. Andy said nothing. "Your grandfather wanted you to have this."

She held the ring out to him with her other hand, and the light from the hall glinted on the lion's head, the figure that Andy always imagined was Gramps when he was a young, powerful skater in the pros. Andy knew this wasn't a game. Mom was serious. Gramps was dead. D-E-A-D. He turned and bolted out the door into the teeth of the wind. There was no one left to share the sendings with. No one.

The storm pounded his face with stinging flakes. He didn't care. Let it come. Let it bury him until he couldn't move. Plastered up, and for a half a century no mortal would disturb him. Yes! Gramps was gone, and that hurt much worse. It was nothing like he'd imagined. Oh, he was free now, free of the dreams like he'd yearned to be. No trapped Fortunato here. No false taste of Amontillado. But the cost was too high. He'd gladly be a prisoner again and have Gramps back. Gladly.

"For the love of god, Montresor!" he cried out.

Tears welled under his eyes, and they also burned on his skin in the bitter cold that rushed across the yard. But the burning faded, as did the shame that had been marked on his cheek by his mother's hand. Gramps had given him the ring he loved, hadn't he? He'd entrusted it with him. Andy felt drained and tired. He turned and went inside. His mother needed him now.

In the kitchen, under the glow of a white globe lamp, Mom sat in the rocker and scratched the fur on the cat's neck. Her face looked broken, the make-up streaked around her eyes.

"There's something on the table for you with the ring. A couple sports magazines I'd bought at the Hub. I know you like to read them at the end of a long day." She blew her nose on a tissue. "God knows, this has been a long one."

"Thanks," he said. By god, maybe she'd heard him this morning after all. Maybe something other than his voice communicated.

"They're not much, but . . ."

"No. You're wrong. They are important. It's like with Gramps." He stood beside the rocker and reached and touched the yellow silk of her hair with a wet hand. She looked up to him, kissed his hand and held it against her ear. "These last days every little thing was important to him, Mom. Wasn't it? You knew."

The melting look of understanding in her eyes comprised the only answer he needed, but, yes, he'd needed it nonetheless. This was real. It would suffice. It was just as important; whether she could send or not, she could communicate.

The storm raged full over the moors and beaches of the island. It sent drifts up to the windows. Flaunted its raw power in the night like a vengeful enemy. Yet though the day wasn't over for them, he thought the howling of the wind had lessened at the eaves, grown quiet, as if Gramps had spoken his last words in a sending, a firm farewell, and let go with the grace of a proud, proud king of the wild.

Andy said, "Before you make the call, I'd like to go up and see him."

Why Pop-Pop Died

Francis J. Matozzo

Francis J. Matozzo has sold fiction since 1980. His most recent stories have appeared in *Pulphouse* and *Modern Short Stories*.

"Why Pop-Pop Died" takes the family motif that we've been following through the last few stories and adds a horrific twist. The innocence of the young narrator juxtaposed against the violence make this one of the most frightening stories I have ever read.

What made it all happen was the Mann's car being parked in front of our house where it should not have been because that's the spot Daddy likes to keep clear for the people who are visitors. Pop-Pop and Grandmom were coming over and Meg's boyfriend too all for Thanksgiving dinner and to watch football so there was no place to park except down the street where they had to walk a long way. Pop-Pop's leg hurts so bad it's hard for him to walk and I watched them coming up the pavement in the sunny light between the big piles of leaves that were raked up all over and to see him lean on Grandmom

who is so small made me think he would break her and if there was
snow they would have slipped maybe. Mommy held the door open and
they smiled and kissed and waved *Happy Thanksgiving* to everybody.
I stood behind the big easy chair to jump out and scare Grandmom
who pretended she was afraid but really wasn't and she patted me on
the head with one hand while she held out the other with the bag of
Grandmom's bread she always makes to give Mommy. And Meg came
running downstairs in her new white dress and kissed Grandmom and
Pop-Pop and told everyone she thought it was Dennis who played
football at the High School where Meg went to all the games to be
cheerleader. Dad called in from the kitchen where he was cutting the
turkey that he was sorry they couldn't find a spot out front to park
because of the Mann's car. Grandmom took off her big furry coat that
smells like Christmas which I always get to bring upstairs and lay on
the bed and said it was some nerve the Mann's had. Mom said it's all
fine and well but they have their own driveway and next time she saw
Mrs. Mann she was going to tell her just that. That's when Meg said
oh Mom don't make such a fuss. Daddy turned his head so that he
could look at Meg without even stopping what he was doing and said
no Mom was right our guests should not have to walk half a block to
come to our house *look at Pop-Pop he could have fallen and broken
something young lady*. Mom told Dad to watch what he was doing or
he could cut himself *God forbid* but Dad was finished by then and he
never cuts himself he said because *I do it the right way* and then he
told me to go downstairs to pour a pitcher of beer from the tap for him
and Pop-Pop. I went down but when I did little Fluff Meg's kitten
which Dennis gave her as a Happy Birthday present ran past me and
right over to Grandmom and Meg scooped it up before it started to
stretch and work its little claws into Grandmom's stockings. Daddy
pushed the turkey bits down the garbage disposal and said to Meg that
she'd better put the cat away because it would be a pest with all the
food around. Then the door knocked and Dennis came in wearing his
High School jacket and a big smile like he wasn't sure of something
and had done something wrong. He said that he was sorry he was late
and Mom said *never mind you're just in time*.

All the time I was wishing for snow and said so to Mom and Dad
but it wasn't the right time they said and anyway Dad didn't have his
snow tires on yet but was doing that next week on vacation. I still

wasn't sure because the sun went down and outside got cold and all the windows steamed up in the kitchen and when I looked out at them it was easy to pretend that piles of snow were all around the house. That made the food on the table really good because it was warm with curls of smoke and smelled nice like winter. Grandmom said God bless me I ate so good for a little boy. And when we were all finished Pop-Pop went into the living room to sleep on the old easy chair while Dad told Dennis about the right kind of paint to get for the outside because Dennis was going to paint the garage for Dad this summer and certain kinds of paint last longer than others. The best kind Dad told him would hold up to the weather for six years although the instructions on the can said eight but *you have to leave a margin for error*. Dad knew because last time he painted the garage was seven years ago this summer *right Mother*? Dad said how important it was to know the details and the right way to do things. By then it was real dark outside so that the windows looked pitch black and as I was praying for real true snow for Christmas the cat meowed because she was locked in the kitchen behind the doors. Dad made Meg do it after Fluff had jumped up onto the dinner table right when we started to pass dishes around and went for a piece of turkey so fast like a tiger that its white tail went right past the hot candle Mom lets me blow out and almost caught fire and *there goes another life* said Mom. Dennis kept laughing at what everybody said and he ate a little bit but not much so that Mom kept asking if he wanted more and he winked at Meg every time he thought nobody was looking and she would giggle. *Go wake Pop-Pop for dessert* said Mom and so I left the table and went into the living room where Pop-Pop was sleeping and snoring in the easy chair. When I saw his big wrinkled face with all the lines and marks and his nose like two black caves that went real wide every time he snored my hand just stopped on his hairy wrist and I was afraid. I went back into the dining room and Daddy said *go back and tickle him* but I shook my head and hung onto the chair behind Grandmom who smiled and said *I'll get him he's so hard to wake these days*. Mom said the coffee was on and the door knocked real loud and Pop-Pop opened his eyes. Dad said maybe it's the Mann's seeing if they could use our garage. Dennis laughed and offered to get the door and Fluff was meowing louder than ever to get out.

* * *

I could feel the cold when the door opened and I thought for sure there must be snow in the air high up in the clouds waiting to come down. Daddy let the first man at the door slap Dennis in the face with an iron pipe so that he fell against the table with the lamp that Mommy always says never to play next to because it was antique. It fell and broke all over but Dennis didn't see it because he was on his knees and another man with a cut face kicked him in the belly. Mom dropped the coffee-pot and Grandmom screamed and so did Meg. Dad started to stand up but the man with the pipe ran past and put one end in Meg's mouth and said he would shove it all the way down until it came out her privates and everyone should *shut the fuck up and go over to the couch*. The other men came in and one who was black brought a long knife under Dennis's throat like a barber would and asked if he knew what was good for him and Pop-Pop was still waking up. *We all have to sit nice* said the man with the pipe but he kept standing and didn't sit with us and the black man put his knife away and stood by the door and said *Kayo is late*! The man with the big scar down his face said *so we wait* and all of us sat on the couch except Pop-Pop on the easy chair and Dennis who was still crawling and coming up all over the floor. He had a cut on his head that dripped big red drops of blood onto our new rug that Mommy always says to make sure you wipe your feet before coming in. Then the sirens started far away like there was a big fire and the three men who were all dressed in the same kind of blue clothes started rushing about and looking out windows and kneeling down and peeking out. The noise was so loud it kept coming and going up and down the streets and once even red lights flashed by the window and a car slowed outside and the little red blinks ran around our windows a trillion times. Everything got real quiet so that you could hear a heartbeat and there was no noise and the colored man with the knife and the man with the cut face stood behind the door and the man with the pipe had a knife out too and was pointing it at us as he moved to the kitchen. He pushed open the door and sure enough Fluff came running out hissing like she sometimes does whenever she doesn't like you bothering her. The man jumped back and turned white like a ghost. Fluff just stopped and looked at him and washed her paws and the colored man laughed and said *pussy*. The man with the cut face watched out the window and the red lights and sirens faded. The man with the pipe screamed and his eyes got so big I thought they would pop out. He jumped at Fluff so fast and picked her up and told how he hated cats and Meg was up off the couch before Daddy could stop her and shouting *leave my cat alone*! The man pushed Meg aside and ran into the kitchen with little Fluff in his big hand. He stuck her legs and tail into the garbage disposal and turned it on until she was all sucked down and gone except for her screeches which were louder even than the sirens and pieces of wet hair which floated onto his hands and he wiped across Meg's dress. Then he went into the dining room and got a big hunk of cake and stuffed it in his mouth and ate so that the crumbs dribbled down his mouth like what Mom would call bad habits.

Daddy let the men go around the house and take all our money. He let them eat all our food and drink all the bottles in the cabinet I'm not allowed to go in and put their feet up on chairs and tables. He let them make fun of Pop-Pop who wet himself when Fluff screeched and now was looking all around and stuttering until Grandmom asked if she could *please give him the medicine in my bag* because he wasn't a well man. They laughed at her too and the man with the pipe said *this medicine will fix him*, and he poured some of the bottle he had right down Pop-Pop's throat. It spilled out into his shirt and tie and he coughed and I thought Daddy was going to throw them out then but he just sat there looking at his hands. And then the men wanted to play and they might as well have fun while they waited and so they made Meg get up and kneel in front of them and they all stood around her. Mommy screamed and jumped at them and they tied her up and stuffed an old sock in her mouth that Fluff played with and put her in the closet where I always like to hide because it's nice and small. And they came back and Daddy let them take Meg's clothes off and throw her on the floor real hard and take turns laying on her and making her cry. Even Dennis was crying and when they were all done they left her lay there and Dennis wanted to *at least put a blanket over her you animals*! They laughed and beat him up until his face was like a squashed tomato and then they went on Meg again. And later when Pop-Pop started to shiver and shake like he would fall apart I asked the man with the cut face if it was snowing outside. He looked at me and said *yeah snow's all over the place* and I asked if I could look out the window but he said no and got mean. I knew he had told a lie anyway because then two big lights were shining in the window and I could tell that no snow was falling past them. I was going to tell him that when the black man started shouting *Kayo my man Kayo*! and all the three of them rushed out the door. Pop-Pop just kept coughing until his eyes and face were red and his hand was digging at his chest like he was clawing himself. I went over to him but was still afraid to touch him and when I saw his eyes turn up white I went to the other side of the room and hid in the corner but no one else moved. They all sat and stared until Meg got up real slow and said *Daddy call someone Daddy do something*! Dad just sat there and waited and let Pop-Pop keep coughing and when Grandmom and Dennis and Meg were finally moving around and Mommy was unticd and out of the closet Meg was the one calling the police and the ambulance on the phone. Dad just sat there and I went over to him and touched him and his hands were all shaking. When the ambulance came it had to park in the middle of the street because the Mann's car blocked the front of our house and they had to carry Pop-Pop around it. Later on that night after the police left when everyone was tired and ready for bed Dad cursed and punched the wall and said if it wasn't for the Mann's and their damn car being in the way we could have saved Pop-Pop in time. He kept hitting the wall until his knuckles bled and Mommy made him stop. Even later when everyone was asleep I went downstairs and opened the back door and went out onto the porch and saw that sure enough it had snowed all over the backyard and street and the trees and tops of houses all around the neighborhood nice and smooth and white.

The Murderer Chooses Sterility

Bradley Denton

Bradley Denton's fiction has always taken risks. From his Nebula nominee, "The Calvin Coolidge Home for Dead Comedians," to his novels (such as *Wrack and Roll*), Brad has proven his willingness to tackle tough subjects. And none is more difficult than making a serial killer a sympathetic viewpoint character.

"The Murderer Chooses Sterility" is a stand-alone excerpt from a novel in progress: *Blackburn: His Violent Life and Death*. Two other excerpts have been published in *Pulphouse: A Weekly Magazine* and *The Magazine of Fantasy and Science Fiction*.

On the day after he killed his eleventh man, Blackburn decided to have a vasectomy. That was because the Monday *Kansas City Times* reported that the victim had been a father of four. Blackburn didn't enjoy reading it. He wished that he had stayed behind the grill instead of taking his morning break.

It wasn't that he regretted what he had done. Late Sunday, Number Eleven had run over a dog and had made a hash mark in the air with his finger, so Blackburn had driven after him and killed him at the next red light. It had been quick—one .357 bullet through the side window, and the light had changed. Blackburn had rolled up his own window and driven on. No one had seen. Kansas City was dead on Sunday nights.

Number Eleven had deserved what he had gotten, but Blackburn thought it sad that the man had fathered four children who would now be warped by his cruelty in life and his ugly death. With that thought, Blackburn realized that he himself would not make an exemplary father and that he might die an ugly death of his own.

After his experience with Dolores (whose paramour he had thrown off the Golden Gate Bridge), he doubted that he would ever take another wife. But he had a sex drive as strong as that of any other twenty-four-year-old man, and women found his sandy hair and blue eyes attractive, so there would be girlfriends and one-nighters. He could not allow himself to impregnate them.

Paying for the operation might be a problem. Upon arriving in Kansas City in September, he had spent most of his cash on documents identifying him as Arthur B. Cameron, and the rest on a scabrous 1970 Dart. He had then landed his job at Bucky's Burgers, but in two months of work, he had saved only fifty dollars. He would have to find a clinic that performed cheap sterilizations.

During his afternoon break, he went into Bucky's office and looked through the Yellow Pages. He found what he needed under the heading of "Birth Control":

Responsible Reproduction of Kansas City
Pregnancy Testing
Birth Control/Family Planning
Abortion Counseling and Services
Vasectomies
Fees Scaled to Income
Open Noon to 10:00 P.M. Weekdays

The ad was followed by a telephone number and a midtown address. Blackburn's one-room basement apartment had no phone, and he didn't want to call from Bucky's, so he decided to visit Responsible Reproduction after work. He spent the rest of the afternoon in a state of anticipation, knowing that he was about to give a great gift to the world.

* * *

Stinking of deep-fryer grease, Blackburn pushed open a glass door embedded with wire mesh and found himself in a room illuminated by fluorescent tubes. Plastic chairs lined the walls. Most were occupied by women, a few of whom clutched the hands of nervous men. Three toddlers sat on the linoleum floor playing with G.I. Joe dolls. An odor of medicine mixed with Blackburn's own smell.

He approached a middle-aged woman who sat at a desk beside a doorway. A sign on the desk read *Ellen Duncan*. "Ms. Duncan," Blackburn said, "my name is Arthur Cameron. I want a vasectomy."

Ms. Duncan opened a drawer and brought out a pamphlet that she pushed across to him. It was entitled *Facts to Consider About Vasectomy (Male Sterilization)*.

Blackburn took the pamphlet and gave it a glance. "Thank you," he said, "but I've considered the facts, and I've decided to have the operation. Could you tell me how much it will cost?"

Ms. Duncan frowned. "Our urologists charge Responsible Reproduction a hundred and ninety-five dollars. The amount that we pass on to the patient varies according to what he can afford." She paused. "Pardon me for asking, but have you discussed this with your spouse?"

"I'm not married."

"Are you in a long-term relationship?"

"No."

"Have you any children?"

"No." Blackburn wondered what these questions had to do with anything.

"Mr. Cameron," Ms. Duncan said, "our mission is to make family planning services available to those who couldn't afford them otherwise. We provide vasectomies to men who have consulted with their partners, whose families are complete, and whose incomes must support those families. We prefer that single men who have fathered no children see private physicians . . ."

A woman in a white smock appeared in the doorway. "Melissa," she called. "We're ready."

Across the room, a girl of sixteen or seventeen stood up. As she stepped around the children, she trembled.

". . . but, in any case, you should read the pamphlet," Ms. Duncan was saying. She opened the drawer again and brought out a sheet of paper. "Then I hope you'll contact one of the physicians on this list." She put the list on the desk and looked at Blackburn as if she expected him to take it and leave.

He watched the girl named Melissa disappear down a hall.

"Why is she going back there?" he asked.

Ms. Duncan stared. "That's none of your business."

Blackburn stared back. "Does she have a family? Must her income support it? Did she consult her partner?"

Ms. Duncan's face flushed. "Please leave."

"Why?"

"Because I don't think you're here for information. I think you're one of those who stand outside and shout horrible things at the people who come to us for help. You're here to harass us."

Blackburn shook his head. "No. I'm here because I don't want kids. I have no partner to consult, but since I work as a short-order cook, I also have no savings account or health insurance."

Ms. Duncan studied him. "All right," she said, picking up a pen and poising it over a calendar. "You'll have to meet with our staff counselor."

"I don't need—"

"It's required. The discussion will deal with your reasons for this decision and with the nature of the procedure. Your cost will be calculated then." She looked at the calendar. "Could you come back tomorrow at 5:45?"

"I'll be here."

"I'm glad I was able to help you," Ms. Duncan said.

Blackburn was glad, too. When Ms. Duncan had begun asking her irritating questions, he had decided to kill her if she turned him away. He had never killed a woman before, and he had not been happy at the prospect.

The sun had gone down, and the air was cold. As Blackburn left the building, he put his hands into the side pockets of his jean jacket and gazed at the concrete walk. He didn't see the people who blocked his way until he was almost upon them. They hadn't been there when he'd arrived.

There were eight of them, clustered beside the drive that led to the clinic parking lot. Each held a burning candle in one hand and a handmade sign in the other. The letters shone in the glare of the streetlights.

Blackburn stopped and read the signs. GOD COUNTS THE CHILDREN, said one. SAVE THE UNBORN, said another. ABORTION IS MURDER, said a third.

A man stepped out of the cluster and asked, "Have you come from in there?" He pointed with his candle, and the flame faltered. "There where they butcher babies?"

"I've just been inside," Blackburn said, "but I don't know anything about any butchering."

A slender woman joined the man. She was dressed in a gray coat with matching gloves, muffler, and cap. Her eyes and lips gleamed with reflections of her candle flame. Wisps of brown hair quivered beneath the edge of her cap.

"If you've been in there, you know about it," she said. Her voice had a rich timbre, but was hoarse. "They do abortions."

"They didn't do one to me," Blackburn said. "Now, please, let me pass. My car is across the street."

"So why are you here?" the woman demanded. "Did you drop off your girlfriend so she could let them kill your baby? Or—" The flames in her eyes brightened. "Or have you killed babies yourself? Are you going to a home paid for with the flesh of infants?"

Blackburn had heard enough. These people were lucky that after his close call with Ms. Duncan, he didn't feel much like killing anyone tonight. He strode forward.

The man who had confronted him jumped aside, and the cluster of six did likewise. The woman in gray stayed where she was.

Blackburn stopped again to decide whether to shoulder his way past her or to try to go around.

The woman dropped her candle and reached into a pocket, bringing out a vial filled with dark liquid. She pulled out the stopper with her teeth (perfect teeth, Blackburn saw; white, smooth), then spat it out and screamed *"Murderer!"* She snapped the vial toward Blackburn as if it were the handle of a whip.

The liquid hit him in the face and got into his left eye and his mouth. He took his hands from his jacket pockets, and as he rubbed his eye, he tasted what was on his tongue: Blood. Cow's blood, pig's blood, maybe even blood that the woman had drawn from her own veins.

She remained before him, holding the vial like a weapon. It was not empty.

Blackburn took a step. The woman stood her ground. He reached out and plucked the vial from her glove, raised it to his lips, and drank. When the blood stopped flowing, he put his tongue inside and cleaned the glass.

Then he dropped the vial to the sidewalk and crushed it under his foot. The edge of his shoe caught the discarded candle as well, flattening it.

The woman gaped at him.

Blackburn walked around her and crossed the street to his car. Once inside, he turned on the interior light and examined the smears on his fingers. He almost reached for his Colt Python, which was nestled under the seat, but did not. He was calling it even with the woman in gray.

When he returned the next evening, the protesters were pacing, their breath wafting in faint clouds. He parked the Dart where he had the day before and walked across, but they ignored him as he passed.

Inside, Ms. Duncan gave him a personal information and medical history form to fill out, and when he had completed it (having lied where necessary) she led him to a cubicle where the staff counselor, a black man in his mid-thirties, was waiting. Ms. Duncan introduced the counselor as Lawrence Tatum.

"Call me Larry," Tatum said as Ms. Duncan left. He was sitting at a desk covered with a jumble of books, pamphlets, and folders. "I'll take that data sheet off your hands."

Blackburn handed him the form and sat down. The desk was against the wall, so the two men faced each other with nothing between them.

Tatum examined the form, then looked up and asked, "What happens if you decide to get married, your wife-to-be wants kids, and you've had your balls disconnected?"

Blackburn tried to imagine the situation, but the only wife-to-be he could picture was Dolores, she of the perpetual white bikini-patches. "I won't be a father," he said, remembering how his own father had shot his dog and then pushed his face into the dirt for crying. "Any woman who knew me and still wanted to have children by me would make a poor wife."

"A vasectomy is permanent, Arthur. What if you turn thirty and all of a sudden, *blam*, you want to be a daddy?"

Blackburn doubted that he would live to be thirty, but he considered the question anyway. "That'll be tough shit for me, I guess," he said.

Tatum wrote on the form. "Okay. Let's talk about what'll happen during the operation, and then Duncan can schedule you for surgery."

Blackburn was surprised. "That's it?"

"For you it is. Couples take longer." Tatum began to rummage through the mess on his desk. "Besides, I figure that any guy who would be sterilized without understanding the consequences is a guy who shouldn't be spreading his dumb-ass genes around anyway."

It was the most honest statement Blackburn had ever heard. He liked Tatum.

Tatum found a card with a diagram of male genitalia and held it up. "You'll be given two shots of local anesthetic in the scrotum, one on either side of the base of the penis." He pointed with his pen. "After they take effect, the doctor will make a vertical incision midway between the vas deferens tubes. He'll pull one vas over to the incision, put a permanent clamp on it, and cut away a section. Then he'll repeat the procedure for the other side and close the incision with a few self-dissolving stitches. The whole thing takes about twenty minutes. Any questions?"

Blackburn stood. "How much will it cost?"

Tatum glanced at the form. "You'll need to bring a money order or cashier's check for ninety bucks." He picked up a telephone receiver and punched a button. "Ellen? When Mr. Cameron comes out, could you arrange the pre-vasectomy sample and schedule him for surgery? Thanks."

"What's a pre-vasectomy sample?" Blackburn asked.

"Semen specimen," Tatum said, hanging up the phone. "You'll need to take it to a medical lab within a half hour of ejaculation. We do the post-op sperm counts here, because then it doesn't matter whether we find the sperm alive or dead, only that we don't find any. For this one, though, we need a live count. You never know—maybe you won't have any."

"What are the odds of that?"

Tatum chuckled. "About the same as the odds of the Royals winning the Series next year. If you don't hear from us before your surgery date, assume that your count's in the normal range."

Blackburn thanked him and went out to Ms. Duncan, who gave

him the address of the lab and told him to deliver his sample on Thursday morning. She also told him that his surgery would take place in one week, at 5:20 P.M.

"Soon," he said. "That's good."

"Every Tuesday," Ms. Duncan said. "There are two underway upstairs right now."

"Could I observe?"

Ms. Duncan said that she didn't think so. Then she gave him two instruction sheets and a baggie containing a single-bladed, blue plastic safety razor. The first instruction sheet told him what it was for.

Before going to the Dart, Blackburn stopped among the protesters and spoke to the woman in gray. "You have the wrong night. There's no baby-butchering today."

"I suppose you call it 'choice,' " she said.

Blackburn smiled. "No. Tonight it's 'crotch-cutting.' Or maybe 'scrotum-slicing.' "

"I can have you arrested for obscenity," the woman said.

Blackburn laughed and crossed the street. As he unlocked his car, he heard footsteps on the asphalt. Turning, he saw that the woman in gray had followed him. She had left her sign and candle on the sidewalk.

"Are you going to throw more blood?" Blackburn asked as she drew close.

The planes of her face seemed frozen. "You already have so much on you that it'll never wash off."

"Yet blood washes away sin."

"What would you know about that?"

He knew plenty, but instead of telling her so, he said, "I'm not an abortionist."

"It doesn't matter. If you work there, if you're *in* there, you're one of them. Condoning it is the same as doing it. It's evil."

"So why come over here? Shouldn't you be afraid of evil?"

She tilted her head. "I need to understand you if I'm going to fight you. How can you believe in what you do, and *do* what you do?"

For a moment, the sureness of her tone made Blackburn fear that she knew who he was, and knew the things he really had done. Then he remembered that she didn't even know him as Arthur Cameron, let alone as James Blackburn.

"You're wrong about me," he said. "In fact, I'm making sure that I'll never be the cause of what you're fighting." He took the baggie containing the plastic razor from his jacket. "This is to shave the hair off my scrotum. I'm having a vasectomy next week."

The planes of the woman's face crumpled, and she spun and stumbled into the street. A car was coming fast and would have hit her, but Blackburn pulled her back.

He was startled at what he had done. He didn't save people from themselves. He left people alone . . . unless they angered him, in which case he either punished them if the offense was slight, or killed them if it was great.

In the past seven years, the only exception to this rule had been that he had not killed Dolores.

The woman in gray clawed at his hands until he released her, and she rushed into the street again.

"Could I have that back?" Blackburn called.

She stopped. Her right hand was clutching the baggied razor. She dropped it and ran to her fellow protesters.

Blackburn retrieved the razor, got into the Dart, and drove to his apartment. All that night, the woman in gray filled his thoughts. He was afraid that he might be in love with her.

On Wednesday, Blackburn worked twelve hours at Bucky's. He needed the money.

On Thursday morning, he ejaculated into an empty breath-mint box and took it to the medical lab. He was embarrassed, not because he was delivering his own fresh semen, but because he had conjured up the ghost of the woman in gray to produce it. She had thrown blood on him, and then they had rolled together, each staining the other.

After a ten-hour shift behind the grill, he drove to Responsible Reproduction. The woman and her friends were there, but none of them seemed to recognize his car. He parked a short distance down the block, and for the next hour he watched them shout at everyone who went in and out of the building. The voice of the woman in gray rose above the rest.

On Friday night, after cashing his paycheck, he approached the clinic from the opposite direction and parked across the street from where he had the night before. He watched longer this time. At nine-thirty, the protesters blew out their candles and stacked their signs in a station wagon. Blackburn slouched low as they went to their cars.

The woman in gray crossed the street alone to a maroon Nova. When it left the curb, Blackburn followed.

He lost the Nova in traffic on the city's east side, but spotted it as he drove past a side street. It was parked under a streetlight, and the woman was standing on the porch of a small house. Blackburn pulled over and adjusted his rearview mirror so that he could see her.

A light came on in the house, glowing yellow through the shades, and the door opened. A thin, backlit figure handed the woman something, and the door closed.

The woman returned to her car carrying bunches of red roses, their stems wrapped in green florist's paper. She cradled them as if she were carrying a child, but when she reached the Nova, she put them into the trunk.

Blackburn followed her again as she drove away. She went far west, into Kansas, but he didn't lose her.

The Nova stopped in the parking lot of an apartment complex in Mission, and Blackburn watched as the woman left her car and entered the complex through a security gate. A bank of mailboxes filled the wall beside the gate, so if he had known her name, he could have discovered her apartment number. But he didn't know her name.

He went to his own apartment and stayed up listening to the radio. The figure who had given the roses to the woman had looked male, but he was not her lover, Blackburn decided. She hadn't gone into his house, and she had left the flowers in the trunk of her car. At most, he was a friend. A friend with roses.

Blackburn worked another ten-hour shift on Saturday, then drove past Responsible Reproduction. The lights were on, but there were only five protesters outside. The woman in gray was not among them. In bed that night, Blackburn lay awake wondering if she had abandoned her post because she had a date.

The next evening, there were no protesters at all. The street was empty, the clinic dark. Sunday in Kansas City.

He went to the apartment complex in Mission, thinking of breaking into the woman's car to find its registration slip and discover her name, but the Nova wasn't in the lot. He wished that he'd had the idea two nights ago.

Shivering and dozing, he waited for her to return. Once he dreamed of shooting a backlit figure, and awoke at the Python's report.

The Nova didn't appear, so Blackburn left at dawn and drove to the house of the roses. The woman's car wasn't there either, but he parked the Dart and watched the house until a skinny man who wore glasses came out and drove away in a Pinto.

Blackburn walked up to the porch and saw that the name on the mailbox was "R. Petersen." He pressed the button beside the door and heard the bell ring. Inside, a dog barked. Blackburn pressed the button again, and the dog kept barking. No one came to the door.

Blackburn went to work. While on his mid-morning break, he read in the *Times* that a pipe bomb had exploded at Responsible Reproduction during the night. It had been set off outside the front door.

The police suspected that the bomber's intent had been to cause minor building damage, but the explosion had done more than that. A counselor named Lawrence Tatum had been doing paperwork in an inner office, and the police speculated that he had heard a noise and investigated.

They had found him in the waiting room with pieces of glass in his flesh. They thought that he had been starting to open the door when the bomb had gone off.

At press time, Tatum was in critical condition at St. Luke's. He had not regained consciousness. The police had no suspects. Ellen Duncan of Responsible Reproduction had announced that the clinic would continue its usual services.

After work, Blackburn bought a six-pack and a *Star*, which said that Tatum was still alive. The police had questioned some people, but they still had no suspects.

Blackburn went to his apartment. Five beers later, he was able to sleep.

On Tuesday, Blackburn left Bucky's at mid-afternoon. He stopped at a branch post office and bought a ninety-dollar money order.

At his apartment, he took off his work clothes and showered. Then he sat on the edge of the bathtub, soaped his scrotum, and shaved with the blue razor. It was a slow process because his testicles kept drawing up, but he persevered. His only alternative was to use his electric.

By the time he had dressed, it was five o'clock. He took the money order and the razor and drove to Responsible Reproduction.

More than thirty protesters were pacing the sidewalk when he arrived, and there were so many cars along the curbs that he had to park almost two blocks away. As he started to walk to the clinic, he saw the woman in gray emerge from a van with six others. He waved to her.

He had almost reached the building when he realized that he had left his money order in the Dart. He ran back to get it, and the woman and some of her companions stepped off the sidewalk to avoid him.

"Tonight I do it!" he shouted as he ran past. The woman averted her eyes.

When he reached his car, he glimpsed a bit of color on the pavement and squatted to pick it up. It was a rose petal. The edges were black and curled, but the center was bright. He crushed and dropped it, then grabbed the money order and hurried back to Responsible Reproduction. Several protesters yelled at him, but the woman in gray was quiet.

The glass-and-wire-mesh door was gone, and in its place was a slab of plywood with a handle. Blackburn opened it and went inside.

He lay on a padded table that was covered with blue paper. His naked buttocks rested on a pad of the stuff.

His knees were supported by saddle-shaped pieces of plastic atop metal posts, and his feet hung in the air, chilling. He wished that he had left his socks on.

The crewcut medical assistant took a spray bottle from a counter and bathed Blackburn's crotch in a cold mist. Blackburn gasped.

"Antiseptic," the assistant said. He returned to the counter, opened a packet, and pulled out another pad of blue paper. When he unfolded it, a hole appeared in its center. He laid it over Blackburn's crotch and pressed down so that the scrotum pushed up through the hole. The upper half of the paper became a curtain between Blackburn's thighs.

"Doctor'll be in soon," the assistant said, and left.

Blackburn lowered his head and stared up. Above him, attached to the ceiling with thumbtacks, was a poster of a kitten clutching a knot in midair. Underneath the kitten were the words,

When you've reached the end of your rope, HANG ON!

Blackburn wanted to tear it down. He wasn't in the mood for cute bullshit.

Then, as the antiseptic evaporated and made his testicles feel as if they were packed in ice, it occurred to him that this room was used for vasectomies only on Tuesday evenings. On other evenings, it was used for other things.

He was lying on a table where women had lain for abortions.

He thought of the girl named Melissa. Would the kitten have meant something to her, or would she have thought it as stupid as he did?

The assistant returned with the doctor, who was wearing a green smock over chinos. The doctor had thinning hair and looked about forty. "Let's get to it," he said.

Blackburn raised his head and watched as the assistant brought a cart and a stool to the foot of the table. When the cloth over the cart was removed, he saw a syringe and an array of stainless-steel instruments.

"You'll be more comfortable if you keep your head relaxed," the doctor said.

Blackburn lowered his head again, but he was no more comfortable. With peripheral vision, he saw the assistant pick up the spray bottle again. A second cold mist hit his scrotum and hissed against the blue paper. The assistant placed the bottle on the cart, then opened a package of latex gloves and helped the doctor put them on.

The doctor nudged the stool with his foot and sat down between Blackburn's legs. Blackburn could see his face, but his hands were hidden behind the blue paper.

"I'll check on the other guy," the assistant said. "The jerk showed up half-shaved." He left the room.

The doctor grasped Blackburn's testicles, pulled them away from the body, and began rolling the skin above the right testicle between his thumb and forefinger. Blackburn's calf muscles contracted, and his feet cramped. He had to grab the edges of the table to hold himself down.

"I have to find the vas," the doctor said.

Blackburn clenched his teeth and glared at the kitten.

"Got it," the doctor said. "Now I'll give you the first shot of anesthetic. It's procaine hydrochloride, like the Novocain you get at the dentist's."

Blackburn had been to a dentist twice, and both times he had suffered. Novocain did not work well on him.

"Here it comes, in the top right side," the doctor said. "It'll feel like a bee sting."

It was worse than that. Blackburn's back arched, and his thumbs tore through the paper covering the table. He strained to keep from pulling his legs off the posts and kicking the doctor in the face.

The needle withdrew, and the doctor began manipulating the left side as he had the right. "One more," he said, and the needle went in. Sweat trickled into Blackburn's ears.

"Try to hold still," the doctor said.

The needle withdrew again. Blackburn lay still for a moment, then raised his head to see what was happening.

The doctor was looking up at his face. "How old are you?" he asked.

"Twenty-four."

"Ah. How many children do you have?"

Blackburn wanted to hurt him. "None. So what?"

"Ah," the doctor said again. He shifted on the stool, and his right hand appeared above the blue curtain. It held a blood-smeared scalpel.

"What does 'ah' mean?" Blackburn asked.

The doctor laid the scalpel on the cart and picked up another instrument, moving it behind the paper before Blackburn could see what it looked like.

"Never mind," the doctor said, looking down at his work again. "I'm going to pull the right vas over to the incision now. You might feel a slight tug."

It was as if a vein in Blackburn's abdomen were being yanked out through the scrotum. Blackburn rose on his elbows.

"*Please* hold still," the doctor said.

Blackburn wished that he could feel justified in killing the doctor, but he knew that he couldn't. He had asked for this.

Much later, the doctor said, "You seemed to experience some discomfort, so I'll give you another shot before I do the left vas. It won't be as bad this time, because you're already somewhat deadened."

The kitten was a yellow blur. Blackburn tried to brace himself, but it didn't help. The woman in gray, he thought, had better appreciate this.

When the stitched wound was covered with gauze, Blackburn got down from the table and put on his clothes and jacket. He couldn't feel the pressure of the athletic supporter, or of his jeans. It was as if he had no genitals.

The doctor gave him a prescription for tetracycline and left the room. Blackburn started to leave as well, but paused at the foot of the table. He was surprised at how much the blue paper on which he had lain was blackened.

The assistant came in with a trash bag and began taking up the paper. He glanced at Blackburn and said, "You're finished, aren't you?"

Blackburn went out. Downstairs, Ms. Duncan smiled at him. "We'll see you in a few weeks for your first sperm check, Mr. Cameron."

"Right." He moved toward the plywood door.

"Oh, you might like to know that I just called the hospital about Larry Tatum," Ms. Duncan said. "He'll lose two fingers and maybe his right eye, but he's out of danger and joking about the whole thing."

"That's good," Blackburn said, and left.

Outside, among the protesters, he stopped before the woman in gray. "I'm sterile," he said.

"Get away from me." She was surrounded by candles, and her face wavered between dark and light.

Blackburn looked back at the clinic. "A bomb went off here two nights ago. A person was hurt."

"That's what they'd like us to think," the woman said, "but it's a lie to make it look as if *we're* in the wrong. If we stopped marching, we'd be giving in to that lie."

Blackburn's wound began to throb. "I admire your strength," he said, and walked on to the Dart. Each step hurt more.

The van wouldn't bring the woman home for at least two more hours, and no one approached Blackburn as he opened the trunk of the maroon Nova. When he was finished, there would be no evidence that he had done it. Trunks were easy.

A bulb came on as the lid lifted, and a heavy scent reminded

Blackburn of compost and funerals. In addition to a tire and a jack, the trunk contained three bunches of wilted roses.

The paper around one bunch was loose, and a few flowers had fallen free. Blackburn picked up this bunch and pressed his face into the dead petals, then put it down and reached for another. This one was heavier, so he left it on the floor of the trunk and unwrapped it.

Among the rose stems was a twelve-by-two-inch iron pipe that was capped at both ends. A cord almost as long as the pipe hung from a hole in the center of one of the caps.

Blackburn picked up the pipe and shook it, listening to the rattle. He had used something similar once, so he knew that the pipe contained a stick of dynamite and a blasting cap. This was the simplest sort of pipe bomb, a bangalore torpedo. When he opened the third bunch of flowers, he found another.

His pulse was trying to break through his stitches, so he began to hurry. He unbuttoned a jacket pocket and took out the razor, dropped it, and stamped on it. He used the freed blade to slice off half of each fuse.

After rewrapping the pipes into their flower bundles, he closed the trunk and gathered up the razor's plastic shards. On the way to the Dart, he dropped them into the gutter.

He had his prescription filled at an all-night pharmacy. Then he went to his apartment, took four aspirin, and lay in bed with an ice pack on his crotch. He couldn't sleep, so he read the "Instructions to Follow After a Vasectomy" sheet over and over.

Instruction #8 said that it would take from fifteen to thirty-five ejaculations to clear the sperm from his tubes. After fifteen ejaculations, he was to bring a specimen to Responsible Reproduction for examination.

Blackburn doubted that he would remain in Kansas City long enough to do that.

The name of the woman in gray, the next Monday's *Times* said, had been Leslie Bonner. She had shared her apartment with her mother.

She had placed her second bomb outside the door of an obstetrician/gynecologist's office in Overland Park. It had gone off when she was twelve feet away, and her head had hit the sidewalk when she fell.

Her car had been found nearby, with another bomb in the trunk. The police were investigating to discover the source of the dynamite.

Blackburn looked at the picture of Leslie Bonner for his entire morning break.

Either she hadn't noticed that the fuse on her second bomb was shorter than the one on her first, or she had thought that it didn't matter. She had trusted the maker. She had failed to understand the consequences.

No one had saved her from herself.

Blackburn dropped the newspaper into the garbage. He worked until the end of his usual shift and left Bucky's without cleaning the grill.

At his apartment, he gathered his possessions and put them into his duffel bag. Then he lay on the bed and waited for night.

She hadn't looked like a Leslie. If anything, Blackburn would have guessed her to be a Lisa, or a Lydia. Thinking about her, he started to have an erection, but the stitches pulled at his skin and stopped it.

At eleven o'clock, he went into the bathroom and examined his incision. The swelling was gone and the stitches were dissolving, but his scrotum was still bruised. He put a new gauze pad over the wound, pulled up his jeans, and took his duffel bag out to the Dart. The weight made him ache. He wasn't supposed to carry anything heavy yet.

He drove to the east side of the city and parked a few blocks from the house of the roses. He tucked the Python into the back waistband of his jeans so that it was hidden by his jacket, then walked the rest of the way. The street was quiet, the homes dark.

The house's shades were drawn, but there was a light on inside. As Blackburn stepped onto the porch, he heard the sound of televised laughter. R. Petersen was watching David Letterman.

Blackburn took the pieces of fuse from his pocket and tied them together. He lit one end with a match, then held the knot in his left hand while he took the Python into his right. He pressed the revolver's muzzle against the doorbell button.

When the door opened, he tossed the fuse inside. R. Petersen turned toward it, and Blackburn hit him behind the ear with the Python. Petersen fell.

Blackburn went inside and closed the door as Petersen crawled across the hardwood floor toward the fuse. Blackburn stepped around him and turned up the volume on the television set.

Petersen reached the fuse and slapped at it.

Blackburn took a pillow from a chair, pressed it over Petersen's head, and fired one round through it. The fuse sputtered out by itself.

He found a roll of tens and twenties in a dresser drawer in the bedroom, and a half-grown, black-and-white mongrel pup in the kitchen. He found a box containing dynamite, blasting caps, crimpers, and fuse hidden among junk in the basement.

When he was ready to go, he carried the box outside and dumped it on the street. Then he returned to the house and lit the fuse he had looped around the living room. That done, he took the pup and left. The pup was heavier than she looked, and she squirmed. By the time Blackburn reached the Dart, he was sore and had to take aspirin.

He didn't think that the single stick of dynamite in Number Twelve's mouth would endanger the neighboring homes, but he stopped at a pay phone and called 911 anyway. He didn't know the house's exact address, but he told the dispatcher which street and block.

Then he drove north on I-35. He would dump the Dart in Des Moines, acquire another car, and go on to Chicago. He had never been there.

"Chicago sound good?" he asked the pup.

The pup gnawed on the butt of the Python and growled.

Blackburn was having trouble thinking of a good name for her. Maybe he wouldn't give her one.

Public Places

J. N. Williamson

J. N. Williamson, like Bradley Denton, has chosen a murderer as a viewpoint character, but he doesn't intend Stenwall to be sympathetic. In fact, "Public Places," which appeared in our first issue, is perhaps one of the most purposefully uncomfortable stories I have ever read.

J. N. has written more than 30 novels and over 100 short pieces, as well as editing the *Masques* series of original anthologies. His most recent book, a short story collection, has just appeared from *Author's Choice Monthly*.

"Y ou done trashed two of Big Buns' little girls over Memorial Day weekend, Stenwall, so he said he ain't gonna give you a chance t'infeck no more of 'em, awright?" Sax Chacker always spoke like a whining parrot, but the self-righteous tone he fell into whenever he quoted his pimp boss made Stenwall feel even more like puking. They were inside the service station, alone, Sax behind the cash register. "Don't you take this personal, but he said t'get yore sick prick into a clinic and keep away from the Farm till you got a clean bill of health. Okay?"

It wasn't close to okay. Stenwall saw Sax glance covetously in the direction of the place they called the Farm, filled with young females, and thought of how Big Buns sometimes gave one of them to this pervert in the western-style hat. Sax, with a razor scar bisecting his pocked face down the middle, whose mug always seemed to be mooning people. Stenwall could care less about the shit Sax Chacker did to the bitches he was paid with, but avid envy was probably already showing on Stenwall's face.

"Since it's the Fourth of July tomorrow, I'm locking up the pumps till Monday." Nervous, Sax tipped his huge hat back on his smooth skull, momentarily stopped gaping out the window toward the Farm, and strove to end their discussion. "So you just get yore doctor's slip and come talk t'Bee Bee in person, awright?"

Stenwall had one more question: the whereabouts of the huge Hispanic gay who operated the Farm. Once he'd learned that Big Buns was in the east, on a procuring trip, he kicked Sax Chacker's ass till the scarred-up pervert couldn't possibly have given a damn how many young hookers Stenwall "infecked."

He hadn't killed Sax, unfortunately. Sax wasn't female.

Meaning to go to the men's for another of his recent, red-hot leaks, Stenwall stormed out of the service station into the broiling desert sun-stream and turned toward the side of the building. Mom Baggit preferred for johns to *look* clean, anyway, and he had Sax all over him.

But sizzling motes of light caromed off the station lot, exploding like tiny mushroom clouds, and Stenwall paused to brace himself against the rusty coke dispenser. Dear Christ, it looked like the edge of the world outside and it also felt that way. If you drove down the one unmarked side road leading off the neglected old oven of a highway, you found an air-conditioned converted farm with ladies who took all the heat off—so long as Big Buns wasn't present. He bought a coke, drank it fast.

But if you drove straight ahead, you wound up in the desert even before the handkerchief in your hip pocket stuck to your butt. Shocked by his insight, suddenly lonely and freshly frightened for the first time in years, Stenwall saw it as a choice between Heaven and Hell. It was another first for the little enforcer, part-time bodyguard and spare-time hitman, to prefer the former over the latter.

Scarcely noticing Sax's hefty three-quarter ton truck left on the lip of the concrete drive, Stenwall headed for the men's, thinking.

Probably it was Phoenix where he had acquired the rash. For a week, that was all he imagined it was. But another pimp who looked after his ladies had rejected Stenwall's money and he'd gotten pissed, then deep down worried and ultimately headed for where he'd known damned well he could get some. Or believed he could.

En route, the fevers—not constant; occasional ones—had begun. In Taos, two days back, he had admitted he wasn't at all well. Blaze, Nevada, had begun increasingly to sound like Heaven. Because hookers were everywhere, but not the sort Bug Buns raised, literally, for fun and profit. He bought on the unwanted baby market or kidnapped the real cuties, then handed 'em over to Mom to get the maternal touch.

And every year, a new "crop" came in, ripe for harvesting. They were nine, twelve, maybe as old as fourteen; depended on the girl, and how ol' Mom ranked her.

But Independence Day—July Fourth—that was, by tradition, the day when the true cream of the crop was marketed, and all of Big Buns' regulars—like Stenwall—had the date stuck to the insides of their brains as if Christmas had started coming twice a year. No moon-faced pervs and no running goddam sores were going to keep Stenwall from groping around under the tree to see what the faggot Santa Claus had left for him!

Woozy, he shoved against the men's door, then swore. He could never remember that this building was so damn old the doors opened out, as if the men's had once been part of a private house. Tottering inside, he told himself he'd have this one last virgin—two if he was up to it—then get medical help. After the treatment, he'd be out of action awhile but he'd have this last romp at the Farm to remember while he healed.

If I heal, Stenwall mused darkly. Part of the truth he was having to face was that he never screwed anyone but hookers, and bought two a week. Unlike Bee Bee and Mom's little darlings, they weren't all exactly immaculate.

Another part of the truth was that Stenwall was street-smart but otherwise stone stupid. He lived just to fuck. He stole and chiseled, sold unsavory goodies and would muscle or kill anyone at all, so he had cash-money for fucking. He boasted, told jokes, ate, slept and occasionally bathed, moved his bowels, and breathed to fuck. And whores were fine, nowadays preferable, for numerous cogent reasons.

He even had a speech for the way hookers were cheaper in the long run; another attesting to their infinite variety.

Other women had drawbacks, but Stenwall had no speech explaining that particular viewpoint.

He squeezed into the room, elbowed the front door shut, locked it. At once, his nose wrinkled. The goddam Sax Chacker made no goddam effort to keep the place clean and the men's reeked. If ghosts had followed the scent of their own urine the way animals did, for I.D., this was surely the most haunted place on earth. Joseph Smith might have stopped to pee on his way to Utah!

It was also windowless, little more than an outhouse that flushed, and Stenwall—whose sensitive nose made him don fresh clothes whether he had washed lately or not—bustled to the solitary urinal, fumbled for his zipper and idly peered down, anxious to get this over with.

Still zipped, he made a face.

The customary mothball-stinking oval shit lay at the bottom of the upright pisser, disinfectants that failed and looked like the testicles of someone who had died in Egypt and been mummified over a urinal. Sax had let the thing back up. Viscous, golden piss lolled round the nuts and, should Stenwall deposit even a drop, the mess would slosh all over his glossy shoes.

Hurriedly—furious to be Out of There, driving to the Farm—he walked between the two modest partitions housing the one commode and unbuckled, sweating. Trousers at half-mast, Stenwall paused, abruptly moved by his recent disposition toward hygiene. He unrolled a couple of feet of toilet paper to spread on the horse-shoe shaped seat, working with the exquisite care of a father wrapping his child's birthday present. And he took particular care with the horse shoe's break, where Brucie, named years ago in high school, would need to dangle.

Stenwall's precautions had nothing to do with the outstanding chance that he'd contracted a communicable disease and wished to protect the innocent. They stemmed from the harsh warnings Ma had given him thirty years earlier, and served—once he was perched cozily in place—to trigger other memories of his past.

As if he had become an aged person grown aware of limited futures, inclined to imagine unlimited pasts.

But it hurt, again, to whiz. He gasped audibly and simultaneously achieved a roiling, thunderously odoriferous dump—as well as a glimpse of the most intriguing graffiti Stenwall had ever found on a john wall. Instantly, his plan for medical assistance was forgotten in the presence of that kind of panorama that had ever urged Stenwall to inquire into the *Weltanschauung* of existence itself.

An epicurean spectacle of foul legends spread across the booth walls on either side of Stenwall and a scanning evoked his complete admiration. A lengthier, more thoughtful perusal of graffiti and he was inspired—*elevated*.

After cramming another yard or so of toilet tissue beneath him and rubbing, Stenwall sought a writing implement; anything! Adding his own observations to the marvelous compilation was essential; he could do no less!

But since he scarcely ever remembered to send even a Christmas card to his mother and rarely dealt in checks, there was no pen or pencil anywhere on his person. The witty, rude jingle he had dredged from memory and meant to write began to fade.

Eagerly, then, Stenwall leaped up. He struck the flush lever, yanked his trousers up, mentally saw himself reaching into his pocket for a knife.

But the gee-dee toilet was rejecting his shit. Already it rose dangerously near the seat itself, blackly swarming—

And he saw the other wall, the wall *behind* the lavatory cubicle, with a gaze of rapture akin to the expression of the supplicants who had first seen the Sistine Chapel.

Cuh-ryst, Stenwall marveled. From fly-specked ceiling to sticky men's room floor, extending the width of the room, lines of graffiti had been scribbled or carved with such a mood of frolicking, fresh *esprit* that the gaze of the muscular little onlooker was magically gripped. By comparison to the works he had admired while seated, these limericks, gibes, Kilroys and innovative genitalia were Miltonian . . . Byronic . . . Shakespearean. There were also feminine names, phone numbers, addresses!

Awestruck, Stenwall edged closer. Space for more was available, narrowly. But what he chose to add could not be the product of whim or a stale imagination. Stenwall withdrew his pocket knife, opened it, held it poised in his palm with aesthetic tension, leaned nearer—and froze, surprised.

Half the drolleries were dated . . . *decades ago*. He scanned an amusing anecdotal verse concerning a lass named Jill—"she will"—and the date: May 5, 1928.

Magnetized, Stenwall grunted. He had known Big Buns' place went back a long way, but he couldn't have conceived the service station building was—

Stenwall began to sweat again. There was a neatly crafted raillery about a female named Flora—and three digits: 916! The date adjacent to the signatory, "Foot Long Frankie," was 1909. "916" was Flora's *phone number*?

To feverish Stenwall, distantly disturbed by a sense of apprehension and twinges of pain, what he was seeing before him was renewal. A hallowed Wall of Memories. Chuckling at intricate cartoons, reading more messages, he licked his lips and nodded his approval. It was possible all the old broads who'd do it, lick it, eat and sit on it, "69ed" and loved "every manly inch" were rotting in the ground today.

Yet the things their men had said about them lived. In a way, Stenwall thought as his heartbeat accelerated, these slits were fucking *immortalized*!

Suffused with enthusiasm, he chose a suitable portion of the Wall and started to carve in it, remembering the little he'd learned about filigree. Sweaty, he dragged the sharp blade, formed a large, magnificent "F" with a flowering tail and curved curlicue for the cross-bar. Making small sounds, satisfied but self-demanding, Stenwall went to work on an enchanting "U."

—Hesitated, believing he had heard, from the other side of the wall, another similar scraping sound.

Intently listening, brows raised, Stenwall edged back. *It's the fucking heat*, he concluded, retrieving his backward step, raising the knife.

The answering noise of carving began once more but was immediately drowned out by the vastly louder sounds of something massive—ponderous—headed, apparently, toward the door of the men's room.

Spooked, Stenwall whirled, stared in that direction. The room trembled—

And he thought he knew what the rumbling was and dashed frantically to the door, tugged on the knob.

Again, he'd forgotten it opened out. Except, it wouldn't do that now; it wouldn't budge. "Hey," Stenwall called in a small voice. He lowered his shoulder, pushed, did it again with more oomph. Zilch. *"Hey,"* he cried, shoving hard—

The door gave, opened. Fractionally, a crack, a half-inch.

And he knew his hunch was right. He really should have killed Sax Chacker.

The scar-faced pervert had backed his three-quarter truck against the men's room door and parked there. The motor wasn't running.

The fucking jackoff pimp's man had *imprisoned* Stenwall!

"Hey!" he shouted, much louder. "Sax, you scuzzball, get your goddam truck outta the way!" A pause. "Come on." No answer. "Chacker? Dammit, man, move that sonovabitch now—you hear me?"

The white glare in the crack to the outside was late-day sunlight, and all was silence but for the hot, silent scream of desert heat.

"Sax, hey? Yo, Sax?" Staring at the sunny glare was beginning to blind him; his face, reactively livid, was pouring sweat. "Well, I got to hand it to you, man . . . Sexy Saxy, you sure caught *me* by surprise!" The flat, mute strange shriek of sand as far as the eye could see crept up Stenwall's arms, neck, whispered hot and blubbery things in his ear. ". . . Please, Sax? Please, man?"

Outside, way out there, a homebound, holiday semi blasted like the last Tyrannosaurus and, giving up, Stenwall spun away from the front door and angrily threw his pocket knife at the closest object, the wash basin. The clatter on the hard floor was a shock. Instantly, he went after the knife and fell to his knees, snatching it up and finding the blade had snapped in two.

Worse, his trouser knees were stained with the crap he had knelt in.

Stenwall ripped a handful of paper toweling from a wall dispenser, hoisted one knee to the basin's edge, awkwardly, turned on the faucet.

It made a croak-*kukkuk* like an animated frog. Nothing came out of the faucet but rusty-looking puke. He worked the second faucet and not even the lily-pad crowd responded.

He looked toward the sealed rest room door, and the place where a window would be if they'd made one. Stenwall sobbed. Sax had said he was locking up the pumps, that he'd be there awhile—but then he was leaving for the holiday. Tomorrow, the Fourth of July, was a Friday. This was a Thursday, late afternoon.

And neither Big Buns nor the goddam pervert split-face in the cowboy hat planned to return—until Monday.

Stenwall was stuck in a rundown men's on the fucking outskirts of hell and nobody except a bastard he'd beaten up even knew he was there. *Jesusjesus.* Claustrophobia Stenwall hadn't known he possessed fluttered up along with the realization that the Farm—the little girls —might as well have been on the gee-dee Gaza Strip!

—*I could die here*, he sobbed. Three and a half days of heat, no food or water—it was getting real to him—he could *die* in a *men's*!

"Wait," he said it aloud, crouched. There was water . . . there *was*.

He sped back to the lavatory cubicle and stared down, heart thudding.

But the john was crammed with the tissue he had used, and it wasn't just water.

Frantic, he began hitting the flush handle. Over and over.

The toilet coughed dryly, overflowed. Stenwall watched the stained and wadded assortment come up and seep under the seat like a goddam swamp monster. Perspiring, involuntarily crying out, he jumped back before it slopped over his shoes, perceived that he was gagging and started to vomit stress-bile. Or worse. Suddenly the stench was foul in such close quarters and his guts were killing him.

Behind Stenwall, the three-quarter's big motor turned over. Spinning, running, he got to the blessed crack he had created in time to hear the tires clutching at the concrete and to wonder if Sax Chacker was driving off or merely taunting him. *"Please,"* Stenwall begged—

At that instant the truck backed up against the door again, neatly slamming it shut without smashing the frame, and turned the old rest room into a nearly airtight container. Glancing down, wildly, Stenwall saw that he couldn't even have slipped a note asking for help between the crammed-closed door and the truck. Then the three-quarter's engine shut down. Silence.

He knelt beside the basin, arms draped over it, cheek pressed to the sink's relative coolness. Partly, he slept; partly, he passed out.

It must be morning, Stenwall thought, standing almost arthritically and pulling up the wrist with the watch on it. Electricity still burned in the men's; a bleary-eyed glance at his watch told him the truth.

It was just past midnight. Not an hour or a day later.

Stenwall started to cry, turned it into a near rage instead. Dammit, there *had* to be water in there and, if there was, he'd find it. Because he might very well last until Monday without food, but thirst, the putrid reek, and the smothering heat were already making him need to shut-down, pass out; combined with his secret sickness, he felt nauseous, desperately frail.

The urinal, Stenwall thought, blinking at it. Sax hadn't considered *that*—and when he got out of there, come Monday, Stenwall would cut the goddamn pervert's balls off and feed them to him, one at a time!

Enlivened, purposive, Stenwall lurched across the tiny floor and halted, head cocked. If Chacker was still in his truck, if he *heard* Stenwall flushing the pisser, he'd turn the water off. That meant saving water, containing and preserving it.

Stenwall's gaze darted every which way but felt his renewed optimism and killing thirst for violence dissipate fast. There were no paper cups beside the basin, not even a soft drink bottle he'd almost brought inside with him; there was nothing he could employ to hold the urinal water.

Once more, he started to weep. He hurt now, everywhere; the walls were ready to close in, and he was hot inside as well as out.

But the aged prophylactic dispenser—a tube marked FOR PRE-VENTION OF DISEASE ONLY—hung from the wall right next to the pisser! Giggling, then covering his telltale lips with both palms, Stenwall slipped over to the faded machine, thinking: If you stretch condoms the way smartass college boys do, making balloons, *condoms hold water.*

Tremblingly, Stenwall fished in a pocket for change. His lips made little bursting bubbles when he laughed, chortled—read the two-for-fifty cents price information and realized it was like time travel in this goddam room! Not that he'd ever used any of those ribbed, pebbled, brightly colored and scented things because real men didn't fucking worry, real men wanted to feel—

He didn't even have the right change. *Cocksucker!* Stenwall mouthed the word, dropping his change and seeing it roll, fucking vanish, into crevices as ancient as moon craters. The sweat was drip-ping into his eyes now and his nuts felt like somebody was branding them. Through the glass on the dispenser, the packaged condoms were like belly buttons—or sunken, staring child's eyes. "Tell *me* no," Stenwall exclaimed and smashed his fist into the glass.

The packets tumbled out, along with red from his wound. Stenwall couldn't tell how deep it was, but it was near the wrist and it hurt like Christ. Shrieking nonsense, he bolted for the basin before remembering there was no water, froze in panic with his eyes rolling everywhere.

Okay. Clutching one package in his teeth, tearing at it with his uninjured hand, Stenwall ripped the condom out and stretched it the best he could. Then he thrust his whole, dripping hand into it. The rubber filmed over with blood immediately but he seemed to remember blood stopped if air couldn't get to the wound. For a moment, the men's jumped before his eyes like an athlete—

Until the unobtrusive carving noises he'd heard first issued from the other side of the wall.

Dizzy and scared, hurting differently in many places, he allowed his body to slump against the wall, believing his cell was starting to shrink in dimensions but uncertain what terror he should fear the most.

And he knew uncannily that the sun was up, a night had passed, and he was being watched.

His wristwatch, past midnight when he had previously checked the time, said it was nearly nine and also announced that it had stopped. Because he had forgotten to wind it.

Maybe, just maybe, he had passed out for thirty-three hours, not nine.

Stenwall started to stand and the wet floor threw him painfully to one knee where he stayed, licking dry lips, noting that the door was still tightly closed, realizing the morning temperature was making the rest room a torture box.

Awareness of thirst instantly accelerated it beyond all rational, tolerable limits. Letting his tongue loll pathetically from a corner of his mouth, he pawed up a dozen or so packets of condoms, cradled them in his arms, and crawled across the floor to the urinal. Tearing the packets open cost him most of his energy and he peeled off his drenched shirt and worked his trousers down and off, howling faintly at the pressure on his bruised knee. While the pisser had overflowed, he sat, didn't even feel the mess sinking into the seat of his shorts. But undressing had worked the rubber halfway off his wounded hand and it was seeping again, a mixture of blood and puss; and by the time he had formed three condoms into the shape of drooping scrotums and was clambering slipperly to his knees, Stenwall was talking to himself.

"Trash the little girls, did I, they were trash already, born trash." He extended one of the rubbery devices, midway up the length of the urinal, sick from the disinfectant fumes rising to his twitching nostrils. After nothing whatever occurred, he remembered the obligation of mashing the handle down. "I'll trash the bitches, the cunts, like they always tried to trash me, tried to make Brucie feel dirty."

Instead of a Niagara from the urinal, there was a trickle. He licked filthy fingers, let the contraption just fall off his hurt hand into the drain. Fuck it. He hit the flush handle again, wondering how much blood he was losing, coaxed water into the deformed, quivering rubber, muttering to the faint flow.

Yet he did better this time! Real water flowed into the condom, pooked-out the nipple, elicited from Stenwall a childlike relief and shaky yet careful attempt to raise the partly filled prophylactic to his lips.

He dropped it into the repulsive mess, gaping in horror toward the floor in front of the urinal.

A pale-brown insect—a huge roach—had been in his water supply. It had been on top of the porcelain contraption and plummeted straight into the condom while Stenwall was endeavoring to fill it.

He knew that because he saw the roach crawl out of the rubber and begin to sun itself on the anemic, testicular cubes.

"All *their* fault, I shoulda killed the bitches, alla them!" His fists were clenched, raised by the sides of his head. "Shoulda killed alla them!"

Cutting sounds. Carving noises—scrape scrape, jab, *scraaape*—nearer somehow—brought Stenwall's head around so he faced the wall behind the partition of modesty.

Impelled, he started slithering on hands and knees toward the wall, the wall he had so admired, a wall bearing the innumerable and timeless scribblings of other men who had no idea how better to make their mark in the world. Other men who shared a loathing created almost entirely by a near-the-surface certainty of their common inferiority.

It's a rat, said a portion of Stenwall's mind, as he scuttled; it was many rats, gnawing on the other side of the wall. And that message, that notion, seemed immeasurably preferable to a different claim entirely asserted by the functioning bulk of his brain.

When he had crept naked through the reeking overflow at the base of the aged toilet, Stenwall stopped, tried to lift his hand. "I wish I'd killed more of them," he wheezed, hauling himself around the side of the bowl on his knees, getting the hang of it now. Sweat and other things were in his eyes and he couldn't see much, but he had never imagined he had to much to see, anyhow. "I do, I honestly do."

The faint bustling sounds—something new to hear—helped him thrust his head above the level of the commode and his stinging vision made out a long jagged line exactly like the one in Sax Chacker's face, splitting the wonderful Wall of Memories. Blinking, he saw the split widen and reveal interior edges colored a pulpy pink. "What the hell . . . ?"

The jagged line divided the flowery letters he had succeeded in carving, ran between the "F" and the "U."

And the segments of the wall crumbled—disintegrated—chunks of plaster raining on Stenwall, pelting him just the way the tampons were that were being thrown at him like weapons. More hit him, hurting; one took an eye out, or he believed it did, the pain was too general for him to be sure. Brucie looked out for himself by trying to climb inside Stenwall and he cupped it with his hands, further protecting the little guy.

Then the attack ceased, or was momentarily suspended. More plaster broke away from the walls, caught him glancing blows, and Stenwall rocked back on his ass to stare with his more or less good eye at what was apparently trying to kill him.

Dozens, no, *hundreds* of nude women ranging in age from the cradle to the grave were pouring through the rent in the wall. Not a one of them had a face, all were skeletal except for their bosoms and genitalia; a few had hair left on their heads, most did not. Because they could not possibly see him with great sockets where their eyes had been, he knew this was nothing personal, understood immediately that anybody, almost, would have done—so long as he was male. *Do it, do it to him*, he thought some of the trashed women shouted; *sit on his face, all right . . . 69 him*! Grins of ivory sought to turn into enticing, lip-smacking puckers but they had no lips left and the mouths split wide, like the wall. Stenwall shrank back against the modesty partition but the bony arms reached out, hands making the kind of obscene gesture he'd always found expressive, more clawing with fingers like the white keys of an old piano. *They* went after him in waves, slopped avidly over him, attempted to mount him any horrible way they were able. The flesh they had left, all that had ever been coveted, slapped against every portion of his terrified body while dozens of furry patches pressed to him, jostling to reach his mouth or penis.

And when he felt he must certainly smother, they stopped.

He opened his eyes to the echo of his own screams and squinted around. The men's room remained barricaded and there was still time to go, days of disease, isolation, and dying for need of water. He found the naked dead women were still there, mostly, pulled back from him, slowly seeping into the split in the wall—some already gone and more going all the time. Those who remained had lowered their arms of bone and their postures were rueful. The one counter-attack they had mustered at last was abandoned because of what each woman essentially was and would always primarily prefer to be: Unlike him.

Before they left Stenwall—none forgiving him but incapable even collectively and dead of the violence that was not of their sex—clearly understanding once more that they alone possessed pity and might generate it—the immortal women shed tears upon their shining, their fleshless cheeks.

And Stenwall knew finally that even one drop of that priceless fluid could have saved him from joining them. Soon. But they had never touched him that way. Not even once.

Perhaps it would happen behind the perpetual Wall of Memories. When all of them were one.

Clearance to Land

Adam-Troy Castro

Sometimes people chastise me for refusing to have a first reader to read manuscripts by unknown writers. But if I had a first reader, I'd worry that stories like "Clearance to Land" would slip by me. The unusual paragraph structure and writing style, and the fact that Adam-Troy Castro had yet to make his first sale would have led many first readers to pass over the story altogether.

Since this story appeared, Adam has sold several more stories to *Dragon Magazine*, *Pulphouse: The Hardback Magazine*, and *Pulphouse: A Weekly Magazine*.

"Clearance to Land" was Adam's first published short story. Of the many first stories we published, this was, I think, the most impressive debut.

Y ou are forty-seven years old

and you have back trouble, and you do not bend easily, and the edge of your belt buckle jabs at your belly like a dull blade

and you are desperately tired, but too scared of death to sleep and your feet, which are the only things you've been allowed to look at for hours now, are tingling so madly from lack of circulation that you ache for permission to stamp them

but the bearded man is a cruel bastard, and has more than once punished frivolous requests with violent beatings

and so you grimace, and you press your head further than you thought possible into the empty space between your knees, and you look at your shoes, which are resting on carpeting sticky from dried blood, and you listen hopelessly for the sound of another murder

but at the moment, nobody is dying loud enough for you to hear them. The engines continue the droning hum audible from every seat in the plane; your daughter coughs under her breath every two or three minutes, to clear that congenitally dry throat of hers; paper rustles, from God knows where, somewhere behind you; somebody three or four aisles away whispers a couple of words to his neighbor, and manages to get away with it, this time; and the blood roars in your ears, like a trapped beast

but nobody's dying. Nobody's being shot in the chest. Nobody's being stabbed in the throat. Nobody's being bludgeoned to death with the butt of a semi-automatic rifle. Nobody's being murdered. And the reason for that is simple: nobody's moving. They're doing what you're doing: sitting on the edge of their seats, with their heads between their knees, and their hands clasped together behind their heads. They're ignoring the pain in their backs and the dizziness from lack of movement and the stench rising from their unwashed bodies, and they're going mad with fear

as they've been doing ever since you left American airspace, when the bearded man stood up in his seat; when you somehow knew, even before his bald partner came running down the aisle, everything he was going to say

and it didn't seem fair to you, then, because this was happening to you already. That was why you were on this damn plane. You were on this plane because your daughter was on this plane, and your daughter was on this plane because two days earlier your son-in-law, in Paris on a business trip, was blown to shreds by a firebomb that went off in a fast food restaurant, and she needed to pick up what was left of the body. The very idea that this could happen in your life two times in one week had seemed insane to you at the time

and ever since then you've wondered just how many of the surviving passengers still regard this as a mere hijacking. At least a tenth, you suppose. Maybe. People are that way. Faced with something impossible, something that becomes more and more impossible with every passing second, they focus on the concrete threat: the bald man and his sadistic bearded partner. They take what the bald man said for granted. This is a hijacking. Right. Cooperate and you won't be hurt. Sure. We want to exchange you for political prisoners. Uh huh. We believe you. We've all seen this kind of thing happening on the news; we may have never believed it would happen to us, but we know it happens to somebody, somewhere, and it might as well be us. This sort of thing is easy to believe in. Easier than the rest of it, anyway. The rest of it is downright impossible. And you ache to know just how many of your fellow passengers have managed to deny

what your daughter's known for a long time. Her eyes are black dots on a doughy white face, and the perspiration seems to be rolling off her body in waves and you're pretty sure that the impossibility of your situation has driven her insane. You'd know for sure, one way or another, if you could only get a substantial look at her, but it's been hours since you've been able to get her to meet your eyes. The last time was—when? this morning?—when the bald man ordered all the window shades lowered. As one of the passengers unfortunate enough to be sitting next to a window, you were permitted to raise your head for all of a second and a half; and you took advantage of that trivial second and a half of freedom to look at your daughter. She was looking past you, at the window sliding shut behind you. Her face was red from the light shining through the glass, then white from the normal electric light of the cabin, then shadowed as the bald man screamed that it was time for everybody to bend over again. Her eyes met yours then, for just a fraction of a second, and there was damned little sanity left in them. There must be less left there now. And you know how she feels. You're so far gone that it's been easily two, maybe three hours since you remembered that the bag of dry blood slumped in the seat between you and your daughter was once your wife

and though you know you should feel grief, or shock, or something like that, you feel nothing. You've always feared having to watch something horrible happen to somebody you loved, and you've always loved your wife, more or less. The affection the two of you felt for each other was never the passionate, all-consuming thing they write about in romances (it was never more than a mildly pleasant affection, at most) but still, you know you should have felt more than a thump of sympathetic pain when the bearded man blew her brains out the back of her head. Of course, by then, you had already realized that something impossible was happening

by then the skies had already begun to take on an improbable reddish hue; by then everything in the cabin was already the color of blood; by then the number to total executions had already left double digits; and by then you'd decided, like just about everybody on the plane, that nobody was going to get out of this alive anyway

but you should still feel more. You should feel hatred. You should want to blind the bastards with your thumbs, and castrate them with your fingernails. You shouldn't be sitting here, head between your knees, obediently staring at the tops of your shoes, for hours on end, feeling only your backache and the tingling of your feet

and it stopped being merely ". . . hours on end . . ." almost two weeks ago, didn't it? It sure did. It's been days on end, now. You know this because ever since the beginning, even since the bald one whimsically ordered everybody into crash positions, your wristwatch has been in clear view. It's an analog watch, of course; you learned how to read a clock at six years of age and you've always considered digitals a form of cheating. It was just about midnight, on a Friday, when the hijacking began; by the time the hour hand was pointing straight up again, twelve hours later, two stewardesses were dead and your greatest concern was that the plane would run out of fuel before the hijackers found a country that would give them permission to land. Your wife was still alive, then, though gripping your hand so tightly that her fingernails drew blood; your daughter was still managing to throw you an occasional brave smile, though they were as transparent as tissue paper; and you still believed that this was just a hijacking, albeit an extraordinarily brutal one, and one you stood scant chance of walking away from. By the time the hour hand rotated all the way back to twelve, seven more people, including three children from one family, were rotting in their seats; the view outside the window was disconcertingly pink; your daughter was asleep; your wife was sobbing quietly; and the only thought in your mind was *dammit, where's all the fuel coming from*? Then the hour hand made another full rotation, and

it was twelve hours later, and the plane still hadn't landed any-where to refuel, and it was still flying, and the sky was the color of blood, and nobody had had anything to eat, and nobody had had anything to drink, and nobody had been to the bathroom, and nobody had needed to do any of these things, and you saw in your wife's eyes, and in your daughter's eyes, and in the eyes of the other passengers, that they knew this was beyond possibility, that they wanted someone else to tell them that they were merely insane. And the bearded man, who never seemed to sit down, marched down the aisle, and shot a college student dead just to prove he was still capable of doing it, and the passengers looked at their own feet again. The hour hand made another full rotation

and a woman in the next section up went crazy. She just stood up in her seat—ignoring her husband, who frantically grabbed at her—and started screaming that this was going on forever, that this was never going to end, that somebody had to do something, that somebody had to make it stop. Her head was in fragments before she said the word stop. And the hour hand made another full rotation. And another full rotation after that. And an eighth. And an eleventh. And a seventeenth. And a twenty first, and

there's no reason to dwell on all of that, when all of that is clearly impossible, since the bearded man is walking up your aisle again. You don't see him, of course; you're still obediently looking at your feet. But you can hear him coming, and you don't need to see him to know he's pointing the machine gun at every head he passes. He's frowning. He's running his black tongue over the surface of his black little lips. His lips are the color and consistency of a dog's. His pores are big and wet. His beard is moist. He's blinking. He's restless. He's bored. His footsteps are getting closer. He's stopping. And

suddenly you know he's looking at you. Or your daughter. And you close your eyes tighter than they've ever been closed in your entire life, so tight it hurts, and you feel the part of you that still cares pray *let it be me, not my daughter*. And eons pass. And you feel him lean over you, and you feel something cold and metallic press hard against your temple, and the part of you that still cares turns selfish and evil and thinks, *no, I was wrong, let it be anybody else*, and

the bearded man says, "Come with me,"

and there's an immediate stir among the other passengers, because up until now the bearded man hasn't been interested in anything other than killing people. Something else is going to happen now. It's unquestionably something worse—everybody knows the bearded man well enough by now to know that it can't be something better—but at least it's something else. And it's happening to you, first. And

you're so stunned not only to be alive, but to be the one person, out of the few dozens remaining alive, to be chosen to break the pattern, that for a moment you don't move. You don't even look up. You just remain frozen, waiting for the other shoe to drop. For him to change his mind and pull the trigger. But when he says, "Come with me" a second time, with the deadly impatience of a man to whom other people are easily disposable commodities, you jerk upright at once, eager to show him just how willing you are to obey. Too quickly. The blood drains from your head. Your knees buckle. The world goes gray. You almost collapse. You force yourself to look into his eyes

and even with the few pitiful glances you've been able to manage now and then, when he wasn't looking directly at you, you've been able to tell that there was something seriously wrong with his eyes, but now you see what it is. They're not eyes. They're what eyes look like, on photographic negatives: white irises surrounded by football-shaped fields of black. The pupils are so bright that by the time you blink, a purple afterimage has been left on your retina. You gasp. You think *there's fire in there*

and then his hand shoots forward and grabs you by the collar and pulls you toward him. He pulls you past the corpse that was once your wife and the cringing wreck that was once your daughter; and when along the way a cold hand closes on yours, there's one truly terrible moment when you think the hand belongs to your wife

but no, it's your daughter; there's life in her yet; she doesn't want him to take you, and she's trying, however feebly, to hold you back. You wish her the strength to manage it, as if strength alone would do any good. But you're yanked from her grip so easily the bearded man doesn't even notice she tried to interfere

and he places you on your feet in the center of the aisle. And he says, "Walk." And for the first time in almost thirteen days you walk. You're out of practice. Your feet don't approach the ground at the right angle. They hit glancingly, on the edges. You stumble. You limp. You have to keep an eye on them to make sure they're doing what you want them to be doing. And even so they try to trick you; once or twice you find yourself veering to the left or right. But you walk on, because the bearded man is following you. You can't hear him, because right now you can't hear anything except the bass drum in your chest; but you can feel him, because the ache in the center of your back feels exactly like a wound, and the hollow at the base of your spine is filling up with puddled sweat that feels exactly like blood

and you can see him, because some of the surviving passengers are stealing glimpses at you as you pass them. Most of those seem to hate you. They quickly meet your eyes, hostility burning in their otherwise hopeless faces, and then they look at the their feet, before the bearded man sees the expression directed at him. Others seem to be pleading for you to do something, though what they expect you to do is a mystery. And then there are the dead, some of whom have complete faces; they glare at you with contempt, murmuring, "Too

Late, Too Late, Too Late." You offer no responses to any of them. You can't. Just walking, without collapsing in a heap and thus surrendering yourself to the inevitable bullet in the back, is as much as you can manage. And so you walk forward—

past the stewardesses who lie sprawled in the galleys, the children who sit sobbing next to dead parents, the blood-splattered old woman who could be either alive or dead, but whose expression, of nearly infinite shock and grief, makes either possibility equally horrible

—and as you walk, it gradually becomes clear to you that you're walking uphill. That the nose of the plane is elevated. That you feel unnaturally light. That the steady drone of rushing wind is growing louder. That, after twelve and a half days, the plane has at last reached final approach

(to what?)

and as you pass the spiral staircase leading up to First Class, the bearded man taps you on the shoulder and says, "Up." What can you do? You climb up. The weakness in your legs, combined with the clumsiness of fear and the slight but definitely perceptible tilt of the stairway, turns the fourteen steps into an impossibly difficult climb. When you stop to squeeze the handrail, as if to confirm that it's still there, the barrel of the bearded man's rifle bumps against the back of your knees, and again he says, "Up." You take a step up. And then another one. And then another one after that. And your head emerges into First Class. The faces of the First Class passengers swivel as one to greet you

shocking both you and them. You're pale and terrified and splattered with blood and brains; they're pale and terrified but clean and, without even a single exception, alive and well. They gasp when they see you; this is the first time they've seen somebody from down below, and they now know, in a small way, what all the shots were about. You try to tell them everything with a look

help, you say with your eyes, they're killing everybody, there's no end to it, please do something, he can't kill everybody if we all just rush him at once but once again the rifle barrel prods you at the base of the spine, and once again the bearded man says "Up," and you proceed upward

into the cockpit

which is so dimly lit that, at first, you mistakenly interpret what you see as thick electrical cables, pulled from the machinery for some reason and crisscrossed about the room like streamers. Each is the width of a child's arm, and each is anchored to one of the seats where the members of the flight crew sit. Their shadows cavort on the curved ceiling. You look down, searching for the light source, which seems to be coming from someplace near the floor, and you find it immediately: a single red candle, standing in a puddle of melted wax. The plane shakes. You look up. The cables are swinging back and forth like jump rope. One of them swings close to your face, and you catch a whiff of something you've smelt before

—most notably a few months ago, when one of the sewer lines in your office building broke open and spilled several gallons of human excrement all over the men's room. The stink hadn't been quite this bad, back then—

and even back then, it had been more than you were able to stand. This time the stench hits you like a physical blow. You gag, and close your eyes, and try to double over. In another second you'll vomit. The bearded man grabs you by the back of the collar and pulls you upright. You try to say, "Please." He won't let you do that either. He pushes you into the room. You duck one of the swinging cables, skid on a slippery spot, and take a step forward. There's not much to see here; the indicator lights on the instruments are all off, rendering the entire console invisible, and the windshield itself is hidden by an expanse of black cloth that covers it like curtains. The flight crew is

dead, of course. There are four of them. Three lie sprawled in their chairs, arms swinging bonelessly at their sides. Their faces, dangling backwards over the tops of their chairs, stare at you upside down with the cold contemptuous indifference of the dead, candlelight dancing in their glazed eyes. In death, they seem to recognize you, in a way you've never been able to recognize yourself, and they seem to be taking a vague pleasure in refusing to tell you about it. You swallow. The fourth sits in the captain's seat, with his hands on the controls; and the second you decide that this one is not dead after all

he turns to greet you. It's the bald man. He smiles at you, with glistening teeth. "Hello," he says, and waits for a reply. And just as you realize that the thick ropy things draped about the cabin are not electrical cables

(you have to press your hand against the control console to keep yourself from collapsing in shock; it's metallic, but it's warm, and it presents for you the only remaining solid surface in the entire universe)

the bald man, oblivious, says, "We're about to land, and we've chosen you to help us with the exchange." Just like that. In this room, his words are like distant babble, in no language known to man. You force yourself to focus on tone instead of meaning, the bland face instead of the atrocity it's committed, and, just barely, manage to choke a reply: what exchange? "The prisoner exchange," he says, as if that's obvious. The phrase means nothing to you. He sees your confusion and elaborates: "The authorities have finally agreed to our demands." What authorities? What demands? You feel yourself trying to faint, but there's no place to sit: all the chairs are occupied by eviscerated corpses. You wonder if they know what's happened to them. You wonder what it's like to be treated like an envelope made out of skin, to be opened up like a letter and have your contents removed and displayed around the room like wall decorations. You wonder if he brought you here to do the same thing to you. The bald man frowns impatiently. "We're not terrorists," he says, seeming to need your agreement. "We're freedom fighters. We're fighting a fight that needs to be fought." You nod dully, eager to please him, eager to show him just how anxious you are to cooperate. Disappointed but apparently not angry, he dismisses you with a wave of his hand, and turns his attention back to the controls. The bearded man behind you claps you on the shoulder and says, "Down,"

to the First Class section, where he places you in an empty seat opposite a pretty young woman in a starched white suit. Her face is tightly locked in the kind of expression fussy hostesses wear when an oafish guest uses the wrong fork by mistake. And it seems to be directed at you

which takes you a moment to understand. Unlike you, she's been safely, if only slightly, insulated, from the bloodshed of the lower decks. And she's been able to place it at the correct emotional distance. Like all these others. You glance at the others—

the priest, the old woman with the bright red lipstick, the cherubic fat man who requires two seats, and the rest

—and though they don't look at you, because they don't want to be caught staring, you can see the same revulsion toying at the corners of their mouths as well. You wonder what it's been like for them, these past two weeks. Oh, they were probably terrified enough, at least at first

but soon enough they noticed that none of their own were being killed, and they decided that the slaughter taking place elsewhere, though a real shame, had nothing to do with them personally. They took comfort in that. They've grown bored. Until you, their first reminder that the massacre has a human face, had the colossal bad taste to intrude upon their antiseptic refuge. Part of you can understand how they feel: two weeks ago, confronted with a figure that reeked of death as powerfully as you do now, you would have shrunken away yourself. You would have done anything to escape him. But the rest of you feels a sudden overwhelming hate for these privileged ones. How dare they sit up here, snug and secure in their luxurious carpeted womb, and pass judgment on you? How dare they look disgustedly at you, when their families are whole and alive and no blood stains their expensive clothes? And how dare they look pretty and clean as they daintily avert their eyes from the gore that's been drowning you? You open your mouth to scream at them, but you don't get the chance, because

all around you

from outside the plane

a sound like a hundred babies being mauled by iron knives. Like a thousand cats being plunged into boiling water. Like a million men having their lower jaws ripped from their faces. Like a billion drill bits being activated inside a billion skulls. Like

nothing you've ever heard, to tell the truth, but it's a sound you recognize immediately, because it's a sound you've known since your conception, even if until now you haven't allowed yourself to know that you knew it. It's

the sound that's been going on forever, in the place you've just landed

the sound of the place that up until thirteen days ago was your greatest fear in the whole world; the place they told you you might end up, the place they preached about in Sunday School

and you can't fly a hijacked plane to the afterlife, but somehow the bald man has managed it

"to free political prisoners," the bald man had said

and as the dilettantes of First Class recognize the sound too, the knowledge hits them with the force of a sledgehammer, and they sink deep into their seats, as if each and every one of them was suddenly three or four times heavier. They're shattered, all of them. You feel your own guts turn to liquid, but you've spent the past couple of weeks hearing a pale imitation of that sound, in the form of senseless slaughter, and you're able to manage a small and inadequate reaction. You start to stand. You start to say something. You have no idea what you're about to do or about to say

and you don't have the chance to find out, because the bearded man is back. He pulls you into the aisle for the second time in ten minutes, looks you over to make sure you still possess at least a small percentage of your innate faculties, and says, "We've landed." And around you, the screaming starts affecting the bearded man not at all. He looks around idly, his face passing over the elegant old woman, the priest, the fat man, the middle-aged marrieds, the couple with the baby

and apparently deciding to do the easiest one first, places his cold dark hand on the shoulder of the pretty young woman you'd just decided to despise, and says, "Help her downstairs,"

and you comply, because there's a machine gun at your back, and nothing can make a human being march another human being into hell better than a machine gun at his back. You place a hand under her elbow and gently pull her to her feet. She doesn't possess the strength to stand. She collapses against you, clutching at the lapels of your jacket, sobbing that there must have been a mistake, that they must have mistaken her for someone else, that she'd never done any- thing to deserve this. "Hurry her up," says the bearded man. "We've got a lot of comrades to free." You pull her into the aisle. She screams louder, but doesn't resist; she just walks with you, helplessly, as if her feet are not her own, as if what she does with them is no longer any of her business. She lets you escort her to the stairway. She lets you make her start descending the stairs. She doesn't try to escape when her position two stairs lower than yourself makes it impossible for you to maintain a strong grip. She doesn't shudder when the bearded man steps onto the stairway after you. She just screams, continuously; and

halfway down the stairs you almost join her. The front hatch, the one which had been connected to the tunnel which had been connected to the terminal which had been connected to the real world, is open. And beyond it churns a sea of molten rock, a sea that crashes and boils and flares as violently as the surface of the sun, and a sea where the loudest sound is the wailing of unseen millions of people. The heat from the open door raises blisters on your skin. You can't force yourself to get any closer than the bottom of the stairway. But the bearded man shoves you and your terrified charge aside, walks right up to the door without any apparent discomfort, sticks his head out, and producing a megaphone from somewhere, shouts: "First prisoner!" And, grabbing the shrieking young woman by the arm hurls her out the hatch like a doll. Somehow, she manages to turn around in mid-plunge to face you

and her expression, all eyes and all mouth, doesn't possess even a shred of hope in it. It's the face of someone who no longer needs hope, or sanity. It's the face of someone unjustly damned. Even as she turns, her clothes have turned to ash and dropped away; her hair is beginning to smolder; her skin is beginning to dance with flame. The ground beneath her is already starting to reach upward, in the shape of a clawed six-fingered hand, to claim her. You catch a glimpse of fire beginning to catch on her tongue

before the fingers close

and you become aware that there's a body at your feet: a body that wasn't there a second ago—the body of a naked man a shade above five feet tall. Horribly blackened and burned, still smoking from the fires that have just released him, and twitching uncontrollably, the only part of him recognizably human is his face, which the flames have left untouched. He looks like nobody special—olive-skinned, brown-eyed, with a big nose and a fine lattice of what to you seems to be acne scars, he could be anybody. You glance up at the bearded man, who flashes the kind of rictus grin that only appears on the faces of electrocuted prisoners, and says the burned man's name. The burned man weeps in response

and as the bearded man disappears up the circular stairway, you can do nothing but listen to the screams. Not the ones from upstairs, of course, or even the ones now coming from the aft sections—

they're still audible, the way a flute is still audible in the middle of a symphony

—but the screams outside the plane. They're screams of a different color entirely. Screams that have attained an awful power that you've never heard in screams before. Screams that make the screams of your fellow passengers sound like weak moans. And though there are millions of them, they don't blend together; somehow, each and every individual voice among that vast chorus remains wholly audible by itself. Each scream retains its own character, and each scream is totally discordant with all the rest. The woman from First Class is still there, of course, and her scream is awful because it's the scream of a new arrival, who is still beginning to understand that this is all she has to look forward to, forever; but surrounding her on all sides are the screams of people who have been here so long that they can't remember anything else, and their screams are immeasurably worse. In between are screams that still contain words. Most are in languages you don't recognize. Others are voices you have a sick feeling you recognize. They're people you used to know, years ago; most of them are people you didn't like, but you didn't hate them, you didn't want to torture them, you didn't want to see them dance in a furnace for your amusement. You want to apologize to them for not joining them in their agony. And you want to do something—anything at all, the specifics don't matter—for them, but

instead you sit where you are and do nothing as the bearded man marches another helpless hostage to the hatchway. This one's the fat priest. Unlike the young woman, he's struggling. He's kicking and biting and, dammit, he's drawing blood. The bearded man is bleeding from the nose. The bearded man is missing a bite-sized gob of flesh from his right arm. The bearded man is having trouble controlling him. But he's still the stronger of the two: inch by inch, millimeter by millimeter, the priest is still being backed up toward the door. He jabs the bearded man in the belly. The bearded man grunts and shoves him onward. The priest's eyes dart toward you. You feel the impulse to move

but your legs remain frozen. The priest is back up against the hatch now. His leg dangles over the inferno; smoke begins to rise from his black pants leg. You can't look away, but you can't move either. And then fingers as brittle as autumn leaves circle your wrist

and pull you down

against your will

to face the eyes of the burnt man. They're surprisingly bright, and filled with both infinite anger and infinite will to enforce it. He despises you. He hates the rawness of your flesh and the naiveté in your soul, and if his arms weren't charcoaled sticks fresh from the campfire he'd gladly peel the features from your stupid face, but

there's fear there, too, coupled with such desperation that for a moment you forget the machine guns and the blood and the millions of screams and move closer to the burnt man of your own accord, to hear what he has to say

and he opens his lips and he coughs out a cloud of glowing embers

and, with breath the odor of burnt meat, he begs you to stop it

he tells you that nobody deserves to be tortured forever; that nobody deserves to be held in the grip of infinite power and infinite sadism; that he can't stand to see anybody thrown into the fire; and he says all this in a language you don't recognize, but even so you understand every word

but even as he begs you again to please, please, do something to stop it the chorus of screamers outside the plane increases by one, and there's another burnt man at your feet. This one materializes face down, though you're unable to tell that at first, because he's so swollen from the heat that one side of him looks the same as the other. But then he turns over, without any help from you, leaving a greasy stain on the carpet where his skin had been touching it

and he peers into your face with dark black eyes set deep on an ugly little face

and he shouts at you impatiently

and you recognize him at once

and you make an incoherent noise, and back away, until the cold metal of one of the seats cuts into your back, and you collapse at its side, helpless to do anything but watch him no tears for this one. No remorse. None at all. He's not even surprised to be rescued. If anything, he's annoyed that it's taken so long. He's anxious to start over where he left off. And he wants to know what's holding up the return trip. And he shouts all of this at the top of his lungs, the same way he did in all those scratchy old recordings, and his delivery hasn't lost any of its power or charisma for its time spent in the flames. Unlike the first burnt man, he's not a shell of what he was; if anything, he's even more than he was. He just needed to be cooked a little more, that's all; he was a shade underdone before, that's all

and he sees these thoughts on your face, and he extends one blackened and oozing hand as far as it will go and starts pulling himself toward you, leaving a trail of soot on the carpet behind him, and there's clear purpose in his face, and you don't know what's so special about you personally that this murderer of millions has to take care of you himself, but by now you want to die, so it doesn't matter

and the bearded man comes down the stairs again, this time cradling the baby

using both arms, and cooing at it; the machine gun is strapped to the belt at his side. He takes a couple of steps toward the hatchway, winding up for a toss. This is going to be a great throw. The baby is going to sail forty feet before starting to fall

and then the bearded man stops. He looks at the carpeted floor. He follows the trail of soot. He does a double-take when he sees what the new arrival is doing. It's a very theatrical double-take. Its straight out of the movies. He looks impressed. He looks at you, expecting you to share the joke. You can't; you're too busy cringing

so he dismisses you and takes a step toward the hatch

and then he stops

and he adds his own voice to the chorus of screams

because the first burnt man, the one you'd first mistaken for an Arab, has shot across the floor like a snake and, with one convulsive squeeze of his clawlike hand

closed around the bearded man's ankle like a vise

and the skin breaks, the bone turns to powder, the calf above the break starts to bulge from dammed blood

and still the burnt man squeezes, until his hand becomes a closed first, and the foot below the bearded man's ankle simply

separates

and as the bearded man shrieks and falls, he drops the baby and clutches at the machine gun latched to his belt, but he can't move anywhere near fast enough—

the burnt man is already on top of him, seizing it and throwing it, so it lands almost exactly halfway between you and the mass murderer crawling toward you

—and the bearded man is begging now, because the burnt man is pushing him across the floor, toward the hatchway, where the flames are jumping, and the heat is building, and the voices of suffering millions have suddenly become almost musical, almost joyful

and the mass murderer stalking you grabs the machine gun by the barrel, his brittle blackened hands making shiny marks on the metal

and the bearded man is dangling from the hatchway now, holding on with his arms, and you can't see much of him, because most of him is hanging over the fire, but you can see that his hair is beginning to smoke and there are pinpoints of flame beginning to build on the surface of his eyes, and the burnt man is peeling away his grip, finger by trembling finger and you realize that somehow your finger has encircled the trigger

and as the red glow streaming in through the open hatchway momentarily becomes much, much brighter, the chorus of screams outside the plane becomes louder by one

and you squeeze the trigger, and the chorus of screams outside becomes louder by yet one more

and you meet the burnt man's eyes

and again, without saying a single word in any language you understand, he tells you about climbing a mountain when he was little, with friends; considering it a game; and it was a tall mountain and he was smaller than the others and he got to the top exhausted and the rest were too impatient and they climbed down without waiting for him and he had to climb down by himself at night when it got cold and he grew up thinking that there was no such thing as loyalty and that friendship was a game for fools and he kept on thinking it until long after the day he died, and he tells you he doesn't offer any of this as an excuse but as an explanation for the crime that sent him to this awful place

and he tells you all of this in an instant

and without thinking you're halfway up the stairs, cradling the machine gun like a baby

and you climb right past First Class to cockpit level, where the bald man is waiting for you, and he tries to kill you as you enter, but he's just candy, and leaping over his body you all but pounce on the microphone hanging from the console and you raise it to your lips and you open your mouth and scream, "Flight Twenty to Tower! Flight Twenty to Tower!"

and through the speakers a Voice older than Earth and colder than ice says, "This is the Tower," and your knees turn cold and you have to force upon yourself the strength to talk, because that Voice is the worst you've had to contend with yet; you know Whose voice that is without having to ask; and somehow you manage to shout, "This is Flight Twenty! The Hijacking is Over! Repeat the Hijacking is Over! Request Immediate Clearance to Return to Scheduled Flight Path!"

and the next second and a half is the longest second and half of your life; then the speakers crackle again and the same Voice says, "You may change course as soon as Our prisoner is returned to Us,"

and you say, "We don't have any pilots,"

and the empty eviscerated corpses of the pilots place their cold dead hands on the controls, waiting for further instructions, and their eyes are cold, and alive, and in pain

and the Voice says, "You may change course as soon as Our prisoner is returned to Us,"

and it's clear there will be no negotiation on this issue

so it's down the stairs again, where the burnt man is standing, with difficulty, at the edge of the furnace. And he is cradling the baby, which looks like it's giving some serious thought toward halting its headlong scream some time soon. And he is crying too. And he looks at the hatchway, and then at you, and then at the hatchway. And you wait for him to make whatever prayers a man already damned may want to make. And then he gives you the baby, leaving hand-shaped soot marks on in its belly, and he turns toward the hatchway, and he stands on the edge of the furnace, and the hot wind lashes at his face, and he turns his back to the fire, and he looks at you, wearing the infinitely sad expression of a man who's atoned for everything way too late

and then he's gone

and you close the hatch

and the baby sobs softly on your shoulder, and the sounds of screams disappear, everywhere outside the plane and you sit down right where you are, in the aisle, on the carpet

and you bow your head in the first prayer you've uttered in years

mourning your wife, and your fellow passengers, and the repentant soul of Judas Iscariot.

Creationism: An Illustrated Lecture in Two Parts

Jane Yolen

When Jane Yolen wrote this prose poem, the news about Salman Rushdie had just broken. Rushdie's *Satanic Verses* had so offended the Islamic world that the Ayatollah had placed a price on his head. Jane's intent with "Creationism: An Illustrated Lecture in Two Parts" was to offend every religion she could think of. What better place to publish the poem than in *Pulphouse*?

Jane has written more than 100 books, many of them for young adults. She edits a young adult novel line for Harcourt Brace Jovanovich. Her short fiction has appeared all over the science fiction field, and she has won awards ranging from the Golden Kite to the World Fantasy, with lots more nominations in between.

In the beginning
>(*click*)

>>God created the heavens and the earth.
The earth was without form.

>>>(*click*)

>>>which is not to say entirely formless, but rather still lumpy and without fixed landmarks. And void, or empty, or unpopulated.

>>>(*click*)

Darkness was over the face of the deep and under it as well. And as the spirit of God hovered over the face of the dark deep, rather like a hovercraft, only without any actual flow systems, the voice of God said "Let there be Light."

(*click*)

Which we take to mean the sun appeared in the sky, though appear may be rather too sudden a word for what obviously. . . .

(*click*)

And there was light and it was good.

Then God divided the light from the darkness, a rather neat trick, and called the Light Day and the darkness He called Night.

(*click*)

and there was evening and morning, the first day.

Then God checked his list and said, "Let there be a firmament in the midst of the waters, a kind of metaphysical dike, dividing them." And He called the firmament Heaven. Or Lower Atmosphere. There are two schools of thought on this.

(*click*)
(*click*)

And there was evening and there was morning, the second day.

And God said, "Let the waters under the Heaven be gathered together in one place and let dry land appear, which are easy to map."

(*click*)

And which appear in any child's telescope. And He called the dry land Earth and the gathered waters Seas or Oceans or Mares, there are three schools of thought on this.

(*click*)
(*click*)
(*click*)

And He bade the Earth put forth grasses and seeds and trees bearing fruit and mushroom and fungi and trailing vines. And God saw that it was good.

(*clickclickclickclickclickclick*)

And there was evening and morning and that was the third day.

On the fourth day God put a multitude of lights in the Heaven further dividing day and night and southern hemisphere from northern. And He distinguished the seasons, making one half Earth freeze and one half Earth bake, an interesting approach to world building.

(click)

Which led, as we shall see, to an odd prolificity of life, the hemispheres each with their own distinguishable creatures. And it was evening and morning, the fourth day.

Then God said, "Let the waters swarm with swarms of living creatures.

(click)

And let birds fly in the Heavens."

(click)

And He created great monsters of the sea which could not live on land and great monsters of the land which could not live in the seas, a great wasting of monsters, whose bones litter both land and sea.

(click)

(click)

Then God saw that it was good, and told the creatures to be fruitful and multiply

(click)

though He forgot to tell them how to stop multiplying, a rather more useful skill one would think. And there was evening and there was morning, the fifth day.

Then God said, "Let Earth bear living creatures, wild animals of every kind," by which He meant creatures other than the great monsters, who were already overbreeding on the shores and polluting the seas with their monster bones.

(click)

So He brought forth cattle and serpents and herds of horses

(click)

(click)

(click)

and wombats, snail darters, and the chicken-eating frog.

(clickclickclick)

And God saw—though we may wonder why—that it was good.

(*click*)

And then God said, "Fuck it. I'm not going to make man in my image. I have total recall, both forward and back. I know what a mess he will make of my Earth. And just when I've gotten all my firmaments and Mares and snail darters and lights just right." And He squeezed His fingers together

(*click*)

which made mush of the piece of clay he had been molding,

(*click*)

and threw it down in the middle of the central continent where it formed an odd ridge of mountains

(*click*)

which we today call *God's Pile*.

(*click*)

And He made our lovely planet instead, ninth away from the sun.

(*click*)

Lights, please.

Now, before I deal with the second part of my lecture, the scientific approach to creation, are there any questions?

—to Salman Rushdie

She's a Young Thing and Cannot Leave Her Mother

Harlan Ellison

In the late 1960s, Harlan edited *Dangerous Visions* and *Again, Dangerous Visions*, works that broke a number of taboos in science fiction and fantasy. Without those ground-breaking books, *Pulphouse* could not exist. So it was only natural that we ask Harlan (who is deservedly one of the best-known short story writers in the English language) to contribute a story to us.

Fortunately for us, Harlan became and has remained one of our strongest supporters. He wrote "She's a Young Thing and Cannot Leave Her Mother" for our first issue, had a teleplay in our third issue, and is working on a three-volume set of short stories that we will publish as a special collection.

This morning I woke to the infinitely sweet, yet lonely sound of *Clair de Lune* coming to me through closed windows, upstairs in a high-ceilinged suite of this century-old hotel; in a land that is not my own. I lay in bed and at first thought I was still in the dream: it was so ethereal and melancholy. Then I heard Camilla stir, where she lay wrapped in blankets on the floor, and I knew the dream was past. The bed had been too soft for her, an old fluffy mattress with a gully down the middle. She had chosen to sleep beyond the foot of the bed.

I lay there and listened to the music, trying to snare just a wisp, even a scintilla, of the dream. It was the memory of something I was certain I'd lost among the ruins of the years that lay strewn behind me. Years in which Camilla and I had fled from place to place, neither citizens of a certain land nor citizens of the world: simply refugees whose most prominent baggage was fear. Years that bore our footprints on their every hour. Years like a pale golden desert stretching back and back, on the side of me that has no eyes; a desert in which lay items from my life's rucksack; items that I had jettisoned so I could continue walking. Because there was no possibility of ending the flight.

I had untied those items and dropped them to lighten my load, because the flight had grown ever more arduous: the walking through years . . . the caretakership of the woman I loved.

Like a wanderer without water, or a soldier separated from his companions, I moved forward with her minute by minute, discarding casual acquaintances and toys I had outgrown; names and faces of people with whom we had briefly traveled; the taste of candy no longer manufactured and songs no longer sung; books I had read simply because they had been at hand when there was time to be filled waiting for a train; all dropped in the shifting sand and quickly covered by time, and all that I retained, all that sustained me, was this love we shared, and the fear we shared.

As far as the eye could see, on that side of me without eyes, empty vessels and odd items of clothing lay vanishing in the golden sand, marking our passage, Camilla's and mine.

And one of those memories I had once held dear bore resonance with the strains of Debussy floating up to me in the cool ambiance of the nascent morning. I lay there in the old bed's gully, Camilla stirring on her pallet, and tried to remember what I wanted to reclaim from the desert. But without eyes on that side facing toward yesterday, looking out across the golden sands of all those years . . . I could not call it back.

It was the music no one was playing that I had heard at Stonehenge, ten years ago. It was the sound of the pan pipes at Hanging Rock thirteen years ago, and the notes of a flute from the other side of the Valley of the Stonebow eight years ago. I had heard that recollection in a cave in the foothills overlooking the Fairchild Desert and, once, I heard it drifting through a misty downpour in the Sikkim rainforest.

The dream abandoned, I have never been able to unearth the

greater substance of that memory. And each time it floats back to me—like the remembrance of an aunt I had adored, who died long long ago, with me again for just an instant in the sweet scent of perfume worn by a passing woman on a city street—I am filled with a sense of loss and helplessness. And not even Camilla can damp the sorrow.

I lay there, knowing it was no dream, weak and without resources, dreading the day to come, afraid to leave the safe gully of the bed, once more to shoulder the remaining gear of my life; for another terrible day in the endless flight.

Then *Clair de Lune* was interrupted by three warm, mellifluous tones—B, F Sharp, D Sharp—and, distantly, as if rising from within a crystal palace in a lost city on a sunken continent, I heard a woman's voice announcing the departure of a train to Edinburgh; resonating through the domed vastness of Glasgow's Central Station; drifting up to me in my bed in the Central Hotel built above the terminal; the murky glass dome lying just two storeys below my window; forming a postcard depiction of the Great Bubble of the Capitol City of Lost Atlantis. If such a place ever existed, it would have looked that way. And if it had ever existed, it could have had no more magical presence than through the strains of Debussy.

Clair de Lune resumed, I sighed, threw back the covers, swung my feet out onto the cold floor, and resumed the walk that was a flight that was the remainder of my time that was my life, on the desert littered with my past.

I tried not to think about what might happen today, and went to the walk-in clothes closet, and took down the brown satchel with the flensing equipment in it. Then I selected something slim and sharp, and dutifully scraped the encrusted material that had accumulated during the night, off the body of the woman I loved.

Out there in Atlantis, *Clair de Lune* died away.

One would think history could never forget them, Sawney and all the rest of them. But not even the great library in Edinburgh had more than vague and cursory references. Nothing in Christie's history of Scotland, nothing in Sharp or Frankfort. A mere thirty-eight words in Donaldson and Morpeth's *A Dictionary of Scottish History*. The library in Enid, Oklahoma, where I was born and raised till I ran off to find my fortune, would have had nothing. I could in no way have been alerted.

One would think such things too terrible to be forgotten. But I understand there are college students all over the world these days for whom the words Dachau and Buchenwald and Belsen have no meaning.

In such a world, I'm grateful to have found love to sustain me.

We drove the rental car south out of Glasgow on 77. It was barely eight o'clock. We wanted an early start, though Ballantrae was less than seventy miles; 111.021 kilometers, to be precise. The southwest seacoast. Galloway.

We had discussed settling down here: Portpatrick, Glen App, or Cairnryan; perhaps take a freehold on a crofter's cottage near Castle Kennedy; or even nearer Bennane Head, possibly on the sheltered southern shore of Loch Ryan. But the councils weren't sanctioning freeholds for Americans, and Camilla had no birth certificate proving she was of Scottish birth, of course. So we had come to visit, at last. After all the years Camilla had begged me for this hometurning in our flight, we passed through Milmarnock, and reached the Firth of Clyde at Prestwick, just as the rain began sweeping the coast. After all those years, it was an unpleasant omen. And my trepidation about returning Camilla to her ancestral environs deepened. But she had implored me so heartbreakingly.

We drove the short distance to Ayr and cut over to 719 that trailed deeper south right along the coastline; it was perhaps an hour, then, to travel the thirty-five miles to Ballantrae, the rain barely increasing in intensity, though the sky blended in gray metal with the water of the North Channel. Sheet metal from top to bottom, and we sloughing along the extruded wetness of the road that edged the moors.

Camilla did not speak, had not spoken since we'd passed Dunure; but she had her face pressed to the window, looking out at the dismal machinery of leaden scenery, leaving for an instant four halations of breath fog on the glass before turning to stare ahead through the windshield. Her breath rasped and puffs of exhalation warned me she was getting too cold. I pulled over and took a blanket from the back seat, and wrapped her more securely. She smiled and mewled softly.

I scratched the nape of her neck, said, "Soon," and turned back onto the road and kept going.

We reached Ballantrae before noon, and Camilla decided to wait in the car while I went to get a bite to eat. I told her I'd bring something back, and she leaned across and kissed me, and smiled, and moved her head in that sweet sidewise way that I adored. "Haggis?" I said, teasing her. She hated haggis. She gave me a look, and I quickly said, "I'm kidding, I'm just kidding," before she cuffed me a good one. "Howzabout some eggs?" That brought back the smile.

I didn't feel like going into the rental's boot for a bowl . . . everything was packed tightly. So after I found Wimpy's and choked down three burgers, I cruised till I found a Woolworth's and laid out three quid for an aluminum mixing bowl. There was a delay in the checkout line, with an old woman in a snood raising such a fuss about something or other that the teen-age cashier had to call the manager. And everyone stood in line, more or less embarrassed by the whole thing, till they stopped shouting and the manager took the old woman off upstairs to his office to sort things out. I was impressed at how kindly he treated her, after all the ruckus. He seemed a nice man, and I felt sorry for the old woman, who looked widowed, cast alone, and hopeless. It made me sad for a moment, but the line moved quickly and I paid for the bowl and went back out into the slanting rain.

There was a grocer's on the way back to the public parking lot where I'd left the little Vauxhall Cavalier, and I waited in another short queue to pay for a half dozen free-range eggs carefully placed in a paper bag by an overweight, ruddy-faced man who carried on a running diatribe with his wife, at the rear of the shop, about how he would absolutely *not* carry Mrs. Bassandyne's box of groceries out to her car, no matter *how* many times she imperiously honked her horn. His wife looked like a typical telly version of a little old mum, and she agreed with him that Mrs. Bassandyne was indeed a right miserable cow. He managed to thank me for my purchase, in the middle of a Bassandyne sentence, and I went out again into the rain, which had grown heavier.

Camilla wasn't in the car.

The rain had soaked through the shoulders of my mac, and every time I took a step my feet squooshed in my wellies. The door of the rental was unlocked, and I put the bag of eggs on the front seat. Camilla was nowhere in sight, and I was an amputated leg. At first distressed, then troubled, then quickly frightened, I began running up and down the rows of parked cars. All I found was casual litter, a penny lying face-up in an oil slick, and the bones of what had probably been a small dog; very white and clean, with the marks of tiny teeth all over them.

When finally I circled back to the Vauxhall, Camilla was there, standing in the rain, the soaking blanket around her. I hustled her into the car, went around and, dripping wet, climbed in. She looked at me mischievously, and I apologized for having taken so long. "There was a line at the Woolworth's and the grocer's," I said. "Are you hungry?"

She told me she was hungry, but she said it with that subtext of tone that reprimanded me for having kept her waiting. I pulled the aluminum bowl out of the deep pocket of my mac, and broke the eggs into it. I put it on the lowered ledge of the opened glove compartment, and she went right to it. I watched in silence, determined not to ask her why she had wandered off into the storm.

When we drove out of the parking lot, a sizzle of lightning illuminated the delicate calligraphy of dog bones that still lay between a Ford Escort and a Mazda.

We left 77 just south of Ballantrae and took a weary, flooded dirt road out along the cliffs above Bennane Head. I could not contain my growing fear, and Camilla's reassuring smile only made me dwell more darkly on the ivory luster of bone in water.

Fame and fortune always eluded me. I laugh when I think how *completely* they had eluded me. I never had a clue. Not the smallest indication how to go about sinking roots, or making money, or bettering myself, or taking hold. There are people—well, I suppose almost *all* people, really—who manage to do it. They find mates, they get jobs, they buy homes, they have children, they furnish apartments, they get an education, they learn the ins and outs of electrical wiring or plastering or office temp, and they make lives for themselves.

I never knew how to do any of that. I couldn't talk to people, I was afraid of women, I never went into a restaurant or bookstore where anyone recognized me a second time. It was just the road, always the road, from here to there, and on again to someplace else. And no one place was even the tiniest bit better than the place I had just left. I was cold as an ice bucket, and had strong legs for walking. A job here, a job there, and I never became good enough at anything for an employer to suggest that I might, to our mutual advantage, stay on, settle down, take a position.

I went everywhere. All over Europe, the Greek isles, Hungary and even those parts of the Balkans that are no longer called Transylvania or Barnsdorf or Moldavia; Algeria, India, all over the subcontinent;

Pakistan, Israel, Zaire, the Congo. I shipped aboard tramp steamers to the China Sea, to Sumatra, as far north as Kiska and Attu, as far south as Brazil, Argentina. I saw Patagonia. I saw gauchos. In another place I saw penguins. I shipped there and back, and never once made a friend who lasted beyond the time at sea.

No one disliked me, no one very much interfered with me, they just didn't take much notice of me. I followed instructions to the letter, but managed to stay away from bad companions or trouble. I just went where the waves hit the shore, and stayed a time, and then moved on.

But I never returned to America, and I suppose all my family is gone now. I never had it in me to return to Enid, Oklahoma: I mean to say, that's where I'd run *away* from, why would I go back?

Fifteen years ago, I found Camilla. We fell in love. I thought I wanted to say something about that, how we came to be together, the time we've spent together since. But I don't want to go into that. It isn't something everyone would understand. I know it isn't enough to say that we just love each other, and need to be together, because anyone could say the same thing. But if I know one truth about people, it is that everyone judges everyone else. People they never met, and only read about in a newspaper or saw on a telly, they decide this or that about them . . . this is a good guy, and that's a sick and weird guy, or this woman is no good and that woman is above her station. It isn't fair. You just can't know why people do the things they do; and if you try to be a good guy, and go out of your way not to hurt anyone, then other people simply ought to let you be.

For instance, and I don't mean this to be smutty, but it's just exactly what I'm talking about, a long time ago I was in Uppsala, Sweden. I was given some magazines full of naked men and women, by a student I met who attended the University there. One of them was full of photographs of a woman having sex with animals. When I first saw it, I was very upset. I'd never seen anything like that. The woman was pretty, and the pictures had been taken on a farm somewhere, I suppose in Sweden, because the bull she was with had ice all matted in his hair. And she was doing things with a pig.

And I was so upset that I sought him out, the student who had given me the magazines, and I gave that one back to him, and I told him I couldn't understand how a woman could do such things. And he told me this young woman was very famous, that she was a simple farm girl, and that she truly loved animals, and didn't think there was anything awful about making the animals she loved happy. So I sat and studied that magazine, with that pretty young woman making love to the bull and the pig, and after a while I could see that she was really smiling, and the animals seemed to be content; and after a while longer it wasn't dirty to me any more. It was just as if she were petting a rabbit, or hugging a kitten.

I didn't see the ugliness others saw. I came to understand that there is little enough affection in the world and, even if everyone finds it necessary to pass judgments that this is proper, and that is obscene, that *this* young woman, even if she was of what they call diminished capacity, even she was better than those who passed judgments, because she loved the animals, and she wasn't hurting anyone, and if that was how she chose to show her love, it was okay.

But try to explain that to most people, and see how their faces screw up as if they'd eaten something sour. And so, if you take my point, that's why I don't want to talk about how I met Camilla in Wales, and what she was doing there, and how we got together, and how we came to find love together.

I'll just say this: she didn't want to be there, and her lot was not a happy one, and I got her away from there, and we started running, and besides being in love, she is the first and only person who ever *needed me.*

And that accounts for a lot. So after fifteen years of her asking me to take her to Galloway, I agreed, and it was a long, hard journey, but I'd taken her home.

Why was it she would tell me anything, had always shared everything with me, but would fall silent when I'd ask her how long it had been since she had seen her family, how long she had been away from her home?

And where in the world could they live, out here at the edge of Scotland, in this desolate place of cliffs and caves and moors? What could people farm out here, to sustain a decent life?

We parked at the edge of the cliffs, and I suggested we wait in the car till the rain had abated. Camilla was veiled in her manner, and tried not to seem anxious. But after a few minutes she wanted to get out, and she managed the door handle, and went down into the rain. I jumped out and came around, and helped her up. She stood there, her head tilted toward the heavens, the pounding rain sleeking her, running off both of us. Then she went to the edge of the cliff and tried to find a way down to the sea. "No!" I yelled across the thunder and darkness. "There's no way down!"

She went low and tried to crawl over the edge, grasping the tenacious twist of a briar bush. I slipped trying to get to her, and went face-first into the running mud where the road met the flattened grass. When I tried to rise, I slipped again. Then I just crawled toward her, as she tried to lower herself down the cliff. "Camilla! No! What're you doing? Stop, this's crazy . . . stop!" It was lunacy, a sheer drop nearly six hundred feet into the Channel, the storm skirling across the cliff-edge, the rain flooding the ground and waterfalling over the rim. I couldn't believe what she was trying to do. Where was she going?

I managed to grab her under the shoulders, and I rolled sidewise, digging my wellies into the mud and loam, making a dam against the water with my body. Then I started scrabbling backward, pulling her with me. She screamed and raked me.

I kept pulling, she was trying desperately to get away from me, I lost purchase as one of my feet slid across the mud, she got loose, crawled away, I reached back and snagged her clothing with one hand, I held on and wrenched back as hard as I could, she rolled onto her back, and I dragged her through the vicious downpour as darkness now fell utterly, dissolving sky, sea, cliff, land, everything. Only once, in the sulfurous whitelight of a blast of lightning close to the cliff, could I see Camilla's eyes. It wasn't the woman I'd loved for fifteen years, it was a mud-swathed creature possessed by a madness to go over the edge. Had she been trying for a decade and a half to return to this place only to kill herself? A lemming seeking oblivion? Had her life before my coming, or since I had joined with her, been so awful that all she wanted was to die? I fought against it. I fought against *her*, and finally . . . I won.

I rolled us over and over and over, back toward the road, away from the cliff edge, and at last came to rest against the side of the car. I held her close and cradled her, and she spat and raged and tried to break loose.

"No, Camilla . . . no, please, stop . . . honey, please . . ."

After a time, there in the cascading darkness, she went limp. And after a greater time she let me know she would not try that route again. But she kept saying she needed to go home.

I knew, then, that there was no lonely farmhouse out here. There might not even be family, as there might not be family in Enid, Oklahoma. But she had the need to find them, wherever they were out here; and I had to help her.

I loved her. That is all there is to say.

When I was certain she would not try for the edge again, I let her go. She rested a moment, then rose and moved slowly away, across the road, away from the cliff and the sea. Out across the moors. Without a word, she made her painful, laborious passage through the gorse, the silvery gray tufts of grass now bending beneath the hammering rain, the craggy rocks black and crippled-seeming leaping out for an instant as lightning illuminated them, then vanishing into blind emptiness as night rushed back in around the image. For a moment she vanished as she moved through a stand of tall reedlike grass, then she was limned against the sky as she crawled over a rock outcrop. I followed, at a short distance, as an observer would track a great terrapin trying to find its way to the sea.

She seemed to know what she was looking for. And I had bright instants of hope that there would be, if not a lonely farmhouse, then the burned-out wreckage of a farmhouse that had been here long ago, before Camilla had left.

But finally, she came to an enormous pile of rocks all grown over with briar bushes, thick with thorns. She climbed the cairn, and I followed; and found her trying to dig away the sharp spikey branches. She was already bleeding when I got there.

I tried to stop her, but again, she was possessed. She *had* to pull away those bushes.

I gently edged her aside and, wrapping the cuffs of my mac around my hands, I strained and wrenched at the bushes where she indicated. After a fearful struggle, they came out of the niches in the rocks, one by one.

The first clot of dirt surrounding the tenacious root-systems brought up a filthy skull. It was a human skull. I thought for a moment it was an animal skull, but when the rain washed it clean, I saw that it was not an animal. It had been human. How long ago it had been human, I could not tell. When I stopped digging, she moved to take over; but I nudged her back, and went at it again.

It seemed hours, just wrenching and digging in the spaces between the black rocks of the cairn. Hours in the slashing storm. Hours and eternities without time or sense. And at last, my hand slipped through into a cool empty place between the rocks.

"There's a hole here . . . I think, there seems to be, I think there's a large hole under here . . ."

She joined me again, and I couldn't stop her or slow her. She dug madly, like a beast uncovering a meal hidden for later attention.

I wedged myself against the larger of two leaning rocks in the mound, and braced my feet against the smaller, and steadily pushed. I have strong legs, as I said. The rock crunched, trembled, moved restlessly like a fat man in sleep, and then overbalanced in its setting, and fell away, tumbling quickly out of sight down the slope of the cairn.

As lightning blasted the landscape, I saw the entrance to the cave. The black maw of the opening gaped beneath my feet. As the rock rolled away, I fell forward, caught the edge of the hole, and dropped. I screamed as the world fell past me, and the water spilling over the rocks filled my mouth with dirt and gravel, stung my eyes, and I hit the sloping wall of the passage, and slid on a carpet of running mud like a man in a toboggan, careening off the rough surface from which roots extended, plunging down and down, feet-first into the darkness. The channel sloped more steeply, and I gathered speed, screaming, and went faster, and could see nothing but the deep grave funneling up past me and an instant of dim light high overhead behind me as lightning hit the night sky again.

Then I was shooting forward on a less inclined plane, still too fast to stop myself though I tried to dig in my hands and ripped flesh for the trouble, dirt clogging under my fingernails . . . and I shot out of the end of the tunnel, like a gobbet of spit, and somehow my legs were under me, but there was no floor, and I dropped into open emptiness, and hit still accelerating forward, and managed half a dozen running steps before I smashed full face into a rock wall, and I lost everything. I didn't even know when I'd fallen.

The light was green. Pale green, the color of moldy bread that seems to be blue till you look closely. The light came from the walls of the cavern. It was an enormous cavern, and the first thing I heard was the sound of a vast audience applauding. I fainted again. The pain in my face was excruciating. I knew I'd broken parts, and I fainted again. The pale green light expanded in the space behind my eyes, and I went away.

When I swam through the pain and the film of swirling shapes, I regained consciousness in the same position, propped against the wall of the cavern. This time I understood that the applauding masses were the sound of the sea hitting the cliffs. At each ovation, water rushed into the cavern from far across the floor, and I realized we had to be at least two hundred yards inside the cliff. The cavern glowed with a sickly green luminosity and I could make out tunnels that led off this central chamber, dozens of tunnels, going off in every direction around the circular centerplace.

I tried to move, and the pain in my face nearly sent me into darkness again. I raised a filthy hand to my cheek and felt bone protruding from the skin. My nose was broken. My teeth had bitten through my upper lip. My right eye seemed to have something wet and loose obscuring the lens.

I dropped my hand to the rock and dirt floor beside me, and my palm slid in something moist and soft. I looked down. The headless body of a young woman lay twisted on the floor beside me. I screamed and pinwheeled away from the corpse.

Then I heard a chuckle, and looked with extreme pain and restriction of muscles to my left. Camilla's father—How did I know it was he? I don't know. It was he—hung head down from the rock wall, sticking to the surface of moist, mossy rock. Watching me.

His scaley surface was not as clean and opalescent as I'd kept Camilla's. Rot clung to the scabrous flesh. There were more teeth in him, and larger than Camilla's.

He came away from the wall with a sucking sound and dropped to the floor of the cavern. Then, without difficulty—and I am a large man—he extended two of his arms and took me by the collar of the mac and dragged me across the floor, toward one of the tunnels on the far side of the chamber, through the river of seawater that ebbed and flowed as the audience applauded against the cliffs of Bennane Head.

He dragged me through the mouth of the tunnel, and we passed chamber after chamber, a vast labyrinth of cave system—and I looked in on Camilla's family, inhabiting the rooms beneath the Galloway moors.

In one chamber I saw nothing but bones, hundreds of thousands of bones, pale green with their gnawed-clean curves and knobs, hollow where the marrow had been sucked out. Bones in mountainous heaps that clogged the chamber from floor to roof, and spilled out into the passage. He dragged me through the history of a thousand meals.

In another chamber were piles of clothing. Rags and garments, boots and dresses, shapeless masses of raiment that seemed to have come from a hundred eras. Plumed bonnets with moss growing on them, jodhpurs and corselets, leather greaves and housecoats, bedroom slippers and deer-stalkers, anoraks and cuirasses, masses of clothing thrown haphazardly and in a profusion that defied estimation, filling the large side-chamber like the clothes closet of a mad empress.

I cannot describe the drying and curing rooms, save to say that bodies and parts of bodies hung from hooks in the low ceilings. Men with their faces gone. Women with their breasts ripped away. Small boys without hands or feet or sex organs. A mound of dried, leathery babies.

And on, and on, and on.

I could not stop him, he was too strong, I was too weak and in pain, and I was able merely to turn my head as we bumped along. Turned my head to see horror upon horror in this seemingly endless charnel house.

Into a cavernous hold far back in the system, where I finally, after fifteen years, confronted Camilla's family. All of them. The children of Sawney Beane.

And there, in the bosom of her loved ones, was the woman I loved. My cool and beautiful Camilla, with a gobbet of human flesh hanging from her lipless mouth, her fingerless hands redolent with blood.

In the center of the chamber was a great stone bowl. And as I lay there, watching, first one, then another, of Camilla's brothers and sisters and nieces and nephews—all the products of incestuous couplings—kneeled before the stone crucible and drank slurpingly from the thick, clotted liquor. I knew the name of that terrible brew.

Camilla's father left me there and went to his wife and daughter. I knew at once who they were. The affection they showed toward one another, and the attention all the others lavished on them, indicated how pleased they were that the prodigal had, at last, returned. And bearing such a tender banquet as oblation to the family.

I saw the resemblance between mother and daughter.

And for the first time asked myself how old Camilla really was. I'd assumed she was young, but what did that mean in a lineal line where one hundred, two hundred years was only early maturity?

I was too terrified to move, and the nausea that swelled in my throat left me weak and empty.

Then Camilla came to me, and settled down beside me, and lifted my head and stroked my face with a bloody hand. And she kissed me. And I smelled the butcher shop on her lipless mouth. I almost cried: she still loved me.

What they spoke was barely a human tongue, a language that had been guttural and ancient when King James the First had tracked them to these caves, and dragged out Sawney and his wife, and eight sons, and six daughters, and eighteen grandsons, and fourteen granddaughters—forty-eight in all—but, ah, not *all*, as he thought— and shrove them all the way to Leith, and condemned all, without exception, to death; and, as the women watched, King James ordered that the men have first their penises, then their hands and feet, chopped off, and were left to bleed to death where they lay; and then he had the women hurled living into three great bonfires, where they, too, perished. But it was not the end of Sawney Beane's clan. For the caves beneath Galloway were deep, and many, and mazelike, and some survived. And literally went to ground, to breed anew.

I learned all this from the woman I loved, who spoke a second language. A tongue that was slick with terrible history.

And she told me that she loved me, would always love me. And she told me that it was cool and protected here. And told me that her family approved of her choice. And told me we could stay here. Together. In the bosom of her family. And not for a second did I see in her eyes the green, hungry glow in the eyes of her immense mother, who squatted across the floor all that night—I think it was still night—watching her intended son-in-law.

Camilla mewled and ran her tongue over me, and held me and rocked me. And spoke of our love.

Then, when I was able to stand, I ran. I turned and ran back the way we had come; and each of the horrors I had passed was a marker: the drying rooms, the hanging chambers, the rows of skulls in niches with tallow candles that had burned down centuries ago, the clothing room and the bone room, where I grabbed a femur and, hearing feet pounding along behind me, turned and swung the longbone as hard as I could, and shattered the head of a scion of the family of Sawney Beane, perhaps Camilla's father, I don't know.

I found the sloping passage, and jumped and went half into the hole, and some rough appendage grasped my legs, and I kicked out, and heard a moan, and scrabbled up the slope and kept going, up and up and up toward the night sky that was now gray-blue with passing clouds and moonlight.

I went up, for my life, with the smell of slaughter from Camilla's kisses, fresh on my lips.

I lie now in this room where I awoke this morning. *Clair de Lune* drifts up to me from Atlantis. I lie here, having left this brief chronicle, thinking of what I must do. I know I will return.

What I do not yet know, as I think of my rootless life and the emptiness I knew before I found Camilla in that gully, is whether I will dive down that hole in the cairn bearing gasoline and gelignite and a flamethrower if I can steal one from some armory somewhere . . .

Or if I will go to taste again the kisses of the woman I love, the only woman who has ever loved me.

This I know, however: Atlantis never existed.

BEAN, Sawney (s.l. mid-1400s). Scottish highwayman, mass murderer, and cannibal. Illiterate and uncouth, he lived with his wife and 14 children in a giant cave by the desolate seacoast along the Galloway region in southwestern Scotland. For over 25 years the Bean family assaulted, robbed, and killed travelers—men, women, and children—on their way to and from Edinburgh and Glasgow in the north. Their depredations included cannibalism as well. Finally, an intended victim who had seen his wife knocked from her horse, her throat immediately slit, and her body cannibalized, managed to escape to warn the Scottish king at Glasgow. Some 400 men and bloodhounds, led by the king, tracked down and, after a fierce battle, captured the Beans in their cave, in which were found numerous mutilated cadavers. Sawney and the rest were brought to Leith, showed not the slightest repentance for their crimes, and were promptly burned to death at the stake without a trial. It was estimated that the Beans' murder victims totaled well over 1,000 persons.

Extract from DICTIONARY OF CULPRITS
AND CRIMINALS

(George C. Kohn; Scarecrow Press; London, 1986)

Chopped Liver

George Alec Effinger

In the early days of his career, George Alec Effinger was known for his humorous short fiction. He then switched his attention to more serious works, which have won him both Hugos and Nebulas. But he still returns to the occasional humorous piece. He called his *Author's Choice Monthly* collection *The Old Funny Stuff*.

Very few stories make me laugh aloud. Even after several readings, George Alec Effinger's "Chopped Liver" still makes me chuckle.

Morton Rosenthal discovered the first piece of his fiendish plan while he was in Mt. Sinai Hospital, recuperating from having his gall bladder cut out. He hated the routines of the hospital, because they seemed to be the only things standing between him and genuine good health. All he wanted to do was sleep; but the nurses came by at eight o'clock and compelled everyone on the ward to walk to the floor's dining hall, even though Rosenthal insisted that he never ate breakfast. After that, when he tried to nap, a nurse's aide came to give him "his little bath." Then when he thought it was all over and he'd finally be left alone, someone else came by to change the linen. When that was done, it was time for medication. And then it was lunch time. . . .

It was early afternoon of the day before he was to be released. He sat in the dining hall in a foul mood, wearing a new flannel bathrobe over the hospital gown, with brown paper slippers on his feet. When the nurse's aide brought his lunch tray, he took off the metal lid, expecting Salisbury steak and carrots. That's what he'd ordered at breakfast. Instead, though, he found fried liver and onions with green peas.

Liver, thought Rosenthal grumpily. He grimaced. The fact that Rosenthal was a butcher didn't make the liver any easier to take. Hardly anybody can stand liver, he thought. He figured that it a national poll were taken, only forty or fifty people in the entire United States of America would admit to having ordered liver voluntarily in a restaurant. *Nobody* eats liver, thought Rosenthal. And even if they do, nobody *likes* it.

The liver was the first piece of the puzzle, and one of the most important.

He was discharged from the hospital the next day, and Rose, his wife, was supposed to be at the hospital at eleven o'clock to take him home. The physician had made out the proper forms, the cashier down on the first floor had been satisfied that eventually someone was going to pay for Rosenthal's renovation, and now all he had to do was sit in the olive green lobby and wait. Wait for Rose to come pick him up at eleven o'clock.

Eleven thirty. Noon. Rosenthal went to the pay phone and called his house. He let it ring ten times. Rose wasn't home, so she was apparently on her way to the hospital. Rosenthal went back to the lobby and looked at an issue of *Sailing* magazine. Half past twelve. One o'clock. Another phone call, still no answer. Rosenthal was furious. He called a taxi and went home. The cab fare came to thirteen dollars and seventy cents. He let the cabbie keep the thirty cents change.

Rose wasn't at home. Rosenthal was so angry that he forgot to be worried. He spent fifteen minutes putting his clothes and toilet articles away. He rolled up the new green bathrobe into a ball and threw it into a corner of a shelf in his closet. Then he opened a bottle of beer and turned on the television. It never occurred to him that his wife might have been in an accident or something.

She came home at five o'clock. Accidents never happened to Rose Scheinek Rosenthal. *She* was the one who pulled her car across two lanes of traffic to make a left turn, and watched the cars around her blam into each other. No, she hadn't been in an accident. She'd spent the afternoon going through dimestores looking for a healthy asparagus fern.

"Morty!" she said, surprised, putting her fern on the coffee table. "I was just getting ready to go for tonight's visiting hours."

"I was discharged this morning," he said, glaring at her. "I told you last night that you were supposed to pick me up at eleven o'clock."

"Oh, Morty," she said, "don't make such a big thing out of it. I just forgot, that's all."

He didn't say a word; he just stared. The second piece of the puzzle was Rose, his wife. Maybe this single incident was trivial on the face of it; but the phenomenon of Rose, The Rose Experience, if you will, the twenty-nine years of living with Rose, that was a nightmare he could never wake up from.

Or so he'd always thought, over the years. Piece number three was a terrible movie that came on at eight o'clock that evening. The movie had not a single recognizable star; it had little story, not even some modest on-screen sex or violence. All that it had to recommend itself to Morton Rosenthal was that the bad guy murdered his shlub of a wife.

"Hey," thought Rosenthal, "you can always murder your wife! How could I have been so blind all these years?"

Right then, before the movie even ended, and all during the television entertainment for the remainder of the evening, Rosenthal considered the various ways of doing away with Rose. He discarded every one of them. There were too many details to be considered.

There was, first of all, opportunity. He'd have to do the job without her catching wise first and without being noticed by the people next door. The means? There was *tsurris*, too. He didn't want to go out and buy a pistol, or seek out an untraceable poison, or rig a fatal accident. He wasn't brilliant, he wasn't clever. Hell, he was only a butcher, a divider of lamb chops.

Anyway, he'd seen enough movies to know that it was always the cleverest criminals who were caught in the end. Morton Rosenthal knew that if there was one thing he wasn't, it was a Criminal Mastermind. So, if it took something he just didn't have to murder Rose, he would have to be content with what he had and what he was: a first-class butcher, a second-class imaginer, a third-class crook.

Piece number four—the key piece—the *wonderful* piece that made them all fit:

"I suppose I'll have to work late for a few days, to catch up. I have to get out Admiral's weekly order, and Bar's Mike and Grill. Schumann and the kid probably didn't lift a finger while I was gone."

"You *always* work late," grumbled Rose. When she grumbled, it was like living for all eternity in late January, maybe early February. Feh.

"I don't *always* work late."

"You *always* work late. You've worked late six days a week every week for the last eighteen years. And you come home with liquor on your breath."

"I work food," said Rosenthal, repeating his old lie. "I have to keep clean. I have to sterilize everything or they put me in jail."

"So what do you do?" asked Rose. "Gargle whiskey and spit it over everything?"

"Watch the movie," said Rosenthal.

A week later, Rosenthal had done all of his homework. He had planned the entire event as carefully as a bride's mother. There were loose ends, of course, but there are some aspects to any murder that are bound to be left dangling. You have to expect that, you have to accept the fact that the perfect crime doesn't exist. Rosenthal was realistic. He didn't get to be a first-class butcher by dreaming his life away. Rosenthal hadn't thought much about how he'd explain his wife's disappearance. He'd say, maybe, she left him for a Latin band leader. With Rose, who knew?

The rest of the murder was simplicity itself. The only difficult thing would be getting Rose down to the shop. She never came in to see him, there was no reason. He brought meat home, she never had to go shopping. Heaven only knew why she couldn't drop by just to say hello. To tell the truth, as far as Rose could testify, Rosenthal might have been anything from a professional bowler to a famous homosexual poet.

One night, Rosenthal decided that he was actually going to do it. He was going to act out his innermost secret fantasy. He was really going to murder Rose. "That's a good thing," he thought. "It's a healthy thing to express yourself. It's best to get these things out into the open and deal with them on a mature basis."

The method he had chosen for expressing himself was a True Value claw hammer. He admitted that it had none of the exotic appeal of obscure chemicals and elaborate mechanisms. It was, however, practical, silent, easily concealed, and one hundred percent effective. No chance here of Rose getting off with just a flesh wound as the neighbors and police break down his door after the gunshot. No chance of Rose almost dying but recovering and the neighbors and police breaking down his door and finding vials of black fluid in the medicine chest. Just a good old claw hammer. A man's weapon.

"So nu?" said Rose. "What do you feel like tonight?"

"I don't know. What do *you* feel like?"

"I don't know. My legs hurt. I thought maybe you'd bring something home for supper. There's nothing in the icebox. I thought maybe we'd go out to the Chinese. There's nothing for tomorrow, either. Why didn't you bring something home?"

"I don't know," said Rosenthal glumly. "It's okay if maybe we go out Chinese."

"And what about tomorrow?" She peered at him over her glasses, waiting to reject his reply.

"Tomorrow I'll worry about tomorrow. You want to go out Chinese, or maybe we'll go by the shop and pick something up." Rosenthal's heartbeat grew louder in his ears.

"I don't know," she said. "I don't know what I feel like, now. The back of my neck hurts."

"Let me put my jacket on. We'll go out."

"No, let's stay in," she said. "You go out and pick up a nice flanken and I'll make it with the spinach and farfel."

"Feh," thought Rosenthal. He went to the closet and took out his jacket. He also got the claw hammer from the tool box. "Anything else you want as long as I'm going out?" he asked. He walked as casually as he could to the sofa where Rose was sitting. She was reading the old *TV Guide*, the one from the week before.

She didn't look up. "No, nothing. Maybe pick up some frozen blintzes. No, I don't know. If you feel like it."

More than at any other time in his life, Morton Rosenthal felt like it. He raised the hammer, but just before he brought it down he stopped himself. "Why don't you come with me?" he asked.

"Why should I want to come with you?"

"So come on. We'll get a couple drinks."

Rose looked up, astonished. "Drinks? Where? You mean the colored bar?"

"No, we'll drive around. Find a nice place. Go eat someplace."

"My legs," she said. "My neck."

Rosenthal tried to keep his grimace form showing. He couldn't. "You'll feel better," he said. "You'll see. Let's get out of the house."

Rose sighed. "All right, I don't want to cook anyway. Let me get ready." She got up and went into the bedroom to change. Rosenthal stood in the middle of the living room, his jacket on, holding the heavy claw hammer. It took Rose fifteen minutes to get dressed. They rode down silently in the elevator and walked out to the car. Rose never noticed that her husband was carrying around a hammer wherever he went.

"I've got to stop at the shop," he said.

"So?"

"So I've got to stop at the shop. I'll bet the kid left the freezer open again. He did it last month and it cost me next summer's vacation."

"So we'll stop. Let's eat first."

"I want to stop first," he said. They didn't say anything else while they rode to the shop. Rosenthal parked his car behind the shop. "Come on," he said. "Come in with me."

Rose wrinkled her nose. "Why? What do I want to come in for?"

"Pick something out for Sunday dinner."

"You pick. I just want to sit here. My legs hurt."

Rosenthal gripped the steering wheel tightly. He felt lightheaded and vaguely unreal. His left hand closed on the hammer. He didn't think he could do the thing in the car. He didn't think he could get enough force behind the blow, and he didn't want to drag Rose's body from the car, across the lot, and into the shop. "Rose," he said softly, "please come with me. It means a lot to me. Do this once."

The tone of his voice made her suspicious. "What are you up to?"

"Nothing," he said. "I don't like the idea of you sitting out here alone in the car. Just come on."

"What is this?" she asked dubiously. "A surprise? Is that it? You planned a surprise?"

"Yes, Rose, you guessed it. A surprise."

She didn't look pleased. "What is it?"

"I can't tell you, it's a surprise," said Rosenthal.

Rose shook her head and got out of the car. She followed him to the back door of the butcher shop.

Inside, Rosenthal told his wife to wait in the back, near the large freezer. He went into the the front of the shop, looked around, listened, tried to get his heartbeat to slow down. He went back to where Rose waited. "What did you get?" she asked.

Rosenthal raised the hammer and brought it down in one smooth motion, trying not to watch as he did it. He crushed her forehead at a point between her silver-tinted hair and her pink butterfly eyeglasses. Rosenthal watched his wife's corpse fall heavily to the floor. He dropped the hammer. He sat down heavily on the floor only a few feet from her body. He was trembling. It took him many minutes before he could bring himself to begin in the next step, the disposal of the evidence.

First and simplest, he washed off the hammer and went back outside. He put the hammer in another tool box in the trunk of his car. Then he went back into the shop, opened the large meat locker, and dragged Rose's body into it. He took off her clothing slowly. He hadn't anticipated that it would be so difficult. He spread sawdust and vermiculite on the floor and put on a clean apron. He chose a selection of tools—cleavers, knives, saws—and, taking a deep breath that came out as a sob of disgust, made the first cut.

The job took longer than Rosenthal had planned. When it was finished, Rose had become sixty-seven packages in the freezer, all wrapped in pale yellow paper, sealed with white tape. It took him another hour to clean up every trace of the night's business, and then Rosenthal let himself out the back entrance. He was startled to see that it was light outside already. He glanced at his watch. It was six o'clock. He had time to go home, take a shower, drink a couple of shots, lie down, and not sleep. He did these things, in that order, and at eight o'clock he dressed again and went back to open the shop.

All day, Rosenthal's mind returned to what he'd done the night before. He began to feel terrible remorse. It should have stayed a fantasy, he thought. He went home early, leaving his assistant and the kid to close up. At home, Rosenthal sat on the sofa and worried. He worried about what he had to do now, because he was certain that the job wasn't ended. It occurred to him that no murder is ever ended. Where was Rose? What would he tell her sister in Florida? What would he tell the neighbors? The paperboy? What was he going to do with his sixty-seven packages?

Halfway down a bottle of Wild Turkey, Rosenthal came up with the perfect solution to that problem. He would go back to the shop, pick up the packages, write LIVER on each one, date them all about five months ago, and sneak them into the freezers of all his friends. Nobody eats liver. Sometimes people buy liver because they think they should, or because they think it might make nice change someday, or because they can't remember the last time they had it. But to the best of his knowledge, Rosenthal had never heard of anyone actually eating liver. And his friends, sometime in the future, while looking through the leftovers and frozen pot pies in the freezer, would come across the packages of old liver. They would all react in the same way: Feh, and into the garbage.

This was the final, masterful piece of reasoning that would cover his trail. About Rose he would only shrug and look sad. He would give all her things to the Hadassah ladies.

In the morning, hungover and surly, Rosenthal opened the shop. He'd spent the minutes while shaving trying to decide what to do with the sixty-seven packages of ground Rose. The frozen liver idea still amused him, but he realized that without a protective buffer of Wild Turkey around it, the notion was basically without genuine merit. The best thing would be to load the packages into large green plastic trash bags and put them out on the curb for the city to dispose of. It would be a waste of a paid-up plot in the cemetery, but, who knew, Rosenthal wasn't so old yet that he couldn't maybe find someone else to fill the ground next to him.

There was a small detail, just a tiny awkward trifle that disturbed him when he went into the large freezer. The sixty-seven packages were now considerably fewer. He counted and found only twenty-nine packages. That was still a lot of Rose, but Rosenthal had more than merely sentimental reasons for wanting his loved one put to rest *in toto*.

"Anybody touch the dollar-and-a-half ground in the locker?" he asked, his voice cracking even though he was determined it shouldn't.

"Order for the Admiral," said the kid. "I made up the difference.

It was, what, it was thirty-eight pounds short. So I took it out of the freezer. Was that a special order or something?"

Rosenthal felt sick. A considerable portion of his late wife had been sold to a hamburger stand on the interstate. He wished he'd never had the inspiration to murder Rose in the first place. Rosenthal realized that the kid was waiting for an answer. "No," he said, "I guess it's all right. It was old stuff, but the Admiral's will never notice. I want you to bag up the rest of the packages and put the bags in my car."

"Sure," said the kid.

Rosenthal left the shop at the first opportunity and put ten dollars of barroom liquor down his throat. Still, the rest of the day his hands shook.

The next couple of days were strange, but quiet. Rosenthal found his home immensely empty without Rose, silent and dark and almost frightening. He finally realized that he didn't have to come home at all if he didn't feel like it. He visited his friends, bringing them all secret remembrances of Rose which he hid in the back of their freezer compartments at the first opportunity. He went out to some bars and drank beer and watched television. He got bored quickly. He went bowling by himself. He could only bowl two lines before loneliness drove him out of the alley. He went to a movie by himself and hated it. He had dinner at a restaurant alone and remembered when he'd eaten there with Rose.

Time moved slowly, but after a while Rosenthal began to get used to his new lifestyle. He admitted to himself that it was not a better life than he'd had with Rose. Sometimes he almost missed her.

One evening after he came home from work, he dreamed that his doorbell rang. He answered the door and saw three men standing there. One man wore the blue sailor's tunic uniform of the employees at the Admiral. He wore a badge that said his name was Doug. His eyes were wild and staring. He stretched out a hand and pointed at Rosenthal. "That's him!" he cried. "That's the man! That's him!"

One of the other men, who wore a vested gray suit and tan overcoat, ignored Doug. He took out a wallet and displayed a card and a badge. "My name is Reed, Mr. Rosenthal, and I'm from the Board of Health. This is Detective Kojak from Homicide. We'd like to ask you a few questions."

Rosenthal woke up in a panic, but then he realized the ringing he'd heard in his dream was the telephone. He picked up the receiver and said hello.

"Morty?" It was Sheldon Wysilewska, his best friend. Rosenthal and his wife had lived next door to Wysilewska and his wife, Bea, for twenty-two years. Sheldon and Bea had been the first of Rosenthal's friends to invite him over when they heard that Rose had "gone away."

"Sheldon? It's you?" Rosenthal still didn't feel entirely awake.

"It's Sheldon, Morty. You have any plans for tonight?"

"Plans? What plans?"

"Well, Bea's making spaghetti for supper, and every time she makes spaghetti, she forgets how much to put in the water and she ends up with enough to feed an army. Why don't you come over and help us eat it? We're only going to throw it out."

Morty wasn't sure he felt like starting a second round of visiting. "I don't know, Sheldon," he said. "I don't have much spare time. I have to see to all the things that Rose used to take care of." He let his voice choke just a little when he said her name. He thought that was a nice touch.

"I'm not going to beg you, Morty, but Bea and I don't like the idea of you pining away in your empty apartment. You need to see your friends, hear the gossip. You can't just shut us out and turn into a bitter old man."

It was true that Rosenthal not only didn't have any plans for that evening, he had no plans at all for the rest of his life. Maybe it wouldn't hurt to drop in on Bea and Sheldon. "Well," he said.

"Good," said Wysilewska. "You'll bring some Mogen David, we'll have supper, then we'll watch a little cable."

"All right," said Rosenthal. He was still reluctant, but he was also tired of sitting alone in the living room with the lights off. He hung up the phone, got up, showered and shaved and put on clean clothes. He felt refreshed, and he realized that he was looking forward to seeing his old friends.

Dinner was almost ready when he arrived, so he and Wysilewska sat at the dining room table and watched Bea bring bowls in from the kitchen. Rosenthal opened the bottle of wine he'd bought at the deli down the block. Wysilewska began lifting a generous serving of spaghetti onto Rosenthal's plate. "You're not bothering us, you know," said Wysilewska.

"I'm sorry?" said Rosenthal.

"We like having you over, Morty," said Bea, smiling at him. She never mentioned Rose's name anymore. Evidently she'd been deeply shocked by the idea of a wife leaving her husband of many years, for whatever reason.

"I'm grateful for all you've done for me," said Rosenthal. "You've been very kind."

"You've been very lucky," said Wysilewska.

"Lucky is not the way I'd describe it," said Rosenthal sadly. He twirled some spaghetti around his fork and stabbed half a meatball.

"I mean, here you've got the greatest friends in the world, and they're hotsy-totsy cooks, too. What else could you possibly want?"

Rosenthal couldn't talk with his mouth full, so he just nodded his head.

"We could introduce Morty to your sister," said Bea thoughtfully.

Wysilewska sipped some of the sweet wine. "Well, maybe Morty thinks it's just a little soon for that. Anyway, didn't you promise me we weren't going to interfere—"

An errant thought crossed Rosenthal's mind, and at first he tried to disregard it, but the notion was just too insistent. He stood up and went into Bea and Sheldon's kitchen.

"Morty?" called Bea. "Are you all right? Can I get you something?"

There it was, horribly, right on top of the garbage—a pale yellow sheet of butcher paper with the word LIVER written in his own handwriting. Rosenthal stared at the paper, paralyzed for a moment, one hand over his mouth. He began choking on the meatball that was now lodged in his throat. He gasped for breath. He stumbled away from the wastebasket, back toward the dining room. This meatball in his throat, it was—

"Morty?" asked Wysilewska. "Are you all right?"

"I think he's choking, Sheldon," said Bea. "Get him a glass of water."

"Are you choking, Morty?"

Rosenthal couldn't cough up the chunk of meatball. He began to panic. His vision was flecked with red and black spots.

Bea was on her feet now, frightened. "Do something, Sheldon!" she cried. "Do that thing, whatever they call it. For choking people."

"The Ludlum Maneuver," said Sheldon. He hurried to Rosenthal, who had fallen to his knees, desperately clawing at his collar. Wysilewska hit him on the back once, twice, three times.

"That's not it!" shouted Bea. Tears had begun to stream down her cheeks.

Tears were streaming down Rosenthal's cheeks, too. There was a loud roaring sound in his ears. He reached a finger down his throat, but he knew he was choking to death. He knew it was all over.

"CPR!" cried Bea. "Mouth-to-mouth!"

"That won't work!" said Wysilewska angrily. "He can't get air down his windpipe. That's the whole problem."

"Sure, it'll work!"

"Then *you* do it!" screamed Wysilewska. His wife primly declined.

Rosenthal no longer heard anything they said. He was floating in his own little world. This is your revenge, he thought. This is your stupid revenge. He felt all his muscles tighten and then suddenly go limp. He fell face forward onto the dining room carpet. Your revenge. Rose, the Meatball of Death.

Nobody's Perfect

Thomas F. Monteleone

After reading the first issue of *Pulphouse*, Thomas F. Monteleone called the hardback a feminist publication. Perhaps. But one of the strongest pro-female stories in that issue was Tom's own "Nobody's Perfect."

Tom has done some editing of his own these days. His 1990 anthology, *Borderlands*, received much acclaim. He has been publishing novels since the mid-1970s, the most recent being *The Magnificent Gallery*, *Fantasma*, and *Blood of the Lamb*.

Lydia thought she might be able to like this guy. He seemed different from all the others. There was something mysterious about him, something exotic, and her intuition told her to expect an interesting evening.

Salazar noticed her . . . *aberration* as he sat in her living room watching her. She stood in the kitchen struggling to open the twist-off cap of a Michelob bottle.

He smiled just slightly. Odd he had not observed the deficiency previously . . .

Not that it mattered much, if at all. If anything, it somewhat intrigued him. He would still dispose of Lydia like all the others, and he was confident that her meat would steam with exquisite flavor.

Salazar allowed himself a small anticipatory smile. He was not certain what excited him the most, what provided him with the most pleasure—the initial search for suitable prey, the stalking-time when one had been selected, or the final act of consummation. There was a grandness about it all which *inspired* him, drove him with a fervor that religious zealots would envy.

The ritual was so wonderful, and the meat always so utterly tasty . . .

. . . It had been a Saturday two weeks earlier when Salazar fixed upon *The City Paper*'s classified ad for volunteers. He had been scanning the "Personals," which had proved to be a good place to find prey—although he had been careful not to establish any patterns which the police might notice—when his eye drifted down to the "Help Wanteds" and read:

> *VOLUNTEERS needed to read and record literature.*
> *Books For the Blind. For details call* 344-8899.

For some reason, he re-read the listing, and a familiar wave of heat rippled his body, exciting him in an almost sexual way. In that single instant he knew the Fates were reaching out to him, directing him to his next mission.

This would be perfect, he thought with a thoughtful nod of the head. Visions of young, single women—most of them probably unattached and bookish—burned in him. Young women with time on their hands. Soulful and naive do-gooders. Yes. This set-up would be perfect.

He called the number and was given an address downtown near the bohemian section of the city. It was a waterfront neighborhood which had recently enjoyed a renaissance in the form of countless new bars with catchy off-beat names, art galleries, little theatres, antique shops, and several alfresco restaurants. Yes, Books For The Blind was open on Saturdays, and yes, they would be glad to have him come down for an audition.

* * *

It was not unusual for Lydia to spend her Saturday doing volunteer work. She found it a pleasant change of pace from her weekday position as a systems analyst for Westinghouse, and since she liked to read anyway, the Books For The Blind seemed ideal. The day had turned out to be bright and crisp, suggesting better weather still ahead.

As Lydia walked through the quaint neighborhood of Fells Point, she did not, as she often did, let herself dwell upon all the pain in the world, all the discomfort and sadness, the injustice and the plainly cruel. Sometimes, when she reflected upon the daily horror in the world, it affected her physically as well as mentally—tiny needles of pain would tingle up the right side of her body, as if a precursor to a special kind of heart failure. Throughout her young life, she had probably absorbed more than her share of the world's pain, but it had left her undaunted, making her even stronger and more positive in the long run.

"You'll do just fine," said Mr. Hawthorne, a reed-thin, nobly balding gentleman, who looked to be in his late fifties. He sat opposite a folding table, wearing headphones which were connected to an ancient, boxy reel-to-reel recorder.

"That is wonderful," said Salazar. "When do I start?"

Hawthorne looked at his watch. "If you can wait until four or so this afternoon, we're going to have an orientation class for all the volunteers we've selected today."

"That would be fine."

"Very good. You'll be getting a schedule for when you can come in at night and read into one of our recorders. We want to make sure everyone knows how to operate them properly." Mr. Hawthorne smiled primly. "Plus, you'll need to know a few basics about how to handle mistakes—so that when the tapes are edited, they will sound as smooth as possible."

"So it will not be necessary to take the machines home with us?" said Salazar.

"No, they're a bit too bulky to be very portable, I'm afraid. If we could get a larger budget, we would like to buy some new equipment, but . . ."

"I see." Salazar did not want his evenings tied up with such obligations. The thought touched him that perhaps this had been a bad idea after all.

"Is there something wrong?" asked Hawthorne. "Didn't I tell you the hours?"

"No."

"Sorry about that. Does your work schedule conflict? Do you work in the evenings?"

"No, not really," said Salazar. "It is just that I am often very busy at night."

"Well, perhaps you'd like to try it for a while and see how it's working out." Hawthorne smiled a weak, thin-lipped smile. "If it sounds like I'm cajoling you, I am. You see, we don't get that many men to volunteer for this kind of work."

"Really?" His waning interest in the project sparked and crackled.

"That's right," said Hawthorne with a smile that tried to be sly. "Lots of young women, though."

Lots of young women.

"It will be no problem. I will return at four."

Passing the audition proved easy for Lydia. She'd always enjoyed theater, and had also done a little singing. Everyone told her she had a pleasant voice, a good voice. She entered the orientation room and took a seat in front of one of the old tape recorders which had been carefully arranged on long tables. Other volunteers were already seated and others slowly drifted in. There was nothing to do but wait for things to get started.

He passed some time by walking around the neighborhood, in and out of some of the art and photography galleries, which he loathed. To see the garbage which passed for true art these days ignited within him a burning anger of righteousness. He wallowed in the ferocity of his outrage, drawing strength and resolve from it. The decadence of art was only one of the many signs pointing to the coming Apocalypse. Such signs, and he saw them *everywhere*, beautifully reinforced his own special preparations for survival.

For March, the weather was surprisingly mild and many people herded along the sidewalks, pretending to be enjoying themselves. He looked closely at many of the couples, immediately despising the males and thinking his usual thoughts about the females.

Despite the intoxicating surges of rage which powered him as he walked the streets, he did not actually prefer being out among the mortals for long periods of time. He felt far more comfortable, more secure in the relative solitude of the Post Office, where he operated his mail sorting machines with mind-numbing efficiency, where he need not speak to anyone other than himself, where he could concentrate on his special thoughts without distraction or interruption. And of course, nothing matched the solitude of his fortress-like row-house in one of the city's forgotten neighborhoods. Like a great womb, the old house encapsulated and protected him. It was the place where he'd been born, had lived his entire life, even after his mother died. It was the place where he believed he would achieve his immortality.

Growing tired of the sidewalks and galleries, and still having almost an hour to kill, he drifted into one of the trendy bars where they served sushi and many foreign ales and beers. The dark interior was more suitable to his mood, even though he found it somewhat crowded as he straddled a stool. He did not like crowded places.

Sipping upon a seltzer and lime, he glanced around the bar to see several young women, and some who were not so young, studying him as well. This did not surprise or excite him, however. His Mediterranean face was softly featured, naturally handsome. His liquid, puppy-dog eyes and warm, resonant voice attracted women. His delicate manner of speaking, the way he carefully pronounced all his words without contractions, charmed most females.

But Salazar ignored them because he knew better than to be seen associating with any of them in public. It was too easy to be seen, to be witnessed and thereby connected.

No. He had his own methods. Methods proved successful over many years.

He arrived at the volunteer center a few minutes late and the receptionist ushered him into a large room filled with long tables and many people sitting at them. Mr. Hawthorne was already droning on about how to operate the recorders as Salazar moved quickly to the closest open chair. Taking a seat in the second row, he looked with great disinterest at the old Webcor which squatted in front of him.

A growing excitement smoldered in him like early bursts of heat from a pile of oily rags. He loved the overall somatic control he conjured up at such times. All his senses operated at the brink of overload; he never felt so incredibly alive as when he plunged into a new hunt.

Salazar absorbed the scent of the woman to his right—a faint blend of Halston perfume and perspiration. It was a natural pheromone to him. His peripheral vision recorded a splash of blonde hair, small movements of her left arm. Stealing a quick glance to his right, he was rewarded with a stunning vision.

Instantly he knew that it was not mere chance which had placed him next to a very special prey. Truly the Fates did conspire to help him, a belief he often pondered. The young woman to his right possessed not the glitz of a Cosmo covergirl nor the sexual artifice of a Playmate . . . just a natural grace, an innocence which seemed to radiate from her soul like a beacon. In an instant, he had mentally photographed her.

Sea-green eyes, long lashes. High cheekbones, and sculpted facial planes. Pert nose and streamlined lips with just the hint of fullness. Strawberry blonde hair, long and full. It was rare indeed that he found one so perfect.

She wore a loose, baggy lavender sweater with macrame laces up the front. It was not something designed to be sexy or revealing. But the way she leaned forward over the table, enabling her to inspect some facet of the recorder's controls, gave him a perfect view of her breasts.

More perfection. Full and upthrusting, but not actually large or pendulous. Delightfully pink aureoles, fully defined, as though swollen, protruded from the rest of the breast. The nipples themselves, while semi-erect, were not thick or obtrusive.

Hawthorne's voice had deteriorated to something less than the idiot-hum between radio stations. Salazar flirted with the state of total rapture.

"Hi!"

The utter cheeriness of the soft voice was like a slap in his face. Stunned, Salazar looked up to the beautiful woman smiling at him. Her age could have been anywhere between eighteen and thirty.

"Hello . . ." he said, trying to keep his voice from cracking. He was not accustomed to be caught staring. "I just wanted to see if we all had the same kinds of machines . . ."

"I think so," she whispered.

Salazar noticed that Hawthorne had stopped talking and everyone was fiddling with their tape machines, obviously testing out some procedure.

"I'm . . . Tony . . . Tony Vespa," he said in a half-whisper. He used the phony name he'd given Hawthorne. "Nice to meet you."

"Lydia McCarthy," she said, still smiling. "Likewise."

"Which category did you sign up for?" He didn't really care, but a desperate urge burned within to preserve their contact. Even though he had not availed himself of any of the other prey available, he *knew* she was the one.

"Oh, I picked the Classics . . ." said Lydia, a seasoning of regret in her voice.

He smiled at her. Most women found his smile disarming and ingenuous. She reciprocated, and his pulse jumped. Salazar was certain she had no idea how she affected men. No teasing. No flirting. Everything was very natural with her. She would be perfect.

"What're you going to be reading?"

"What?"

"The tapes," she said. "What category did you pick?"

"Oh . . . I'm doing some spy thrillers and some mysteries." He could care less about the goddamned blind . . .

"All right, now, I think you've all got the basics," said Hawthorne, his voice intrusive and alien. "Don't forget—it's okay to make mistakes . . ."

Lydia's attention returned to the front of the room. Salazar stared at her, invaded the front of her sweater with his hungry gaze. She would be so sweet . . .

"I'm going to call you out by the category you selected," said Hawthorne. "When you hear your group called, please come up and get your assignments and schedules. If you have any conflicts, you can work them out with our receptionist. Are we ready? All right . . . let's take the Classics first."

"That's me," said Lydia, gathering up her purse and down jacket. "It was nice meeting you . . ."

Salazar was stunned by her sudden movement. His gaze left the front of her sweater and searched out her green-flecked eyes. But before he could say anything, she had turned away, slipped into the stream of other readers moving quickly past Hawthorne's table. A surge of panic choked through him. He should change his category! He should follow her.

But he could do no such thing. He could not draw attention to himself, or worse, connect himself with her in any way. Occupied with precautionary thoughts, he was barely aware of her receiving her book-assignment and exiting the room.

Hawthorne, meanwhile, had moved down his list, calling on Bi-ography, General Non-Fiction, Contemporary Fiction, Romance—Goth-ics, and Science Fiction, before finally hitting Spy & Mystery. Salazar played out the charade, accepted his schedule with feigned interest, then exited as quickly as possible without appearing to be in a hurry.

The hallway was empty and so was the lobby, other than the receptionist's desk. Lydia McCarthy was gone and if her phone number was unlisted it was possible he'd lost her forever. But he didn't give up that easily, retreating back down the hall to Mr. Hawthorne's vacant office. Moving quickly, Salazar rifled through a folder full of appli-cations on the pristine blotter.

More quickly than he expected, he found Lydia's form, instantly committing her phone number to memory. Right away, the familiar, explosive sensation of great warmth suffused him. Intimate. Comfort-ing. He felt full of power and confidence as he strode triumphantly out into the hall, through the lobby, and out into the cold, late afternoon.

It had been so easy after all. The digits of her phone number blazed in the center of his skull.

The temptation to rush home to call was seductive, almost over-powering, but he told himself he would wait until Tuesday.

Tony Vespa.

At first the caller's name meant nothing to her, but he ignored her initial confusion and re-introduced himself. The handsome, dark-eyed guy at the volunteer center—she suddenly connected the name and the face. He had seemed so very nice. So polite and charming. And as he spoke, he continued to reinforce that first impression.

She was pleased that he'd called, and she was not really all that surprised that, after some small-talk, he asked her out—some drinks and maybe some dancing at Edgar's. Saturday night, around eight?

"Yeah, that would be great," she heard herself say, perhaps a little too enthusiastically. "I've never been there, but people at work say it's real nice."

He confirmed her address, then prepared to end the conversation.

"Gee, do you have to go so quick?" asked Lydia, hoping she didn't sound too forward.

"What do you mean?"

"I thought maybe we could talk for a while. Maybe get to know each other a little better . . ."

He chuckled softly. A seductive sound, even through the receiver. "Plenty of time for that, Lydia. Good night."

Saturday night, eight o'clock. She had opened her apartment door to him wearing a dark blue jacket-and-pants ensemble over an ivory satin blouse. The silky material conformed to her flesh in such a way it was obvious she was bra-less.

And then she'd asked him if he wanted a beer while he waited for her to finish getting ready . . .

. . . and Salazar now watched her working hard to twist off the cap with her left hand while she held the Michelob bottle awkwardly in the crook of her flipper-like right arm.

How had he not noticed it?

He could not keep his gaze from the deformity. Foreshortened, stick-thin, slightly twisted. Just beyond the permanently half-bent elbow protruded three stiff, semi-formed and useless fingers. A withered arm.

The thought lit up his mind like a cheap neon sign. He looked away from the kitchen, trying to seem interested in the contemporary decor of her living room. A withered arm.

So taken had Salazar been with the perfection of the rest of her, he had somehow failed to notice. He had not actually seen her . . . *all* of her. He wondered if this sudden knowledge would make any real difference, and his first inclination was probably not. His image of perfection was of course destroyed, but he could still feel his hot blood pounding in his head. No, it would be all right.

"Here we go," said Lydia brightly as she exited the kitchen and extended the bottle to him with her left hand.

Looking up, he tried to smile, tried to keep his gaze from drifting down to that hideous thing sticking out of her sleeve.

"Thanks . . ." He accepted the bottle and took a careful sip. It was not a good thing to drink alcohol, but the charade must be played out. He knew that one bottle would not foul his plans.

"I'm almost ready," she said, turning down the hall towards her bedroom. "Just a few minutes, really."

"We have all the time in the world," he said.

* * *

A single, unsetting thought that something was not quite right touched her mind as soon as she climbed into his beat-up Chevrolet. The interior was rimed with a furry patina of grime and dust, the windows so fogged with dirt she could barely see the streetlights in the distance. An aroma of Lysol spray, trying to mask a deeper, more hideous odor, assailed her as he closed the door. There was something familiar about the smell—a slightly rancid, yet somehow metallic redolence, but she couldn't place it. She had never been in such a filthy car.

In addition, he never spoke to her after slipping into his seat and keying the ignition. Watching him, Lydia noticed how he gripped the wheel with both hands, knuckles taut, arms rigid. He stared straight ahead, eyes not even blinking. There was something chilling about him, *a sudden coldness that was reptilian.* She could almost *see* it lurking beneath the surface of his handsomeness like the creature in the black lagoon. How could she have not noticed it before?

The Chevrolet accelerated quickly under his unflinching control, changing lanes in the heavy city traffic like a checker zig-zagging across its board. Landmarks blinked past her window and she realized they weren't headed for the hotel district where Edgar's was located. With a shudder, Lydia knew she wanted out of the car—as soon as possible.

She tried to make a few jokes, to get him talking, but he ignored her completely. His coldness radiated outward, touched her, and the inside of the car felt like the bottom of a well.

"Where are we going?" she asked sternly.

He turned a corner roughly, leaving a wide thoroughfare for a narrow, neighborhood street. Poorly lit, the street assumed a mantle of foreboding shadows.

"I said, where are we going? Why won't you answer me?"

This time, he turned and smiled at her.

"We're almost home," he said in a reverent whisper. He sounded stagy, but also frightening.

She knew she didn't want to be anywhere near this creep's home. As the car slowed for a red traffic light, she whirled awkwardly in her seat so her left arm could reach the door handle.

Yanking it upward, she grasped when nothing happened. Almost without effort, he lashed out with the back of his hand. The force of impact almost unhinged her jaw. Stinging flashes of pain lit up the inside of her skull; nausea and dizziness welled up like a black geyser behind her eyes. She collapsed into the corner of the seat and the door, fighting the urge to pass out, to give in to him.

No. She would never do that. She kept repeating the thought as though it would give her strength.

Her mind raced with half-panicky thoughts. How could she have let this happen? He'd seemed so normal, so nice . . . and she had so few dates, so few chances to get out and be like everybody else.

But even her earliest memories confirmed she'd never been treated like everybody else. Just because her pregnant mother had been prescribed a drug called Thalidomide, Lydia had survived as an Outsider. She learned as a small child how to live with the special pain of rejection, of words like *freak* and *monster*. She knew intimately the simple cruelties, and countless, unseen injuries. Like a grey, mottled tumor, her pain clung to the depths of her soul. But rather than allowing it to become a malignant destroyer, she had used her pain as a source of power, of soul-energy. She had learned to accept the pain, break it down into its molecular parts, and rebuild it into a driving engine of confidence and inner strength. Lydia had always faced the torment with a special dignity, always growing more formidable in the process.

But now, she faced something far darker . . .

Salazar was feeling very strong since slapping her across the face. The contact with her flesh exhilarated him. Electricity danced upon the tips of his fingers, singing to him in a chorus of power. Whipping the steering wheel to the left, he jockeyed the car down another side street, then left again into the alley behind his house. As he braked to a halt, his passenger lunged for the door latch. He smacked her again—this time hard enough to break the skin across her cheekbone and to stun her into semiconsciousness. Moving quickly, he grabbed a roll of duct tape from the glove compartment, tearing off a strip to seal her mouth. Then before she regained her senses, he pulled her from the car and fireman-carried her towards the house. Draped limply over his shoulder, she felt almost weightless to him. His entire body *hummed* with infinite vitality; the sensation was intoxicating, sensuous, almost divine. He moved with stealth and silence even though the high fences shielded him from the eyes of any curious neighbors. The light of a half-moon cut a pale blue path through his trash-littered backyard. Salazar followed it to the outside cellar steps and descended with his prey into the familiar darkness.

Tiny flames wickered in the distance. With a great effort, Lydia lifted her head to stare at the candles casting orange light and long shadows across the cellar. She forced herself to sharper awareness. Something was restricting her good arm, holding it almost straight up, and she gradually realized he'd manacled her against a damp, chilly wall of stone. A second bracelet and chain hung past her right shoulder, rendered useless by her withered arm. But the cold metal looped both ankles; short chains tethered her spread-legged to the wall.

The bastard . . . !

Her anger threatened to banish the numbing chill of the cellar. The first tendrils of rage were reaching into the core of her being, seeking the energy which seethed there. She would—

The tape was ripped savagely from her mouth, twisting her neck to the side. Stinging pain ate into her face as she detected movement in the shadows. He appeared out of the darkness, his eyes wide with pleasure. He appraised her with a grin and chuckled to himself. The taut muscles of his chest and arms strained against a plain white T-shirt, over which he wore a thick leather apron. Slowly he raised a barber's straight razor until it was level with her eyes. The blade looked insanely sharp.

Lydia recoiled from the shining weapon, thrashed against the chains, but no sound could escape her throat.

"It's okay if you want to scream," he said in a whisper. "Nobody can hear you down here. They never heard any of the others."

Behind him, next to a work bench full of tools, an old gas stove heated two large stewing pots. Adjacent to the stove at the end of a large, darkly stained, wooden table sat an electric rotisserie. Its interior glowed a deep orange from the glow of its heating elements.

An alarm was going off in her head. It was the klaxon of sheer panic. Naked fear capered like a demon across her mind. She was going to *die*. She was going to be sliced and gutted like a sacrificial pig. For an instant the alarm screeched so loud, so insistently, she felt she was plummeting into the abyss of madness.

"Going to cut you up," said the monster in the leather apron. His face moved to within inches of her own. His breath smelled of decay, his eyes as flat and dead as a shark's. "And then, I'm going to eat you . . ."

No.

The single word went to substance in the very core of her being. It rose up in her, gathering the stuff of anguish and suffering, and plating itself with it like newly forged armor. A vortex of anger whirled into life, kicking out sparks of defiance. A silent cry of pure, sweet outrage streaked out of her like an explosion of radio waves from a star going nova.

In that single instant, she hated him. Completely. With a cosmic finality.

Her anger and her hate fused into something new, becoming a tapline which drove down into the deepest core of her soul.

"Here we go," said the monster as he slipped the razor's edge into her blouse, bringing it down with slow precision. The blade separated her clothing effortlessly, slicing it away like rice paper. He continued down until he had opened her garments as if they'd been zippered. With a technique smoothed by years of practice, he began removing the tatters of her clothes. As the last of her blouse fell off her right shoulder, revealing her deformity, he paused as if to study the withered appendage. His gaze seemed to traverse the short length of her slightly twisted humerus. Twig-thin, punctuated by the suggestion of an elbow and a stump of misshapen flesh, it looked unfinished. Three proto-fingers jutted stiffly from the stump.

He reached out and touched her right arm, slowly running his fingers down the useless travesty of a hand. She wanted to recoil from his touch—for most of her life had avoided touching her right arm as much as possible—but she refused to give him even the slightest satisfaction that he had offended her. The limb had always been numb, essentially dead, but as his fingers played along its length, she felt a slight warmth beneath the shriveled skin.

"Never seen anything like this," he said as though to himself. "Maybe I'll save it as a souvenir."

He looked up from her twisted arm, smiled widely.

"Why don't you scream?" he asked softly. "It's okay if you want to scream."

More expert snicks of the blade, and everything fell away except her panties. Her pale skin goose-fleshed from the chilly dampness, then flushed as a wave of humiliation passed over her.

But she would not let the indignity deter her from the climax of her rage. The maelstrom of hate for him continued to expand inside her, faster and more deadly than a metastasizing growth. Like a hungry cancer it fed upon the storehouse of her pain and humiliation—a lifetime's worth. In a frenzy of building pressure, her loathing sought an outlet . . .

"This will be nice," he said, slipping the edge of the razor inside the elastic band of her panties. Slowly he moved it down, paring away the last boundary of her nakedness. Lydia stared straight ahead into the distant shadowed corners of the room as her underpants fell away in ribbons. He placed the cold steel of the blade flat against her lower abdomen, moved the blade downward over her mons, scything her blonde pubic hair like wheat, until he reached the beginning of her labia. Slowly he rotated the blade so that its cutting edge faced upward and perpendicular to her body.

"This seems like a good place to start," he said in a half-whisper. *No!*

The rage from the core of her being, engorged from the surfeit of her pain, sought form. She blinked her eyes, flinching away from the blade, and sensed that things were somehow slowing down. The warmth in her withered arm surged, bursting forth with white heat in all the places where he'd touched her.

All the years of suffering, the humiliation and exquisitely distilled anguish of her were taking substance now. Time almost stopped for her. The catalytic moment had arrived. Something shifted in the cosmos, and the great wheel of being sought a new balance-point. When he touched her dead flesh, he'd unwittingly switched on the radiant energy of her soul.

He moved the blade upward; the cold edge of steel touched her. It was only an instant, but she could feel the heat expanding, suffusing her arm with a life it had never known. Time slowed, spiraling down into a dark well. A total spectator, Lydia watched as her withered arm moved—moved for the first time in her life. Its pale flesh almost incandescent with vengeful energy, her limb lengthened, swung forward.

Things were happening so fast, and yet she could see it all unfolding with exacting detail. Time fugued around her like a storm.

He looked up as her arm moved, for the moment forgetting his intended upward thrust of the razor. His eyes widened as the stump of flesh flattened out and the stick-like projections swelled and grew into taloned, grasping fingers. Like a spade-claw, it raked his face, and she could hear him scream slowly through the underwater-like murk of distended time.

The sound of his own pained voice, his scream of pain and terror, stunned him as much as the transformation he was witnessing. As his own blood warmed his ruined cheek, he found himself marvelling at the exquisite tang of his own coppery fear, his own pain-fire burning. So different . . . so ironically reversed . . . fascinating as much as horrific. The girl's face had become twisted into an unrecognizable mask. The gaze of her sunken eyes stared through him, past him, and into a timeless place. Her transformation was a gift from the gods, he realized in the final moment. It was a miracle, and only he had been chosen to witness the event. Salazar smiled through his pain and his fear, and awaited her special anointing . . .

In an instant the hand reached *into* his face, index and middle fingers puncturing his eyes, the newly-formed thumb hooking the roof of his mouth. Gristle and bone collapsed from the unrelenting pressure; the razor fell away from his hand. Then the arm shot out, straightening, as the hand held his head like a ten-pin bowling ball. For a moment, he hung there, suspended, a grim marionette, legs and arms flailing through a final choreography of nerve-shock and death.

Then, like a crane jettisoning its cargo, the hand released his stilled body; and powered by the last sparks of her rage and her pain, it yanked free the manacles from her wrist and ankles. Lydia blinked her eyes in the candlelight as her time-sense telescoped back to normal. The right side of her body seemed aflame and her heart raged in her chest as if it might explode. The monster lay at her feet and she'd killed him. Her stomach lurched, sending a hot column of bile halfway up her throat.

The horror of knowing she'd actually killed someone was tempered by her realization of how it had been done. Looking down at her new right arm, her new hand, it seemed impossible that it could really be there.

She kept waiting for it to fade away, to shrink back into the desiccated parody she'd always known.

But it never did.

The Soft Whisper of Midnight Snow

Charles de Lint

Charles de Lint's stories are antidotes for the dark visions that often fill *Pulphouse: The Hardback Magazine*. His work has appeared in almost every issue, and he has written for our other lines as well, most notably four novellas in our Axolotl Press series. He is a prolific author. His most recent book, *The Little Country*, is getting wonderful reviews.

"The Soft Whisper of Midnight Snow" is a good tale with which to end the volume. This gentle fantasy is a story of warmth, beauty, and hope.

Night. The fields lay stark as a charcoal drawing—white drifts, the black clawed talons of the trees, the starlight piercingly bright. A gust of wind-driven snow swirled across the nearest field and he was there again. A shape in the twisting snow. A whisper of moccasins against white grains of ice. One step, another. He was drawing closer, much closer. Then she blinked, the snow swirled with a new flurry of wind, and he was gone. The field lay empty.

Tomilyn Douglas turned from the window and let out a breath she hadn't been aware of holding. The cabin was warm, the new woodstove throwing off all of its advertised heat, but a chill still scurried down her spine. She walked slowly to where her easel stood by an east window, ready to make use of the morning light. Her hand trembled slightly as she flicked a lamp switch and studied the drawing in its pale glow. It twinned the scene she had just been witness to, complete with the tiny shapeless figure, its details hidden in a swirl of gusting snow.

This morning she'd thought it had been a dream, that she had only dreamed of waking and seeing that figure in the snow, moving towards the cabin. Her fingers smudged with charcoal, she'd stood back and smiled with satisfaction at the rendering she'd done of it, that momentary high of a completed work making her a little dizzy until she'd had to go sit down. A useful dream, she'd thought, for it had left her with the first piece of decent work she'd completed since Alan . . . since Alan had gone. It was an omen of things to come, of a lost talent returned, of an ache finally beginning to heal.

Tomi flicked off the light and the room returned to darkness. It'd been an omen all right, she thought. But she was no longer so sure that she understood just what it was that it promised.

"This is where the dream becomes real," he'd told her when they bought and fixed up the cabin. It was meant to be only a temporary arrangement. The cabin stood on a hundred acres of bushland south of Calabogie. Alan had the blueprints all drawn up for the house they would build on the hill behind the cabin. It was his dream to build a home for them that would be the perfect design. The house would grow almost organically from its surroundings. A stand of birch grew so close to where her studio would be that she would feel as though she was a part of the forest, separated only by the glass walls of the room. Solar heating, a vegetable garden already planned out, enough forest on the land that they could cut their own wood . . . Self sufficiency was to be the order of the day and she loved him for it. For the house, for the land, for the dream, for . . . for his love.

They could afford to live out of the city. They were both established in their careers—architect and artist. Alan's clients sought him out now, while her work sold as quickly as she could paint it. They were the perfect match for each other—she loved it when people told them that, because it was true. For eleven years . . . it was true. But the dream had become a nightmare.

Last spring the foundations of their dream house were a scar on the landscape, like the scar on her soul. The forest began to reclaim its own. By the time the snows came this year, the sharp edges of the foundations were rounded with returning undergrowth. The scar she carried had yet to lose its raw edges.

Morning. Tomi bundled up and went out into the field but if last night's visitor had left any tracks, if he hadn't just been some figment of her imagination, the night's wind had dusted and filled them with snow. She stood, the wind blowing her brown hair into her face, and stared across the white expanse of drifts and dervishing snow-eddies to study the forest beyond the fields. The quiet that she'd loved when she moved here from the city, that she'd slowly come to love again as she dealt with her pain, disturbed her now. Too quiet, she thought, then she spoke the clichéd words aloud. The wind took them from her mouth and scattered them across the field. Shivering, Tomi returned to the cabin.

She spent the day working at her easel. Sketch after sketch made its mysterious passage from mind through fingers to paper. And they were all good. No, she amended as she looked them over while having a midafternoon soup-and-tea break. They were better than good. They were the best she'd done in over a year, perhaps better than before Alan—

She shut that train of thought off as quickly as it came. She was getting better at it now. But while she thrust aside the ache before it could take hold, she couldn't shake the uneasiness that had followed her through the day. Night was coming, was almost here. Just at dusk it began to snow. Tiny granular pellets rasped against the door, rattled on the roof. She wanted to turn all the lights on so that she'd be blinded to the night outside, but not seeing made her more nervous. One by one she turned them off, then sat in the darkness and looked out over the fields at the falling snow.

One day he just never came home. She could draw up that day in her memory with a total recall that always struck her as a sure sign that she was still a long way from getting over it. He left in the morning to do some work down the road at Sam Gould's place—Sam having helped them when they were having the foundation poured. When he still wasn't back by dinnertime, she gave Sam a call, but he hadn't seen Alan all day and, no, he hadn't been expecting him.

That night wasn't the worst one in her life—those had come after, when she knew—but it was bad. She hadn't been able to do anything but worry, staring at the phone, waiting for him to call. She tried some friends of theirs in the city. No luck. She thought of calling the police, hospitals, that kind of thing, but knew for all her worry that it was too early for that. Then around eleven o'clock the phone rang, startling her right out of her seat with its klaxon jangle.

"Alan?" she cried into the mouthpiece. "Alan, is that you?" The words came out in a rush like they were all one word.

"Whoa, Mrs. Douglas. Slow down a bit. This is Tom Moulton." Her relief shattered into pieces of icy dread.

"Sorry to be calling you so late, but I was talking to Sam a few minutes ago and heard you were worried about your man. Thing is, I saw your jeep parked out on 511, a couple of miles down from my place. I knew right off it was yours, but I figured you all were out for a little hike or something, you know what I mean?"

She called the police then, and they began a search of the surrounding bush. It wasn't until a couple of days later when she had to go to the bank that she discovered half the money in their joint account had been withdrawn.

Night. The snow had tapered off, but the wind was still shaping and reshaping the drifts around the trees and fence posts and up against the cabin. Tomi was half-hypnotized by the movement of the snow. Time and again she thought she saw a figure, but it was always just a shadow movement, a tree branch, a fox once. Then just as she was ready to give up her vigil, something drew her face closer to the window and she saw him again.

He was closer still. Not moving now, just standing out there in the field, watching the cabin. Tattered cloth fluttered in the wind, muting his outline against the snow. He was still too far away to make out details, but something about the way he stood, about the way he held himself erect, not hunched into the wind, told her that he wasn't who she'd feared he'd be. He wasn't Alan.

"Who are you?" she whispered. "What do you want from me?"

She didn't expect an answer. He was too far away to hear her.

There was a thick glass pane and an expanse of white field between them. There was the wind and the gusting snow to steal her words. She wanted to shout at the figure, to run out and grab him. The window frosted up under her breath. She cleared it with a quick wipe of her hand, but in the time it took the figure was gone again.

Hardly realizing what she was doing, she grabbed her coat and a flashlight and ran outside, stumbling through the snow to where he'd stood. When she reached the spot there was no sign of him, no tracks. The field was virgin snow all around her, except for her own ragged trail from the cabin.

She began to shiver. Returning to the warmth of the cabin, she closed and bolted the door. She tossed her coat onto a chair, the flashlight, never used, on top of it, then slowly made her way to her bedroom. She began to undress, then stopped dead as she glanced at the bed. A long raven's feather lay on the comforter, stark and black against its flowered Laura Ashley design.

"Oh, Jesus."

On watery legs she walked over to the bed, stared at the intrusion, unwilling to touch it. He'd been inside. Somehow, while she'd been out looking for him, in those few moments, he'd come inside. Slowly she backed out of the bedroom. It didn't take long to search the cabin.

There was the main room that included her studio and the kitchen area, a bathroom, and her bedroom. She was alone in the cabin. In a trancelike state, she investigated every possible hiding place until she was positive of that. She was alone inside, but he was out there. What did he want? What in God's name was this game he was playing?

She was a long time getting to sleep that night, starting at every familiar creak and groan of her cabin. When she finally did sleep, restless dreams plagued her, dreams of shapeless figures and clouds of raven's feathers that fell like black snow all around her while she ran and ran, trying to catch an answer that was always out of reach. Underpinning her dreams, the wind moaned outside the cabin, whispering the snow against its log walls.

The deed to the cabin and its land was in her name and, once the initial shock was over, she was quick to remove what money remained in their joint account into one under her own name. She kept thinking there was some mistake, that this wasn't happening to them, to her. But as the days drifted into weeks, she had no choice but to accept it. To believe it, even if she couldn't understand it.

At first she was confused and hurt. Anger was there too, but it came and went as if of its own will. Mostly she felt worthless. If they'd been having fights, if there'd been another woman, if there'd been some hint of what was coming, maybe she could have accepted it more easily. But it had come out of the blue.

"It's him," her friends tried to convince her. "He's just an asshole, Tomi. Christ, he never had it so good."

Neither had she, she'd want to say, but the words never got beyond her thinking them. He'd left her and she knew why. Because she was worthless. As she tried to lose herself in her work during the following weeks, she saw that her art was worthless too. God, no wonder he'd left her. The real wonder was that he hadn't left her sooner.

And even later as she, at least intellectually, came to realize that it *was* him and not her worthlessness that had made him leave, emotionally it wasn't that easy to accept. Emotionally, she retained the feelings of her own inadequacy. She'd stare into a mirror and see her face drawn and pale with her anxiety, the brown hair that framed it hanging listless, the body that could have been exercised but instead had been left to sag.

"Who'd want me?" she'd ask that reflection and then would retire deeper into the shell she was building around herself. Who'd want her? She didn't even want herself.

Morning. Tomi had the jeep on the road and was halfway to Ottawa by the time the nine o'clock CBC news came on the radio. She turned it off. Her own troubles were enough to bear without having to listen to the world's. But once she was in Ottawa, she didn't know why she'd come.

She'd had to get away from the cabin, from the figure that haunted the fields outside it, from the black feather that was lying on the floor of her bedroom, but being here didn't help. There was too much going on, too many cars, too many people. She almost had a couple of accidents in the heavy traffic on the Queensway, another on Bank Street.

She'd been planning to visit friends, but no longer knew what to say to them. Running from the cabin wasn't the answer, she realized.

Just as withdrawing from the world after Alan had left hadn't been an answer. She had to go back.

That first spring alone had been the worst. She hadn't been able to look at the foundations without wanting to cry. Unable to paint, or even sketch, she'd thrown herself into working around the cabin, fixing it up, removing every trace of Alan from it, putting in a garden, buying a new woodstove, discovering talents she'd never known she'd had. She might not be able to keep a husband or express herself with her art any more, but she could handle a hammer and saw, she could chop firewood, she could do a lot of things now—do them without ever worrying about whether or not she was capable of them.

The first night that she made a vegetable stew with all the ingredients coming out of her own garden, she celebrated with a bottle of wine, got very drunk and never once wanted to cry. She stood out in the clear night air and looked up the hill at the foundations and was surprised at what she found in herself.

The ache was still there, but it was different now. Still immediate, but not quite so piercing. She might not be able to paint yet, but the next day she took out her sketchbook and began to draw again. She wasn't happy with anything she did, but she wasn't discouraged about it anymore either. Not in the same way as she'd been when Alan first had deserted her.

Night. Tomi had forgotten how quickly it got dark. She decided to return to the cabin, but since she was in town anyway, she thought she might as well make a day of it. It went by all too quickly. From grocery shopping to haunting used bookstores and antique shops, it was going on four o'clock before she knew it. By the time she was fighting the heavy traffic on her way home, it began to snow again, big heavy flakes that were whisked away by the jeep's wipers but were building up rapidly on the road and fields. When she reached old Highway 1 going north from Lanark, she was reduced to a slow crawl, even with the jeep's four-wheel-drive. The build-up of snow and ice made for treacherous driving, especially on roads like this without as much traffic.

After Highway 1 turned into 511 and crossed the Clyde River, the driving grew worse. Here the road was narrow and twisted its way through the wooded hills that were barely visible through the storm.

The wind drove the snow in sheets across her windshield. The jeep ploughed through drifts that had already thrust halfway across the road in places.

Not far now, she told herself, and that much was true, but a half mile from the laneway leading in to her cabin, the road took a sudden dip and a sharp turn at the same time. She was going too fast when she topped the hill and hit an icy patch. Already nervous, she did the worst thing possible and instead of riding the fish tail and easing out of it, she slammed her foot on the brake.

The jeep skidded, came sideways down the hill and missed the turn. Its momentum took it through and then over the snow embankment until it thudded to a stop against a tall pine. The shock of the impact brought all the snow down from its branches in a sudden avalanche.

Panicked and shaken, Tomi snapped loose her seatbelt and lunged from the jeep. The snow came up to her hips as she floundered through it back to the road. She was breathing heavily by the time she reached it, the cold air hurting her lungs. When she looked back, she saw the jeep was half covered with the snow that it had dislodged from the pine.

She was never going to get it out of that mess. Not without a towtruck or tractor. But she couldn't face seeing to that now. She wasn't far from home. She could walk the half mile easily. Trying to ignore the chill that was seeping in through her clothes, cold enough to make even her bones feel cold, she forced her way back to the jeep, fetched her purse and groceries, and started the short trek home.

The snow was coming down in a fury now, the wind slapping it against her exposed skin with enough force to hurt. Neck hunched into her coat, head bowed, she trudged up the road, fighting the steadily growing drifts. The half mile had never seemed so long. Her boots—fine for town, but a joke out here—were wet and cold against her feet. The stylish three-quarter length coat that was only meant for the quick dashes from warm vehicle to warm store couldn't contend with the bone-piercing chill of the wind.

She got a scare when she stumbled and fell in a sprawl on the highway, her grocery bag splitting open to spew its contents all around her. But she was more scared when she found she just couldn't get up to go on. The shock of the accident and the numbing cold had drained all her strength.

She could lie here and, with the poor visibility, the snowplow would come by and bury her in the embankment, never knowing that its blades had scooped her up and shunted her aside. Or a pickup could come by and run her down before its driver even realized what it was that he was about to hit.

Right, bright eyes, she thought. So get the hell out of here.

She managed to sit up and tried to scrape together her scattered groceries, but her fingers were too numb in their thin gloves to work properly. What a time to play fashion horse, she thought hazily. But then again she hadn't been planning on playing the arctic explorer when she'd set out this morning. What a dramatic picture this would make, she decided. The woman fallen in the snow, her groceries scattered around her, the wind howling around her like a dervish. . . .

She blinked her eyes open suddenly to find that she'd laid her head down on the road again as she'd been thinking. This. Wouldn't. Do. She forced herself back up into a sitting position. Screw the groceries. If she didn't get out of here quickly, she wasn't going to get up at all.

But the cold was in her bones now. Her teeth chattered and her jaws ached from trying to keep them from doing so. Her hands and feet just felt like lumps on the ends of the arms and legs. She realized with a shock that she was almost completely covered with snow. Only her upper torso was relatively free, the snow covering it having fallen off when she sat up.

Up. That was the ticket. She had to get up, put one foot in front of the other, and get herself home. She tried to rise, but the cold had just sapped something in her. There's been a lot of times over the past spring and summer when she'd simply wanted to die, but now that it was a very real possibility, she wanted to live with a fierceness that actually got her to her feet.

She tottered and took a couple of steps, then fell into another drift, frustrated tears freezing on her cheeks. Which was weird, she thought, because the snow actually felt warm now. It was cozy. Just like her bed in the cabin. Or the big easy chair in front of the wood-stove . . .

As she began to drift off, the last thing she saw was a dark shape moving towards her through the billowing snow. Incongruously, for all the howling of the wind, she heard a rasp of bead and quill against leather, a whisper of moccasins against the crust of the snow, smelled a pungent scent like a freshly snapped cedar bough, and then she knew no more.

She blinked awake. The air was thickly warm around her. She was lying on something soft, cozily wrapped in a coverage of furs. Dim lighting spun in her gaze as she sat up. When her head stopped spinning, she stared groggily about herself.

There was a fire crackling in front of her, its smoke escaping upward through a hole in the roof. Roof. Where was she? The walls looked like they were made of woven branches. She could hear the wind howling outside them. Movement caught her eye and she looked across the fire. He'd been sitting so still that she hadn't noticed him at first, but now he leapt out at her with a thousand details, each one so clear that she wondered how she could have taken so long to see him there.

He sat cross-legged on a deerskin, the firelight playing on his pale skin, waking sharp highlights in his narrow features. His clothing was a motley collection of tatters. A black shirt, decorated with bone. A grey vest, inlaid with beadwork, quills and feathers. A raven's skull hung like a pendent from his neck in the middle of a cluster of feathers and shells. He wore a headdress, again decorated with feathers and bones, that lifted high above his head in the shape of a pair of horns. She thought of the wicked queen in Disney's *Sleeping Beauty*, looking at those horns, or of Tolkien's highborn elves, taking in his pale features. But there was more of the Native American about him. And more than that, a feeling of great sorrow.

"Who . . . who are you?" she asked. She spoke softly, the way one might speak to a wild animal, poised for flight. "Why were you watching my cabin? What do you want with me?" She knew it had to have been him.

He made no reply. His eyes seemed all white in the deceptive light cast by the fire, all except for their pale grey pupils. His gaze never left Tomi's face. She was suddenly sure that she was dead. The plow *had* come by and scraped her frozen body up from the road, burying it under a mountain of snow. He was here to take her to . . . to wherever you went when you died.

"Please," she said, fingers tightening their grip on the fur covering. "What . . . what do you want with me?"

The silence stretched until Tomi thought she would scream. She plucked nervously at the furs, wanting to look away, but her gaze seemed to be trapped by his unblinking eyes.

"Please," she began again. "Why have you been spying on me?"

He nodded suddenly. Movement made the bones and quills click against each other. "Life," he said. His voice was husky and rough. He spoke with a heavy accent so that Tomi knew that whatever his native language was, it wasn't English.

She swallowed thickly. Fear made her throat dry and tight. "L-Life?" she managed. She looked for the door of the lodge, trying not to be too obvious about it. She didn't know if she'd have the strength to take off, but she couldn't just stay here with . . . with whatever he was.

He pulled a strip of birchbark from under his tunic and took a charred twig from beside the fire. With quick deft movements, he began to sketch on the birchbark. Curiosity warred with fear inside Tomi and she leaned forward. When he suddenly thrust the finished drawing at her, she floundered to get out of the way, then chided herself. So far the stranger hadn't hurt her. He'd brought her in from the cold and snow, bundled her up in his furs, saved her life. . . . And the drawing . . . it was good. Better than good.

Tomi taught art from time to time, week-long courses at the Haliburton School during the summer, a few at Algonquin College in Ottawa. Not one of those students' work could hold a candle to the lifelike sketch of a snowhare that her curious host had thrust at her. His quick deft rendering of it was what she always tried to instill in her students. To go for feeling first. She smiled to show she appreciated it.

"It's very good," she began.

"Life!" he repeated. Taking back the drawing, he blew on it, then laid it on the ground beside the fire.

Fear clawed up Tomi's spine again as the lines of the drawing began to move, to lift three-dimensionally from the birchbark. A hazily shaped hare sat there, its outline smoky and indistinct. Nose twitching nervously, it regarded her with warm eyes. Her fear died, replaced with wonder. She reached out a hand to touch the little apparition, but it drifted apart like smoke and was gone. All that remained was the birchbark that it had been sitting on. Its surface was clear, unmarked. "You," her host said. "*Your* breath."

"I . . . I can't breathe like . . . like . . ."

"You must."

"I can't breathe—" Suddenly the lodge was spinning again. The fire turned into a whirlpool of glittering sparks, that twisted and danced like snow-driven wind. Tomi's words froze in her throat. Gone. It was going. It was—

—gone.

"—can't breathe. . . ."

Something was shaking her. She blinked rapidly, trying to slow down the spinning.

"Miz Douglas? Miz Douglas?"

The world came into focus with a sharp snap. A face was leaning into hers. For one moment, she was back in the storm, or the storm had torn apart the strange man's lodge, blowing everything away, then she recognized the face. Sam Gould's strong features were looking down into hers. Worry creased his face. He looked at a loss.

"Sam . . . ?"

"It's me, Miz Douglas. Found you lying on the highway. You're damned lucky I didn't run over you with the plow, I'll tell you that."

"You . . . found me . . . ?" Then the lodge, the man—that had been a dream?

"Sure did. Funny thing—thought I saw someone standing beside you, just when my highbeams picked you out, but that must've been you standing for a moment, just before you fell. Hell of a storm, though, and that's fact. Had a look at your jeep, but it's in too deep for me to do much about it till the morning. I'll come round with the tractor then, if you can wait."

"I . . . I can wait."

"Not much damage, considering. Headlight's gone on the driver's side. You might want Bill Cassidy to have a look at that fender. I figure he could straighten her out for you, no problem."

"There was . . . someone standing . . . ?" Tomi managed.

"Well, I thought there was, I'll tell you that. But it was just a trick of the lights, I'd say. Storm can fool you into thinking you're seeing just about anything sometimes."

"Yes," Tomi said slowly. Like what she'd thought she'd seen. A dream. Just. . . .

"Anyway, I brought you up to your cabin," Sam continued. "Thought you might'a had a touch of frostbite on your wrist there, but I wrapped it up tight and kept it warm. The skin wasn't broken, so it'll be all right. You were lucky, and that's fact. I coulda plowed you right up into the bank and no one would've known to go looking for you till your jeep was spotted in the morning. I put you to bed, but 'cepting your boots and coat, I didn't . . . you know . . ." He blushed. "I just covered you up, Miz Douglas."

"Thank you, Sam." Tomi sat up slowly. "You saved my life." A dream?

Sam shuffled his feet. "Guess I did at that. I woulda called up an ambulance, but by the time it would've got here, well . . . I did what I could, I'll tell you that. You want I should call up the doc now, Miz Douglas? Or maybe get someone to stay with you for the night?"

Tomi shook her head. "I'll be all right, Sam. But thank you." Just a dream?

"My pleasure. I'd best be going now. Weather's not getting any better and I've got a load of plowing still to do. Keep me busy most of the night, I'll tell you that."

Tomi started to get up, but Sam laid a hand on her shoulder and gently pressed her down. "I can see myself out, Miz Douglas. You just lie there and take her easy. I'll lock up and be back in the morning with the tractor. You just get some sleep now. You've been through a rough time, and that's a fact. Sleep's the best thing for you now."

Tomi nodded and lay back, knowing that he wouldn't go until she did. She listened to him clomp across the hardwood floors in his workboots, heard him tug on his parka, the sound of the zipper, the door opening. "I'll see you in the morning!" he called, then the door slammed shut. The door handle made a click-click noise as he checked to make sure it was locked. Silence then for a time. Except for the wind. The snow being pushed against the cabin, the windows. The big snow plow starting up. Gears grinding as they changed. The truck backing out of her lane. Silence again as the sound of the engine was swallowed by the wind.

Tomi stared at her ceiling. Just a dream?

She listened to the wind and the whisper of the snow against the window panes and logs outside. She might have drifted off, she wasn't sure, just dozed there, until suddenly she had to get up, had to see, *had* to. She padded out of her bedroom into the main room of the cabin. Sam had left the lights on and she turned them off, one by one, then went to stand by the window.

The snow was still falling, the wind blowing it in great sweeps across the field. She stared out at the field, willing her stranger to be there again, for it not to have been a dream. She wasn't sure what she wanted, what she expected. She had been frightened in the lodge, but remembering it now, there had been no reason for fear. Just the strange man with his totemic clothing, and the drawing that came to life with a breath, with just a whisper of air drawn up from his lungs. . . .

She moved to her easel and turned on a light, aiming it so that it pooled over the easel, leaving the rest of the room in shadows. From the closet, she took out a virgin canvas, a sketching pencil, her acrylics. The sketching went easily. Background first, light, hazy as though seen through a gossamer curtain of falling snow. Then the figure. But close now.

She knew his features and quickly sketched them in. Left their look of sorrow, but imbued them with a certain air of nobility as well. She made the clothing not so ragged, not so tattered. The totemic raven skulls, feathers, beads and quills, came readily, leaping the gap from memory to canvas with an exhilarating ease.

Oh, lord. This was what it felt like. This was what she'd missed, what Alan had stolen from her, what the stranger had given her back.

She didn't know who or what he was, realized that it didn't matter. Dream or real, it didn't matter. Some spirit of winter, of the snow and wind, or of the forest . . . or a creation of her own blocked creativity. It didn't matter.

When the sketching was filled in as much as she needed, she moved straight to the acrylics, mixing the paints and applying them, scarcely paying any attention to what she was doing. Her subconscious remembered, her fingers remembered. She only had to give them free rein. She only had to breathe life into what took shape on her canvas. God. To have forgotten this . . . to have lost it. . . .

She leaned close as she worked, mixing colors on the seat of the stool, too enrapt in her work to search for her palette. The shades came easily. The painting grew from the rough black and white sketch into a being almost composed of flesh and blood, almost as though she was back in his lodge, seeing him across the fire, the light playing on his features, his steady gaze never wavering from hers. She listened to the wind, to the hiss and spit of the snow against the windows, and smiled as she worked.

It was long after midnight, but still far from dawn, when the main figure was completed and she only had the background to fill in. Her gaze locked to the gaze of the figure in the painting as she brushed in the pines and cedars behind him, the swirl of the snow as it gusted through the trees, across the field. But for all the movement in the background, the figure in the foreground was still. Only his eyes spoke to her.

Her fingers were cramping when she heard, under the moan of the wind and the whisper of the snow, the sound of her locked door opening. A draft of cold air touched the back of her neck as the wind entered, the wind and something more, something she had no name for, but she knew she owed it a debt.

It didn't matter what he was—her imagination running wild, or something out of the wild night sparking her imagination. She was repaying what he had recovered for her from that first moment she'd seen him in the field, just a dark shape in the blurring snow, repaying what had been lost and now regained with life.

The door closed, but she didn't turn around. The painting in front of her was like a mirror and she continued to breathe on it as she finished the last cedar.